WITNESS NO MORE

Arthur Kevin Rein

OPEN
BOOKS

Published by Open Books

Published by Open Books

Copyright © 2024 by Arthur Kevin Rein

Interior design by Siva Ram Maganti

Cover image © DavidTB shutterstock.com/g/DavidTB

For my children and granddaughter

CHAPTER ONE

Max

I wasn't an innocent, and neither was Jonah, but the resemblance didn't end there. Of course, our lives were separated by centuries, but that was of no consequence. We'd both been swallowed by whales, that was the point. And while Jonah spent but a short time in the belly of the beast, I had no illusions about release, not in three days, not in three years. Jonah was lucky, his whale was not the United States Government. There was no bolt of divine intervention in the script I'd been handed. Too late for that now. Too late for innocence.

I splashed water on my face, awake finally, and looked in the mirror. My story wasn't going to end here, in Moreau, South Dakota, the wide-open plains, where you can see everything well before it arrives: a car, a thunderstorm, the next town. Though over a thousand miles from either ocean, I'd found out too late. Whales were not the kindly beasts of the Bible, and not all swam in the sea. I had no idea what to make of Jonah's whale. Was his white, like mine? White as the Capital in D.C. or the president's residence? I wiped the water from my face and realized I wasn't Jonah, but Ahab, the sailor. Because his whale wasn't benevolent and kind, but white and malignant, just like mine. I had to laugh. I was comparing myself to characters in the Bible and Moby Dick, two of the most over-rated books ever written. I looked in the mirror and studied my eyes. Did I see signs of crazy? "I'm fine," I said to no one there. But then again, I didn't look for very long.

Our house was small, late twentieth-century modular. We lived here rent-free courtesy of the Witness Protection Program. In the bedroom next to mine, Nadine, my stepmother, was getting dressed, but not in the Neiman Marcus slacks or the Bottega Veneta Booties that used to fit her like she was born on Fifth Avenue. She would shake out the wrinkles in the slacks she'd worn the day before and check the blouse for grease stains. On most days both would pass inspection because that was easier than doing an extra load of wash. For twenty-seven years she'd been Nadine Cherhasky, nee Colum, until a federal bureaucrat who'd never spoken to her transformed her into Nadine Farmer. Just as quickly, our entire family had dropped through four tax brackets and landed in a world of push lawnmowers, TurboTax, and the Affordable Care Act.

The new names the feds had given us were a pain in the butt and easy for us to forget. How many times had she called her husband J.R. instead of by his new handle, George? A slip like that in front of the wrong person at the wrong time could put the mob onto us. Besides, she wasn't any more a Farmer than I was a Malibu Beach Bum.

I put on my shirt, stepped past the living room to the kitchen, and got a cup of coffee.

My father sat down on a kitchen chair. "When did you get in last night?"

"And good morning to you." I warmed my hands on the cup. "I don't know. After one. We had a gig."

"A gig?" George tapped a pack of Sweet n Low into his coffee. "Why don't you stop pretending at this rock n roll business?" Bagel in hand, he waited for his coffee to cool. He'd gone grey in the last year, but the rest of him still looked younger than his forty-one years, and he knew it. About his brain, I wasn't so sure. Somehow the incisive wit, insight, and quick thinking he'd so easily displayed as J.R. Cherhasky had left him, "died" as it were, when George Farmer was born.

George stirred his coffee. "Get a real job, work up the ladder like I did. When I was your age I was running not one, but two filling stations—"

Not this again. "Come on. We've been over this. I'm going to college. That's what you want."

George held up two fingers. "Two stations: *By myself.* The old man came by once a week to sign the orders from Standard Oil, pay the bills, and make sure nothing had blown up. Otherwise, it was up to me."

I stood in the doorway, legs crossed, and focused on the mug in hand. It was supposed to be a launching pad, this year of my life. And yet, every morning, there I stood, in the same dreary kitchen, my stomach curdling on something, and it wasn't the coffee. The gas-station verse was as familiar as a rock song refrain. Now, I flicked them away like a guitar pic tossed to the audience at the end of a set. "And where did it get us? Your real-world job?" I said, smirking. "The band cleared one twenty-five apiece last night. That's pretty damn good if you ask me." *And more than you make pushing TVs and microwaves*, I thought.

Reduced to a salesman because he had committed felonies, in the plural, over many years with the nastiest people imaginable. In the end, he'd found the nerve to testify against them and stay out of jail. But not all prisons have bars. Our options became either go into the Witness Protection Program, or let the mob have their pound of flesh.

The transition was a bitch for all of us, hardest for George, as it should be. I watched as my father's life slipped through his fingers. He'd become a bit player in his own band, J.R. the lead singer had become George on tambourine on his way to roadie.

"Music is no way to make a living," snorted George. "You're no John Mayer, for chrissakes. And that cover band of yours, well, they know how to 'cover' their mistakes, that's about it. Come up with something real and you might have a shot."

"At what?" I asked. "Even if I am a *pretender*, it's better than sleep walking through an appliance store all day. And don't worry, when I leave I'm not taking Heart Shaped Rock with me. I'm a front man. In a college town, rock drummers and bass players fall out of the trees."

There was a path out of this town called music, but I had to make it my own. I was smarter than Elvis, not as needy as Janis, or as screwed up as Cobain. "Don't join the twenty-seven club," that was my mantra. That gave me nine years to get it done: date bikini models, party with vid actors, marry a starlet, and buy a disgustingly expensive residence in every state that started with the letter C.

The other members of Heart Shaped Rock didn't buy my vision for the band. In fact, when I suggested the band stop doing covers and play original material, I was shouted down by the other three. Obviously, I wasn't going to hitch my star to those guys.

Nadine walked in the kitchen dressed in a waitress uniform, tennis shoes on her feet. I noticed a brown blotch on one toe. Gravy from yesterday's special, no doubt, but it looked like something worse. "Gross," she muttered, then moistened a napkin with her tongue. She grimaced and wiped at the stain until only a shadow remained.

"Did I interrupt something?" She pulled her thick, auburn hair back into a ponytail. "I heard you mention the band. Are you guys playing this weekend?"

"No, you didn't interrupt," I said. "Yes, we were talking about the band and no we're not playing. I was just leaving for the Thrift Store. I'll be there all day." I pointed my cup at my stepmother. "You should keep your hair down, get a lot more tips." Not that she needed any advice from me. The amount of tip money she plucked from the modest bunch of farmers and truck drivers at the local mom-and-pop restaurant was astounding. One look from her emerald green eyes was worth fifteen percent on the bill before she even took the order. She was born with a certain type of capital, and knew how to bank the dividends.

"Have a little respect." George took a sip of coffee and winced. Still too hot. "Someday you'll see. Maybe, when you get a job."

I knew what that meant. George had the Fox News take on Millennials, bought into all the stereotypes, and included me in that group. We were selfish, sensitive, job-hopping malcontents who lived with their parents and spent all our time on the Internet. Well, he wouldn't have to worry about me hanging around.

Nadine checked her look in a hallway mirror. "You also told me to wear high heels." She dabbed her lips. "During breakfast shift. If I had a set of those Blush Napa Sarah Flint's, I'd think about it." She glanced in our direction. "Look in my closet. Nothing but T.J. Maxx and Famous Footwear."

"What the hell is wrong with you?" George snapped the morning paper and gazed at me over the top edge. "We can't draw that kind of attention. This family can't afford it."

You mean you can't afford it, I thought.

Nine months had passed and I wasn't yet over the morning sickness, a hollow nausea that woke me every day before the sun came up. It started the week we arrived in Moreau. I now answered to a different name, spoken by a different circle of friends. My past was lost. My truth a year ago was now a lie. So why did I have to go on listening to the same drivel from my father after every gig?

George growled, "For god's sake, man. Wearing high heels in a small town like this before noon? You think people won't talk?"

"They're already talking." I spread my arms. "Nobody ever moves here. They only move away. People ask me why we came here, what do I tell them? Because the mob wants to kill my dad and they'd never look *here* to find him? And Nadine, she's only ten years older than me. You think people don't notice *that*?"

"Lower your voices, both of you," Nadine said. "Somebody'll hear. We'd have to notify Witness Protection and boom, we're gone to another outpost." She looked sharply at her husband. "Well, I'm not moving *again*."

I smirked. "I'll play my Stratocaster. No one will notice us then, right, George?" My appetite was gone. I walked out the back door and toward the Ford Ranger, rusting like a bolt in a junkyard. The frame creaked as I climbed in and drove away.

———

The Thrift Store building began as a brass works factory back in the 1900s. The business went bankrupt, and the building went through several owners until a community self-help organization purchased it for their retail outlet. I opened the service door and walked into the rear of the store where I had been a regular for the last three months. When I'd first "volunteered" to work here, it was to fulfill the community service credits I needed for graduation. I thought the whole idea was bullshit. I had better things to do than work in a Salvation-Army wanna be. But after working a month of Saturdays in the receiving department, I found the people unpretentious and friendly. A welcome break from home.

Community Service ended but I didn't want to leave, so I asked the store to hire me. I needed the money. That was the kicker. Nadine and George brought in enough to cover expenses and that was about it. There was nothing, zero, nada, coming in from anywhere else. And, there was a pretty artist with a workshop next door who had the sexiest, ice-blue eyes I'd ever seen.

I threw my jacket on a stack of cardboard boxes. "Hey, Trevor, what's happening?" My friend had arrived at work ahead of me, as always.

"About time, Farmer. Little ol' lady dropped off a load of furniture and I can't move it alone. Built like iron, weighs like concrete." Trevor tripped on the power cord to the lamp he was carrying, stumbled sideways, and crashed into a box of toys. Somehow, the lamp was undamaged, but he moaned.

"Whoa, take it easy on the merchandise, dude." Had it been anyone else, I would have rushed over to help, but I had seen Trevor stumble and fall so often and come out unscathed, I no longer even blinked. "Be there in a second," I said.

Neither one of us was built to last in a warehouse. The day I met the manager, he took one look at my thin arms and shallow chest and pegged me as a cashier. Trevor was no more fit-for-duty, but in the other direction—big-boned with plenty of flesh that hung as loose as his personality. But Trevor's word carried a different kind of weight at the store. He told the manager I could handle the lifting, and I got the job.

Trevor was none the worse after the fall. He got up, kicked angrily at the cord, and went back to work. I got a drink of water and joined Trevor next to the sofa.

"What the hell is with the couch condom?" Trevor asked, prodding the thick, plastic fabric cover with the toe of his shoe.

"Maybe the house had animals," I said.

"Or maybe she had animal sex in the living room."

"Get the other end, ya perv." I grunted with the lift. "Thought you said she was an old lady. Or maybe she's on your Tinder list, so you'd know about the sex."

"Up yours." Trevor moved the furniture dolly under the sofa. "Ready to roll."

"Try not to crash into anything, Ricky Bobby."

Moving the entire set took a good part of the morning. A few pieces went out to the retail space, some into the storehouse. Other pieces, already in the showroom, had to be moved to the back of the building and the site of my proudest achievement—reorganization of storage. The first time I walked through the area my skin crawled. Cardboard boxes set on tables and pallets. Aisles of items winding here and there like a cow path in a pasture. For three months, a pitched battle raged between me and this helter skelter hell-house until finally my fussy compulsion and Trevor's muscle prevailed. We now walked amongst a highly organized, neatly stacked collection of lightly used items.

As lunch approached, I took a look toward the hall that led to a couple of private offices in the back.

"Yeah, she's here," said Trevor, knowing where my mind was at.

"How do you know?" I stretched my neck to see. "Oh yeah, the lights are on. Maybe I'll go—"

"She's not down there."

I stopped. "But you just said—"

A woman's voice spoke, "I told you before, Max, you've got to grow a pair." She paused. "Of eyes, I mean, in the back of your head."

Startled, I turned around. "How'd you *do* that?"

She said, "Now that's entertainment." Sitting on one of the antique chairs we had just moved was Leah Walters, a dark-haired, blue-eyed, woman in white bibs with a blue t-shirt. Multi-colored streaks of paint were scattered everywhere: on the pant legs, sleeves, on her cheeks. Shards of plaster were in her hair and affixed to the paint.

"Dude, it's easy to sneak up on you," Trevor said.

But no one did it with as much flair and unpredictability as Leah, who'd been doing it to me since before we started going steady in February. I walked slowly toward her, waving a finger. "We had a deal."

"Oh, get off it." She waved me off. "What deal? You didn't think I was serious about giving it up, did you? Why would I?"

I played at picking away some of the paint on her t-shirt. "Tormenting me. I think you get off on it."

Trevor smirked. "She's the only one gets away with it."

Leah said. "Now, are you taking me to lunch or what?"

CHAPTER TWO

Max

The Prairie Kitchen was on Watertown Street in the old section of downtown Moreau. The owners had been at the location even before the city's recent renewal plan upgraded the sidewalks and light standards. The owner of TPK's, as the locals called the place, liked to say she had now gone through three such "rejuvenations." Her clientele, on the other hand, was just getting older. Trevor loved their breakfast menu, served all day, but he worried I would feel uncomfortable because Nadine worked there. I snorted. "I see her every day. It's not like we'll explode if we see each other outside the house."

Because we had a pickup scheduled after lunch, we climbed into the Thrift Store's sixteen-foot van for the five-minute drive to the restaurant, Leah between Trevor and me. I pulled onto the street.

Leah nudged me with her shoulder. "But I agree with Trevor. There was a time when you and Nadine, you know." She raised her fists. "You told me."

She was right. Back in Wisconsin, I wouldn't have given Nadine the time of day, and she wouldn't have asked. I thought I'd told Trevor that, but then again maybe I hadn't. Since the move, Nadine and I had slipped into some kind of uneasy truce. And sure, from time to time both of us would violate the moratorium and backslide into our own version of trench warfare. "Yeah, but that was before," I said, smiling ruefully. "Back then, after she married my father, the battle lines were everywhere. We went to the mat on everything. We still argue, but I got other things to think about, and so does she. I mean, perfect example—a year ago there was zero chance of seeing her in a waitress uniform."

We parked in TPK's lot, went inside, and seated ourselves in the last available booth. Busy as it was, it took Nadine five minutes to bring ice water and menus to the table. She apologized for the delay.

"No problem," Trevor's voice was like syrup. "We can see how busy you are." He usually got tongue-tied around girls. Nadine was the exception, and I wasn't sure why. She was older than the girls at school but every bit as hot, so he should have been a stumbling moron around her too. The change came after he'd seen Nadine at our house at various times of day in casual dress. The conversations between her and I were not affectionate, but they had the tinge of the commonplace. Trevor grew into it, although only after several false starts which were invariably short and awkward. I think he picked up on my ease in her presence and suddenly Trevor felt more comfortable.

"Hey, Nadine." I looked up from the menu. "I think we all know what we want. Leah, you wanna go first?"

Leah waved at Trevor. "Get the guys. I'm still deciding."

I ordered the French Dip with fries and water.

"Me too on the water." Trevor folded the menu and used his hands to describe his order. "I'd like the blueberry pancakes, but instead of the sauce and whip cream, can I get butter and syrup?"

"Sure," Nadine said, her eyes shining.

"Thanks. You're awesome."

She smiled again. "Do you need more time, Leah?" She shook her head and ordered the chicken salad and soup special and coffee, black. "Okay, I'll put in the order."

Trevor turned his head, watching her walk away, still gazing when there was nothing to see but the kitchen door swinging on its hinge. I flicked a packet of sugar and hit Trevor in the head. He flinched back to the table. "I couldn't do it. How can you live in the same house?" Leah and I, both astonished, stared at him.

"Trevor! Come on. Leah's right here." I said, "She's reason number one. Reason number two, she's my *stepmom*. Reason number three, she's ten years older and m-a-r-r-i-e-d."

"Yeah, I know but…" I swore Trevor to silence about the age difference. I didn't want that to get around town.

I said to Leah, "I don't know if I can be seen with this guy anymore."

She glanced about the restaurant. "Find him a girlfriend. He'll be fine." He amused her, and she didn't hide it. But she had to be careful with the personal attention. She didn't want to lead him on.

I sat forward. "Truth is, I don't think things are so fine with my father and her. If you know what I mean. In fact, I know they're not." I mentioned thin walls, late nights, and strained, hushed conversations I didn't want to hear.

"Oh, that kind of talk," Leah said.

"Yeah, and she's not happy about it."

Leah grabbed hold of my upper arm and pulled me close. "Let's go back to reason #1. What was that one again?" We rubbed noses.

"Okay." Trevor waved his napkin in surrender. "Let's just keep the PDA under control, all right? We're in a restaurant here. People are trying to eat."

Leah turned to Trevor. "No, no. My point is, reason #1—why Max shouldn't go to the University of Iowa. It's too, too far. Eleven hours away, and for what?" She tilted her head in my direction. "South Dakota has a lot of schools half the distance, and Black Hills in Spearfish—"

"Stop right there." I held up my hand. "You know Black Hills if off the table. Too close to home."

"Why? What's the problem?" Trevor asked. In the fall, he would be attending a Tech school in Rapid City. He liked the Black Hills argument because I would still be in Moreau.

I took a look around to check for eavesdroppers, but the restaurant was bustling and noisy; no one was paying us any mind. I said the people at the table were the only ones who knew that when I left for college I planned to rarely, if ever return home. I was bolting. Present company excluded, I felt no connection to anything or anyone in Moreau. "And then there's my family's past," I said. "You both know how I feel about that."

I had to stop there and make my case without mentioning the WPP. They had magnified my family's dysfunction a thousand-fold and poisoned everything I saw, smelled, or touched in Moreau. I couldn't leave the WPP, George had made that clear. My original plan had been to go to a Westcoast college and never come back—a perfect plan until I met Leah. She had both complicated my life and saved it. What the last twelve months would have been without her made me shudder. "So, I said to the beautiful artist, 'Come with me. Iowa City is a college town, artsy people, you'll fit right in.' But…" I pointed at Leah. "Your turn."

"I don't want to leave Moreau. My family, my friends, people who love and inspire me. Everything that has gone into my art started here. But I don't want to lose Max." She looked at me. "But why so far? South Dakota State is only five hours. I could drive there. You could sneak back into town to—"

"Wait, wait," I said. "It's almost impossible to sneak anything in or out of Moreau." I knew that wasn't exactly right; my family had done it. I pointed at Trevor. "What do you think? Who wins, Trev?"

"Whoa, wait. I'm not getting in the middle."

"Go ahead," I said. "Say whatever you want."

He clearly felt uncomfortable as the center of attention. But after reassurances from Leah and me, he spoke his mind. "But I'm leaning into this compromise thing, maybe because I'm selfish." His eyes danced back and forth between Leah and me, begging for some sign of approval.

The order arrived. I sat back while Nadine filled the table with plates of food, the coffee, and put the bill face down next to my plate.

Compromise: I hadn't seen that one coming. There'd been so little of it in my life, I barely knew the word. Mine was an all or nothing world. Stay out of trouble or go to a boarding school; no in between. Then there was the nanny my father hired to watch me during the summer. I liked her, George did not. She was fired and I was off to two boarding schools in two years, the second one military. I wasn't cut out for either of them but that didn't matter to my father. While I was away he found enough time and freedom to date and marry Nadine, who had the maternal instincts of a snake and no interest in who I was or what I was doing.

Black and white was all I had known.

We used to live in "the most exclusive property on Red Wolf Lake," my father used to say, but it had all the soul of a worn-out boot. No wonder I'd spent half my nights at Noquebay Resort last summer. It was owned by Sam Robel's parents. His family lived in the lodge, a one-hundred-year-old building that had no air conditioning and floors that slanted from room to room like a Tilt-a-Whirl at a county fair. And I loved it.

For one summer, the Robels had become my family. Sam had two brothers and a sister. I had started to feel like I was part of that, part of a group for the common good, eating meals with them; and Mrs. Robel claiming me as one of her own anytime I was under their roof. And the cooking, the smells of casseroles and spaghetti, baked cakes and pies in her makeshift kitchen were enough to put me on a regular eating schedule for the first time. Jim Robel, at the head of the table, held everyone to the same manners and expected everyone to help around the resort, including me. These were the things I had during the summer of 2013, had never had before, and would never have again.

Most of all there was Diane Warren, a girl I'd been dating for only a couple weeks. I had to end it, of course. In a tearful meeting, I mumbled a half-baked apology about how things just weren't going to work out. She looked at me through moist eyes, not understanding, not believing, not wanting to hear what was being said, but in the end, courageous.

And therein lay what made Leah Walters special. I'd dated several other Moreau girls before meeting Leah, all of them pretty, one of them gorgeous, another as bright and smart as Emma Watson. But none of them made me forget Diane. Only Leah was able to do that.

Between bites, Trevor said, "What you're really shooting for is to break with the family but not with Leah. But you said your dad has this mysterious deal that says you have to live here and we can't tell anyone."

"That's right," I said. "You both swore."

"Yeah, yeah, yeah. I'm down," Trevor said. "You're going to slow play it, go to college, slip away. Everyone will fall asleep and poof, you're gone."

I said, "Right. I'm not asking for anything extra."

Trevor pointed at me. "Clint Eastwood. Outlaw Josie Wales!" He sat briefly, considering. "But with Leah's plan, you can do it just the same." He nodded. "She wins."

I shrugged. "It was a losing battle. If I was really serious, and Leah wasn't around, I'd strap the guitar to my back, hitchhike to L.A., and join a band." I knew Trevor was right. The one thing I couldn't lose was Leah, the only person I'd ever met that gave me a sense of wonder. The first time I saw her art, I was astonished. Then, sometime later, she allowed me to watch her work in the studio, and I fell in love.

Trevor insisted on leaving the tip, very generous because it was for Nadine. We stood at the front register. I handed the cashier a twenty. Leah brushed hair from her face and saw Trevor holding his cell. "Are you texting?"

"No, checking an address." He expanded the screen. "We have a pick-up for the store." He showed the address to me. "Supposed to be there in thirty minutes."

"I gotta go, too," Leah said. "I'll walk back. I like the exercise." She asked me about our plans for later and since we had tapped out of options in Moreau, suggested we drive to Rapid City. We'd meet at seven. Leah walked away, teasing plaster from her hair.

Trevor and I climbed into the panel truck, a reject from a rental company with over 350,000 miles on it. The air conditioning was shot and so were the springs in the seats.

With the end of our senior year fast approaching, our talk turned to graduation plans and Prom, a week away. Trevor didn't have a date. I was going with Leah. Even though she'd graduated last year, this would be her first prom. She was sick her Junior year and had to cancel. Senior year she wanted to go, but wasn't asked by the right guy, so she stayed home.

"You should ask somebody," I said. "It's not too late. Ask Elise Anderson. She's cute."

"What? She's a soph. She wouldn't understand my sophisticated humor."

"Neither do I, but I still laugh." I turned onto the County Highway to take us out of town. "All the girls in the Junior and Senior class are pretty much gone."

"Elise, hey," Trevor said. "She *is* cute. And not as crazy as most of the Sophs. If I tell you something, you can't repeat it."

"Whatever, sure."

"For a while, I had a thing for her."

"No shit. When was this?" I asked.

"The first time I saw her. Love at first sight."

"See what I'm telling you?"

Trevor waved that off. "Hell, I can do love at first sight every fifteen minutes."

I laughed. "So, call her. The worst she can do is say no."

"She wouldn't go with a pudge like me." The truck labored up a rise. He asked, "What about you? I hope you're playing straight with Leah. She knows why you're here, right?"

I shook my head. "No one knows everything, not even you."

"Wait a minute." He glared at me. "You've had sex with her and she doesn't know the most important thing about you?" Trevor sat back, astonished. "You don't have to tell me the whole story, but you gotta tell her."

"It's for her own good."

"There it is again." Trevor paused. "One of these days it's going to bite you in the ass."

I agreed with him more than he realized, but arguing this through was pointless, so I let it drop. There were times I felt guilty telling Leah anything at all. What if something happened to her? Here was an artist, starting a medium I had never seen before: layers of color and plaster and strings of different lengths and strengths, embedded together like a lasagna. Except, after it set, she ripped the strings from the plaster in what looked like random destruction, but was really a carefully choreographed disassembly. In the end, underneath, there emerged an image. Fascinating really. She was an artistic savant waiting to be discovered. If somehow, she got tied up in my father's past and the mob, I would never forgive myself. I looked at the map on the cell. "Couple miles yet."

I'd fallen in love with the art right away. But with the artist? That took a little longer. When I said her talent was too big for a small shop, she hesitated. She wanted to remain in her studio. That was where the vibes were strong, the light was pure, the colors spoke. But she was spinning her wheels in this town, and so was I. Why couldn't she see that? Sometimes she could irritate the hell out of me.

The pickup call took a couple of hours. A family was cleaning out the home of their father, who'd died after living in the house for decades. Some of the linen was so threadbare it would be thrown in the trash, as would most of the clothing. As always, I held my breath for that one-in-a-thousand find—a classic Taylor acoustic guitar, tucked away in a worn guitar case, dusty and forgotten, lying in a back closet. The perfect partner to my Stratocaster. The best part of this haul would be the small appliances. The old boy must have been a junkie for the Home Shopping Network. Dozens of countertop gizmos, and they would sell pretty well at the Thrift Store. But no guitar.

On the way back to town we were hungry and the truck needed a fill, so I pulled up to a pump at a station just outside of Moreau. Trevor took care of the gas. I went inside to buy some drinks and a couple burgers.

I slid the prewrapped sandwiches toward the register and ordered two regular coffees. A commotion out by the pumps caught my eye. I stepped to the window. Trevor had his hands up, trying to apologize to a biker, who was setting his Honda back on its stand and cursing at Trevor. I assumed Trevor had accidentally knocked over the bike. The rider turned and I saw his face. A knot stuck in my throat. The round, puffy, pink face of Tugger Jonsson was unmistakable. So was his bloated belly, oozing neck, and the stained overalls that saved the world from exposure to the rest of his mass. Tugger and Trevor were the worst kind of enemies, foes from the same side of the tracks. Neither knew when the animus had started nor why, and now, Trevor had committed the ultimate insult: damage to Tugger's bike.

It would be no contest. Tugger was the heavyweight from last year's wrestling team, and even though he hadn't done much as an athlete, he was still nasty. Trevor was a little taller and could match him in weight but not in muscle nor temperament. Tugger hand-checked Trevor backward into a concrete pillar. He winced and cried out in pain. I went back to the register. "Make that two jumbo coffees." I swiped my card and left.

"You forgot the burgers," called the attendant.

Tugger put the gas nozzle back on the pump, moved toward Trevor, and grabbed him by the throat. Tugger backed him up against a pillar. I walked over to the Honda, sipped coffee from one cup and pulled the keys from the bike's ignition.

When he saw me sitting on his bike, Tugger let go of Trevor and yelled. "Hey! What the fuck are you doing?"

I tried to keep my voice calm, "Dropping these keys into the gas tank of this piece-of-shit rice-grinder you call a bike." The keys plopped.

Tugger growled and elbowed Trevor in the stomach. He folded in half. Tugger charged. I threw a jumbo of piping-hot in his face, the other on his shirt. Tugger roared in pain. I pushed the bike over, then kicked Tugger in the balls.

Trevor was hands on knees, eyes wide, and mouth gasping.

I pointed. "Trevor! Truck! Let's get the hell out of here."

CHAPTER THREE

Max

The Red Wolf High School Annual was contraband, as illegal as anything within a fifty-mile radius of my bedroom. If the Feds got even a sniff they'd be on me like ravens on roadkill. I sat down on my bed and ran my fingertips across the textured finish. Three weeks after I'd ordered it from the Red Wolf High School website, UPS delivered it right to the front door. Whoever did the cover design had nailed it. A wolf's head in shades of grey, eyes of red, the school colors, with the same tones on the border, *2014* inscribed in a lower corner.

The Annual wasn't thick. There were only seventy-three in the graduating class. One of them, Sam Robel, had done as I asked, got my real name in the Annual even though I hadn't spent my senior year there, not a single day. The pages leafed open to the Senior picture section. At the bottom of page nine there was a grey box that said "Picture Not Available." The name below was the one given by my mother eighteen years ago—Max Cherhasky. Had I still lived there, I would've been on my way to pick up Diane Warren for the Red Wolf High prom. I wished I had a picture of her, but just like Leah, she had graduated a year ahead of me, so she wouldn't be in the annual.

I hated myself for falling into this sticky nostalgia. Yearning for what used to be was stupid, a waste of time. And yet, I couldn't help it. I deplored this life of eggshells and mirrors, where everything was fragile and nothing as it seemed. If my father found me with the Annual the consequences would be immediate and prolonged—bitching and recriminations were the last thing I wanted to deal with. What was the harm, as long as the Feds and the Mob didn't find out? I placed the Annual back in the boot box and put it on the top shelf of my closet. I grabbed the eight-dollar three-piece suit I'd bought from The Thrift Store off the rack and got ready for the prom at Moreau High School.

The shirt was simple white, the tie stolen from my father's Gerry Garcia Collection, psychedelic orange, blues, yellows, and blacks. But my favorite were the shoes, boots really, Caterpillar steel toes, Thrift Store specials, solid black. Leah would do some artsy, hand-stitched dress, over-the-top-Hollywood made out of material I could only guess at. All the signs pointed toward a great night, so why did I feel as if there was a stone stuck in my throat? I left the house without notice from George or Nadine, started the Ranger and drove.

The Walters lived in a side-by-side duplex rental in an aggressively bland neighborhood. Tract residential buildings to the end of the block, roadside mailboxes, and no sidewalks. Again, I was struck with the idea that Leah, this striking human, capable of something so complex and breathtaking as her art, had come from these dull surroundings. Ken, the old man, was an over-the-road trucker and rarely home. A big step up from the old days, when he was occasionally employed, frequently parked in the living room, and generally drunk. I turned onto the gutterless street. No truck parked across the street, so Ken Walters was working.

I pulled into the gravel driveway and walked up to the front door, flowerbox in hand. A wrist corsage, she told me, and when she answered the door, I saw why. Leah's dress appeared to be made of white feathers edged in pink—artificial I was sure, given her love of animals—and strapless, off-the-shoulder. There was nowhere to pin a corsage. She looked ready-made for a wedding except the hem was too short. She was thinner than me and tall, at 5 foot, 10 inches, so in heels we were about the same height. The only thing she had in abundance was hair, thick and black, which made her blue eyes and red lips smolder like ice and fire.

The late afternoon sun was filtered by the screen door, which

I was still holding. The light caught Leah's face and stopped my breath. "Don't move." I pulled out my cell phone. "I need a pic."

"Here, at the door? I don't have my heels on."

I grinned and checked the pic. "Can't see your feet. Guaranteed." In the photo her gaze was direct, her mouth open with the hint of a smile, the tip of her tongue visible between her teeth. I looked at the image and then turned the phone toward her and said, "Beautiful."

"Come in," she said. "Can't wait to see you dance in those boots. I'll get my shoes, then you can give me the flowers."

I sat down on her father's Lazy Boy. I watched her walk away and felt a pang of remorse. In every idle minute, I had it: the underground stream of a guilty past, the oppressive present, a future already tainted by lies and half-truths, and the relentless thumb of the WPP growing more onerous. Neither Leah nor Trevor knew, but I'd packed and repacked my suitcase a dozen times. For months, I'd been hoarding cash, waiting for fate to give me a reason to leave Moreau. Was I compulsive? Probably. Paranoid? I had never been so, not back in Wisconsin.

She walked down the hall in three-inch heels, white to match the dress.

Mrs. Walters walked in from the kitchen, held up her phone, and said, "Pictures."

––––––––––––––––––

We had dinner alone. I'd asked Trevor to come along, but he hadn't asked Elise Anderson in time. She was going with a group of girlfriends, so maybe they would meet at the dance. The supper club was busy with other couples, foursomes and two parties of eight, all pre-prom groups because Snider's Steak House was the only decent gig within a twenty-mile radius of the school. Leah didn't eat red meat, so she had the scallops. I ordered a T-bone, no salad, no soup, just plenty of bread and butter.

We started people watching. Which couple was trying too hard, which guy was too loud, which dress too tight. Even more fun were the faces on the older crowd as the prom-goers walked by. Eventually, the conversation stalled, mostly because I grew quiet. Leah asked if I was all right. "It's been a tough week."

Leah put a napkin on her lap and leaned forward. "The fight with Tugger?"

"Spending too much time on the Internet. Shit I shouldn't be looking at."

Now I was stuck. Of course, she would want to know more. For months I'd been so careful not to spill hints about my past. But like Trevor said, Leah deserved to know who I was. "It has to do with my family and where I used to live."

"You never told me. I asked but—" The anticipation in her eyes made me look away.

My tongue stumbled. "I know, and I still can't. It's not up to me. If it was, I'd tell you in a second. It's for your own good." All the same old tired lines I'd dragged out a hundred times before, just like my WPP handlers had instructed. I'm sure she was sick of them. I was too, and sick of the sound of my own voice.

For long seconds, she was ominously silent. The emotions passing across her face were unnerving and changing so fast I didn't know where her head was at. Her eyes were looking left, vacantly gazing at the couple at the next table. Then, a breath in and suddenly I was in her sights. "Why don't you let me decide what's best for me? I've had enough of this 'for your own good' crap. Where do you get off telling me what I should know and not know? That's b.s., Max. The secrets have to stop, if you want to stay with me."

She was so beautiful in that dress, and yet her words had bite. It was almost surreal. And she wasn't done. "If you're not okay with that, say so. I'll be fine. Breaking up now would be hard, but better than waiting for someone or something to do it for us."

I shouldn't have been stunned by her reply, but I was. I needed some breathing room, so I tried to backfill. "What do you mean?" I asked softly, hoping to defuse her frustration and anger. "I don't tell you what to do. You act like I'm trying to control you."

"That's not what I said." Her eyes had the intensity I'd seen in the studio, when she was ripping strands of twine from a canvas. "It's about trust. It's about closeness. Do you really think we can make it together if one of us"—she leaned forward, her face framed in black curls—"if one of us has secrets?"

There was nothing to argue. And she'd mentioned the idea of breaking up, which was the last thing I wanted to do. "Okay, I get it. The secrecy is eating me up, too. And I don't know what to do with it."

"Share them, with me." A red fingernail tapped on the table. "You can have your secrets with the rest of the world. But not with me."

I nodded.

She swallowed, shifted. "Okay, what about the Internet?"

I looked about, as if to check for prying ears, but I didn't have to. The place was humming, noisy, the excited voices of prom-goers had taken over. "I've been following news reports from back home." I paused while bread and butter were put on the table. "There's this lake, they found a body at the bottom. A skeleton really, dead for years."

Leah's eyes widened.

"Don't worry." I put a finger to my chest. "*I* didn't put it there. We, my friends and I, we were the ones got them to look for it. Right before I came here." I ripped apart a roll. "We thought we knew who it was. We were wrong. It's been almost a year, and they still haven't identified the... remains. They have a list who they think it might be." I bit into the roll.

Leah finally took a breath. "You've always avoided talking about 'home.' I thought of a dozen reasons why. A body at the bottom of a lake was not one of them. Keep going..."

I said, "My mother, my real mom, died fourteen years ago. The cops say they know how she died, but I think the story is b.s."

She wanted to hear the story, b.s. or not.

"Mom and my father were on a camping trip in northern Wisconsin—"

"Oh! So, you're from Wisconsin. Go on."

My neck burned. "My dad said a renegade bear mauled my

mother while he was off on a hike. They found a trail of blood leading from the tent to a river. Her body was never found." I paused for a breath. "She's on the list, you know, of cold cases. They never found her."

Leah's jaw dropped. "My god, Max. How would your mother's body get to the bottom…?" She couldn't finish the sentence.

"Of a lake?" I held up the butter knife. "That's what I'd like to know. My father always told me this story—" I stopped myself. "Shit, sorry. I've got to stop. See what I mean? Second guessing everything. Don't know who to believe. Like this bear-in-the-woods crap."

"How do you know? You should have said something to someone."

I bristled at that, but glad she couldn't guess at what was in my head. Suddenly, the clinking of glasses and silverware bothered my ears. "I didn't say I *know* it. And who would believe anything from a four-year-old anyway?"

"Well, no. Not back then," she admitted. "I see what you mean. Who would listen, even to a teenager?" Tears welled in her eyes. "I'm sorry. What was your mother's name? Can I ask that?"

I nodded. "Madelyn."

The waiter served Leah's salad. I said thank you, the bread was fine.

Leah stabbed at her greens. I went on. "You can see why I don't want anything to do with my family. I mean my dad, the appliance salesman who thinks he has the world by the ass. But the more I read about what's going on back home…" It felt like the eyes of the room were on me. I slowed down. "I don't know if I want to go back to Wisconsin and see what the fuck, or run the other way."

"That's awful, Max." She dabbed her lips with a napkin, then froze. "Do you think your father had something to do with your mom's… disappearance? You're skeptical about something obviously. Maybe there's more you're not remembering."

My knee banged into the underside of the table. The plates and silverware rattled. "No! Remember? How could I remember? I was too young." I sat back. "I think her name is on the list just because she's a cold case, a missing person. But yeah, I don't trust my father any farther than I can throw a truck."

"Have you ever talked to him about Madelyn's death?"

I said, "No, never. I don't think he'd be able to look me in the eye. He knows I blame him."

"Then he's lying. I agree, or somebody is. Sooner or later he'll have to come clean."

Something lurched in my stomach. "Come clean? What does that even mean? Everyone has a stain that won't come out."

She tilted her head like a bird listening, trying to figure out which direction the sound was coming from. The look on her face was quizzical and knowing at the same time, and it shook me.

"Sorry, sorry. I shouldn't have said that." I knew I'd made a major blunder. How was I going to get away from that one? Leah was too smart to fool. What was it about these women I'd dated? When I told Diane the same camping story, she'd said it was bullshit, a cover. I thought she had the best b.s. detector in the world, until I met Leah. The difference between the two was that Diane was calling out the story on a hunch. Leah made it personal: she'd all but accused me of not telling the truth. "They're gonna do DNA on the body. You know they will." I gazed sideways. "They might already have my DNA. What if I'm a match?"

"Don't go there. It's too awful to think about. Besides, she wasn't *camping* near your home, was she?"

I sat back. "No. Up North in a National Forest."

"Far away?"

"Pretty far, yeah." I tapped the roll on my plate. "Okay, I see your point."

"Max, who has your DNA?"

I was walking a line between a full confession and keeping my involvement with the Federal Government a secret. I couldn't tear my heart out and show it to her. That would put her in the same awful predicament I was facing. The DNA was a complication I may have bought on myself. I didn't want to talk about it anymore. "I'm being paranoid. Just forget it. Please?"

Hesitantly, she nodded, then asked an unrelated question. "I've been thinking about Nadine. How you used to fight like cats and dogs. And now this thing with your mother, do you think you resent Nadine for trying to take her place?"

"I remember very little about Madelyn, so I don't think so. Nadine and I are just too different."

She ate a forkful of salad. "And now you get along, not great, but better. What's that about?" I shrugged as if to say 'you tell me.' "I think it's because now you have something in common."

"Like what? My father? That's not new."

"No. The moving. The stress of a new life. I'll bet she hates it as much as you do. She wasn't working until you moved here, right? Bet that doesn't sit well. And now, she's stuck in a marriage... How would you describe it?"

"Bad." I bit into another role and regrouped my thoughts. Leah's intuition was overwhelming and, in a way, intimidating. I had hinted at some of the things going on at home, but she'd fleshed out the details all by herself.

The entrées were served. I ate without tasting the steak. The tone of the conversation had taken my appetite. We were sharing a one-and-done lifetime event, and I was making a mess of it. My graduation was looming over the table, and so were the questions that came with it. In spite of the debate at TPK's, I still hadn't decided about college. Leah spent most of her time watching me. The minutes rolled by.

"If I Google 'George Farmer, missing wife?'" Leah asked. "Will I get any hits?"

"I don't know. Lots of George Farmers out there, but you won't get the one in Moreau. The people who moved us here have made sure of that."

"What if I Google 'Max Farmer'?"

"I don't know. Forty-nine-year-old cabbie in Boston maybe. But not me."

An attempt at humor, but she didn't find it amusing. "Hmm." She stopped eating. "Max, I'm scared."

"Scared? Why?" I wondered if the family history was too gruesome for her. "This business about bodies and missing persons, it's just talk. It's not me."

She wrinkled her brow. "Not about that. I'm worried about you. About us."

I grabbed my water glass, took a drink, then set the glass down very slowly. "Enough. No more about me. Terrible dinner conversation. How are the scallops?"

"The scallops are fine." She leaned forward. "I want you to know—"

"I know what you're going to say," I said, too loud for the room. I pursed my lips. "I hear you. I do." I was afraid of the end of the sentence. Leah's emotional intelligence was off the hook. She knew I was holding back. If she didn't know all the details, that was nothing. She could simply ask. But she needed a partner who'd give an honest answer, and I wasn't sure how I felt about anything, not even myself.

"No, you don't."

"What?" I asked.

"You don't know what I was going to say." She lowered her voice. "I was going to say you can tell me anything you want about you and your past, about Wisconsin, your family. It makes no difference to me. I'll still love you."

Struggling to speak, I blinked two, three, five times.

"Okay?"

My voice cracked. "Okay." I cut into my steak. How had life become so tortured? I pushed the past out of my mind; tried not to think about Sam and Diane anymore, or the night we'd brazenly broke into a boat house and brought down the Manticore dynasty. Friends I loved once and couldn't have. Now, life had sent me Leah, a jewel I wanted above all others and which, somehow, was moving beyond my reach.

Had the heavy conversation over dinner set the tone for the evening? I thought so. I couldn't even look forward to the music. Disc jockeys and mirror balls never did it for me. But once we got past the Grand March, I was glad I came. Leah was lovely. The dark cloud hanging over us at the restaurant had disappeared. Her miniskirt gown drew looks from everyone. One of the senior girls asked to buy Leah's dress on the spot for a bachelorette party. Trevor showed up in his father's suit and provided comical distraction. He played lunge and parry with the knot of sophomore girls that included Elise Anderson. Finally, the throbbing bass of hip hop ended and a ballad played.

I moved close to Leah's ear and asked, "Dance?"

She put her hand on the back of my neck and kissed me.

The dance with Leah was the peak of the evening. On the other hand, the entertainment was just starting. Elise got Trevor on the dance floor. Skillful and subtle he was not, but when it came to intensity and abandon he didn't take a back seat to anyone. Elise needed the reflexes of a gymnast just to stay out of his way.

"Is that girl in dance?" Leah asked.

"She ought to be," I said. "If she can make Trevor look good, she could be in vids."

Leah locked her hand in mine and held it up. "And here are the fingers," she said. "That will play the music, to the vid that Elise will dance in."

I blushed, not because of the music video, that was my dream, but because she implied I'd be *in Moreau* to do it. Then it hit me. I couldn't make a video. Hell, while I was in the WPP I couldn't even write a Letter to the Editor of the Moreau Times.

The song ended. "Well, we won't be seeing much of Trevor for the rest of the night."

While I obsessed about tomorrow, Trevor was having a hell of a night. Why couldn't I live in the moment, this one time? Leah was so good at it; could I not learn this simple skill from her? Forever with me it was a preoccupation with the past, the future, with stacks and stacks of old furniture at the Thrift Store, for god's sake. I could keep things in order everywhere, except my brain.

The night was winding down. I tugged on Leah's elbow. "You ready?"

She grabbed her lipstick purse. "Let's go."

The night had cooled. We could see our breath as we sat in the cab of the truck. The windshield fogged. I draped my suit coat over her shoulders. She sat close to me on the bench seat and put her hand on my thigh. I drove slowly, waiting for the engine to warm enough for the heater to work. I asked if she was going to try fashion design. She laughed me off, but I persisted, arguing there were more shows on cable for fashion than there were for artists.

"Do you know how many fashion designers have been discovered in South Dakota?" Leah asked, using my own line against me. "Less than zero. But I'll make you a deal." I looked at her skeptically. She leaned in. "You take one of the songs you wrote, let's say *19 Counts*. I like that one. You record it in a studio. I know you can do the guitars and drums. Then make a homemade vid and put it on YouTube. Just like Bieber did."

I scoffed. For one thing, I couldn't afford studio time. Leah said she'd pitch in as a producer. If I did the video, she would take a shot at fashion. I didn't say no, because I'd love nothing more than to try studio work. But there were hurdles. I'd have to borrow a bass guitar. And drums have to be practiced to be any good.

"Excuses," Leah said.

I parked in the drive behind her father's Peterbilt Cab. "Looks like your dad's home."

"Looks like." Leah put her hand on the door handle. "You want to come in? Dad won't mind. He likes you."

Leah unlocked the front door, which woke up her father. He'd been sleeping in the Lazy Boy, beer in hand, the TV flickering in front of him. He lowered the foot rest and rubbed his face. She apologized for waking him. Her father said he was just about to go to bed and asked about the prom. Leah said it was great, and she and I were going up to her room for a while. Her dad went up the steps ahead of us. The duplex had two floors, all the bedrooms up. Leah and I could hear her dad getting ready for bed as we sat barefoot, cross-legged on her bed, knees touching. We talked low, sometimes in a whisper.

"This is why," Leah said. "I want to move out of here. Dad said not until I'm married." She rolled her eyes. "It's embarrassing. I'm nineteen."

I thought her father had nothing to worry about, that Leah could take care of herself. I privately grinned when I remembered she let me into her bed before she allowed me to watch her work in the studio. "That's nothing," I said. "I know people twenty-nine and still at home. Older than that." I put my finger under her chin and kissed her. "But I wish you had your own place too, man do I wish and hope and pray and want." I grabbed one of her big toes and wiggled it. "Your dad seems all right. There was a time I hated my father, when he was working, making the big bucks. It was all he ever thought about."

"I'm the opposite." She kissed me. "Before, when he was out of work, he did nothing but sit home and complain and drink. This job—" She kissed me again. "Is a godsend."

Chapter Four

Max

"I don't care what you say," Trevor said. "There is no way the word *compromise* and Leah Walters appear in the same sentence." Knees bent, feet on the low concrete wall outside of school, he and I sat together eating our lunch. I felt his eyes on the side of my face. "That is cold. Who are you, man?"

"Dial it back, for chrissakes. That's not what I said." The campus was busy, conversations lost in the hum of a hundred other voices near and far, carried on the first breath of spring. The sun warmed our faces and hands. I picked at my tennis shoe. "I said her *solution* was a compromise. But like I said, Iowa is three times bigger than South Dakota State. If I'm looking to put a band together, my chances are way better in Iowa City. It's all about the talent pool, man." Heart Shaped Box was a perfect example. They were the best guys in Moreau, and not nearly good enough. "I wish she'd just come with me and see the world."

"And that's another thing." Trevor swung his legs around and looked away. "What's with all the talk of leaving? What is that? You don't have to. There are people here who like you, who love you, for chrissakes, if you haven't noticed. Stay here and keep Leah. It's a no-brainer."

"South Dakota State is a bad deal for me. Really, what do I get there that I don't already have? In fact, it's less. Less Leah, it's not Big 10, and it's too close to home."

Trevor pointed his sandwich at me. "Do you hear yourself? You bitch about your father, then say something like that." He raised his eyebrows. "Like father, like son."

"Spare me the curbside psychology. Freud says I kill my father and bang my mother. Well, the old man is still breathing, and Mom is dead a long time ago."

———————

My arms were folded on the history text on my desk. Eyes closed, lips moving silently: *The run to California*, I thought. *fare $300, food twenty dollars a day ... I could do it.* The bus stops clicked through my head. Buffalo, Wyoming; Denver; Las Vegas; Riverside.

Trevor, sitting across from me, shoved me in the shoulder. I flinched. "What?"

Trevor nodded toward the head of the classroom and Mr. Crawford. The intercom spoke. "Is Max Farmer present?"

"He is now," Mr. Crawford answered.

That's why I hadn't heard the name in the first place. "Farmer" still didn't register in my brain, never would.

"Have him come to the office, please."

"Yes sir, Mr. Tonn." The teacher turned toward the board and added, "Max, take your books." It was almost the end of last hour so there was no point in coming back. Graduation was only a few days away, so my grades were already made.

I had no idea what the principal was calling about. In the last few months, Trevor and I had scaled back the classroom interruptions and hallway mayhem, just as Mr. Tonn had demanded. In return, we retained our driving-to-school privileges. I entered the secretary's office. She pointed toward the open door to her left. I stepped in. "Mr. Tonn, you wanted to see me? And before you say anything, I had nothing to do with that campaign poster for next-years student council. You know me. My pornography is a lot classier than that."

Mr. Tonn smirked. "No, not that. I got a call from your mother—"

"My mother died when I was four."

"Ah, right, sorry. Stepmother. Nadine is quite upset, and she wants you to come home right away."

"Why? What happened? Why didn't she call me?"

"I don't know. Maybe she assumed you'd need permission to leave class, so she called my office. Something to do with your father."

I frowned. "Now what?"

"You should go."

I turned to leave but remembered I had to drive Trevor home as well. Mr. Tonn said I could take Trevor out of class and notified Mr. Crawford.

The springs on the Ford Ranger groaned as Trevor and I climbed in. Trevor had the glow of early release all over him. I frowned at the traffic, which was heavier than usual.

"Crawford had a minor stroke when you came to get me," Trevor said. "But my spot at the technical school is a lock. What do I need with a history grade?" He wasn't as confident as he sounded. Graduation was a prerequisite for the welding degree he wanted, and he had to pass all his classes to get a diploma.

The brakes squealed as we pulled in front of Trevor's home.

"Thanks for the ride. See you tomorrow," Trevor said. "Call later?"

I threw him a 'will do' wave as I pulled away.

My place was another mile down the road—a small ranch on the edge of town with a single-car garage, no sidewalk, a single tree on the side lot, and a lawn that was half sand, half grass, half weeds. I parked the truck on the gravel driveway and walked in through the garage, picking up a spent beer bottle as I went in. Stepping into the kitchen, I called for Nadine, but there was no answer. I called again, set my book bag on the counter, and found the eight-pack of seven empties under the sink. I replaced the eighth and looked to my left. Nadine appeared from the living room, tissues in hand, mascara running down her face, her usually clear, green eyes as pink and pale as unripe strawberries.

"Max." She came to me and wrapped her arms around my chest. "You're here."

I was stunned. Through all the court cases, the trial, the lawyer deals, the grand jury testimony, she had little more than touched my hand. Because of all the whispers about my father's trophy wife, I had steered clear too. I put the empties on the counter. "Nadine, what's going on?"

She stepped back, put her hand on her forehead, and said, "It's George, your dad. They've arrested him." She put the tissues over her mouth. "Oh, Max, I'm so sorry."

I thought we'd gotten beyond worrying about Dad and his legal hassles. We'd paid that price when we left Wisconsin. I grasped her by the shoulders. "Why? What happened to him?"

She looked down. "I told you. Arrested, again…"

I let her go. "I know that, but for what? Is he cheating customers on the appliance contracts? Bait and switch?" I snatched the eight-pack in disgust. "What?"

"Oh, it's much worse. They think he killed…" Her throat seized. I didn't think she would say another word. Sobbing, she took a step back and leaned against the stove.

Killed? Killed who? I wondered. I was surprised but not shocked. Because of my father's ties to the mob; anything was possible. Nadine was the bigger mystery. I'd only seen her like this one time before. Eleven months and two weeks ago she had locked up the same way. Tissues in hand, she'd shuttered in a corner of our kitchen, surrounded by granite counters and giant, stainless steel appliances, while a team of FBI agents slapped a search warrant on the table and handcuffs on her husband.

With my free hand, I took hold of her upper arm and braced her. "Nadine, what are you talking about?"

"It's…It's your mother." She'd rarely mentioned her to me, and never called her by name. I would tolerate no comment, nor listen to any opinion, be it positive, negative, or otherwise from Nadine about my mother. She looked in my eyes and gasped. "They found Madelyn. The body in Red Wolf Lake. It's her."

The eight-pack crashed to the floor.

Chapter Five

Max

I spent the weekend in isolation. My mood was so dark, I didn't want to see anyone, not even Leah. We had a daily call routine, so rather than raise any suspicions, I dialed her up. I feigned illness and told her I didn't want her to catch it. She picked up the bad vibe, so right away she had me sputtering nonsense. I hung up and realized if I didn't tell her about the arrest, she'd hear it from someone else. News travels fast in a small town when there's a murder suspect in their midst.

On the second call, I told her the truth. It took everything I had to convince her that I needed some space. I'd been torn in half, and I didn't want her to see me so full of indecision and doubt. I promised to see her on Monday.

I had more loose ends tossing about than a Leah Walters canvas. I should have been in a better mood, elated, but I wasn't. They had finally nailed my father. Maybe this would be the turn of events to free me. Hang a murder on a black bear? How stupid. I knew enough not to believe it, but because I'd repeated the story for all those years it left me with a guilt I felt every day. Even with George in jail, I still had plenty to fear. He'd always been something of a loose cannon, and if he became desperate he might try to take me down with him.

Then there were the feds. The disaster thrust upon me, I now had to either fish or cut bait, as Sam Robel had once told me. Fishing meant sitting tight and waiting for the WPP hammer to fall. They'd take Nadine and me and move us to yet another backwater town. I hadn't asked her how she felt about that, but I could guess. And if I let the ham-fisted government take the reins, I'd be leaving yet another girl behind. In Wisconsin it had been Diane. This time I'd lose Leah.

Cutting bait was more my style. Pack up and hit the road. Take as much money as I could find, go off the grid, and run. But how to reconcile with Leah? She hadn't even gone along with a move to the University of Iowa. She didn't know the backstory then. Now, I would tell her, and change her mind.

I blew off school Monday morning, and hoped never to see the inside of Moreau High again. Standing in front of the bathroom mirror, my eyes rimmed in red, hair helter-skelter, a shirt sagging like my prospects, it occurred to me the whole idea about California was stupid and lame. Leah and Trevor were right. Nobody knew me anywhere else, except Walnut Creek, Wisconsin, and I couldn't to go back there. And who was I trying to fool? I had no road skills, little money, and living off the land was something I'd only seen in movies. I headed for the shower.

Dressed in old jeans and a sweater, I went out to the kitchen. Nadine was at the table drinking coffee, staring out the small window over the sink. She said her night had been no better than mine. Running on high-octane anxiety until the early morning hours, she gave up on sleep, went out to the living room, and turned on the TV. She'd never been a practical, common sense type of woman. Now, she needed to find both, and do it alone. She had fewer friends in town than I did. During the last nine months, not once had I seen her bring a friend over for coffee. I couldn't help but wonder what was going through her mind.

I got a bagel out of the refrigerator, opened a jar of jam, and poured myself a coffee.

"No school today?" Nadine asked without looking at me.

"Not for me." I cut the bagel in half. "I heard the phone. Who was it?"

Nadine said the lawyer wanted her to know the extradition hearing on George was moved to next Tuesday. Eight more days of waiting. I kept my voice toneless and flat. "It's not like it's a mystery. They're going to ship his ass back to Wisconsin."

I sipped the coffee. "And another thing. Enough with the fake names. Jeremiah Roman Cherhasky killed my mother, not George Farmer. From now on, I'm not answering to Max Farmer." Nadine nodded. I took a bite of bagel. "Anyway, I don't care what they do to him. Look what he's done, screwed me, screwed *us*… again. They'll ship him back." I sat down at the table. "I'm not going to wait for the feds to relocate me."

Nadine looked away. "You're leaving him to rot… in jail?"

"Are you kidding? Nadine, he's a killer. Prison is too good for him. I hope he burns in hell." I ripped the bagel in half. "You should hope so too."

She sat across from me, a quizzical look on her face. "What am I supposed to do? I can't stay here alone."

"Whatever," I said. "I'd divorce him if I were you." But I could see it in her face, in the way she held herself: she couldn't run her own life, could barely run a house. What would she do if I left and my father was extradited? I honestly didn't know. Unless the Feds took her under their wing, she could end up homeless. Whatever money she had would be gone in no time.

She said she didn't like Moreau either. I got up from the chair, took a couple steps, then turned toward her. "Don't you get it? You're leaving here too, one way or another. Either the Feds do it again, or you beat them to it and bolt." I sat down again. "You better wake up and smell that coffee in front of you." I looked away. "I'm taking option two."

She swallowed hard, as if the coffee was hot. "Where are you going?"

I lifted my cup. Not knowing where this question was headed, I didn't want to give too much away. "Nowhere, out there. Who knows? Anywhere not here."

She sat up straight. "I want to go."

"What?"

"Take me along."

"But… hell no. We don't even, we barely speak the same language."

"I want to go."

"Are you out of your mind? I'm a loner. You'd slow me down. Besides, they'll be looking for us."

"Who? Why?"

"Because we signed a contract with a tiny organization called the Federal Government. Remember? And… Just so you know, I'm stealing the Ranger. Already sold my guitar and amp."

The sale of the Stratocaster astounded her the most. I'd sold it to a pawn shop in Rapid City and got a screwing on the deal.

"Whatever amount of money you have, I got more." Nadine poured some more coffee. "My name is on the title for the truck. What about that?"

"I'll sell it hot."

"I've got a car," Nadine said. "We could sell that, too. And I have cash in the bank."

I was astounded. Nadine hadn't come to this plan on a whim. She walked into the kitchen prepared, all the way down to the savings book she pulled off the counter. With a flick of her thumb, she showed me the names on the joint account, and then the balance, well over twenty thousand dollars. A pittance compared to what my father *used* to throw around, but for some reason, the figure shocked me. Probably because my current net worth, minus the Ranger, was south of twelve hundred dollars.

I told her I was going to California. With barely a crease at the corner of her mouth, she said she didn't care about George—"I mean J. Roman"—either. Her dream was to go back to Wisconsin, and that wasn't going to happen.

I leaned back in the chair and told her that, before leaving, I was going to steal as much shit from that bastard as I could carry. "So, if there's anything in this house you want, tell me now."

"What if the cops come after you?"

"That's why I'm going off the grid. But you don't have to." I tapped the bank book.

"It's not as simple as all that." She clicked her fingernails. "There are details about your father's past that I want to leave behind."

I studied the distant gaze, the half-hooked tilt of her mouth. There was a part of J.R.'s past I didn't know about. I hadn't been privy to every meeting, listened in on all my father's phone calls. She hadn't either. But there were dinner parties she'd attended, business trips she'd been a part of that had nothing to do with me. And I was fine with keeping it that way.

She said, "Your plan, or what I've heard of it, sounds pretty thin. If we join together our chances are better."

"Okay, let's say we sell your car. What else?"

"I go to the bank, withdraw ten thousand dollars, for the defense 'of my poor husband.' They know me down there and they'll have heard the story by now."

A chill went down my spine. Credit cards were easy to trace, so we'd have to pay cash for everything. The plan was taking on a new shape. I needed cash. She needed a ride out of Moreau. As long as we kept to that simple formula, I could put up with her. I couldn't think of a better option. I held up a finger. "Screw up one thing ..."

She held onto her elbow and shook her head. I knew enough about her past to have a good idea what she was thinking. She'd been born to a family barely anchored; had grown up in a shack with too many siblings and a couple of hard-scrabble, hard-drinking parents who had money about as often as they had jobs. She'd escaped that scene and wouldn't go back again. But the road out of Moreau was poorly lit, and if she took a wrong turn, it might take her to someplace truly strange.

Did I want to be on the road with someone carrying that much emotional baggage? I squirmed in my seat. "It's my plan. No questions asked. Anytime you and I don't see eye to eye, we go our separate ways."

She stiffened. "Once we're on the road, Max, don't leave me behind. That's my only condition."

I nodded curtly. "We travel light and fast. One suitcase each. Small, with wheels. No exceptions."

She wondered if Leah was coming along. "Already asked her."

And she'd said no, I thought. *But then it was a 'what if.' It's real now. She's got to change her mind.*

From my seat in the waiting area of the bank, I watched Nadine through the partially-louvred windows of the Accounts Manager's office. He looked to be about fifty, short hair, graying, suit and tie, a standard issue banker-for-life. He hadn't taken his eyes off Nadine since she walked in the door. She wasn't wearing anything special, the same outfit from the breakfast table, a pair of flats; simple, untucked, light blue shirt; and black tights. From the expression on Keith Lightfoot's face it was obvious, he was going to make sure "Nadine Farmer" got whatever assistance she might need.

Nadine folded her hands on her lap. She looked comfortable, in charge. I hadn't seen her like that since we left Walnut Creek. She took her time. I could hear the chit chat through the open door; a few conciliatory words from Keith. A secretary entered the office with the requested funds. Nadine paused to count it, then tucked the cash in her purse, and walked out. She played the role of the distraught wife right up to the second Keith closed his door. He wouldn't know the truth for days, and by the time he figured it out, she and I would be on the other side of the Continental Divide. She winked at me and we left.

There were two vehicles to sell, the Ranger and Nadine's Chrysler 200. The Ranger would have to go eventually, but pickups were easier to unload in the Dakotas than a sedan. We drove to Rapid City and sold the Chrysler for cash.

On the drive home, the afternoon sun behind us, I wondered when Nadine would hear again from the lawyer. She wasn't sure because his contact with her had been erratic, but she didn't expect more from a public defender. I asked about it because the cell phones would be gone once we hit the road. I pointed at the two burner phones we'd purchased that day. She was fine with going offline, but wondered why I wasn't sticking around to get my diploma, only four days away. I massaged my forehead with the fingertips of one hand. In spite of all we'd talked about, she still hadn't grasped how vulnerable we were.

"Four days! Nadine, we talked about this. We may not have four hours." My lips formed a tight, straight line. "Do you want to be a waitress for the rest of your life? 'Cuz that's what'll happen if they get their hooks in us. Besides, I don't need no stinking diploma." The road sign said *Moreau 4 miles*. "When I get back, I got to talk to Trevor. Where do you want to drop?"

"We're still leaving tomorrow?" Her voice was suspicious, as if now that I had the money, I was going to up and leave without her.

I tuned toward town. "And bring your old Wisconsin driver's license. Might need it." I looked at her sideways. "You still got it, right?"

"Yeah, yeah." She scowled. "Take me home, then. I got packing to do. After Trevor, you're coming straight back?"

"What? Yeah, of course. What's it to you?" She shrugged. Suddenly tired, I turned my head lazily. "Don't worry. I'll be there."

CHAPTER SIX

Max

Late afternoon. The walk from school to Trevor's house was a mile. His routine rarely varied, so I knew where to look for his long, loose stride that time of day. Trevor heard the old Ford before he saw it. I stopped. He slipped into the Ranger and thanked me for the lift. He'd been worried about me, thought I was sick or something when I didn't show at school and hadn't texted him.

"Nah, skipped school. I should've shot you a text. Sorry. Gotta minute? I want to drive down by the river."

The city park was deserted, the water in the Moreau River running high, the grass waiting for its second cut of the season. I parked the truck and opened the door. The smell of spring surrounded us, the odor of the nearby woods waking from winter. We'd often do some fishing at this spot, but we didn't have any gear, so Trevor wondered what was up.

I said, "We're going to the stumps." The two cottonwoods, cut off next to the bank of the river just upstream, was a place we'd discovered last fall. There was no trail, so we didn't have to worry about eavesdroppers. I stood, tossing stones into the river.

Trevor sat on one of the stumps. "What's up?"

"I don't even know where to begin." I wanted to talk to Trevor before Leah because it would give me time to find a little courage. If I could talk to Trevor about leaving without falling apart, maybe I'd have half a chance with Leah.

"Then start at the end."

"What?"

"Everyone always says start at the beginning," said Trevor blithely, trying to ignore a heavy vibe. "I say, start at the end, that's where the meat is."

"All right. I'm leaving tomorrow. I'll probably never see you again."

"Seriously? Dude!" The light in Trevor's face flickered away. "I'm an idiot. Don't listen to me. Skip the ending."

I sat down. "My dad's in jail again... on murder charges."

"Again! You mean he's been there before?" I nodded. Trevor slouched. "Oh, shit. That sucks... I mean," this time more softly, "I'm sorry man. Who'd he kill? When did you find out? What are you going to do?"

"Believe it or not," I hesitated. "Oh, why not? The charges are out there. My mom, they say he killed my mom. We should skip the details. Even if I could say it, you wouldn't believe me." I felt guilty treating him like this, like he couldn't be trusted. The truth was, I didn't trust myself. It was too hard to talk about.

"Why the secrets if you're leaving. What difference does it make?" He broke a fallen limb in half." "What *can* you tell me? Where did it happen? Was it around here?"

I held up my hand and paused. There was frustration, even anger in Trevor's voice, and that was rare. I said, "It didn't happen around here or even... it happened a long time ago. Listen, my dad was involved with the mob, and I don't want them looking for you. Which is what they'll do if you know too much." I picked at the bark on the stump. "It's complicated, I'd need a whole night to tell you." I looked at the sky and thought *I'll bet the Feds about took a crap when they found out their murder suspect is in the WPP.* "Anyway, I'm getting out. I'm leaving tomorrow before they show up to relocate me."

"Gawd, could you be any more mysterious?"

I shot him a withering look.

"Okay, have it your way," Trevor said. "So, next stop, California."

"I'm going to save rock 'n roll. Springsteen is getting old. He's held the banner long enough. Someone's got to pick it up and run. Might as well be me."

"Springsteen started in Jersey. East Coast." Trevor grunted. "What about your band?"

I shook my head. "Traveling light."

For a minute or more there was the sound of the water rushing by and nothing more. Suddenly, I shot off the stump. "What was that?"

Puzzled, Trevor leaned back to get a look. "What? Where?"

I backed toward Trevor a step. "Right there. In the grass. Shit!" I climbed up on the stump. "It's a snake. Slimy bastard. Get it. Get it."

Still seated, Trevor said, "Probably a grass snake. They're all over. They can't hurt you."

"I hate 'em. Where is it?"

Trevor pushed off his perch. "Never seen you this way." He toed the grass. "There he goes. See? He's gone."

"You sure?"

Trevor rolled his eyes.

I jumped down and took a breath. "I am scared shitless of those things. The scene in Raiders on the Lost Ark, where he's with all those vipers, I almost puked." Arms crossed, I stepped toward the stream. "Hey, don't repeat any of this." Trevor waved as if at the snake. "Not the snake. I meant the part about me leaving."

"I wish you hadn't told me."

I glanced at Trevor. "Stay away from Tugger."

"White trash."

"Hey, I know," I said. "He's so dumb he lost a game of rock-paper-scissors to a paper towel dispenser." Trevor laughed, and for the first time in days, so did I. "Stay out of his way though, seriously. I'm going to ask Leah to come with me. I think she'll say no. If she does, look after her for me, will ya?"

Trevor's chin trembled. He looked down. "Ah man, don't ask me that." He sniffled.

I sat down on the stump, elbows on knees, eyes down. "Now don't start that shit or you'll have me doin' it."

Trevor straightened. "Let's go."

While walking back to the pickup, I dialed Leah's cell but she didn't pick up. I left a voice mail, something I rarely did. It was likely she was working in the studio and may not get the message for some time. While Trevor went ahead to the Ranger, I shot a text to her on the off-chance she wasn't working:

Must see you ASAP. Am driving to studio RN. Be there in 10. Call if not there. ILY.

I drove to Trevor's home. As we approached, I had a strangeness in my throat, an emptiness I couldn't swallow.

Trevor said, "So, just drop me off. Don't say goodbye or nothin'… I want to think it's just another Monday afternoon."

"Okay, dude. I'm good with that." I didn't turn my head to watch him exit the cab, but after the door shut and Trevor had taken a few steps I allowed myself a glance. Trevor turned at the same time. We offered each other the smallest wave.

I checked my phone. Still nothing from Leah. Two minutes later I was parked in front of the studio. While I was jogging down the hall, my phone went off—Leah's ringtone—but I didn't bother answering. I flew through the studio door, around the atrium wall, to Leah's workspace where I found her pacing, a concerned look on her paint-streaked face, goggles on her forehead, the phone planted in her ear.

She silenced the phone. "Max! What is it?"

I wrapped my arms around her.

She held me too. "I'm full of paint. You'll—"

"I don't care." I held on, kissing her first on the ear, then the cheek, finally her lips. I stood back a step, looked at my shirt, blotched in dobs of bright colors, and said, "I'm keeping this shirt forever."

She bit her lower lip. "Max, what's the matter?"

My minute of grace was over. Lead flowing in my veins, I leaned on the large, heavy, work bench behind me. "Leah, all those talks we had about this fall, which college, what you and I should do… my whole life's been trashed."

She stood only a step away. "What do you mean? How? Did

your father die? Was there an accident?"

I rubbed my head and looked down. "No. Nothing that simple."

She took my hand. "What then? Tell me."

I swallowed, struggling. "You know the story I told you about... the body... in Wisconsin... in the lake." She answered softly, yes. I collapsed into a chair. "It's my mother, Leah. My mom." I tented my hands over my face. Tears seared my eyes.

She stood me up and held me in her arms. "I'm so sorry. Oh my God. But how?"

I rested my head on her shoulder. "That's not the worst of it. They arrested my father. He killed her. They have an eye witness." If I'd have stopped right there and thought about what I'd said, it would have changed everything that was about to happen. An eye witness to what? The actual murder? But my memories of that time were more radioactive than Chernobyl, so like the Russians I'd entombed them in concrete. "And the DNA matched."

Leah let out an anguished cry but didn't let go. "DNA?"

"I sent in my DNA to one of those online places to get more information on my family tree, especially my mom's side, since my father never talks about it. Well, the cops traced it back to the body in the lake. They do that now with cold cases."

For a while, she just held me close. Then she said we should sit down on a love seat in the atrium. She locked the front door, put out the closed sign, and asked what would happen now. I mentioned the call from the public defender, extradition, and the biggest worry of all, the impending arrival of federal agents, probably within hours, to take Nadine and me to parts unknown, repackaged, renamed.

"But how can they do that?" she asked. Finally, the story poured out of me: the WPP, the Chicago connection, my father's malfeasance and how it put us finally in exile, in Moreau.

Leah's hand went to her chest. "But if they do that I'll never see—"

"I know. It's a lose-lose deal. If I stay, the WPP sucks me in and I lose you. If I hit the road, I lose you." I looked in her eyes. "Unless... unless you come with me."

"Holy hell, Max. Don't say that. Don't do this to me. To us."

Abruptly, I stood and threw my hands down. "It's not me. I didn't make the rules." I paced away; then turned back. "Well, I'm not following their rules anymore." I clenched my hand into a fist. "What other choice do I have? You tell me."

Still seated, spine erect, but her shoulders showing the weight of the moment, she said, "Face them down, the feds."

"What are you talking about? Leah, they don't negotiate."

"Make them. Tell them you're not going anywhere until this thing with your father is settled. You can't be expected to make a decision like this in two minutes, or even two weeks."

"You don't know. I do. I was there when they packed us up in four hours and we were *gone*. Do this, don't take that, lock the door, get in, bye, bye." I flapped my hand at her, then paced again. "Gone, Leah. That's how they work."

"Running away from this is not right, Max, so no, I can't come with you." Fingers buried deep in her hair, she lowered her head, and quietly sobbed.

I stopped pacing, stood before her, and spoke softly. "Listen, I've done a terrible job explaining this off-the-grid thing. It's not permanent. We set up a new life somewhere out west, and when no one cares about us or me anymore, we come back, see your family again.

"We got some money, Nadine and me. We figured out how to get some cash. Nothing's forever. You're so talented, you can work anywhere. I'll get a job. We can do it."

Leah watched me, tried to hear me out, but her courage was running low. By the time I finished she was sucking on her lips, her head bowed. Silence was her only answer, but it was clearer than anything she could have said.

"Oh, Leah." Gently, I held her head between my hands and kissed her hair. Tears mingled with the paint on her face and fell, dotting the knees of her painter's pants. I stepped toward the door and turned the latch. Leah stood, rushed to me, and wrapped her arms around my neck. My knees got weak. I knew I had to leave immediately or never leave at all. I tilted up her head, kissed her nose, and let her go. Shabby tennis shoes silenced my steps as I walked down the hall.

CHAPTER SEVEN

Max

Early Tuesday morning, Nadine and I left Moreau and headed north on highway 75, then to 85 for the six-hour trip to Williston, North Dakota. Nadine looked out the windshield, a confused expression on her face. We weren't out of South Dakota, and already she was anxious.

"I didn't ace Geography in high school," she said. "But I'm pretty sure the *West* Coast is not North of Moreau." In other words, what kind of road tripper didn't know North from West? My answer was dismissive and brief. To that point she'd shown no interest in the travel details. She wasn't going to do any driving, so why should she? I had only told her what she needed to know. I worried that given too much of the schedule, she might unknowingly give away information to the wrong person at the wrong time.

The sign for *North Dakota* passed by and the questions were back. I told her the plan was a lot more complex than a straight shot to Los Angeles. I expected the police, FBI, or both to be looking "for our collective asses" so we had to think like fugitives. That still didn't explain Williston.

"There's an Amtrak station there."

"Ahh," she said, as if she understood. I hummed my assent, knowing she didn't get the half of it.

A new hole in the Ranger's muffler reminded me the vehicle wouldn't make it through the Rockies. We passed the Little Missouri National Grassland and the Theodore Roosevelt National

Park. We were still an hour from our first break: a gas station north of Williston, the last stop before the state turned into the great northern plain and essentially, the big empty. The city went by in a blink.

Nadine twisted in her seat as the city shrank in her rear view. "Wasn't that Williston?"

"Don't worry, we'll be back." I pointed ahead. "See that gas station? It's the last one for a long time between here and the Canadian border. We're going to gas up and use our credit card for the last time. It's all cash after that."

"So why use the card now?"

"They'll come here looking for us and assume we're going to Canada."

We purchased gas and some food for the trip. I took a quick look inside. The cashier was an older man sporting a stubble and dressed in Dickie slacks and a green, John Deere shirt. I handed the credit card to Nadine and said, "We'll go in together, but you pay. Make sure the guy notices you."

"How do I do that?"

"Don't worry. You were getting noticed before you could walk." I scanned the highway for other cars. "Flirt with him or something, just long enough for him to remember you."

We went in the front door. Nadine smiled at the man as we walked toward the food aisles where we each selected chips and snacks. We dumped our selections on the counter.

"Guesh you'll want a bag for all thish," said the cashier through a lisp. His nose was too red for the fair weather and he sported a belly—not half-moon yet but a waxing crescent for sure.

Nadine batted her eyes. "Yes, if it's not too much trouble."

The cashiers face lit up. "Not a problem, ma'am."

She handed him the card. "I guess it's a lot. Hope I don't get fat eating all this."

Something tugged at the corner of the cashier's mouth. "Hasn't so far, not as I can see." He handed her the receipt and the bag.

"Thank you so much."

At the pumps, I cut the card in half, took her's, and did the same. We drove out and went North for a mile, just in case the cashier was paying attention, before I turned around and headed back to Williston.

"We're going to have to ditch the truck," I said. "It's not worth selling. We'd get, what, a few hundred bucks? And if you sign the deed it would put them onto us." Two miles from the Amtrak station, I drove past Williston Memorial Hospital; its parking lot full of vehicles of all types and ages. And since the turnover was continuous, perfect cover. We threw the vehicle's identification papers in the trash. She got out her cell.

"What are you doing?" I asked.

"It's too far. I'm calling a cab." We'd both left our personal phones in Moreau and brought the burners.

"Like hell you will. Cabs keep logs. Cabbies remember faces. We're walking. That's what the Nikes are for. You carry the food for a while, then I'll take it."

The sun at our backs did nothing to warm our faces, and the northeast wind had a bite that put a charge in our gate. Our cheeks flushed with cold, we arrived at the terminal with plenty of time; the eastbound Empire Builder didn't depart until 6:59 p.m.

"Are you shittin' me?" Nadine asked, "Eastbound? That's Wisconsin. You know we can't go home."

"What did I say?" I tapped my temple. "Think like a fugitive or you'll end up next to your husband. The guys chasing us are smart. They'll look up the credit cards and, if we're lucky, head for the three or four border crossings into Canada. They'll come up empty and come back here. They'll find the truck; it's only a matter of time. Then, Amtrak is obvious. They'll ask after you and me. They'll ask about cash customers."

"You really do have a plan." She still sounded apprehensive, but I thought that she was finally putting it together. "Then what'll we do?"

"You'll see."

We purchased two one-way tickets to Milwaukee, Wisconsin. Roll-along carry-on suitcases at our sides, we sat on an inside bench and waited. Nadine clicked her heel on the floor. I said,

"Don't worry. We're not going all the way to Wisconsin. By the time they figure it out, we'll be on step five."

"That's exactly what I'm worried about. You've got some kind of crazy scheme going, and I don't have a clue."

I opened a bag of chips. "Leave the technical stuff to me. When you need a heads-up, I'll let you know." She side-eyed me with a wary and skeptical gaze. I sensed if she'd had an alternative, she'd have walked away. Better she didn't know what was ahead, because the next step was crucial. The success of my plan would come down to twenty minutes in Minot.

On the train, two hours later, the sun had set. Nadine was reading a magazine. I got out my burner cell and tapped in a phone number. She asked who I was calling.

"A guy we have to meet at the next stop. He's going to sell us a camper." On the other end, a phone rang.

"If we're not going all the way to Milwaukee, why did we waste all that mon—?"

"It wasn't wasted." I put up a hand. "Yeah, hi. This is Max. Is this Phil? Yeah. I called about the camper. We're twenty minutes out."

Phil said, "Ah, listen, okay. Been wondering about you," the voice said. "Um, sure. I'll meet you there. You got the money?"

"Of course, I do," I said. "What's going on, Phil?" I wondered if he was planning an ambush of some sort. Luckily, we were meeting in a public place, because I didn't have any kind of weapon stashed, not even pepper spray.

"Ah, yeah. Right. I'll see you in… at the station."

Call ended. "Damn," I said. "This guy is one weird egg."

"What's the matter?" she asked.

"Nothing, I hope."

We could see the lights of Minot from miles away. The train pulled into the station. The conductor announced a twenty-minute stop. I told Nadine to bring her ticket and suitcase. We exited the car and walked across the platform toward the station's front entrance where Phil was supposed to meet us. Most of the people in the area were exiting the terminal and walking toward waiting rides, and there weren't many of those.

Nadine pointed at a middle-aged man, standing under a streetlight smoking a cigarette. He watched nervously as the people walked by. "Is that him?"

"Better not be."

I didn't see anything larger than a pickup truck parked anywhere, so I hurried toward the man, whose hip rested on an old Toyota Camry. "Phil? Is that you?"

"I'm Phil. Are you Max?"

"That's right. What's going on? Where's the camper?"

He was about the same height as me, balding, coarsely featured with a large nose and a heavy brow that cast a shadow over his eyes. "Camper's gone. Got a better price. Been calling you about it all day. You didn't answer."

"What the hell. We had a deal. You said so yesterday."

Phil blew smoke out of his nose. "Deal ain't a deal till it's done. Now, if you'll cool off for a second, I bought this along as a peace offering." He stepped away from the lime-green car. "'93 Toyota Camry. Legend in its own time. Sell it to you for five-hundred less than we agreed on the camper."

"What are you talking about?" I kicked my suitcase. "I don't need a car. I need a camper." My eyes went to the Camry. There was rust in the wheel wells and under the doors.

"Don't let the body fool you," Phil said. "Engine runs like a sewing machine."

"You can't be serious. You sold it? Why didn't you tell me twenty minutes ago?"

Phil shrugged. "Figured I should say it in person. And I have an alternative. Take it or leave it."

"Shit!" I spat. It was a good thing I didn't have any pepper spray, because I would have given him a blast, just on general principle.

"What now?" Nadine asked.

"All aboard," called the conductor.

I pressed my lips into a slash. I looked at the car, then the train, the car. I grabbed Nadine's arm and said, "Let's go."

We turned and sprinted for the loading platform, our suitcases clanking and jumping behind us.

CHAPTER EIGHT

Max

I stood before the window seat and slammed my forearm into the headrest. Not even a day out, and already a major miss. Phil was supposed to sell me a used, fully functional camper that would have been our transportation to California and provide shelter if the money ran out. If we ended up sleeping under a highway overpass, it wouldn't matter how well I played or sang.

"What the hell was that all about?" Nadine asked.

I told her the bones of the truth without fleshing it out. The day had been long. The night, stretched out as broad and empty as the interminable plains, and we were about to spend it on the train. Exhaustion settled on my shoulders like a dreary rain. My head felt heavy. I wanted to sleep, but that wasn't going to happen. Between Minot and Milwaukee, I had to find a way off the Empire Builder. Cellphone in hand, I brought up the train schedule and checked the upcoming stops. We'd cross most of North Dakota and Minnesota during the night. The next serviceable break was Minneapolis around breakfast time. Then two more stops before crossing into Wisconsin and the La Crosse terminal. By then it would be mid-day Wednesday. The longer it went, the more likely we'd be missed, and the higher the chances we'd run into a search party dressed in blue.

The train came to a stop and woke me from a fitful sleep. After a glance out the window, I nudged Nadine awake and asked, "Hungry?"

She shook her head, stretched, and asked where we were.

"Minneapolis. Food machines, maybe a breakfast counter. We got thirty minutes. Bring your stuff. We might not be back."

As soon as I saw the size of the terminal, I realized we could get lost here. Distractions at each corner, storefronts around every turn. That wasn't good. Complacency would come easy here. Winding through the crowd, my head on a swivel, I looked for a quick-hit food counter. A right turn took us into the middle of a teeming, major thoroughfare. Nadine halted.

"What's the matter? Bathroom?" I asked.

She looked at something or someone, but instead of stretching her neck, she crouched, as if looking through a fence. "No, I guess not."

I hurried her along. We couldn't decide on what to eat so it was McDonald's in a bag and two coffees. I pointed toward the front of the building. "Gotta find the bus desk." We were moving easily with the crowd when she looked over her shoulder and put an elbow into me.

"Something's wrong," she said.

"Again? Listen, I know the train is the other way. But I want to get a bus. Don't be an anchor." She stopped me. A troupe of girl scouts went by. I tugged back to get her moving, but she was a boulder.

"No, something else. I saw a guy. Twice. I think… I should know him." She crouched again, backed toward an empty storefront.

"What are you talking about?" I followed her to the wall. "Know him from where?"

"Where do you think? Walnut Creek. Chicago." Her grip crushed our breakfast bag.

Those were disturbing answers. I bent closer. "Who is he?"

"I don't know." She sat down on a folding chair. "It was a face, for a second, but the kind you don't forget."

"Great, are we having a panic attack here? Over what?" I pulled the suitcases closer. "Is he in uniform? Is it a cop?"

Head bobbing, shoulders shifting, she was too distracted to answer.

54

"Nadine! Who am I looking for?"

"We can't stay here. He saw me." She stood. "I think he saw me."

Then I saw a stern, stout man a stone's toss away making his way toward us, his eyes boring in, more intense than they should have been. Was this the guy she was talking about? Even at a distance, he didn't look official. No uniform, and he was pushing through and around knots of people as if they weren't there.

"Drop the food." I grabbed her. We ran close to the wall away from him. I forgot about the bus. We needed to get back on the train. But how? Doubling back was not an option. And the building was a maze. Hallways, direction signs, each with arrows pointing in every direction. A corridor branched to the right off the main hall. It was less crowded, so we could make better time. "Come on," I said. "Run."

The clatter of our suitcases echoed off the hallway walls. We were running parallel to the train, not toward it, so I took another right into… a dead end. Stopped cold. We ran back. Went right again. Stumbling. My suitcase flipped off its wheels. I looked back.

"Do you see him?" Nadine asked.

"No. I don't know. Keep going."

The smell of diesel creased my nose; I followed the pungent odor to the train platforms. We jumped aboard and looked through the windows. The stocky man was not in the loading area. Stumbling toward the front of the train, we passed through three cars, then stopped and looked again. Still nothing, but it was hard to keep an eye on the entire length of the train, and we couldn't see everyone in the departing area. A single man could be missed. I shrugged toward a set of open seats, and we settled in. Both of us took a deep breath.

"Fun and games already." I glanced at Nadine. "Still have your ticket?" She showed it to me. "I don't like that guy. He looks dangerous, Nadine."

"It was like a flashback or something." A door slammed shut and she flinched. "Maybe he just gave me the creeps."

I slipped into a seat. "What? Now you're not sure?"

Her glare was hard enough to break glass.

I whispered, "Gawd. Listen, I'm already paranoid. You don't have to make it worse by imagining old boyfriends stalking you in the station." She flipped me the bird. I rubbed my eyes. "You got any Tylenol? For a headache."

"Ibuprofen." She tipped out a couple tablets and I swallowed them dry.

We were in the front car with backward facing seats, so we could keep an eye out. The train moved along the Mississippi River, going south through Red Wing, then Winona. I was on my cell, looking at options. With each fail I swallowed a "damn" or "shit" while she squirmed. Finally, I uttered "yes." She leaned into me and asked what I'd found.

"Bus connections. Next one is in La Crosse. We get off there. It's a much smaller terminal. If anyone is tailing us," I looked at her sideways, "we'll see him for sure."

CHAPTER NINE

Nate

The teller behind the counter at the gas station said he'd been working all week, but it was a busy place, and he couldn't be expected to remember every Tom, Dick, or Mary that sashayed past a fuel pump. He was standoffish, not unusual in western folks when agents from the federal government came knocking. I was used to it, and tried to disarm him as best I could. The list from the credit card company spread between us, I pointed to his store and the time and date of the charges.

"An' jush because dey use a credit card." A lisp filled his mouth. A retiree making money to pay the gas bill, I thought. He shrugged. "Most folksh pay at the pump."

I asked him to take a look at the pictures anyway. The headshots were better than we were used to getting, two 4x6 recents of fairly high resolution and good lighting, full color, straight from their Witness Protection Program files.

The joints of his fingers were bony, big, and bent as if someone had taken a hammer to them, but nimble enough as he took the photos. "Who'd you say you were again?"

I had already showed him my badge. I repeated, "Nathaniel Bauer, Special Agent—"

"Yeah, yeah, yeah, FBI." He took his first look at the shots. "Ohh, yaa, now dem I remember. Who wouldn't? Good lookin' as dey are, 'specially the girl."

"What do you recall?"

"Not much. Dey gassed up, got food, an' left."

"See which direction they headed?"

"Nort. I remember because I wash thinkin', lookin' at that truck a' his, I didn't know how far dey'd get. Plush, you know, not many goes nort from here, 'cept the locals. And I know them. Between here and the border, not much there."

"Guess that's right." I left my card with a request to call anytime if one or both of them showed up.

"Sho. These two, they like Bonnie and Clyde dangeroush or what?"

"No, we don't think so. But they're skiing in powder over their boots, and the blizzard hasn't started yet."

I got back in the car. Max and Nadine Farmer, participants in the WPP for less than a year and therefore still considered high risk, had suddenly, just over a day ago, left their home and headed north. During a stop at a service station north of Williston, North Dakota, they used Nadine's credit card and then continued on toward the Canadian border in a broken-down Ford Ranger. The logical assumption was they were a couple of amateurs making a mad dash out of the country, presumably to escape the inevitable relocation they knew was coming after the arrest of George Farmer. If so, their plan was poorly considered, and I really had to wonder who was calling the shots. My recollection of both Max and Nadine from a year earlier was a little hazy, but there were details I'd never forget. At that time, of course, they went by different names. But today they had used their WPP names, and freely so in front of the cashier.

The first time I saw this family their circumstances were vastly different. They were named Cherhasky then, not Farmer. Nadine was the beautiful wife, younger than her husband by more than a decade, standing in the kitchen of her husband's lakeside estate in heels and a bikini; wearing a summer cover-up that, well, if she'd purchased it for more than a few bucks, she'd overpaid. My hands were empty, but had I been holding a box of office files, I might have dropped them on my foot.

Seconds later, her husband was under arrest and she was in tears. A rather odd sight, crying in a swimsuit: a combination

I'd not seen before. Her husband scolded her for the display, as if she were a child. Of the three, his son comported himself best, showing more cool under fire that his father did. If I had to guess, Max was now making the decisions, not Nadine. But his age was showing, because mistakes were dropping right and left. If his slip-ups continued, this would be a short assignment. My girls had soccer games that weekend; I was more optimistic I'd be home to see them.

I called the regional office and had pictures of Max and Nadine Farmer, along with descriptions and relationship, emailed to the five closest U.S.-Canadian border crossings. I turned the car north and drove awhile. Within ten minutes I was in the Big Alone, or at least that's how it felt. Very few homes, even fewer crossroads, no gas stations, and the farther I drove, the more it became so. If Max's old Ranger broke down out here, he'd have been hard pressed to find so much as a cell signal, much less roadside help. Bringing a crippled vehicle into this country was a foolish gamble, but then going on the lam with his stepmother told me all I needed to know about how much thought he'd put into this cross-country joyride. His trail glowed in the dark. He used a credit card. And showing the "girl" to the attendant, for chrissakes. She could have showed up with the ghost of Freddie Mercury and talked to the only gay man in the Dakotas, and still he'd have noticed her.

I drove back to Williston and looked around for an hour, hoping for a little luck. But it was wasted time. The Amtrak Station was in the middle of town. The ticket agent on duty had not been working the day before, so couldn't help with the pictures. I needed to see the roster of tickets sales for the previous thirty-six hours in both directions, but he couldn't give me that without authorization. I told him he'd have it within the hour and left.

My instincts told me they weren't in town. Max wouldn't have made it *that* simple. I called into my Milwaukee office and told them I needed clearance for the Amtrak manifest. Lance, my assistant, was to check for names of interest and let me know of any hits. He also told me there'd been no positive IDs on the pics sent to the border. I was stuck in the middle in Williston. I could drive to the border ninety minutes north, do the requisite leg work with the immigration agents, and spend the night there. There were a handful of crossings they might have used. Visiting every one of them was time intensive and *maybe* worth the effort. Or head south, get the five-hour trip back to Moreau out of the way. The credit card hit had taken me straight to Williston, so I had some back-tracking to do in the Farmers' "hometown." If I spent the night in Moreau, I'd get a start fresh tomorrow interviewing friends and family. Any experienced field officer will tell you that every investigation presents dozens of decision points that can and do have a profound effect on how a case unfolds. They're like crossroads on a journey, some of them are minor and alter the case only slightly. Others are like a major exchange on an interstate highway: take the wrong exit and you end up looking at a glacier in Alaska. The agents that climb the department ladder are usually the ones who apply common sense, instinct, and analytics in equal measure. I decided on Moreau. Border traffic at most of the nearby crossings was fairly light, so I thought the eyes onsite were a reasonable proxy for my own.

One of the downsides of not having a partner, was the time spent alone; too much time to think, to remember what my career looked like one year ago. At that time, my position in the FBI was solid. I'd been one of the lead agents on the bust of a syndicate operation that involved two states, two prominent Wisconsin families, and the Chicago mob. While my associates raided the Wisconsin Headquarters of Square M Construction and a well-known mob leader in Illinois, I led a team to the home of J.R. Cherhasky. It was a high-water mark for me. Not long after that, luck or circumstances threw me a pitch that fooled me so completely, I didn't even take a swing. Struck out, without ever taking the bat off my shoulder.

That dismal showing hadn't changed my rank or position within the organization, not officially. Behind closed doors was another story. I'd been dressed down by my section chief, Rick Atwater. He stopped short of firing me but made it clear that for the foreseeable future, I was on a short leash.

True to his word, Atwater busted me to the minor leagues. For nine months, I hadn't gotten within sniffing distance of any significant investigation or operation—until this week. The arrest of George Farmer (formerly J.R. Cherhasky) must have set off some kind of chain reaction in the offices on the fourth floor. I was charged with bringing in Max and Nadine, the two non-felons in the sordid affair. It sounded like a softball assignment or a test. It was both. I was the obvious choice because of my familiarity with the Cherhasky family and their position in the Witness Protection Program. The toughest part of the job would be getting to Moreau. The criminal in the family was already in custody, so my role amounted to little more than babysitting. Atwater's message was clear: *Let's see how you handle this, then we'll talk about your future.* Instead of working with a partner, I'd go alone; in place of an airline ticket from Wisconsin to South Dakota, I was assigned a rental car—a compact, no less.

By the time I got back to Moreau I was beat. The temptation to blow off another AA meeting was strong, but I knew if I did, the second I called my wife she'd sniff me out. And it would have been my third miss in a week. My personal standard was two or less. The local chapter was in the phone book. I drove over for the evening meeting and got some local scuttlebutt in the bargain.

In the car afterwards, it was finally safe to call Brooke, who would have been done with her training by then. I was a three-sport star in high school and without doubt, the poorest athlete in my family. Brooke was a consistent medal winner in the over-forty CrossFit Games for the Upper Midwest Region. And my two teenage daughters were soon approaching the day they could kick my ass in most any sport they chose.

Even on FaceTime, Brooke looked good. Everything was fine at home. The school year still had three weeks to go. Would I be back in time for Claire's eighth-grade graduation?

"Tell her I'll try my best."

"Tell her yourself," said Brooke. She handed the phone to my thirteen-year-old, her mouth braces-full, her eyes gleaming. We talked a bit and she passed me on to Mila.

"Well, look at you," I said. "You got your hair cut."

"Ugh! Dad, I got it cut for prom… two weeks ago."

"Oh, right. Of course. It looks different on FaceTime."

Brooke asked me about the case. After Austin died, she retired from the ATF to raise the girls, so she understood the stress of working for a federal enforcement agency. I gave her a brief rundown and signed off a few minutes later.

By then it was almost nine p.m. I got a room at the only hotel in town, took a meal at a mom and pop, then turned in after watching the news.

CHAPTER TEN

Max

Between Winona and La Crosse, I slept the sleep of a man with a plan. La Crosse would be a turning point. I sensed it as sure as the four watches nestled safe in the depths of my travel case. I'd stolen them from my father's safe.

My father had "smuggled" them from Wisconsin; now I was doing the same thing, this time to California. *Poetic justice, or something like that*, I thought. Having packed and repacked my bag six times before deciding on how best to store the booty, I knew exactly where they were—lower third of the carry-on, a pair of shorts and a shirt on one side, three pair of underwear on the other.

Bus fares in all directions from La Crosse were reasonable. What was more, another mode of transportation would make it tougher for anyone trying to track us down. I still had to pick a short-term destination, a decision I would make when I saw the departure board in the station. It didn't fit with my OCD, but I prided myself on finding the correct, random event to fit my needs. I still wanted a used camper. They weren't parked in every farm yard, so I had to keep my eyes open.

I looked over at Nadine, eyes closed, her cheek resting on the back of the seat. It didn't seem reasonable, as bright as those green eyes were, but she was more beautiful asleep than awake, or maybe she just looked younger. She wasn't very tall, five foot five I guessed, but everything, from the length of her legs to the size of her hands was in perfect proportion. It wasn't as if

I'd never noticed before, only that it never mattered. She was so different from Leah and yet the sight of her made me heartsick for the girl I'd left in South Dakota. Leah was not in proportion at all. Though not skinny, her legs were too long for her torso and her hands too large for her body. She had a pretty, pert little nose but it looked puny above her wide, generous mouth. The package wasn't perfect, yet I loved how it all came together. I sighed and bumped Nadine's elbow. She stirred.

"La Crosse, coming up. You ready?"

She stretched her neck and groaned.

"Ticket? Jacket? Bag?" I asked.

She drew a lazy-V shape with her index finger. "Check."

"Okay. After we get off the train, we go to the bus station downtown. It's almost two miles away, but a municipal bus will take us there."

There were only a few other passengers on the platform. I said very little, using hand signals and touch to direct Nadine away from the train, through the station, then to the bus stop. I looked back as the train pulled away and something jolted in my chest. The half-balding, stocky man from the Minneapolis terminal was standing at the corner of the station. Stunned, I stopped for a moment. Was this guy some kind of magician? How could he show up like that out of thin air? I had been so careful when we got off the train, checked every passenger. There weren't very many. It would have been impossible to miss him. In Red Wing I'd watched as well, and all the other stops to see if the man had exited the train. I never saw him.

I grabbed Nadine's arm.

"Ouch! What the—"

"It's him. This way. Quick."

Suitcases rattling behind us, we stumbled across the road and ducked behind a stand of trees into a backyard. We passed a swing set, ran through a vegetable garden, and stopped behind a grapevine in the next yard. Peeking between the leaves, I saw the man trotting along the sidewalk in our direction, one hand in the pocket of his long coat.

"What are you doing?" she said. "What's the matter?"

"It's him, damn it," I said. "Move."

We ran across an alley to an adjoining yard, then between houses to the road and turned away from our pursuer. Half a block later we repeated the move, between houses, two yards, to the next road. Nadine was struggling with her case, so I took it and carried both. In no time, I was wasted. Sidling alongside a garage near an alley, we stopped. My chest heaving, I took a look around the corner. Hands on her knees, choking between breaths, she asked, "See him?"

"Nah."

"Think he's gone?"

"No." I took three or four deep breaths and looked again. "Shit! There he is. Three blocks up." I stepped back. "Take a look. Careful."

She crept closer, looked, then pulled back.

"Do you know him?"

"I don't *know* him; not like I know you." She licked her lips. "But I know he shouldn't be *here*, and he better not find us, or we'll *never* get out of here."

"Great. Damn it." I looked the other way. "All right. Stay off the street."

Running silent on grass, we went as far as we could until the backside of a huge lumber yard loomed over us. My arms were dead. I put the bags back on rollers and handed one to Nadine. Using parked cars for cover, we walked quickly through the parking lot to the nearest major street. The downtown bus station was still two miles away, and there was a river flowing between us. We'd have to cross a bridge at some point, which would expose us again to our pursuer. I had no time to decide otherwise. We took a right turn out of the lot and came face to face with the bridge.

We crossed the street and walked on the far side of the span, keeping a steady, leisurely pace to avoid attention. Nadine kept her head down, eyes forward, silent.

My head was up, back and forth, looking everywhere. "Christ, this valley is wide. For such a stinking little river. We're doing hundreds of steps here, and the river can't be more than sixty feet wide." A look back. "I don't see the cue ball. Do you think we lost him? I think we lost him."

The river's meandering course made the valley, a wild combination of grass, low brush, and trees, wider than it otherwise would have been. There was a bike path on the south side of the stream, sheltered by a tree line for most of its course. Standing above the hollow to the north were pole buildings for light construction companies and service stations. We were walking away from that toward a more residential neighborhood. We crossed the bridge without incident and found an entrance to the bike path that appeared to go downtown. Our luck was turning.

"How are you doing?" I asked as I checked for cover. "Can you jog?" She thought she could. I said, "Let's go."

This weekday in May, we saw few bikers. The current in the river was brisk, the course ox-bowing like a seizing snake. Our goal was 3rd Street, coming into view about a quarter mile ahead. I was feeling better. This was an area of town I'd studied. Municipal Bus Route 6 had a bus stop on 3rd Street two blocks south of the river. We'd been on the path for almost two minutes when we stepped into sunlight. Suddenly, the tree trunk next to Nadine splintered, then shattered and fell. A concussive *thud* knocked the suitcase out of my hand. Nadine screamed. I grabbed her arm and pulled her to the ground.

The hand that had been holding my case buzzed like a nest of hornets. "Are you hit?"

"Hit! With what?" she asked.

"He's shooting at us, the bastard. He must have a silencer." I yanked my suitcase closer. "Stay low. That way, behind the trees."

We scurried forward into the shade again. I craned my neck. "Can you see him? I can't see him."

"There." She pointed. "Way over, by that big, green building. The railing. There's a red truck next to him."

"And I was worried about the Feds." I dropped my head. "Who wants to shoot us? Got to have something to do with Witness Protection. But that was to protect Dad, and he's locked up."

Nadine got on all fours. "The shooter guy, he's moving,"

"What are you not telling me?" I grasped her arm. "Nadine, I'm putting my ass on the line. I want to know why."

"Nothing." She yanked her arm away. "If I knew his name, what difference would it make? The bullets don't care. He's setting up again. Look!"

We started down the path, our cover holding until the river turned precariously close to the trail bed. For about forty feet there were no trees on either side of the trail. We'd be walking from the shadows into a fully exposed position. I held out my hand to stop her.

"We're going to have to sprint, fast as you can, here to there."

Nadine wiped sweat from her eyes. "I don't think I can."

"I can't carry you. Come on, Nadine, those legs will take you anywhere."

"Maybe we should call it off." She blinked quickly. "Get your cell out. Call the cops."

I tested my case to make sure the wheels were undamaged. "Go ahead. But I'm not going back. I don't think that asshole cares about the cops. Either way," I waved at her jacket, "you have a phone. You do it." I turned toward the trail. "I knew this would happen. I should never've brought you along. First sign of trouble, you fold like an accordion."

The mist in her eyes dissipated. "Excuse me and my fear of bullets. I don't remember any mention of assassins in the brochure."

"That's pretty good. 'Assassins in the brochure.'" I smiled at that. "Anyway, I'll draw his fire, you call 911. Save your pretty ass."

"Wait." She held my wrist. "I'm fucking out of my mind, but shit, let's go."

On three, we ran. Five steps in, the gravel spit and the air sang. Something seared my thigh. I stumbled. Nadine came to my side.

"The river," I cried.

We jumped in feet first. The water sputtered. The current dragged us to the middle of the river. The water was four feet deep. We bobbed along, my feet stumbling over the uneven riverbed, Nadine behind me. I held both suitcases as shields. A shot hit my bag flush. Nadine stumbled, almost pulled me under. No sooner had she regained her feet and I lost mine—first my right slipped, then left, then right again. My thigh felt ready to explode. The river turned away from the trail.

"Grab that root. There!" I said. "Coming up."

She missed the root but got a low-lying branch. I threw one, then the other case onshore and grabbed hold of another bush downstream. The flying lead had stopped. I looked back. A large stand of trees on the opposite bank had saved our lives. We got back on the trail. Nettles and Buckthorn had poked and stuck to Nadine in a thousand places. Both suitcases were soaked, mine worse because of the bullet holes.

"Are you in one piece?" I asked.

She shivered in the shade. "I'm wet. You're bleeding."

My left thigh was on fire. The pant leg was torn; my flesh throbbed through the denim, blood streaking like watercolor. I flexed my leg. "He only grazed me. Let's go, we still have to get on the 6 before he sees us."

Almost to 3rd Street without any more shots from the gunman. We climbed the approach to the sidewalk and veered left. Two more blocks to the bus stop, where we huddled and waited. Nadine pulled nettles off her clothing. As the bus approached, I put the suitcase in front of my leg to cover the blood stain. The woman driving the bus opened the door and looked us up and down. We dropped the $1.50 fare and didn't stick around for questions. Our heads were dry, the clothing wet but not dripping. Such could not be said for the suitcases. Our shoes were filthy and squishy, the smell river-bottom bad. We took a couple seats in the back on an almost empty bus. Four stops later we were downtown.

A modest number of passengers milled about the Transit Center Station. Another bus pulled in. We saw no sign of the shooter. Nadine and I hopped out the back door and shot across the alley to the Greyhound Terminal. My original plan was to take either Greyhound or the Jefferson Bus Line to Madison or Minneapolis. I knew Madison well, having visited there several times while living in Wisconsin. Both places had the advantage of size: big enough to hide with plenty of people our age. I scanned the schedule. The wait for the Twin Cities was too long. The bus for Madison left in a few minutes, but I thought that choice too obvious. Our pursuer would figure it out. On the other hand, we couldn't stay put. I was pretty sure we'd gotten on the bus unobserved. But we were in a relatively small town. We needed to leave. Outside the window, a bus idled, a driver at the wheel. The overhead schedule board said Next Departure: Iowa City, IA. I stepped up to the window and held up two fingers.

CHAPTER ELEVEN

Max

The bus felt more confining than the train. Caught in a situation I couldn't control, my OCD went full throttle. From La Crosse to Rochester, Minnesota, my eyes never stopped twitching—out the window, behind me, through the windshield of the bus, even at empty seats. Within an hour, Nadine couldn't take it anymore:

"Knock it off. You're driving me crazy. If he was on the bus we'd have known by now." I mumbled something and picked up my coffee. She took the cup away. "Oh no. You've had enough." She handed me a water. "You're off the hard stuff."

I took the bottle. "Pardon me if I'm a little jumpy. My body doesn't take well to bullets either." *A following car!* I thought. I hadn't checked for a car stalking the bus. I stood up but stares from other passengers put me back in my seat.

"All right, Mr. Die Hard, let's look at it, your leg." She turned on the overhead light and gently probed the tear in the thigh of my jeans. Blood had stiffened the material. "I can't see the cut." She looked at the driver and the other passengers. "We're good. Pull down your jeans."

"Hell no."

"No one gives a shit about you. Come on, you've got boxers on, right? We gotta know if it's infected."

I knew she was right. Ignoring a bullet wound, even a superficial one, was a bad idea. I undid my belt and slid the jeans to my knees.

"Well, the bleeding's stopped, but it's swollen." She pressed lightly. I jumped. "Sorry."

I pulled a damp-but-otherwise-clean handkerchief out of my pocket, tore it into three strips, then tied them end to end. I wrapped my thigh, adjusting the bandage so a flat area covered the wound. "I'm going to pull this tight. You tie the ends."

This she did. After my pants were on, I took another look around. We'd drawn the attention of an elderly lady across the aisle and one row back. I smiled and waved; she frowned and turned away. "Can't believe I'm riding with this mangy bunch." I took a drink of water.

"Slow down on the water."

"I'm thirsty." Another drink. "I think we got away clean." I drank again. "You think we got away?"

She told me to think of something else.

I put the bottle in a cup holder, sat back, and ran a hand through the disorganized mop that passed for hair. 'Something else' was a good idea, but the minute I stopped thinking about the gunman, I knew what would happen—Leah would take over my brain in a Minnesota minute.

Out of the blue, she said, "Fill me in about the Jean Manticore mystery."

I raised an eyebrow. "Didn't think you cared."

"Don't care! She was my BFF in high school. We used to hang out all the time. And we both worked at Carter's Candy Store. So yeah, I care. And this arrest thing with J.R. made me think of her."

I looked at her. "You know about the belt buckle Sam snagged out of the lake." She nodded. "Okay, and the pump at the boathouse—"

"Yeah, yeah, old news. But how did you get them to look for the bones?"

Telling her the story settled me down a bit. It occurred to me that, since the body had been identified as my mother, we still didn't know who the belt buckle belonged to.

Nadine said, "We spent a lot of time during the summer on Red Wolf Lake. We'd go down to swim at the city beach and bum boat rides from the swim platform."

"Sounds like you kinda miss it."

"That was what, ten years ago." A forlorn look at the ceiling.

"Can't believe it—missing my twenties and I'm not even thirty."

I asked, "Was it hard to leave your family behind when we moved?"

Nadine stared hard at me for a long moment. Then she grabbed her travel case and tried to find a tissue, but failed. Blinking hard, she wiped away tears with her fingertips.

"Sorry. You don't have to answer."

"No, it's just that… you're the only, it's the first time anyone has asked me."

I felt empty now, too, because no one had bothered to ask me either.

Finally, Nadine said, "Sure, I miss them. My mom and dad are a strange kind of people. Very opinionated, even though neither one got through high school. Get something in their head, couldn't pry it out with a crowbar. They were happy when I married Roman, but for the wrong reasons." She rubbed her thumb and fingertips together in the universal sign for cash. "They expected some Cherhasky money to slide their way. I sent them what I could. Roman held the purse strings. He's a control freak; you know that. Anyway, a couple years ago my father's car needed a ring job, very expensive. He asked Roman for a loan. Roman knew he'd never see the money again, so he said no. There was a huge blowup. Mom and Dad were so mad they couldn't spit. It's been sorta cold between me and the family ever since."

"Maybe things would be different now," I said. "If you could go home."

"I don't know. Maybe." She crossed her arms and looked out the window, into the darkness. "Like that's ever going to happen."

The sun was down by the time we got to Rochester. The stop was ten minutes, so there was only time for two things—the bathrooms and the food machines. The time felt even shorter because we had to keep an eye out for the shooter. He wasn't there. Cellophane-wrapped food in hand, we climbed back on the bus in clothing that was mostly dry. Ever smaller puddles still formed under the luggage. The stink on both of us had improved only slightly.

In minutes, the food was gone. Nadine stuffed the trash away and pulled a dog-eared magazine from the back of the seat. Before I fell asleep, I set a mental alarm to wake me at each stop. Another surprise from the shooter and we'd be history. An irresistible, otherworldly force closed my eyes. The hum of the wheels walked me back from the inside of my eyelids to the center of my exhaustion, along the frame of the bus and even through the dark Midwest soil to the warmth at the center of Mother Earth.

Through the next four hours, the driver made three stops. I woke but once, made a cursory check of the passengers, and couldn't sleep again. The smell of the river wafting up from my clothing had tripped a mental switch. The last twenty-four hours replayed in my brain like a loop recorder, the images of the brawny, balding man, the impact of the bullet as it hit the suitcase, even the man with the lisp at the gas station.

The questions wouldn't leave me alone. Who was trying to kill us? Was it a personal vendetta or was he being paid? I'd assumed the FBI would be after us for violating the WPP agreement, but assassination of American citizens wasn't their style. And then I saw Leah, sitting in front of me on her bed. I'd never admit it to Nadine, but when we were back in La Crosse on the bike trail, before she'd said anything about calling the cops, I'd heard a voice in my head telling me to do the very same thing. *Call the cops. Call them now.* The voice was Leah's.

73

Chapter Twelve

Max

Thursday morning, one a.m., Iowa City. We dragged ourselves off the bus, strung out from the road, and beyond caring about anything. We walked away from the terminal in solitude, searching for a place to crash. After a few blocks, a flickering VACANCY light caught my eye from around a corner. The "T" was missing from the MOTEL sign and only a few cars were parked in the lot. Orange doors and mosquito-free yellow lights put a garish funk around the place; so did the moth-eaten asphalt and teeter-totter rain gutters.

The front desk area was damp and deserted, but then an older man limped out of the laundry room, grey hair pulled back in a ponytail, wearing bib-overalls a size too-large. He rented us a room, no questions asked. We paid in cash, which didn't faze him a bit.

We dragged ourselves down the walk to the last door in the line. The room was stuffy and too warm. I turned off the heat and collapsed in a chair.

"You want to shower first?" I asked.

"Yeah, all right, but I have to sort my stuff." She opened her suitcase, flipped it open, and dumped it out. She toed the pile of clothes. "All my worldly goods. What a fuckin' disaster."

"At least yours doesn't have a bullet hole in it."

I slipped a finger in the two holes on the side of my suitcase and exhaled. One of the shots had gone completely through. Something had stopped the second bullet, which was a good thing because it would have scrambled my skull. I unzipped the suitcase, flipped it open, and rifled through soggy shirts and shorts—all my careful packing replaced by chaos. Tucked in the middle was the wooden box that held the four watches I'd taken from my father's safe, exploded into five or six pieces. Carefully, I dissected wood from watch from soggy mess. The Rolex and the Bell & Ross were pristine, but one of the Piagets was shattered, a mushroomed bullet lying right on its face.

I dumped the remaining contents from the suitcase onto the lowboy chest, next to the television. We'd hit the laundry room in the morning. I shoved the suitcase into a corner and searched for a dry set of underwear. Nadine came out of the bath dressed in a wrinkled nightshirt and a pair of shorts. "I'm done," she said. "in more ways than one. Don't wake me up tomorrow unless I'm dead."

I took my shower. We fell asleep in separate beds and stayed there for the next eight hours.

The morning air was clean and the sun warmed my skin. I'd done some necessary shopping, all I needed now was a good breakfast and a clean set of clothes.

I looked both ways down the street. The motel-room door opened with a grunt. Nadine was still asleep, her head buried in a mass of red hair, cascading over her pillow. Her foot stuck out from under the covers. I grabbed a couple toes and said, "Wake up, Nadine. I'm starving. And we have a lot to do."

Nadine sat up in bed, pushed hair from her face. "Where are we again?"

"Iowa City."

She nodded at my purchases on the desk. "What's all that?"

"The suitcases are shot, and we're too slow with them anyways." I held up the backpacks. "We'll be faster with these. Come on. They have a laundry here. There's a pancake joint a block away. We'll get a bite and after that, we'll get started."

She got up, pulled her t-shirt down to her thighs, and watched me unpack the plastic bag. "Scissors. Hair color. Shaver and a newspaper," she said. "What the hell?"

"We're too easy to spot, especially you. I got sunglasses too. Bandages and ointment. I'll tell you about it while we're eating."

She picked up the hair color. "Are you going brunette? 'Cause I'm not. I've never used hair color in my life. Why should I? Women kill for my hair."

"You almost got killed standing under it." I paused. "We've got to cut it too."

"Cutting!" she said, horrified. "And who's going to do it? You?"

"Hey, I'm shaving my head and growing a beard. Buck up, sister."

The argument didn't end there, continued in fact, all the way to the Pancake House. But it had no effect on our appetites, which plowed through eggs and bacon with a side of hash browns, and coffee. There was a brief reprieve while I paid the bill.

One thing we did agree on was clean clothes. We stripped down to the minimum and threw everything else into two piles. She carried the whites; I carried the colors. We loaded the washers and slid in the quarters.

Back in the room, I unpacked the clipper/shaver and spread some newspaper under a mirror hanging over a desk. "I'll need your help where I can't see, on the back of my head."

"Are you kidding?" She stared at me in the mirror. "Max, I've never done this before."

"Neither have I. But I gotta do it." I turned on the clipper and ran it over my scalp. Large clumps of hair plopped onto the paper.

Nadine gasped. I kept going. Clump after clump, the dark pile grew. When I'd done all I could, I extended the clipper toward Nadine. "Around the neck and ears. Anything I missed. Go on." She cringed, as if the buzzing was bothering her ears. "Nadine, go ahead. It doesn't hurt."

She took the shaver with both hands and took some short strokes at my neck. Those went well, but on one pass up the back of my head, she dug in. I flinched. "Oh, sorry." She rubbed her finger over a tender ridge. I shrank away. "It's not bleeding. Sorry."

"It's all right. Keep going. Go slow. There's no rush."

She was careful around the ears and had me sit down so she could see the top of my head. When she was done I rubbed my bald, pale scalp and looked in the mirror. "Man, that is weird. Not bad."

"Oh, it's bad," she said.

The clippings went in the trash. "Your turn." I looked up. She had tears in her eyes. I pursed my lips and said, "Look, it does no good if only one of us is in disguise. We can't have a repeat of yesterday."

She shook her head. I wasn't sure if she was agreeing with me or refusing the haircut.

"Okay. Let's wet your hair. Yours is so thick, it'll be easier."

She put a towel around her neck, stood next to the tub, and stuck her head under the shower. After a towel dry, she came back and sat on the desk, facing away from the mirror. I tugged lightly on her long, auburn hair, cutting off variable lengths with the scissors. Her eyes were closed; an occasional tear escaped. She asked me to leave it just above the shoulder. I did my best.

I said. "It'll grow back in no time."

She remained silent.

She had no idea how to dye her hair, so I read the directions. "Oh crap. Your hair has to be dry. All right. Let's go finish the laundry. We'll do this after we get back."

Avoiding the mirror, she towel-dried her hair and we left. The laundromat was deserted. We transferred the loads to dryers, paid the machine, and left. In ten minutes, we were back in the room.

She sat down on the toilet lid and I got the dye ready. The fold-out instructions were laid over the sink. I showed her a pair of plastic gloves. "You've got to put these on, you know, to spread out the coloring." There were two bottles in the kit. I mixed them together and shook.

"I can't do it." She handed the gloves back to me.

I put them on. I squeezed the bottle carefully. My gloved fingers passed through her hair a dozen times. "Now, it says, we have to wait thirty minutes. I'll go get the laundry."

"What am I supposed to do?" she asked.

"Wait. Take it easy. Watch TV. Read the newspaper. Whatever you want."

The dryers had finished. I folded the clothes into his and her piles, making the chore last as long as I could. Twenty minutes later, I walked in the room. I put her clothes next to her backpack. I packed mine away, then looked at my watch. She hadn't said a word to me, only sat motionless, looking without expression at a TV gameshow. I turned on the shower and said, "Come on. It's time."

She got up, pulled a towel tight around her neck, and walked into the bathroom. She leaned into the stream of warm water. Again, I ran my fingers through her hair, this time until the water ran clear. "One more step, there's a conditioner." I reached for a small white bottle. "Stand up a second." I dabbed in the conditioner. "Okay, rub it in."

She did, then rinsed again. I handed her a fresh towel and thought to give her some space while she reapplied her make-up. I said, "There's an internet place down the street. I'm going to see if I can get some online news. Be back in twenty."

It was a very productive twenty minutes. When I got back, I tossed the key on the bed and looked up. Nadine stood in the bathroom door, eyes flashing, her new, brunette hair tussled.

"Wow. Brilliant," I said. "I like your disguise a lot better than mine. But you didn't get those eyes in a box of Clairol. What do we do about those?"

She'd also put on a clean outfit and packed up her clothes. She raised an eyebrow. "Where are those sunglasses?"

I hung them from my index finger. She snatched them away and said, "I'm going for a walk."

"Not too long. I figured out the next step."

She stepped past me and rubbed my bald scalp. "Okay, Dwayne."

"What? Who's Dwayne?"

"Dwayne Johnson. The Rock."

CHAPTER THIRTEEN

Nate

The hotel in Moreau served a complimentary breakfast. It was a good place to catch up on the local news, get a bite, and wait for the town to wake and my office in Milwaukee to open. My first interview was Trevor Manning, Max's best friend. I wanted to catch him at home because, if he wasn't eighteen years old I'd need a parent present to interview him.

I knocked on the front door of the Manning home at 7:20 a.m. A middle-aged woman in a sweater, blue jeans, and slippers answered. I introduced myself and asked if I could speak to Trevor.

"Why? Is he in trouble?" The woman asked through the screen door.

"No, ma'am. I'm asking about his friend, Max Farmer. Seems he's disappeared."

"Oh, my." She pushed the door open, invited me in, and called her son's name. I followed her into the kitchen where she offered me a cup of coffee and a seat at the table. Trevor appeared from down a short hall, a big boy, soft in the middle, hair cut short on the sides and long on top.

"Trevor," Mrs. Manning said. "This is Nathaniel Bauer from the FBI. He's here about Max. Do you know where he is?"

With a bemused expression, he shook his head.

"If you'll sit down, Trevor." I motioned to a seat. "I'll try to make this quick. I'm sure you have school, and Mrs. Manning, you're busy too, I imagine."

"Work. Eight o'clock, but it can wait. I'm self-employed."

I nodded. "I use my cell phone as a recorder." I held it up. "Hope you don't mind. It's my second brain. Trevor, I'm here in Moreau to help your friend, Max Farmer. You may know, his father is currently in jail."

Trevor nodded. I thought it strange he didn't ask why an FBI agent would be interested in his friend, so I made a note. "I went to the Farmer home yesterday and the house was empty. He wasn't at school, either. Any idea where I can find him? It's pretty important."

"No, sir." He blinked several times. "He wasn't at school, like you said."

"When was the last time you saw him?"

"Monday, so three days ago, after school. He drove me home like he always did."

"You don't expect him to be doing that anymore?"

Trevor raised his eyebrows. "What do you mean?"

"Only that you said, 'like he always *did*. As if he wouldn't be doing it again."

"Like he always *does*," said Trevor. "That's what I meant."

His mother frowned.

I pursed my lips. "Okay. How'd you get home yesterday?"

"Walked."

"Did you try calling him?"

"Yeah, every day. No answer, so I left a voice mail. Text, too, but." He flashed his palms. "Nothing."

"Trevor, why didn't you tell me?" his mother asked. He shrugged.

"Frustrating," I said. "I know how you feel. In the last few weeks, did he mention anything about leaving town? Any plans after graduation?"

"He wasn't one to talk. He only moved here last year, and I don't think he ever felt at home."

"Was he going to go to college?"

"He got accepted at a couple of places. He wanted to go to U of I, but I think he blew them off, last he told me anyway."

"Iowa's a good school," I mused. "Kinda far away."

Trevor raised an eyebrow. "Not far enough. Or not close

enough to the West Coast, more like it. He was always talking about it. The music scene. He thought he could make it there. We called bullshit on that, of course. Not that it ever bothered him."

"Anywhere particular out West? California? Seattle?"

"Southern California, I always assumed."

"He any good?" I asked.

"Singing." He tipped his hand back and forth. "Passable. But the guitar, those fingers could fly."

His mother added, "I told him, he has a gift."

I flipped the page on my notebook. "Just a couple more questions. I appreciate your time, really. Max has a stepmom, Nadine. How well did he get along with her?"

A distinct hook formed at the corner of Trevor's mouth. "Not at all. When those two got into it, I took cover."

"That worries me because she's missing too. Did she have any friends? A job?"

Trevor shrugged, but his mother said, "Waitress. I saw her a few times at The Prairie Kitchen. It's downtown. But friends, none that I know of."

"Thank you." I flipped my notepad shut. "Fill me in, Trevor. What's he running away from? His father? A pregnant girlfriend? What?"

"I don't know. He broke up with his girlfriend, so I don't think it's that. He was a strange kind of guy. Very self-confident."

There it was again, the past tense. Trevor had already said goodbye to Max, in one way or another. I stood up, thanked Mrs. Manning for her hospitality, and left them my card.

The Wheatland County Courthouse, the biggest building in Moreau, occupied almost an entire side of a downtown square that had a bandstand and park in the middle. The downtown wore a thin veneer of prosperity without being gaudy or brash, probably because it was the county seat. Empty store fronts were few and most of the businesses well-kept. I walked the steps to the second floor, passed though security after surrendering my sidearm, and registered to interview their celebrity lock-up, George Farmer.

When Farmer entered the interview room, I thought they'd

brought the wrong guy. This George barely resembled the J. Roman Cherhasky I'd arrested in the kitchen of his lakeside estate a year earlier. Dressed in orange, manacled to a belt cinch, shoulders slouched, his hair grey, and skin as white as a cut root, he took a seat opposite and gazed at me with dull eyes.

"Bauer isn't it? What do you want? Couldn't wait till they dragged me back to Wisconsin to sink your claws into me?"

I took out my cell phone and notebook. "It's not about you, not entirely." He lifted his head a little. I went on. "I'm charged with the safety of your son and wife."

"What the hell kinda help do they need? They're not in lock-up. I'm the one accused. Get me a decent lawyer. This guy from Rapid City's an amateur. I'm being railroaded back to Wisconsin and he's not doing a damn thing. This is bullshit Bauer, and you know it." His expression was as bitter as day-old coffee. "I signed an agreement, protection for me and my family so long as we live within the bounds of the law. Then you shove me in this backwater town in a job fit for a vagrant. And do I complain? No! Because I signed on the dotted line. Now it's time for you guys to do your part. You can't put me in prison. The only way I'd leave that place is belly up, dead as a fly in a window well. And you know it. You can't do it. That's what Witness Protection is all about."

I tipped my thermos and poured myself a coffee. "Interesting take. The devil, as they say, is in the *fine print.* You are released from any and all violations particular to the agreement. All *other* felonies are fair game."

"Alleged! Alleged! And you've already blown my cover."

I took a drink. "Have you thought for even a moment about how your arrest puts your son and wife in danger? Especially your wife?"

If he paused for a second, I missed it. "Small fries, both of them. Do you understand anything about my former associates? Kill the head and the body dies. Well, I'm the head." He clutched his hands to his belly. "I'm the one they want."

"When did you last see your son?"

A fishy gleam came to his eye. "I don't know. Before the arrest."

"He hasn't come to visit?" I wasn't surprised when he shook

his head. I told him he'd been missing for thirty-six hours and I was worried he was on the run. "Any idea why he'd leave town?"

"He's a big-headed, impulsive, irresponsible kid. What other reason do you need?"

Regarding his wife, he was even less responsive. I expressed my concerns about her disappearance and that she may have lit out on her own.

George chuckled softly. "She's got all the independence of a baby kangaroo." When I suggested the two of them might be together, he erupted in laughter. "Yeah, I think you can forget that little theory. They'd rather boil in oil."

I asked about friends, but he said Nadine had precious few of those around here. "What about access to money, checking, safe deposit box?"

His gaze flared. Suddenly I had his attention. "Her name is on the savings account." He banged his knuckles on the table and winced. "There's a safe, in my house. Check it. There should be four watches in there. That bitch. She'd be able to pawn them in a minute." He gave me the safe's combination and a description of the timepieces—all high-end and very expensive. I turned off the cell recorder, left the lock-up, and headed for the bank.

My credentials got me immediate attention and, after they received oral permission for access from George Farmer, immediate answers. Nadine had made a $10,000 withdrawal two days ago. She'd been accompanied by a younger man they assumed to be her stepson.

The Farmer home was not locked. The safe was open. There were no signs of forced entry, so whoever had opened it knew the sequence. The watches were gone.

It was time to touch base with my office and get something to eat. Mrs. Manning had made my lunch decision: it would be The Prairie Kitchen. It was pretty busy, but I got a booth, ordered a sandwich, and dialed. Lance answered right away. He's a good agent and had gone through the Amtrak manifest as I asked and found no sign of Max or Nadine Farmer. He'd also checked the bus lines in the area, precious few as they were, and came up empty. I had him email the Amtrak information to me anyway and asked if there was any news from Chicago.

"Nothing, Nate. Sorry. I'll let you know."

The meal was good, right down to the coleslaw side and the chocolate malt. I complimented the waitress. On the way out, I showed my badge at the register and asked to talk to the manager. No one was in trouble; I just had a few questions about Nadine Farmer. She returned with the owner, a fit-looking, middle-aged woman in slacks and blouse, her hair back. "I'm Susan Dunbar, the owner," she said. "What can I do for you?" Her handshake was all-business, and so was her make-up—only a whisper of eye shadow around her brown eyes and a thin veil of pink lipstick.

I re-introduced myself. She showed me to a small office off the kitchen. "Busy place. I had a fine meal. Thank you," I said.

"That's why we're busy." I noticed her clothing was clean and pressed. Her hands looked soft, the nails were manicured.

"I'm here about one of your employees, Nadine Farmer." Susan's face grew some new worry lines. I said, "I'm here to talk to her about her husband, and I can't locate her. I thought you could help me."

Susan sat down behind a small desk and pointed to a chair for me. "Did something happen? Is she all right?"

"I don't know. I'm trying to find out."

"I've been worried about her since the day I hired her." She tapped on the edge of her desk. "Good worker, always on time. Customers like her, especially the men. She's a doll, if you've ever seen her…"

I nodded. "I think she left town. Her husband is in jail and she's in some danger. I need to get to her ASAP."

"That S.O.B. What did he do now?"

I said I wasn't at liberty to discuss the case. "Did she mention anything about leaving? Being dissatisfied with house and home, that kind of thing?"

"No mention of leaving, but she dropped plenty of hints about her husband. Pardon my French, but frankly, he sounds like a prick. She has a stepson but the only time I heard anything about him was when they were fighting; but then again he'd come in here and they were fine together."

"Did she ever mention a place she'd go, or want to go to, if she left town?"

"No. Very tight-lipped about things like that. Didn't do the *girl talk* thing at all, especially about her past."

I gave her my card and asked her to contact me if she stumbled across anything else. "One more question, why do you worry?"

"I had… I have this sense Nadine gets through life with her looks and a little luck. And as the years march on, we both know what happens to both of those."

"I guess I do." I asked if she could suggest anyone else for me to talk to, another waitress for instance she may have confided in. She wrote down a name and phone number, but she thought the lead would be a dead end. I thanked her and left.

I stepped out the front door and reached for my car key.

"Hey, mister, you looking for the Farmers?"

I turned. To my left, leaning against the front of the restaurant was a tall, solid, young man dressed in a t-shirt, weeks past its last wash. He had a ruddy, almost burnt complexion and the look of a high-school athlete gone to seed: thick neck, big forearms, but a gut that was getting away from him. I'd noticed him at another table in the restaurant and wondered if he heard me mention Nadine's name to the cashier.

"Yes, I'm looking for Max and Nadine Farmer." I stepped toward him. "Name's Nate Bauer. Do you know them?"

"Yeah, I know them. Nadine works here at TPK's. I wouldn't eat breakfast here once a week if she didn't."

The guy looked creepy, but in her line of work I supposed Nadine was used to putting up with attention from his sort. "I see. I didn't catch your name."

"Tugger, Tugger Jonsson."

I flipped open my notebook.

"That's two 'g's' and two 's's' and no 'h.'"

"Okay, Tugger, help me out here. Nadine is missing. Any idea where she is?'

"Not a clue. It's her piece-of-shit stepson I'm after."

"Why's that?"

"He owes me money, that's why. He messed with my bike and the repairs are costing me. And look at my face."

I said I'd noticed.

"That bastard threw coffee at me. Hot coffee! First and second-degree burns." He flashed his profile at me, right and left. "Had to see a doctor. When you find him, you tell him, Tugger's got a score to settle." Before I could ask for any contact information, he turned in a huff, climbed into a beat-up, full-size pick-up, and drove away, the muffler roaring. The license plate was disfigured, so I didn't get that, either.

CHAPTER FOURTEEN

Max

By the time Nadine got back from her walk, I had both backpacks ready to go. She stopped short at the door, then let it shut behind her and sat on the bed next to her open satchel. While refolding a blouse, she told me she'd stopped at the front desk and bargained the next night's rent to half-price, since we'd come in so late the night before. She didn't want to get back on the bus, not right away.

"Neither do I, but..." I put a small, walking knapsack over my shoulder. "I found a camper. A little expensive, but it's just what we need, only a few blocks away. Let's go check it out. Leave our stuff here." She didn't budge. "Nadine, we have to keep moving. After what happened yesterday, I shouldn't have to explain." I opened the door and held it for her. She stuffed the blouse back in the backpack and led me out the door.

Our destination was a little over a mile. A bridge took us across the Iowa River and toward the university campus, a spot I had wanted to see for years. Well, see it I would, and that was it: no classes, no scouting the music talent, no Big 10 football games. The Winnebago was visible from a block away, parked in the driveway of a two-story home with an outside staircase to a second-floor entrance, an old-fashioned front porch, and a detached garage. I phoned the owner and told him we were outside. A moment later, a man came out of the second-floor door, waved, and descended the steps.

"Hi. Are you Max? I'm Stan Dettmann. You interested in the camper?"

"Max Cherhasky. This is Nadine." I didn't get into the details of our relationship. No point in answering questions that hadn't been asked. "And yes, we're interested." I had done some online research on the 1983 LeSharo, but I let Stan do the talking. He was not the original owner but was responsible for most of the 139,000 miles on the odometer.

"Got an in-line four, oil-burner," Stan said.

"It burns oil?" Nadine said. "That's not good."

"I'm sorry, miss." Stan cupped his ear with a hand. He had hearing aids on both sides. "Diesel, it runs on diesel. I done most of the mechanic work myself, oil changes and the like. It's mostly up-to-date except the battery. It's about four years old." He opened the hood. "You can see, it's all there. Not bad for a thirty-seven-year-old machine."

Stan walked us around the outside. There was a fair amount of rust on the body; the rest of the paint looked passable. We went in the side door for a look at the interior. The two captain's chairs up front were worn, the two in the second row were in better shape.

"My wife and I, my second one, we were gonna see all forty-eight states in this thing. Maybe even Alaska, who knows? But then she got the cancer and died. I been empty as an old shoebox since then. As it was, we never got outside of Iowa and South Dakota."

"Sorry to hear that." I nodded at the sink. "Does the plumbing work?"

"You bet."

"It's showing its age, but I'm still interested. Can I take it for drive?" I asked.

"Let's step outside, and you don't have to shout." Stan tapped on his hearing aid. "My batteries are fresh." Back on the asphalt, he asked for my driver's license.

Without a second thought, I pulled out my wallet and showed him my South Dakota license. I knew my mistake immediately.

Stan's face tightened. "Well, that's you, maybe, when you had hair." Stan held the picture next to me. "Now you're bald as an eggplant. And your last name is wrong."

I looked down. "Yeah, it's a long story."

He handed the license back to me and turned toward the house. "Been nice talkin' to ya."

I couldn't let it end so easily. Truth was, this was the only camper I'd found in the Iowa City area that was affordable and fit our needs. And Nadine was right about one thing—I didn't want to get back on the bus either. A Greyhound schedule was too easy to trace. And buses were like prisons on wheels, once you got on, you weren't getting off until the next stop. I wanted, needed this camper.

"Hold on." I jogged after him. "We can pay cash." My father used to be a salesman, a darn good one, and he had told me if a big sale was in jeopardy, he would "take them out for a meal." I cleared my throat. "Listen, Nadine and me, we're good people. Give us a chance to show you. It's lunch time. Have a bite with us. Do you have a favorite spot? It's on me. After that, if you still want to walk away, no hard feelings."

For the first time, Stan gave us the once-over. "Nothing to lose, I guess," he said. His favorite was a pizza and salad place on the corner. The walk was half-a-block, and he was hungry, so he agreed. The pizza-oven warmth inside was a pleasant break from the brisk spring day. Brick walls and rough-hewn furniture gave the place an old-time ambience even though most of the fixtures were polished stainless steel. We sat down at a booth, checked the menus, and gave the order to a waitress.

Stan surprised me when he ordered a salad. He pointed at me. "Do you know how much salt and fat there is in that pepperoni pizza you ordered?" I shrugged. "Well, I do, and I swore off it. You should too." Stan pointed at the ceiling. "Doc told me, 'if you can't rinse it off your plate, it's probably stickin' to your coronaries.'"

I laughed and said if I ever quit pizza, I'd be slapping pepperoni on my skin like a nicotine patch, just to stop the shakes. I told Stan that I understood why he was suspicious, so I was going to play it straight with him. Nadine and I were running away from the same thing—a man who'd betrayed us. I got out my phone, Googled the story from South Dakota, and showed it to him. He took the phone and read the post.

"So, what?" Stan said. "He's in jail. That don't explain the fake I.D. or why you're on the run."

"Right you are." I nodded. "Ever heard of the Witness Protection Program, Stan?" I asked. He had, but only vaguely, so I explained how we came to be in South Dakota and under the thumb of the Federal Government. "We're not criminals," I said. "You read the story. We're mentioned, but only because they don't know where we are."

Stan handed the phone back. "You're taking a big chance. How do you know I won't call the cops?"

"I don't." I looked at Nadine. "We don't. So, yeah, it's a gamble."

"And this 'Cherhasky' name?" Stan asked.

"That's our real name," Nadine said. "From Wisconsin. Before WPP. Before my husband put his foot in the crap."

"We're headed to California," I said.

The waitress brought the drinks.

Stan was a little overweight, and the overhead lighting bought out a high forehead that sloped into a straight nose and finally a double chin. He nodded, then took a sip of coffee. "I have a dream of goin' there."

"California? Why don't you?" Nadine asked. "You still working or something?"

"No, I'm on disability. Got a few too many stents. Time is not the problem."

"Why California?" I asked.

"Not so much the State, it's a person." Now Stan had our attention. The salads arrived. He told of an old flame from high school he started to email a couple of years after his second wife died. Through the years, they had never lost touch, and she lost her spouse at about the same time as he lost his. Yes, they had dated in high school, he said. He'd even taken her to prom.

"An old flame," Nadine said. "I knew it." She dug into her salad. The pizza arrived. I took a bite.

Stan smiled. "Asked her to marry me, that very night. We weren't even out of high school but I didn't care. She was perfect, the only one for me." He looked across the table, both of us with food in our mouths but not chewing. He waved us away with his fork. "Nothing came of it. She said no."

"Oh, how could she? On prom night!" Nadine wiped her lips. "What's her name? Have you asked her again?"

"Her name is Sandy. And no, I haven't asked again. But I'm thinking on it. I think a second request stands a better chance if I do it in person. Don't you?"

"Definitely. Got to be face to face," I agreed. "Why don't you fly there and do it?"

"Nope. Never. Fear of flying. And I'm not up to driving. Doubt I'd make it past the Rockies." He took a sip of coffee. "Guess I was born to live and die in Iowa."

Given our limited resources, the price on the vehicle was steep. Stan was asking $6,500, and I worried that kind of hit to our cash could hurt us in the long haul. A few thousand dollars less would make a huge difference. I wanted to make a deal.

"What if we drive you there?" I asked.

Stan took a drink, then set the cup down. "You'd do that?"

"Honestly, Stan, Nadine and I, we can't afford sixty-five for the camper. If you take, say $4,500, we'll take you any place in California you want to go."

Stan shook his head. "Can't go that low."

I watched as Stan moved some greens around with his fork. Clearly, the old guy was considering the offer, which was a surprise given how the morning had started.

"Fifty-five is doable," Stan said. "You do the driving. I'll be your mechanic… and I get the back bunk."

"Five thousand. I do the driving. Share the cost on food." I looked at Nadine. "We'd have to figure out the sleeping arrangements. But okay, you have the back."

Stan squinted a bit at that, but was noncommittal for the rest of the meal. I'd finished my pizza and he still hadn't answered. The waitress brought the tab. I paid in cash and left a tip. We walked back to the house and stopped on the sidewalk in front of the camper. Stan put his hands in his back pockets. It felt like bad news scribbling the air.

"Listen, I'd like to help you out," Stan said. "But I can't sell the camper to you. I always said I'd find it a good home and, no offense, but I just met you two. If you were residents of Iowa City, or I'd known ya, it'd be different. I'll have to pass on your offer."

"But Stan, just give us a chance," I said.

"And what about Sandy?" Nadine asked.

"Sorry, that's the way it is." Stan turned slowly toward the house. "Best a luck."

"Yeah, thanks." I wrote down my cell number on a piece of paper and gave it to Stan. "Just in case you change your mind."

As Nadine and I walked back to the motel, I cast a forlorn look back toward the university campus. We talked about our options, a brief conversation because there was little to discuss. The purchase of a used car came up. An older SUV could get us to the West Coast well enough. We could even sleep in the back on an air mattress or in a couple of sleeping bags. But that arrangement gave me a strong sense of claustrophobia. And because of everything we'd gone through together, from dodging an assassin's bullet to the cutting and coloring of her hair, I didn't want a situation that would bring us closer together. More importantly, the camper was one of the lynch pins of my California plan, and I wasn't ready to bury that idea, not yet. There'd be other towns, other campers for sale.

Mid-afternoon, I had just gotten back to the motel room after a visit to the bus terminal.

"Did you buy us tickets?" Nadine asked.

I opened my backpack and went at its contents as if there was a rabid racoon inside. "Where the hell is that Rolex?" I pulled out shorts and a shirt and found the box.

"What are you going to do with that?"

I carefully replaced the clothes back in the backpack. "Pawn it. No sense carrying it around."

"You sure? Might stop the next bullet." She looked back to her magazine. "No tickets then. We're staying here?"

"No! Leaving tomorrow. Denver. All the departure times are for crap, don't matter where you're going. Late afternoon. Another day wasted."

Nadine rolled her eyes. My phone rang. "Who's got your number?" she asked.

I didn't recognize the area code or the number. I said hello. The caller answered. I stood up and covered my other ear. "Yeah, sure Stan. What's going on?"

Nadine dropped the magazine to her lap.

Stan's voice was different, as if he was talking around a stone in his throat. "I got a call from Sandy, you remember, my girlfriend from California." I said I did. "Well, she's been worried about her daughter for some time now. Losing weight, no energy, that sort of thing. Anyway, she found out she's got cancer, the daughter I mean."

"That's bad news," I said. "I'm sorry to hear it." I shrugged at Nadine, who was silently gesturing questions to me.

"Yeah, yeah. Well, the reason I'm calling... I just feel like I should be there with her. All I could hear was the pain in her voice."

"You gotta do what you gotta do," I gestured hopefully to Nadine.

"Your offer, $5,000 like we said. That still on the table?"

"Absolutely. One hundred percent."

"Time is not on my side here," Stan said. "She's pretty bad, I guess. But I got business to take care of at the bank. I'll come to your hotel. Sign the deed and you can pay me. Leave tomorrow?"

"I'm down for that. And thank you," I said. "Oh, by the way. We're not staying out by the interstate. I'll give you the address."

"What? A false address? Why did you do that?"

"We didn't know you either, Stan. You might have called the cops."

Chapter Fifteen

Nate

I headed for my last appointment of the day. The music coming from Leah Walters' studio was so loud I knew she wouldn't hear my knocking. The door was open. I entered and called hello. The volume went down and a rather tall woman in a white t-shirt and white painter pants spattered with dabs of color came out of the back room, a pair of goggles on her brow kept her raven-black hair from falling across a pretty face.

She said hello. I returned the greeting and told her who I was and why I was there. Clouds darkened her blue eyes at the mention of Max's name.

She waved me toward her studio. "I'm in the middle of a piece so I can't stop. But we can talk while I work." I agreed. The room was unlike any artist's space I'd ever seen, but I'd only seen a few. This one had blotches of paint and particles of multicolored plaster all over three walls and the ceiling, like Sherwin Williams had blown up inside a giant microwave. Bolted to a heavy-duty tripod was a three by five canvas, strips of string and thread sprouting from its edge on two sides.

She put on a pair of blue Nitrile gloves and the goggles. "I wouldn't stand there if you value that jacket. It'll end up looking like the wall behind you." I took cover behind the tripod. She took one thread between her fingers, and with a snap and a jolt, tore it free. There was a short, sharp *zip* from the canvas, like fabric tearing. A fleck of red flew into her hair. A slash of red and yellow creased the wall where I had been standing.

"Can I look?" I asked.

She shrugged with one shoulder. "Not much to see."

The painting, which was split diagonally, half black, half in a rainbow of greys, was now scarred by a pencil-thin crevasse of yellow-tinged red, coursing right to left like a thunderbolt.

"Wow," I said, standing back. "Judging from all the string-ends, you've got a lot more to do."

"Each one is a different pattern, color, depth, and width. Sometimes I stop before doing all the strings. It depends on what I'm seeing. And the process is time sensitive, so if you have questions, you'll have to ask them while I rip."

I retreated again, showed her my phone, and asked her to turn off the music. The shrug again, but she picked up a remote and granted my request. "When is the last time—"

Rrriipp.

"—you saw Max?"

She tossed the spent string aside. "Four days ago." Another string.

I took extra notes because of the noise. "Looks like he left town Tuesday. You saw him Monday?"

"Yeah. We broke up." She reached low. "Coming up top. Better duck."

I did. The force from bottom to top came through the canvas like it had been torn by a chainsaw. "That one must have cut pretty deep."

She dropped the thread at her feet. "You talking about the painting or the break up?"

The look in her eyes answered for me.

She grabbed another thread and swung violently. Blue and green pocked her arms and shirt.

I said, "I think he could be in danger. Do you have any way to contact him?"

"Why would I? I mean, up until a minute ago? You tried his phone?"

I pulled a couple of cells out of my pocket and held them up. "Do either of these look familiar?"

She pointed with a nod. "That one, with the crack in the case, that's his. Don't know the other one."

Max's phone was black. "I think the blue one belongs to Nadine. I suspect they're together, wherever they are."

"What? His stepmother? You selling tickets? That's a show I'd pay to see." She slid her goggles to her forehead. Cloth in hand, she dabbed at one of the fissures like it was a laceration on someone's forehead.

I watched. "Will it need stitches?"

Her first smile, and it was so beguiling I almost dropped the phones. "Don't laugh. I've used sutures on a few of my pieces. Learned from a doc in the ER. I've grown rather fond of them, the stiches I mean. Everyone knows what they are, they always elicit an emotional response, and no two people react the same way." She touched the roughened canvas again, ran a finger along the serrated edge of the rift she'd just created. "For me they represent calm among the chaos. Some pieces need that." She set down the cloth. "But not this one. I want it to bleed."

Max seemed adept at leaving others with strong emotions in his wake—Tugger and now Leah. "I think Max left town. Any guess as to where he's headed?"

"Left? Hmm. There's something new in his head every week." The blue of her eyes were ringed in black. Nothing particularly unusual in that. But in her case, it unsettled me, as though she was seeing more than was in the room. "Last week it was the West Coast. Week before, algae was going to save us from global warming." She replaced the goggles and *rriippp*. "The next biofuel. He was going start a farm." She looked at me over the top of the canvas. "I know this isn't helping. It's not because I'm playing the loyalty card. It's because I thought I knew him, and I was wrong."

I had the impression she was being too modest. Usually, those I interview who don't think they can help the investigation are the ones that help the most, and I told her so.

Her lower lip pouted a bit. "If you're interested in his childhood, I can tell you a little about that. Max avoids the topic like a disease." She tore away at the canvas. "From what I can tell, his childhood ended when his mother died. He'll tell you he was only four or five years old when it happened, but that's not true. He was six, and I think he remembers a lot more than he'll say."

I stood taller to get a look over the tripod. This sounded important, and I wanted to see her face as she was telling it. "How do you know that?"

"That he was six? I caught him on the year his mom died. I looked up the story, did the math."

I circled the note in my book. "Why would he do that?"

"I don't know." She tore another strip top to bottom, and splattered my shoes in gray and blue. She said, "Maybe it makes it more believable, that he doesn't remember, I mean. I told him what I found online. That was a mistake."

"He didn't take it well?"

"He went glow-in-the-dark nuclear. Said I was spying on him. I was, I suppose. I never believed the camping story, not for a minute. He was holding back, I could see it."

She was confident when she said this, remarkably so. I wondered how someone not yet twenty had become so adept at reading between the lines. I asked her about it.

Leah had grabbed a thread, but my question stopped her in midair, the thread of green and red still in her grip, the tear only halfway across the canvas. I thought she'd hit a snag. I came around the tripod to take a look. "Are you stuck?"

She let go the string; it plopped onto the picture, leaving a broken trail of color that pointed straight to the floor. I thought the work was ruined, but she didn't seem to notice or care. Instead, she removed the gloves and rubbed forefinger and thumb together, mixing the colors into a gray button. She pushed her thumb into the corner of the picture, as if she were signing it with a fingerprint. "There are only three people who know what I'm about to tell you, Mr. Bauer, and they're all sworn to secrecy. Can I trust you?"

The look on her face, even with the goggles on, was so arresting I almost agreed. But, of course, I couldn't do that. "I don't know. I can't promise until after I hear it."

She parted her lips, hesitated, then said, "Turn off your phone or our conversation is over." I complied and, contradicting what I had just told her, said we were off the record.

"Do you know what synesthesia is?" she asked.

"I don't know. Maybe," I said. "It has to do with people who sense flavors as colors, that kind of thing?"

She grabbed a scissors off a nearby table. "For some yes. I have another type. I see auras around people, colors, like a full-body halo. How the colors change, how intense the halo is, they tell me things. Not facts. I can't tell what you dreamed last night. More like an emotional barometer." She snipped the end of the dangling thread at the lower edge of the work. "Whenever Max says anything about his mother's death, his halo shrinks and becomes a darker blue, more intense."

I looked at her hands, the piece of string lying across her palm like a scar. "That's remarkable." My first impulse was to ask what she was seeing when she looked at me, but I resisted.

The corner of her mouth twitched. "Green with an edge of yellow—the color of surprise," she said.

It takes a lot to embarrass me, but I felt a flush go up my neck. "And what's Max's normal color?" She said it was blue, but a brighter shade. "Wow," I whispered. Then to her, "You better get back to work." She said the piece was finished. "You're going to leave that piece of thread on there?" I asked.

"Yes. It'll fuse to the canvas when the paint dries. It says something. It has a story."

I held up the phone to indicate I was turning the recorder on. "Did Max ever confirm your suspicions about his mother?"

"No. And we almost broke up over it, I'm pretty sure of that. I get it. If I was him, I wouldn't want anyone digging around in my past either."

"Does he know about your—" I twirled my finger, as if at her vision.

She shook her head. "He's not one of the three. I should have. Here I am calling him out about dishonesty, and I was lying to him just the same. I feel terrible about it."

I motioned to the canvas. "May I take a look?" She nodded.

I stepped back and took in the colors, the parallel lines and the asymmetry which somehow worked off of each other. She asked if I liked it. I took a final look at the painting. Or was it sculpture? Modern or impressionistic? I wasn't sure. I thought it was amazing.

She paused for a moment, then said, "Mr. Bauer, bring him home. If you do, you can have any work in the studio. Except this one; it's not going anywhere."

I never completely understood the adage, *that person wears their heart on their sleeve.* But this woman revealed truth through her eyes. I wondered if all artists were that way, was that what made them so? And there was something else about her presence in the room. Or was it that she was standing in her studio, a room that bore so completely the marks of her existence? I didn't think so, but I thought best to interview her next time, if there was to be one, at a neutral location. Because I was noticing things beyond the pale, outside of what I could legitimately call my professional curiosity. The length of her fingers as they tended the canvas, the arc of her arm, the curve of her lower back as she dangled the released string in the air. I thought I should end the interview, because it seemed it would be too easy to fall in love with her.

We talked a while longer. I turned to leave, then she said, "Improvise."

"Your art?" I asked.

"Yes, and that's the part he liked the most. He's a planner, but what comes most naturally to him is improvisation. If he doesn't want to be found, all of your work…" She took off the goggles and tossed her hair. "is still ahead of you."

———————————

I drove to a coffee shop to catch up with my office and check my email. I reached for my cup and noticed a swirl of blue paint on the back of my hand. Immediately, I was back in her studio, listening to her voice, feeling her. *A blue almost a match to the color of her eyes*, I thought. It was also the color of her mood, but that, I sensed, was a much darker shade since she'd split with Max.

Her reaction told me more about him than any other part of the investigation. I took a sip of coffee and laughed at myself. Had some of her synesthesia rubbed off on me?

My phone rang. The news from Lance was bad. Our informants in Chicago confirmed a contract was out on Nadine Cherhasky, value north of $75,000. Serious money from serious people. No word yet on Max Cherhasky. The reports from the Canadian-U.S. border were negative.

The final chapter of my time with the agency had yet to be written, but if at any point I washed out, it wouldn't be because of Lance. If it wasn't for his loyalty I might have been dismissed a long time ago. He could have bolted, hooked up with another agent with less baggage and better prospects and no one, myself included, would have blamed him. I told him as much in a conversation we had four months ago. He'd never given the question serious consideration. I have no idea how to pay him back.

Next, I opened my laptop and reviewed the Amtrak information from Williston. Based on what Leah had told me, I scanned the names for westbound first, and came up empty. Halfway through the eastbound roster I spilled my coffee. Lance was right: no Max or Nadine Farmer. Because they had already changed back to their old identities. Max and Nadine Cherhasky were two days ahead of me. And now Leah's description of her former boyfriend struck home, because either the San Andreas fault had moved California two-thousand miles away from the Pacific, or Max had pulled a feint—maybe his second or third. They were headed east.

Chapter Sixteen

Max

Not exactly the way I wanted it to play out, but bad news for Stan was good luck for us. A small celebration was in order, so that evening Nadine and I went to an inexpensive Mexican place for supper. She predicted good food because the parking lot was full. The same was true of the dining room and the bar, where it was so crowded we couldn't have fit a nacho between us. Finally, two stools opened at the rail, and we ordered from there. Nadine had a margarita and chimichanga; I ordered a water and a Mexican platter. The clientele was a mixture of college and young professionals, so we felt at home. T.V. monitors were everywhere. Music thumped from invisible speakers. We sat close enough to avoid shouting over the din.

She raised her glass. "Here's to one hell of a day."

"To thirty-six hours of crazy." We tapped glasses. "I think I got a pretty good price on the camper. What do you think?" I paused. "I think I got a damn good price. Don't know about Stan, though. If I'm looking at the Winnebago, he's not the best mechanic."

She took a sip of her drink. "What about his heart, with those stints? What does that even mean? What if he gets sick on the way?"

"Stents, Nadine, they're stents," I said. "They're for blocked blood vessels. If he gets sick, we take him to a hospital."

"Yeah, and then?"

The bartender set a bowl of chips and salsa in front of us. "Depends. I don't worry about shit till it happens."

"Depends?" She cast a grave look at me. "Then we'd have to

stay with him, you know, until he was better. You ready for that?"

"Man, this beard." I scratched my chin. "Speaking of which, I have news about *your husband.*"

She stiffened and looked down at her drink. "Don't do that. Don't hang that *husband* crap on me. How many times have you told me not to call him your father? Well, I feel the same. Let's stay with J.R. or Roman or whatever."

"All right. Fair enough." I kept my voice as even as I could in the noisy bar. "I was online this afternoon. Roman's extradition is going to happen next week. The charges have been filed in Wisconsin. Our Witness Protection is history." I dipped a chip in the salsa. They were good and I was starving. Nadine hadn't touched them.

She took a long draw on her margarita and swallowed hard.

"Are you okay?" I asked. She stared straight ahead, silent. Uncertain how she was feeling, I turned toward her. "Maybe you didn't want to know. It's too much, too soon. You're still married—"

"It's not that."

I watched the side of her face, the complexion ever-changing along with the TV monitors, waiting. There were no tears. The bartender brought more chips and salsa. I shook him off. I took a sip of water. "Then what is it?" I tapped her on the forearm. "Go ahead. Who else you gonna tell?"

She flared her nostrils, her lips a straight, tight line. "We haven't been *married* since we moved to South Dakota, if you know what I mean."

I squirmed in my seat. I already knew too much about this. "Oh, you mean... *that.*"

"Yes, *that.* When the money dried up, so did he. And you know what? I don't even care. Why the hell should I? After what he's put me through. And now, this arrest. I'd divorce him in two seconds if I had the time." She shoved a chip in her mouth. "Screw that bastard."

"Okay, so don't shoot me."

"Don't step in front of a loaded gun." I thought she might snap the stem of her margarita glass with her fingers. "All these years I've been living with a murderer. We've been on the road for three days. Run down, shot at… fuck. I guess I'm a little stressed out." She finished the drink. "Bartender." She pushed the glass forward, then side-eyed me. "Why don't you have one? Loosen up a little. They won't card you. You've got stubble all over. You look older than I do."

"No way. I'm not flashing my I.D. for anyone unless I have to." Of course, I'd drank alcohol before. I grew up in Wisconsin, after all. But I wasn't a slave to it, and disliked that *loosen up* effect she was after. I preferred control over chaos, a clear head over beer brains. When I was with friends I trusted, sure, pass me the bottle. But I still didn't trust Nadine. I raised my glass. "But stress? Yeah, I hear you."

We tapped glasses. She asked, "Do you think there's a chance? Even a little one?"

"Chance of what?"

She spun the cocktail glass on the coaster. "That I'll… we'll ever be able to go back?"

I ate the last of the chips. "Back home?"

She raised her eyes to me. I think she was a little embarrassed by the question. I tried to answer as if we hadn't talked about this a dozen times before. She looked so forlorn, I couldn't blame her for hanging on to a thread of hope. "I know what you're saying and believe me, I'd like nothing better. But it's not going to happen."

The food arrived. We unwrapped silverware from thick-paper napkins and rearranged the food on our plates. I have a love-hate thing going with Mexican restaurants. I'll eat anything on the menu. But the way they filled the plates! Rice mingling with the beans, my sour cream oozing into the enchiladas. And I don't know what's going on with the cheese. I spent the next five minutes trying to separate everything from everything.

She asked, "What do you think? Does Roman in Wisconsin bother you?"

Suddenly my blood felt like tar. "Sooner the better," I said with false bravado. I had the sickening sense of the other shoe, waiting to fall. Whatever interrogations they did in Moreau, they'd be double that after his extradition. The Wisconsin prosecutors were sure to turn the screws. I knew my father's fear of prison. Anyone who'd snitch on the mob had an obvious aversion to doing time. He'd try to negotiate a deal. He could implicate others in the murder but not without making his own position worse. He was smart enough to know that, but fear could do crazy things, and not knowing what my father was going to do when the DA turned up the heat made me cold inside. And all the more certain I'd made the right decision to run.

Nadine attacked the chimichanga with a fork and knife. "Do you think we should change our names again? This shooter guy, he scares me."

I didn't hear what she'd said. She nudged me and repeated her worry. "Hey, I'm with you on that. But what can we do? We don't know who he is. Keep moving, that's our best option. You want my salad?" She shook her head and pointed to her own. I said, "And not just because of that guy. I signed the deed today, for the camper. If anyone one is tailing us, they can do a document search and find us. I don't know how long it takes for that kinda crap to show up online, but it'll tell the world we were in Iowa City." Waving my fork, I leaned into her, eyeing her food. "You don't want that guac."

"Hey!" She pushed me away, but only a little. "Then I'm taking one of your shrimp." She tapped her glass with her fork. "And another one of these."

She'd had enough already, but I knew that with a little alcohol flowing in her veins she could be very funny, and make for an entertaining Friday night. But there was a danger too. The story about the night Nadine and Roman met was a well-worn thread in the fabric of Walnut Creek. Following a night of drinking with her girlfriends, she'd tipped off her heels in front of a supper club—some said by accident, some said on purpose—right into the arms of the richest, unmarried man in town. I didn't want any part of that rerun. She was not the same woman. I was not my father. And after the year, the week, the day she'd had she deserved—we both deserved—a little distraction. I raised my hand for the bartender and ordered the drink.

As far as the gunman was concerned, with each passing hour I was getting more confident, more convinced we'd given him the slip. We'd had no sightings in Rochester, Minnesota or Iowa and if everything went according to plan, come tomorrow afternoon we'd leave Iowa City forever.

We paid the bill and left. On the way home, Nadine's feet were barely touching the ground. She glommed onto my left arm. I had all I could do to keep her on the sidewalk. I took the long way back to the motel to burn off some of the tequila.

"Good thing I have heels on," said Nadine. I didn't think so. She'd have been a lot steadier in flats. She looked up at me. "No, no, they make me taller. I know you only like tall girls."

I shook my head. "What are you talking about?"

"Look at your last girlfriend. She was up to here." She released a hand and raised it well above her head.

I chuckled. "Leah? Yes, tall. An Amazon." I was surprised Nadine would bring up her name. Could the legendary Nadine, she of red lips and fingernails, be jealous of a woman hundreds of miles away?

"Not just that. She's talented. And I like her."

I grasped her hand, the one on my arm. "Me too." She squeezed my arm, drawing my eyes down, showing off her signature look: white blouse, two buttons open. I said, "You're not short. You must be 5'5", that's only about an inch shorter than Diane."

"Five foot *six and a half.*"

A car came to a stop at the intersection ahead of us. I tensed and stopped.

She pulled up, too, and her heel spiked me in the toe. "What's the matter? Is it him? Did he find us?"

I grunted in pain. "No. It's a cop." Her heel had nailed my shoe to the concrete. "Lift your foot, quick! I'd like my foot back."

She looked down and lifted her pump, then bent a little at the waist and laughed. "Oh, sorry."

"Still can't believe you packed those." I looked at her. "Red high heels are on your absolutely necessary list?"

"Yes, they are. Men don't understand about shoes." She looked forward. "What about the cop? He's not moving." She covered her purse with her arm. "Maybe he knows you're a guitar player, and he thinks I'm an innocent groupie who needs protection."

"Then he obviously doesn't know you." I propped her up and shook my foot. "Next time we have dinner, I'll buy steel-toe boots. Keep walking. I don't think he's interested in us."

"Why would he? We didn't do nothing."

"I told you days ago. I took my father's watches, four of them. One stopped a bullet in the suitcase. Saved my life."

She straightened. "Why didn't you tell me?"

"I just did." The squad car turned toward us but passed by. "When they go through the house, they won't find them." She said the cops wouldn't even know they were ever there.

"Roman won't let 'em go." I said. "Maybe he'll tell his lawyer to get them. He'll know I took them and report it."

"Well, watches, watches, watches." She tugged on my arm. "Big fuckin' deal."

"These are. Five thousand a piece."

She whistled. "I've got to see these watch-es."

A block from the motel, I turned for home. We'd wrung out most of the stagger in her gait. I opened the motel-room door and she walked directly to the bathroom. I straightened the room and readied the backpacks for the morning. When she came out, she had showered and put on a night shirt.

"All yours." Her hair was only towel dry, the shorter, dark cut shimmering. With her fingers on her scalp, she tossed her locks and said, "I could get used to this. Less hair is so much easier. I'm not going to need the blow dryer. What do you think?"

"Looks fine. Yeah. Whatever." I walked to the bathroom. "Sleep well. We have to get up early tomorrow. No hangovers allowed."

Hands still in her hair, she walked by me. "Oh, don't worry. My stress is below zero. I'm going to sleep like a log. What about you?"

"Yeah," I said. "I'll be fine."

I went in the bathroom. Earlier in the day, I'd placed a bandage on the left-thigh wound. I removed the dressing and showered, carefully washing the ragged cut on my leg. I toweled off. A trickle of blood ran from the lower corner of the laceration. I stanched it with a tissue, applied antibiotic ointment to the wound, and replaced the non-stick bandage. I put on a pair of boxers, turned off the light and crawled under the covers.

"Max? I'm cold."

I paused a moment. The room still felt a little warm to me, so I really didn't want to turn off the air. Besides, sleeping came easier in a cool room. I would make the adjustment now, wait for her to fall asleep, then turn it back on. "Hang on." I walked to the under-window climate unit and opened the latch on the controls. "Your hair is still wet. That's why you're cold."

"Max?"

"Yeah?"

"You're still a musician, right? Even though you sold your guitar."

I looked back at her. "Of course. What you own doesn't make who you are." The only light was the glow from the parking lot slicing through the drapes. Covered with only a sheet, she was on her side, propped on an elbow. "And where's your blanket? No wonder you're cold."

"You're the first, you know," she said. "The first musician I ever *knew*. If you can call it that."

The way she said "knew" distracted me for a second. Then I saw her eyes, wet in the light. The smell of her shampoo still hung in the air, waves of brunette falling across her cheek.

Her finger traced something on the mattress. "I suppose you'll dump me, when we get to California and you get big and famous, I mean."

"I'm not dumping anyone. I don't own you." I adjusted the controls. "Anyway, we're not in California, not by a long shot."

"Close enough." The tip of her tongue glided between her lips. "How's that bullet burn doing?" The sheet fell away. Her fingertips skimmed across the sheet, touched my thigh.

"Still sore, a little." I shivered. She didn't look chilly, not at all. Her eyes, in fact, were crackling with some kind of fire I'd not seen before. "I thought you were cold?"

"Leave the thermostat alone."

Chapter Seventeen

Nate

Seconds later I was back on the phone with Lance. "They bought tickets eastbound under their previous names." I gave him the information, asked him to call Amtrak, find out their destination, and if they had arrived. "I'm going to check out of the hotel. Call you back in fifteen."

I folded the computer, left a big tip because of the mess, and bolted. A few minutes later, I was in my room throwing my gear together. My cell rang as I was checking out. It was Lance.

"Talk to me."

"They bought tickets to Milwaukee, but they didn't get there. Probably got off in La Crosse."

"La Crosse! Damn it." I waved goodbye to the clerk and walked out of the hotel. "There can't be any easy flights from Rapid City to La Crosse. What's the drive?"

"That's affirmative on the air carriers, boss. I checked. Thirteen hours minimum. Layovers up the butt. Checking drive time." A pause. I clicked open the trunk on my car. Lance was back. "About nine hours. Interstate 90, straight-shot. Now, if you were to lease a Cessna 172… It's about 650 miles and you'd have a tail wind. Cut your time in half."

"Don't think it hasn't crossed my mind. But there'd be no reimbursement, and I can't afford it." I shut the trunk and got in the car. "I'll run them down the old-fashioned way, get in about midnight if I leave right now. Get me a hotel room, so I can crash. In the meantime, find out if local law enforcement has run into them. See if Cherhasky has connections in or around La Crosse, friends, you know the drill. Call me."

Highway 73 took me to the interstate. I set the cruise control on eighty-five miles-per-hour. The compact rental I was driving shimmied at anything faster, and the engine buzzed so loud I could barely hear the radio. The towns got closer together as I drove toward Sioux Falls, but the miles longer. I passed into Minnesota; the trip was barely half done.

Worthington, Minnesota, was passing on my left when my phone came to life; a welcome interruption from Lance. I was ready for some news, be it good or bad, to occupy my brain for the next few hours.

"How are you doing, boss?" Lance asked.

"My butt is moaning like an old cow, and I'm bored to death, otherwise fine." I propped the phone on the dash holder and hit record. "What do you have?"

"I think we know who got the contract. His name is Antoni Kopec, Polish National. Last Passport I.D. Miami, five weeks ago. Fifty-five years old. We've seen him before. Suspect in the disappearance of a person in Joliet, Illinois, and one in Zurich, Switzerland. Also, a couple in Trieste, Italy. I'm sure there are others we don't know about."

"Jesus Christ on a bike, this guy gets around."

"Yeah. Got some more," Lance said. "Born and raised Krosno, Poland. Army, two years. Police after that; detective six years. Washed out of training for their counter-espionage organization, the name of which I couldn't pronounce even with a Polish sausage stuck up my ass. Married. One son, one daughter, two grandkids. Height 1.77 meters, Ninety kilos—"

"Lance!"

"Oh, sorry. Five foot nine inches, two hundred pounds. Pretty good with a gun, his preferred M.O. Strong hands and shoulders. Not a quick study, but relentless." Lance's keyboard clicked. "Made his reputation in eastern Europe. A one-way hallpass to hell."

"What about La Crosse?"

"Almost done. Call you back."

I ended the call and replayed the conversation. I didn't know Kopec but I knew the type. They were common enough. In one way or another, life had screwed him and to make it right, he would use his meaty grip to take anything within his reach. The Eastern Bloc training worried me. They usually selected men who were brutal and amoral, single-minded and determined. I was sure it was these characteristics the mob found so endearing, Kopec's family trappings notwithstanding. It was past seven p.m. when I stopped for gas and a bite to eat. I wondered what was taking so long on the second call. But at this hour of the day, Lance would be working alone. A pang of guilt shot through me. The hourly staff was not allowed overtime on a small-time case like this. Lance was salaried, so the department could abuse him in any way they pleased. I tried to avoid falling into that trap; a partner was not something to be taken for granted. My former partner, Caleb, had to retire early from the service. I had yet to forgive myself for that one.

Interstate 90 was as straight in Minnesota as it was in South Dakota. Twenty miles west of Albert Lea the phone rang again. "Sorry for the delay. I'm working as —"

"No worries, Lance. Give me what you got."

"Right. Checked up on both of our people. Friends, relatives, nothing both times. Hotels, car rentals in a ten-mile radius, no hits. But I got a positive on a police report."

"What? How bad?"

"Sounds like a near miss. Shots fired, six, maybe more, across the La Crosse River Valley, not far from the Amtrak Station. Police suspect the perp was shooting at someone on the bike path that runs along the river."

"You said 'near miss.'"

"Right. No blood. No hospital reports, etcetera. Here's the kicker. There's a Greyhound bus station downtown, two miles from Amtrak. A young couple bought tickets to Iowa City. The agent remembered them because they smelled so bad."

"Iowa City! What's my route?"

"What's your Twenty?"

"Approaching Albert Lea."

"Checking." A pause.

Max and Nadine were on a roll. They'd now gone in three different directions via three separate modes of transportation. The first two could have been planned, they had that feel. But this last one in La Crosse did not. The gun shots must have forced Max's hand. What Leah said came back to me. The story she told started with J. R. Cherhasky. I'd studied the man through two Federal felonies and still didn't understand him. He'd sent Max away to two different boarding schools in two years. Must have been tough. Not even in high school and already hardened to the world.

The car was running on fumes, and so was I. A truck stop glowed on the horizon. I stood next to the car, the pump ticking off the sale. Max had lost his mother years ago, but when he learned J.R. was involved—and after seeing the evidence, I had no doubt that he was—Max lost his moral rudder. Leah's insight was remarkable: instead of learning love and acceptance from J. R., he'd learned calculation and manipulation.

The pump handle clicked off. A few minutes later I was back on the interstate. A year earlier, while building a case against J.R. for interstate racketeering, our Wisconsin office did hours of research, including a psychological profile that detailed his penchant for stealth and misdirection, unconventional thinking and composure under pressure. His disregard for emotional barriers and personal relationships also stood out.

Max would deny it to the end, but the truth was clear: he'd learned from his father all too well; had grown up too fast. He was an only child in a well-to-do family and infused with a sense of entitlement. "Stop thinking of Max as an eighteen-year-old kid," Leah had said. He didn't see himself that way, didn't think that way, so neither should I. "Improvisation." I can still see the colored string in her hand, the same color in a streak across the front of her bib overalls. "It's what he does on the guitar. It's what he'll do on the road."

Lance was back. "Take I-35 South. The exit will be east of

Albert Lea. Drive time three and a half."

"Got it. And Lance?"

"I know. Same drill, Iowa City. Already on it. Get back to you."

"Thanks, man. I owe you."

I found the exit that took me into Iowa and spent the next hour replaying the interviews with George Farmer, Trevor Manning, and Leah Walters. The information on Antoni Kopec was ominous and didn't require an extra listen, it stuck with me like wet leaves on a driveway.

And then there was the La Crosse police report. There had been no fatalities. Even though I was two states away at the time, had one or both of my charges been killed or injured, it would have looked bad for me, left a black mark on the agency, and been disaster for Max and Nadine and their loved ones. We were all lucky, but the tone of this assignment had taken a drastic turn. What began as a simple witness pick up was now a search and rescue operation. And all too reminiscent of the Cordell kidnapping. Sweat formed on my upper lip and the palms of my hands.

Finally, Lance's number flashed on my screen.

"Boss, where are you?"

"In country flat as a pool table. What's up?"

"They got off the bus early this morning, like one a.m. at Greyhound. No further ticket purchases. There are a lot of hotels. Iowa City is a classic university town. But I think I found them. A fleabag called the River Bend Motel. Nate, we got 'em!"

I slapped the dashboard. "Good work. Get the police over there. Have them held until I arrive. I still have two hours plus."

"On it."

"And Lance."

"Sir?"

"Tell them these are unarmed civilians, non-violent fugitives. Use discretion."

Chapter Eighteen

Max

Did I worry about the moans, the thumping headboard, and the cheap motel-room walls? No. I was just trying to keep up. Nadine was frantic. Racing against some unseen foe, she seemed to release twelve months of sexual tension in a single detonation. A patch on my back burned from hash marks left by her fingernails. Sweat trickled off my brow. I was on my knees, one hand on her hip, the other entangled in her brunette hair. She grabbed the pillow in front of her with one hand, a fistful of bedsheet in the other. Making love like the strangers we were.

"Oh my god," She groaned, "There, there."

We were far off script, ready to fall off the page.

"Yes… yes…yesss!"

Exhausted, we collapsed. I laid on her back, our skins sharing a thin veneer of sweat. We panted out of sync. With every gulping breath I seemed to bury her petite, prone form deeper into the flimsy mattress. I slid off, stood, and walked stiff-legged to the bath.

I emerged from the bathroom in boxers and a t-shirt, fatigue close behind. Nadine was standing by the air conditioner, her hand pulling aside the drape. Dressed in boxer panties and a long t-shirt, street lights silhouetted her usually inspiring figure, but I was beyond that. She had worn me out. Then I noticed them, bruises on her left leg. I asked about them.

She turned a bit toward me, but not enough to meet my eyes, and told me it was because J.R. was right handed. I was sick for a second, repulsed, but then felt compelled to get a closer look. I saw the edge of another discoloration on her left shoulder. I raised the short-sleeve of her shirt and asked, "This one too?"

She nodded and looked through the crease in the curtains. A single tear traced down her cheek.

I let go her sleeve, my eyes burning. "So, he was beating you too."

"I never saw him hit you. I mean…" She looked me up and down. "You don't have any marks."

"Not me," I said. "Mom. I was too young to understand then, but I do now. The bastard." For a moment, I couldn't say anything more. A thousand images raced through my mind, scenes from a life I thought I'd long left behind. The light from outside changed to a pulsating red and blue.

"What are you looking at?" I asked.

Nadine said, "Cops, a car just came, the other side of the front desk."

"Is that their lights?" I rushed forward and nudged her aside. "Holy shit. There's another one coming. Put on your shoes. Grab your bag. Now! We gotta run."

She opened her backpack, searching. I snatched it away from her and said, "What are you doing?"

"Looking for pants."

"No time. Put on your shoes."

"Panties and a shirt. Are you kidding me right now?" she asked. "I can't run around like this."

"Suit yourself. The cops'll give you something to wear." My shoes were on. I opened the door a crack, and watched. "Ready?" I shoved the bag into her chest. "We go, but no quick moves. Follow me." A light rain was falling. I shut the door quietly.

After a quick right turn around the end of the motel, we jogged to a parking area away from the road. We stopped to don the backpacks. We were still close enough to hear the knock on our motel-room door and officers making the usual demands to open up. Soon after, the door clicked and, "They're gone. Search the area."

I tugged on her hand. An alley down the middle of the block led us to the next street. Two blocks away, more flashing red and blue coming our way. A large, open parking lot loomed to the right, so we went left. Running close to buildings made us harder to spot and kept us out of the weather. Heading north toward the Greyhound Depot, we made good time with the backpacks, but I knew carrying the weight rather than pulling it would soon wear us out. We stopped to catch a breath on the far side of the Army Recruiting Company. A cruiser with a spotlight showed up a block away, scanning the large parking lots surrounding the County Courthouse. We had to move.

Skirting the bus station, we ran into a major thoroughfare, busy with traffic. Rain made visibility tough and our bones stiff. Jaywalking across the four-lane road was a risky negotiation with the drivers. Two blew their horns, one skidded to a stop. We stepped on the far curb. The squawk of a squad half-a-block away stopped us.

"Shit! He saw us," I said. "This way!"

We sprinted three-hundred feet down an alleyway and ran into a large, triangular courtyard. An empty police car was parked at one exit. The squad car from the street turned toward us and blocked the alley. Two officers exited the car; one appeared to be using the radio.

"We gotta hide, fast," I said. The buildings surrounding the triangle were Italian architecture, marble and granite, curving surfaces everywhere but too well-kept. In front of us was a building that appeared to be historic, with a classic, ornate facade. I noticed we were no longer getting wet. I looked up at the heavy-canvas awning that was keeping us dry. "That's it." I stepped to the end of the window. The long, iron crank spun in my hand. The awning rose and folded.

"For chrissakes, Max, what are you doing?" Nadine asked.

"Climb up that planter, then on the end of the frame. When I tell you, throw your backpack into the canvas then follow it in."

"Are you crazy?"

"Lay in the crease. Do it!"

She shivered. Her hair and shirt were wet. But in three quick steps she clambered up the concrete planter to the windowsill and then to the crotch of the awning support.

The canvas was nearly collapsed. "Toss your pack." I kept cranking. "Now you. In." She scrambled forward and slithered between the iron stays.

I went to the next crank and spun it until it was almost shut. Running footsteps were too close. I climbed the side of the frame, slid in, and didn't move. I didn't even breathe. The clattering shoes stopped right below me.

"Where'd they go?" asked an older, gravelly voice, obviously winded.

"Don't see them." A woman, younger. "Whose squad is that?"

"Go find out. I'll call it in and check the doorways."

The footsteps faded. I took a breath and willed Nadine to stay quiet. From a distance, I heard the woman's voice: "That's Boone. He's patrolling East College tonight. Hasn't seen them. Said even with the rain, the mall is busy. Students in spring, you know."

The gravelly voice said, "We had two exits covered. Only way out is west toward Starbucks, but we've always got someone on South Clinton this time of night. Who's covering?"

"I'll check."

"Let's go. I need a cup of coffee anyway. You bring the squad. I'll get a table. We can watch Clinton from there."

"What about the perps?" the woman asked.

"Just a couple runaways. I'm not busting a gut on those two."

The steps faded and so did the rain. After waiting ten minutes, I thought I could hazard a look. The triangle was empty. I slipped free of the metal framework but discovered escaping the awning was more difficult than getting in. I dropped my pack to the ground, pulled myself out feet first, and dropped to the sidewalk.

"Nadine, hold on, I'll open the awning."

"Not too much," she whispered. "I'll drop like a rock."

But opening it even a quarter of the way was hard work. "You're too heavy."

"Thanks," she hissed. "You didn't think so an hour ago."

I stifled a grin. "You have to crawl out. Toss me your backpack."

She dropped it to me and I set it aside. When I looked up, she was halfway out going the wrong way, one leg in, one leg out, as if straddling a horse. "No, no. Toward the —"

The canvas was slippery. She lost her grip, fell sideways, and hit me with a thud. We crashed onto the sidewalk, Nadine sideways across my chest. She told me later that when she dragged herself off me, I didn't move. She kneeled next to me, put her hands on my shoulders, and shook.

"Max! Max, are you all right?" Another shake. "Wake up!"

My eyes popped open, staring blankly at first, then focusing on her. I felt her hand around the back of my head. "Ouch! What are you doing?"

She leaned over me, the rainwater dripping from her hair onto my face, and wiped the moisture from my cheek. "Shut up. Checking for blood."

I exhaled and blinked. "My head." I put a hand on my scalp. Then suddenly, "The cops, where are they?" I stood too quickly and wobbled.

She grabbed my arm. "We gave them the shake."

I dropped my head, reached for the building, and held on. "They'll be back." The cruiser was still parked near the north entrance of the triangle, and there were too many people watching around the Starbucks. "Double back, this way."

The squad that had chased us was gone from the street, but we did not go south. A left turn took us past a hotel and within half a block of a pedestrian mall. "People. Lots of people walking around," I murmured. "Perfect cover."

We walked toward the busiest part of the city on the busiest day of the week. The rain had stopped, but our skimpy, soaked clothing was drawing too much attention, particularly Nadine. One guy locked eyes on Nadine's breasts and rubbernecked himself into a light standard. I said, "You're a walking poster for a wet t-shirt contest." I stopped and pulled a long-sleeve, button shirt out of my bag. "Here, put this on before you put someone in the hospital."

She shrugged off her backpack. "I'm freezing half to death, walking around like a hooker, and just now you offer me a shirt?" She snatched it from me.

"Up till now, I was busy keeping our asses out"—I stuffed the rest of my clothes into the backpack and zipped it up—"of the County jail."

"Why? Were we doing something 'illegal in Iowa?'" With a smirk, she slipped on the shirt. "What now? Sleep in a doorway? Get another room?"

"No way. Cops. On us like white on rice. But you're right, we can't stay out in the cold and rain until we meet Stan tomorrow."

"That's it." She rapped me on the arm. "Stan, call him."

"Yeah. We'll take a taxi and crash at his place."

Chapter Nineteen

Max

We found a taxi right away. I opened the door and followed Nadine into the back seat which, after getting soaked by a cool, spring rain, felt like a capsule of radiant, life-giving warmth. We rode in darkness over the river. The driver had more than the usual amount of curiosity. His frequent glances in the rearview made me nervous. I took care not to make eye contact. I'd have told her to do the same, but she'd have made a scene which would have made us memorable. At some point the cops would wonder how we got away, and the first people they'd call would be the cab companies.

The yard light was on over the Dettmann garage. Everything else was in darkness, including the windows on both floors, but with nowhere else to go, we got out of the cab. The driver took cash for the fare and moved away at a suspiciously slow crawl. I dialed up Stan's phone, but it went right to voicemail. We trudged up the rain-slick steps and set down our backpacks. No doorbell, so I knocked. No one stirred. There was a small window in the door, but I could see nothing through it. Nadine knocked harder and longer than I had, but to no good.

"I'll try the phone again." I knew I had the right number because I could hear the phone ringing inside. I knocked once more.

"Who the hell's making all that noise up there?"

Nadine and I went to the railing and looked down on a buxom, older woman, a little overweight, wearing a pink bathrobe and slippers. A couple of cats wandered about the hem of her house-coat. "Come down from there so's I can see you."

She didn't appear to be a woman to be trifled with. As we shinnied down the steps, I said, "We're friends of Stan."

"Not at this hour, you're not." Backpacks held like a shield in front of us, we stood before the woman. The lights in the lower flat glowed and the front door was open. "Friend or foe, he ain't going to hears you now. He takes his hearing aids out when he goes to bed. Deaf as a stump." She leaned sideways and eyed our clothing. "You always dress likes that in this weather?"

"No ma'am," I said. "Truth is, we bought the camper from Stan—"

"Oh! So, you're the ones." The woman's face suddenly caught light from a window. Her hair was pulled back from a broad face with inquisitive eyes. "Why didn't you say so. You're taking my brother to meet his long, lost love. My name is Kitty. Come on in." She and the cats led the way. "Still don't explain why yous lookin' like drowned rats. Let's get you dried off anywho. Then we'll figures out the rest."

The backpacks were waterproof, so we had dry clothes to put on. Kitty gave us cups of hot chocolate. She added a donut and said, "better you eat them than me," because she had "the diabetes" and had to watch her sugar, a problem she shared with her brother. She found towels to dry our hair and threw our wet things in the dryer, which was in a small room right off the kitchen. "But I worry about my Stan. He's worse off than me. All I gots to watch are the sweets. Stan, he gots one rule to his diet—'if it tastes good, spit it out.'" That drew a smile from both of us. Kitty went on. "No salty stuff, no fats! What's the point of livin' if yous can't eat cheese? I gotta have that, and so do my girls."

I looked around for a picture. "You have kids, then?" I asked.

Kitty shook her head. She hadn't bothered to sit at the table, but shuffled about the kitchen, cleaning this and wiping that. In spite of her age and weight, she was surprisingly light on her feet, dancing around the cats like they were part of a well-rehearsed waltz. Her hair was thinning and turning white, but I got the impression those changes didn't bother her at all. Her skin was pale with only a rare blemish, as if she hadn't seen a lot of sun. The aforementioned cheese made an appearance, a yellow block that must have weighed a pound. She cut several cubes and dropped them to the floor for the cats. "Daughters? No." She pointed with the knife. "These are my kids—Eggplant, Shameless, and Smudge."

"Sorry about waking you up," Nadine said. She reached down and stroked Smudge.

"Ah, I wasn't sleeping. I heard yous walking up the steps."

"Weren't you worried?" Nadine asked. "I mean, we could've been bad guys, burglars, or worse."

"But yous ain't," Kitty replied confidently. "Guess my mind just don't works that way. You can't be a single woman livin' like a fraidy cat." She looked down at her pets. "No offense, girls."

Then she wondered out loud why we'd be out at this hour, with our belongings, looking for a place to stay. "Stan said you had a room in town."

I looked sheepishly at Nadine, then back at Kitty. "Yes ma'am, we did."

"Well, what's happened?"

I glanced at Nadine for a little help. She raised her eyebrows and took a drink. I put down my cup and lowered my eyes. "It's like this, Kitty. We got kicked out."

Kitty shrugged and asked if we'd paid our bill.

"Yes. It wasn't that," I said.

"Well, whats then? You don't have a pet."

I couldn't very well tell her the truth. "We were making too much noise."

Nadine side-eyed me. Kitty looked at our satchels. "I don't see none of those boom boxes neither."

"No, see," I said. "It was us." I nodded at Nadine, who was now wide-eyed. "We made the noise. If you get my meaning."

Stunned for a moment, Kitty recovered. "Oh well, you're young. To be expected, and one complaint—"

"Well, it was both our neighbors. But you know those motels, the walls are like paper."

Nadine clucked her tongue, clearly not enjoying the ruse.

"All right, so you gets a warning and you settle down." Kitty waved a hand. "For God's sake, you don't boot out paying customers after the first—"

"Third," I interrupted.

Nadine slapped the table.

There was a silence, then I said, "This is really good hot chocolate. I'm going to sleep like a log."

Nadine was staring chainsaws at me that said, "And you're going to do it alone."

"I should think so," Kitty said. "But not because of whats you're drinking."

Chapter Twenty

Nate

I arrived in Iowa City well after midnight, punch-drunk on coffee and Hershey bars, trying to work up a lather before I confronted the local police captain. They'd botched the pick-up of Max and Nadine Cherhasky and it had complicated my life in ways I didn't even know. They were going to hear about it.

The long drive had gotten to me, and I hadn't slept well the night before. It wasn't the bed or bad food. I hadn't been bedfellows with a good-night's sleep since before I met Troy and Adriana Cordell. On a cold, damp November day they'd knocked on my office door, told me of the abduction of their daughter, Charlotte, and changed my life forever. After weeks of work, we broke the case just before Christmas. But during a gunfight, my partner was badly injured. It was my fault. Right after that, on the first of January, just over five months ago, I was transferred to clerical support. "Agency policy, Nate. You know the routine." That's what my boss had said. And just like that, the hand that used to wield a Sig Sauer .40 caliber now held nothing deadlier than a staple gun. I couldn't go back to that again. I looked down at the pistol lying on the seat, and dried my palms on my pant leg.

I slowed the car as I drove through town. The streets were wet and visibility poor. I had a hard time picking up the downtown vibe, if there was one. Perhaps it was too early in the morning, or the long day had made me numb from the neck up—probably both. Captain Blain Baker was waiting for me as I entered police headquarters. Our greeting was professional from both sides.

He offered me a seat, which I declined, citing my long drive and overworked backside.

I dropped my satchel on the seat. He sat down and reviewed the report as given by his patrol officers. I shook my head and asked to interview them, but both were off duty and not available until the morning. I leaned against the wall and pinched the bridge of my nose. "They were on foot, soaking wet, with a team of cops on their tail, and still they managed to escape. How'd they manage that?"

"We had two squads on point, with extra units on-call should the chase enter a patrol area."

"Rather light, Captain, for two fugitives."

"Two non-violent fugitives, Mr. Bauer, on non-felony warrants. Both AWOL from the WPP if I'm not mistaken. Hardly cause to breakdown my entire force on a busy weekend night."

"I don't think you understand the gravity of their situation." I walked in front of him, hands clasped behind my back. "These two are being hunted down by a professional hit man. He took six shots at them in La Crosse. If we're not careful, he'll take them out right here in river city. Do you want that kind of action on your watch?"

Baker paused, his expression suddenly strained. "None of those particulars were in the information, Mr. Bauer."

"Call me Nate, please."

He leaned back. "I'll get the patrolmen in ASAP tomorrow. Seven a.m. all right?" I asked him to make it 8:15 a.m. and sat down. He nodded and continued. "You can walk the route with them if you want. Canvas people in the area, but it's likely most of your eyewitnesses are long gone. On the other hand, evidence might be easier to see in the light of day; whatever you want. What have you got on your shooter?"

I reached into my satchel and pulled out a two-page rap sheet on Antoni Kopek and handed it to him. "I have a digital file I can send as well." He gave me the department's email.

I put my elbows on my knees. "Thanks. What I really need is some sleep. Can you direct—"

"Ask at the front desk. They'll help you out. The file on your bad guy will be on the street pronto. We already have pics on your runaways."

I got the name of a nearby hotel, checked in, and crashed.

Patrolman Fred Wexford had coarse features emphasized by the morning sun and a full head of dark hair. Like too many veterans of the force, he was thick through the middle, and I doubted he'd be able to run down Max Cherhasky even with Nadine strapped to his back. His partner, Nancy Hickman, was younger and looked up for a chase. Not as fit as my wife, but with a little more time at the gym, she could have been. Between the two, she would have been the one to get a better look at the two runners and where they might have gone. I thanked them for meeting me at 8:15 a.m. rather than seven. An hour earlier I had been in an AA meeting, but I didn't tell them that. We started at the River Bend Motel, where I interviewed the manager. He knew next to nothing about his renters except their linen needs and the color of their cash. They had arrived very early Friday morning and paid for two nights. He never saw a car. The man who checked them in wasn't immediately available and lived twenty miles away.

After that, Wexford, Hickman, and I followed the course of the chase as best they knew it. Wexford filled in details and mentioned twice how Max and Nadine had avoided open areas and other patrol officers. Their closest encounter was the result of luck. Wexford and Hickman caught them jaywalking through heavy traffic and chased them to a relatively small business court near downtown. We walked the alley in which Max and Nadine were last seen before they disappeared into the triangular pedestrian area.

"I thought we had them." Wexford pointed to the north point of the plaza. "There was a cruiser parked there. Ronnie Boone was standing watch. I doubt they'd even try going his direction. If anything, they'd have gone left, toward Starbucks, but on Friday nights we have a heavy presence on Clinton Street. By then the alert was out; I think they'd have been spotted."

We walked slowly along an old building that had been restored. "Could they have hidden somewhere on the triangle?"

"That's what I thought," Hickman said. "But all the doors were secure. No sewer grates. No sign of forced entry. It's like they vanished."

We walked to the north apex, stopped, and looked back. A few pedestrians crossed in front of us. The sun was just high enough to peek into view. The façade of the old building on the east side was in shadow, so the difference between the two awnings on the far end of the building was hard to pick out. But I was looking for any little thing. Two of the awnings were only half open. When I pointed this out, the officers were as perplexed as I was.

Hickman cranked the handle on the middle awning, it opened without incident. Moving down to the end one, she noticed a slight bend in the cross support, as if it had born a weight in the middle. Wexford and I stood back. The awning extended fully open and a blue and white piece of cloth dropped to the sidewalk. Hickman picked it up. "Looks like a woman's sock."

"I'll be a sonofabitch." Wexford scuffed his heal on the sidewalk. "We were standing right here, talking. They were rolled up in the awning, three feet away, listening to every word."

"Okay, fine, but after we left, they were still up shit creek in a bucket of suck." Hickman pushed a strand of hair behind her ear. "Nowhere to go. Terrible weather. On the run. What were their options? We had an alert out to all the hotels."

I nodded. "Max wouldn't make the same mistake twice. He had something else. He had planned to go to school here in the fall, but never enrolled. My office found no friends or connections. He didn't go back on the bus."

"Taxi?" Hickman suggested.

CHAPTER TWENTY-ONE

Max

Morning sunlight poured in from the living room window and warmed my face. The clock said six-thirty a.m. Somewhere in the house something was rumbling. It took me a minute to figure out it was Kitty snoring loudly in her bedroom. After dressing and washing my face, I woke Nadine and took a look out the window. No sign of Stan, but there were sounds of movement upstairs. Yesterday, we'd agreed to meet at seven a.m. At 6:45 I thought it safe to venture up the steps and knock. Stan was making last-minute preparations: turning down the heat, turning off the water, turning over glasses on the shelf. He had packed light, a suitcase, and a handbag. Clean linen and towels were already in the camper, along with his tool box.

I told him about our night with Kitty and the hospitality she'd shown us. "I was ready to sleep underneath the camper. Kitty really saved our ass." She wasn't up yet, and Nadine and I wanted to thank her before we left.

"She's late to bed, late to rise," Stan said. "And don't wake her early, not if you value your life. We'll call her later."

After a quick breakfast, we loaded the camper. The engine started after a few cranks and ran rough when it was cold. I took a quick look at the controls and then backed out. We made our way to southbound Highway 1. My plan was to stay on small, state and county highways, reasoning that once law enforcement found out we weren't on the train anymore, they'd assume we'd be traveling by car or hitchhiking. The interstate system was the first place they'd look. And I liked single-digit numbers, easier to remember, so I took 1 south to 2, west to 5, south to 6, which would take us to St. Joseph, Missouri, and the first major stop of the day, five hours out.

Nadine rode shotgun to start, with Stan in one of the second-row captain chairs. He leaned forward and said, "She rides pretty good for an old gal, don't she?"

It had been only eight hours since Nadine and I had messed the sheets on her bed, so when he talked about a good ride, my mind went sideways. "Rides well for an old girl?" I turned toward her, raised my eyebrows, and said, "Oh, you mean the camper."

"Shut up." Nadine slapped me on the arm. "You're already on thin ice after that story you told Kitty last night."

"Story? What story?" Stan shook his head. "Of course, I mean the camper. What are you talking about?"

"He doesn't know *what* he's talking about," she said.

I turned away so they wouldn't see my smile. We were just like those Midwesterners from the depression, disillusioned and disheartened, heading down Route 66 to the West Coast. For the first time, I felt the allure of the road. *Ahab never felt it. Maybe Jonah did after his three days of hell.*

I looked at Stan in the rearview mirror. "What kind of mileage do you think we'll get?"

"Fifteen to twenty miles to the gallon depending. That was as good as it got back when it was new. 'Course, it's got no guts, so don't try passing no one except maybe Granny Goodpants on her way to church."

"The seats are awesome," Nadine said. "Way better than my car."

"That's my wife. She took care of the interior." Stan leaned back. "We better look for a bathroom."

"Already?" I pointed toward the back of the camper. "We got one back there."

"You don't want that, and neither do I," Stan said. "It works fine when we're hooked up at a campground. But right now, on a warm day?" He wrinkled his nose. "And hey, I just took a water pill."

We took two bathroom breaks within the first ninety minutes.

But only one more for the rest of the morning. About an hour outside of St. Joseph, Stan fell asleep in his seat.

Nadine had sunglasses on even though the day was cloudy. She asked, "Why are you carrying all the money?"

I turned down the radio. "Where did that come from?"

"Well, it's my money, and I haven't seen it for days."

"I got it stashed in the backpack. What, now you don't trust me?"

"It's not that." She bent forward. "But how would you feel? Besides, safer to split it up, just in case."

"Now I'm not reliable or trustworthy. Great!"

"Max! Knock it off."

"What?"

"You're twisting everything I say. Self-centered ass."

"Bring it down a little." I tossed my head. "You'll wake him up."

"You bring it down." She flipped me the bird.

"We're doing great, the cash I mean." I squeezed the wheel with both hands. "If it means that much to you, next time we stop, I'll show you. You have no worries. And I know it's your money." I glanced at her. Arms crossed, she was still annoyed and unconvinced. "Nadine, come on. Why don't you call Kitty and tell her thanks?"

She changed the radio station instead, her attempt at rebellion. "No CD player. Why didn't I notice that before?" A minute later, she took her phone off the dash and dialed. Kitty answered and Nadine's face transformed in a second from overcast with a chance of rain to mostly sunny. Although I doubted she knew we were just outside of St. Joseph, Missouri, I reminded her not to give our location to Kitty. Then Nadine shook Stan awake and asked if he wanted to talk to his sister. He did, but only for a minute. It was time to eat.

He stretched to look out the windshield. "Look for a Denny's. I like their pies."

"Pie!" Nadine turned in her seat. "What about your diabetes?"

"What? Who told you that?" Both of us were silent. "Kitty! Damnit." Stan looked out a side window. "I'm watchin' my salt and fat. Ain't that enough? A man's gotta live."

An online restaurant search led us to a strip of places on the south side of town. Nadine spotted a Blue Lion convenience store and insisted we stop so we could stock up on snacks and drinks. While she did her thing in the store, I topped off the fuel tank.

Coming up short of a Denny's, we picked a locally owned diner because Stan liked his chances there for homemade desserts. The service was slow, but I didn't mind. After the long-haul driving, it was a much-needed break.

We got back in the camper. I propped my cell on the dash and opened a navigation app. A woman's voice chirped and told me to "turn in four hundred feet onto Highway 59."

The towns along the way, small as they were, often straddled the highway, which made for a perfect speed trap. I'd seen the scam before. Moreau made lots of money ticketing motorists passing through above the limit. The last thing I needed was the State Police checking my plates or worse, my license. I couldn't relax, even for a second. I wanted to spend some time planning the next few days, but I couldn't do that and check the mirrors and watch the highway. The idea of sharing the driving never entered my mind. I'd seen Nadine behind the wheel. How she hadn't yet totaled a vehicle was beyond good luck. Stan had driven the LeSharo thousands of miles without a glitch. But the last time was several years ago, and he didn't look up to the task anymore.

"Listen, you two," I said. "You gotta help watch for cops. I'm on cruise control, but if I miss a traffic sign and get pulled over, we're screwed." The license plates were another problem. Next chance I had, I'd switch them out.

My passengers had the attention span of a three-year-old. Nadine got bored and Stan started to nod off again. She went back to her phone, her fingertip sweeping through Instagram posts faster than she could read them. I peeked around the edge of her dark hair and got a glimpse of her profile, her slightly upturned nose and red lips. She got by on her looks, a more reliable asset than the money stashed in my backpack. I looked ahead. Remembering the night before, I realized her sexual advances weren't out of character. Back in the day, she'd made quick work of my father by investing the same kind of capital. She'd become one of his prize possessions, a role she was born for. Was I falling for the same act? The possibility didn't seem outlandish, not at all. Could she see I was missing Leah and turning that into leverage?

Nadine squared up in the seat and threw the phone on the dash. "Stan, do you have a deck of cards?"

Suddenly, Stan's eyes were open. He hadn't played cards since his wife died and never dreamed Nadine would be interested. He slowly rose from his chair and pulled two decks of cards and a Cribbage board from a storage drawer. He was partial to Cribbage but would play anything from Pinochle to Poker. They sat at the dining table in the back, slapping cards, and calling out the score, their competitive juices flowing. I was missing out on the only fun this trip had produced. But I didn't pull over. The West Coast trumped any silly card game they could think up.

"I'm thirsty," Nadine said. "Chauffeur, send back a couple cervazas."

CHAPTER TWENTY-TWO

Nate

There were two taxi service companies in town. Nancy Hickman gave me their names and numbers but said she and Wexford weren't on a regular shift, so I'd be on my own from here. I thanked them for their help and drove to the first name on the list, a storefront on the east side of town. I wasn't sure what to make of it. Most of the cab companies I'd ever seen were run out of garages. A bell chimed as I walked in. The office was small, a counter, no chairs, and a door leading to a back room. A heavy woman dressed in a blue t-shirt, slacks, and a sleeveless vest came through the door. I introduced myself, gave her Max and Nadine's description, and estimated time of pick-up. The woman scoffed at my information and said that in Iowa, a couple answering that description was as common as corn. Nothing rang a bell, and a review of the company log seemed to bear it out.

It was late morning by the time I got to the second business, run out of an auto repair shop only a few blocks away from the first. The office was locked, but the garage door was up. I followed the sound of a compression wrench to the back of the service bay. A thin, dark-haired boy, barely out of mother's arms, greasy baseball hat on sideways, was working on a taxi on a lift. The work area was a mess, tools strewn about, a radiator lying here, a tire and fan belt over there. Nothing was clean, including the windows.

I approached the boy, identification in hand, and said hi. He wiped his nose on the shoulder of his shirt. "What do you want?"

"I have some questions about a ride from last night. I'll need to talk to the dispatcher."

He snickered. "Dad," he yelled, and went back to work.

A voice from another room bellowed, "What is it now?"

"Guy here to see you."

A man appeared from what looked like a parts room, but it was hard to tell. He looked tired and fed up with something, his son, the business, what he ate for breakfast? I couldn't tell. His blue jean shirt was clean, but the khaki slacks were worn and tattered. "What do you need?"

I again recited my name and purpose for interrupting his Friday morning. "I need to look at your logs—"

"Log." He leaned on a tool chest. "We only got one."

"Okay, your log for all your drivers—"

"One log, one driver," he said.

"Fine. If I can talk to him that would be—"

"You already are."

I exhaled, a little exasperated by his truculent tone. "You're the only driver for this taxi company?"

"Was last night. When you're the owner, you take the shifts nobody else wants."

"I see. I'm looking for a couple. Male, eighteen years old, six-two about one-eighty, dark, long hair. And a woman, five six, red hair, green eyes—"

"She's not a redhead."

"What's that?"

"Got green eyes all right. They look right through you. But if I'm thinking of your couple, she's not a redhead. And the guy shaves his head, three-day beard.

"Then how do you know these are my people?"

He wiped his hands with a rag. "They didn't fit in. Both drenched from the rain, shivering like fish in a net. And back packs, big ones, like for hiking. Paid in cash. Dropped off at a place with nothing but a yard light. That sound normal to you? Don't sound normal to me."

"I'll need that address."

I punched the information into my GPS and sped away from the shop. The place was across the river, not far from the university. I parked in a rather long driveway that went straight to the back of the lot and a detached garage. The house was past its prime, but well kept. It was well into the noon hour when I walked onto the front porch and knocked. The woman that opened the door had the look of a day barely begun. The house coat and unkempt hair implied she had not been out of bed for long. All the shades were pulled. She appeared to be the only occupant, save a swarm of cats circling her slipper-clad feet.

"Good afternoon," I said.

"Afternoon?" She turned and looked at a wall clock. "My god, is that the time? Who are you?"

"Nathaniel Bauer, field agent, FBI. My credentials." I told her about my interest in Max and Nadine Cherhasky, their flight from the motel, and my conversation with the taxi driver. She was not impressed with any of it, I could tell by the shape of her mouth and cobbled forehead.

"Have you seen anyone answering to that description?"

"Don't knows that I have, but my brother lives in the upper flat. Maybe he's seen 'em."

I nodded. "Did you hear any commotion, anything unusual last twelve hours?"

"No, but I have sleep apnea. I puts on my machine and I don't hears nothing."

"Thanks. I'll go check with your brother."

She shrugged away a cat with her foot. "Go ahead, but he's probably gone."

"I'll wait."

"If you gots that kind of time."

"When will he get back?"

"Didn't ask."

"Where'd he go?"

"None of *my* business," she said, implying that neither was it any of mine.

I looked across the lawn. "That patch of long grass over there, by the driveway. Looks like something was parked there."

"You think so, Mr. Bear?" She squinted her eyes nearly shut. "I might've missed it last time I cut grass."

We both knew that wasn't true. "It's Bauer, ma'am."

"Stan's camper was there."

"Stan's your brother?" Her face was blank. I asked, "Can I assume Stan left in his camper?"

"You can do many things on such a nice day, Mr. Bar. But as for me, I have breakfast waiting."

She was about to dismiss me, I could always tell. I put my hand on the door. "I'm worried he's in trouble, and the people he's with."

She tossed me a doubting look. "I know Stan a long time, and one thing for sure—his life is 'bout as exciting as overboiled spaghetti. Good day."

I walked to the car and called my office for information on Stan Dettmann and a camper registered in his name, Iowa City.

"Glad I have you on the phone, boss," Lance said. "Just got a call, a hit on a Blue Lion Discount Card. It's a convenience store chain, this one's in St. Joseph, Missouri. The card is held by Nadine Farmer."

I rubbed my neck. "St. Joseph!" It sounded too far away. "Do I want to know what time they used it?"

"Little over an hour ago," Lance said.

"Don't say it, let me guess. No easy flights. Right?"

"Checked every airline. It's almost like you can't get there from Iowa City. Sorry, Nate."

Chapter Twenty-Three

Max

In the afternoon, it wasn't the water tablets filling Stan's bladder, but his diabetes. Turns out, a high blood sugar will make as much urine as the best pee pills. During our second stop, Nadine told him he needed another wife to "straighten him out." He went to find a bathroom. I punched PAY INSIDE on the pump and lifted the latch. She followed. I tossed my head toward Stan and said, "He looks older than his age."

Hands on her hips, she said he looked fine to her. "What are we doing tonight?"

I played it dumb and said we'd find an RV campground easily enough.

She leaned casually on the pump. "That's not what I mean, and you know it."

I kept working the diesel nozzle as if I hadn't heard. Her new look had me confused, as if I wasn't sure who I was talking to. Was she playing me? Was there some kind of complex darkness behind it? I didn't think so. She didn't have the right stuff, didn't possess the personal corruption necessary to use sex as a weapon.

The diesel pump was slow. Nadine gave up on the conversation and went inside. I couldn't see into the store very well, but I saw no sign of Stan.

The wrong stuff: that was my father. I remembered how J.R. had manipulated Tapper Manticore and so many others like him, not with sex, of course, but with personal charisma. J.R. had shaken off the yoke of my grandfather, forged a path with rules all his own, and turned himself into a whale, the kind they love in Vegas. And he wasn't above bragging about it, even to me. Before the FBI bust at the Red Wolf estate, our father-son talks weren't about sports or music or who my friends were, it was about J.R. and his filling stations, J.R. the Captain of Industry, J.R. and his genius for making others do what he wanted them to do.

Stan and Nadine were back. The tank was full. I went inside, paid for the gas with cash, and we were back on the road. Then it was miles and miles of sprouting Kansas wheat. Once more, I lost Stan and Nadine to the card table.

The sign for Highway 99 south to Sedan, Kansas, reminded me to have Nadine search for campgrounds near the Oklahoma border. I called her away from the card table.

"I can Google that from here," she said.

I replied, "Come up here so we don't have to yell at each other."

Swearing under her breath, she dropped her ass into the front seat. "Okay. Happy?"

I shook my head. Whatever we'd gone through in the last days, her attitude was the same. The major changes I saw in her were the ones I'd insisted on. And I had to grab the clippers and run the dye through her hair, or that wouldn't have happened either.

After fifteen minutes of trial and error she found the Caney Creek Campground and RV Park. Stan came forward and nodded off again. Once we got off the train in La Crosse, there'd been no plan, just an idea of what might come next. Even with Stan's hearing aids in place, this was a chance to talk with her alone. Speaking softly, I asked if she'd been thinking about our friend with the rifle. Had she any luck placing the face? I thought we'd given him the slip in La Crosse, but anyone willing to chase us across two or more states for a chance at a kill scared the shit out of me.

"I don't want to think about him," she replied. "He gives me the creeps. Besides, why should I? Like you said, we fooled him. He'll never find us now."

"Let's change the subject."

"Agree," she said sharply, then looked out the window, squinting into the evening sun. "I miss swimming."

"Swimming? I haven't seen a lake in hours."

"They don't have any in Moreau, either. And I'm not swimming in a river." Her nose twitched as if she'd smelled a dead fish. "If we still lived on Red Wolf, we'd have the pier in by now. Go for a swim, paddleboard a little, then lay on the dock and let the sun dry my skin."

"I hear you."

"What do you miss?" she asked. "From Walnut Creek, I mean."

"Friends, the boat, the lake—all of that. But that's not the worst part."

She bent a knee, sat on her foot, and faced me. "So, what? Tell me."

"None of that stuff is really gone. If we could ever go back, it'd still be there."

"But…"

I scratched my forearm. "You remember the picture I had of Mom and me?"

"Yeah. It was always next to your bed."

"I lost it. Vanished. Kaput." I shook my head. "I remember packing it, but I haven't seen it since we moved to Moreau. I tore that house apart. After Middie died, it was the only thing I had to remember Mom."

"Middie. I never got along with that dog, but I could tell you were really bummed."

Everyone assumed Middie was my dog, so when she died our first winter in South Dakota, my sadness was a surprise to no one. What J.R. and Nadine were forgetting, was that before me, the dog belonged to Madelyn. She was Maddie to her friends. Maddie and Middie, together forever, till death do they part. No one imagined Madelyn would be the first to go. I grew up thinking the little, tail-wagging bundle was the funniest, most fascinating thing I'd ever seen.

The end came slowly. First her eyes started to fade, then her hearing went. She'd rise from her padded donut to eat and "go outside" but had no energy for anything else. Finally, Middie stopped eating, and I realized I was making her hold on only because I couldn't let go. I walked into the Vet's office with her cradled in my arms. I must have looked a wreck because the receptionist knew right away why I was there. Nadine and J.R. didn't come along. "It's not our dog," they said, and indeed she wasn't. Nor was it mine. I was only the caretaker; had been since the day Mom died. I held Middie on my lap, my fingertips gently stroking her head the way she loved, her gaze fading. The medication grabbed hold and took away the only piece of my mother's life that I could still see, hear, and touch. Middie closed her eyes for the last time, the technician took her away. Weak, stunned, and crumbling to my core, I was able to hold off the tears until I was back in my truck, alone. Forehead resting on the steering wheel, I said goodbye to both of them. Middie, for staying with me to the very end. And to Maddie, my mother, because I'd never before had the chance.

"You looked everywhere for the picture?"

I lowered my brow at her.

"Gone?" she asked.

"Gone."

By the time we arrived in Caney Creek, all the time behind the wheel had turned me into a mound of mush.

We grabbed a light supper before arriving at the park. To get the senior discount, I had Stan sign the register. The rates were pre-season anyway, so the price including electric and sewer hook-up was budget-beautiful. There were plenty of open spots. Number 21 was not far from the front desk and secluded without being remote, but as I turned in, something slithered across the drive.

"Oh, crap." Wide-eyed, I backed the camper out. "Was that a snake?"

Nadine rolled her eyes.

Stan said, "Yeah, but a small one. Round here they don't bother you. Get down to Oklahoma and Texas, now that's a different story."

That wasn't going to change my mind. I drove past several good openings before finding another, presumably snake-free spot.

After setting up the Winnebago, I went for a short walk while Nadine and Stan made the interior ready for sleeping. As negotiated, Stan got the rear bunk. By nine p.m. he was ready to "cash 'em in." He removed his hearing aids, took six prescription bottles out of his grip and lined them up on the table. Then he brushed his teeth and climbed into bed.

I returned and told Nadine about a shower building I'd found a short walk away. We grabbed towels and soap, locked the camper, and spent twenty minutes at the showers. Back in the LeSharo, we checked on Stan. He hadn't moved.

We stood next to the second bed, made by the transformation of the two second-row seats. "Okay, you can have the bed." I was in my shirt and boxers. "I'll take the front seat."

"Oh." Nadine sat down on the bed.

There were a dozen ways I might have taken that single syllable. I crawled past her, across the makeshift bed, between the front seats to my resting place. "Can you toss me—" A folded blanket whacked me in the face. "What was that for?"

She lay down. "I don't know what you're talking about." A short pause. "It's her, isn't it? You're still hung up on Leah. You're not listening to your own advice. All this talk about the past, it's gone. Forget Moreau. Forget Wisconsin, that's all I hear from you. And now"—she kicked the back of my seat—"you can't even forget one, single person."

The blush on my face didn't show in the fading light. She was right, of course, but there was no point in going through any of it with her. So far as I knew, she'd never left a lover behind. And J.R. Cherhasky didn't count. "This has nothing to do with Leah. You and I hooking up, I just don't think it's smart." I spoke in a hoarse whisper. "Think about Stan. If he caught us, he'd have a stroke."

She punched her pillow. "Why are you whispering? Remember last night? His hearing aids are out. He could sleep through a tornado, for chrissakes."

"Whatever. Good night." I set the seat back and closed my eyes. A minute later. "Max..."

"The air conditioning isn't on."

There was rustling. My seat creaked and suddenly, there she was, astride me. Her throat, still smelling of soap, only a nose-length away. "One night. What's the big deal?"

I straightened in the seat. "Nadine. In the front seat? Are you serious right now?"

She leaned forward, put her mouth next to my ear. "Hello. Paging the guy from the Iowa Motel. Your presence requested in the camper." She ran her fingers across my scalp. "There was a time I wondered what it would be like to run my hand through all that black hair, but..."

I said, "It's gone now." She frowned. My hands squeezed the arm rests. "Listen, we had a night, a fantastic night. But, let's leave it—"

She stopped me with a long kiss. Then traced a fingernail along my cheek, across my lips. "What happened to the Max I heard about? You know, the guy that had the girls calling day and night."

"Nadine," I whispered. "This is bad."

"Of course, it's bad." She pushed aside my t-shirt, then slipped her hand into my shorts. "That's what makes it so good."

My breath caught. "Nadine... come on." Just as it had in Iowa City, her skill, the boldness of her hands stunned me.

"So, where is he? That guy? The one that's so much fun." She tugged me straight. "Oh, there we go. Your honor, I withdraw the question."

"Oh my god."

"Say what you want." Another tug. "But don't try to tell me you're not into it."

I slid my hands under her shirt, grasped her waist so that just my index fingers and thumbs touched her lower ribs. At that point, I could have pushed her away or simply held on.

I opened my mouth to give an answer. She put two fingers upon my lips. "Shh. I already know," she whispered. "You hate your father as much as I do. What could be better"—she slipped a finger past my lips and then across my tongue. She withdrew the moistened finger and found a wetness of her own. She gasped. "Better than"—she slipped me inside—"fucking his wife."

My hands slipped down to her hips. This was not the rushed, frantic act from the night before. The vibe was completely different; the summation of a new life encapsulated in one desperate yet meaningless act.

I nuzzled between her breasts and knew I was lost. Like a snake, I was shedding my past, becoming someone else. The Max that had loved Leah was nothing more than a dried husk of skin lying on the camper floor. And I really didn't know why. What was turning me into a molting reptile?

I bit gently at her nipples through the thin fabric of her shirt.

A breath caught in her throat. "Where did you learn that?"

"An Amazon I... knew... once."

CHAPTER TWENTY-FOUR

Nate

Kitty Dettmann had not made for a good start to my Friday afternoon. Whether she had a natural suspicion of law enforcement or was protecting someone, I couldn't tell, but as I pulled out of her driveway I was sure she knew more than she let on. A pizza-by-the-slice place on the edge of campus looked busy. I stopped in, went through the order line, and found a seat. I took a deep breath and rested my feet. After traipsing across half of the upper Midwest, I was no closer to my goal than I'd been at the start.

I hadn't worked solo on a case for more than ten years. Most of my assignments had been either high-profile or top priority and required a team of two or more agents. Field work had always been the best part of the job, and I was good at it. It didn't hurt that I'd always been blessed with fabulous partners, especially the last one, Caleb Lambert. Never one to take life or himself too seriously, he became the perfect foil for me and my over-wound, buttoned-down demeanor.

The fact that I was chasing down Max and Nadine by myself was no accident. I understood why my boss, Rick Atwater, hadn't assigned a second agent. First of all, this case should have been a lay-up, the easiest two points on the court. Second, that kind of support was for rookies. My career was at a stage where competency was assumed, and if it wasn't there, either make it right or empty your locker. I could understand the logic, especially given what happened to Caleb. Truth is, after he retired from active duty I didn't want a partner. The flashbacks were finally starting to fade—not gone but less frequent and nowhere near as intense. Working alone wasn't making them any worse; but a new partner might.

My pizza, a small salad, and a tea arrived on a tray. I opened my laptop and signed onto the free Wi-Fi. I was way behind on my emails, but interested in only one. Lance had sent along information about Antoni Kopec. He was thought to be driving a dark-green Buick mid-size with Illinois plates. Law enforcement in three states had been notified to report any sightings, but there'd been no sign of him. And he had not been on the train. My best guess was he was traveling by car, ghosting Max and Nadine.

Then, some real gold. Stanley Dettmann was the owner of a 1983 Winnebago LeSharo, Iowa plates. This had to be Max's latest form of transportation. He was thinking on the run. Leah Walters knew her man, and if I was going to make up the distance between us, I had to realize I wasn't chasing just any eighteen-year-old. He was elusive, canny as a fox, and had no business walking around with the street knowledge he seemed to possess. I needed a new strategy.

I texted Lance and instructed him to alert the Missouri, Kansas, and Oklahoma State Police about the camper, and the possibility Antoni Kopec might be in their area with mayhem on his mind. As a coda, I mentioned I'd be "calling Brooke," knowing he'd understand that the car chase was over—I was going to try and get my Cessna, but I'd need her help.

I caught my wife at Mila's soccer game. Claire was at a friend's house, so I couldn't talk to either of my daughters, which wasn't good since I was counting on their support to bolster my request. Brooke and I spent a few minutes catching up with family matters and with each other, then she asked about the case. As a former ATF agent, she knew about the stress that builds as an assignment drags on, especially when the protection of a state's witness was involved.

"I wonder," Brooke said. "if Nadine knows why you're chasing her? Did you get a chance to tell her about the mob? Her life's in danger, she's got to know that."

"If she knows, she didn't hear it from me. Somehow, she lived with these people for four years and never realized how dangerous they are."

"And Max, he's running because...?"

"He's stubborn and selfish, to be blunt. He wants nothing to do with WPP. Well fine. But don't put another person's life on the line. Jesus H. Christ."

"What was Atwater thinking?" she asked. "No one works a case without a partner anymore. Especially when you're dealing with organized crime."

"WPP retrievals usually don't amount to much. No one expected Max and Nadine to bolt."

She paused a beat. "Have you been getting enough sleep?"

"I think so. I'm fine, really, but I'm treading water, Brooke. I talked to Max's girlfriend. She thinks there's something driving Max, besides the WPP."

"Like what?" asked Brooke.

"I don't know. She had her suspicions but wouldn't tell me what they were. She has a sixth sense about people." I didn't want to get into the synesthesia business, because I wasn't sure I could answer any questions about it. "It's nagging at me like a toothache. But my biggest problem is the chase. He's resourceful and slippery as an eel. Brooke, I need the Cessna to catch them." Silence on the line. "I know what I'm asking. Your flight would only be to Waunakee, an hour. I could meet you there in four hours. How far along is Mila's game?"

"Second half."

"You'd have time to get her home, drive to the airport, and fly to Waunakee. I'll give you my rental to drive back to Appleton."

A sigh came through the phone all the way from Wisconsin. "All right. Four hours. Waunakee. I need some flight time anyway."

"Can you bring the girls?" I asked. "I really need to see them."

———————

Thirty minutes later I was driving northeast toward Madison,

Wisconsin. The closer I got to the airstrip, the more convinced I was about using the Cessna. Max was taking the chase south and, based on what his best friend told me, then southwest. More wide-open spaces. Less of anything man-made and in some ways, more places to get lost. Covering big chunks of mileage in short clicks would be crucial if I was going to get to them before Antoni Kopec.

The four hours to Waunakee turned out to be the longest I'd spent on the road in a long time. I was sick of the compact rental I was driving, sick of the road, sick of not making headway. With every minute I was another mile farther from Max and Nadine, and that worked against every instinct I had. But more than that, I missed my three girls. Brooke hadn't promised to bring Claire and Mila; you can't guarantee anything with two teenage girls in the equation. I knew Brooke would do her damnedest. Since Austin died two years ago, we've watched out for each other and especially our lifeline, our remaining children.

Brooke's question about my sleeping wasn't far off the mark. There were a couple of things that kept me up at night. One was the Cordell case. The other was the memory from a couple years ago when the phone rang at exactly 1:21 a.m. Austin was a senior in high school and had played well in a baseball game the day before. He wanted to go out with the team for pizza, then hang out at a friend's house. Did I miss the signs of my son's substance abuse or, like me, was he expert at hiding them? I was drinking at the time—again—so if they had been there, I missed them. Brooke had told me countless times she missed the signs too, and she only drinks at weddings and on her birthday. This is what I try to remember when guilt bloats my throat and sweat licks at my collar. Fact is, Brooke would not say otherwise no matter the truth. In the wake of Austin's death, I stopped drinking. Brooke gave up her job and started a relentless cross-training program.

I got to the airstrip ahead of Brooke. The small community airport wasn't busy. I saw one other pilot, his plane on the tarmac, doing a walk-around. On the right were two moderate-sized hangars and a fueling station. There was a small office, unmanned at the time, and no control tower. I had to file a flight plan. The office had the sectional aeronautical charts I needed. Sunset would be arriving in a couple hours. My license allowed for night flight, and the weather south was favorable. If I stayed the night in Wisconsin, I'd lose another half-day on Max and Nadine. A self-imposed flight limit of four hours was reasonable given the time of day and time spent driving the car. The plane cruised at 140 miles-per-hour, but I'd be flying into a headwind variable five to ten miles-per-hour. The best I could safely do was 500 miles: that would put me in St. Joseph, Missouri—the same location Nadine had used her card at noon.

Brooke did a low altitude fly-by to check the airstrip and wind direction, then made the turn for her final approach. Heart thumping in my throat, I watched her land and taxi to the end of the strip. The engine stopped, the doors opened, and out came my daughters. I met them halfway and gave them a group hug, my two blondes, hair color being one of the few things they inherited from me. I thank God every day they got their mother's high cheekbones and winning smile. Mila still had her hair in a ponytail from the soccer game. Brooke was right behind, dressed in black jogging pants and light-blue, long-sleeved golf shirt. It was a brunette ponytail for her, and milk-chocolate eyes that always made me melt.

CHAPTER TWENTY-FIVE

Max

When Nadine slid onto my lap, I was at the end of a five-day marathon. She'd quickly snuffed my last ounce of energy. I guess I should have thanked her for the first few hours of sleep. But by three a.m. the glow was gone. The seat was stiff and I felt every ridge and lump in the upholstery. I thought of my father and what he might say that could entangle me in his spider's web of murder and deception. What better reason to make myself invisible. I propped my head on the side window and tried not to dream.

The next thing I heard was the coffee maker, spitting and hissing. Stan was up, his bunk converted back to the dining table. I tried to ignore the commotion. Then Nadine got up and started talking to Stan, who clearly had not yet turned on his hearing aids. I crept out of the seat and stood.

Nadine put bread and cheese out for breakfast. I poured a large bowl of cereal and asked for a coffee. Nadine brought it over. Stan grabbed four pharmaceutical bottles out of a line-up of six, and dumped out a single pill from the first two bottles, and two pills each from the last two.

"Holy shit, Stan," Nadine said. "With all those pills, who needs breakfast?"

He looked up. "What's that?"

I spun a finger around my ear. "Turn on your hearing aids."

"Oh!" Stan put a finger on each one. "Go ahead."

"Nothing," Nadine said. "How do you keep track of all those bottles?"

"Been doing it so long, it's a habit." Stan slid a small fishing tackle box closer, put the bottles inside, and shut the lid.

"So that's why you have that," I said. "I couldn't find the fishing rods."

"Yeah, it's pathetic." Stan put the box on the shelf. "I should dump the pills and go fishing."

We left the RV park before eight a.m. and headed south out of Kansas. In northern Oklahoma we caught Highway 60 westbound, going through or around towns like Lamont and Nash until we ran into an even less-traveled road—Highway 64—which would take us through the rest of the panhandle. I'd picked a bad day to travel through this part of the world. The wind was up in "No Man's Land"—a good name because bovine out-numbered humans here by a wide margin. Every time we passed a cattle lot, dust clouds stinking of cow shit blew across the road and through the Winnebago. A dozen or more of these farms, each one with hundreds of cattle, dotted the landscape and produced a scent that, on a warmer day, might have melted the radiator.

On the outskirts of Jet, Oklahoma two State Police squads, lights on, sirens wailing, were suddenly on my tail. Every sphincter in my body went Code 4. I pulled over along with two other vehicles, fully expecting the troopers to bookend my Winnebago. They shot by. I dropped my forehead onto the wheel. "That's it. I'm sick of my own paranoia. Next town, we change the license plates."

The town of Cherokee was bigger than the last six we'd seen. After driving through miles and miles of brown grass, brown sand, and gravel sideroads, it was good to see a flash of green from the occasional tree. Two blocks off the highway we found a church with a large parking lot, full of vehicles. "Services? On a Saturday?" I asked.

"Don't have to be that," Stan said. "Could be a basketball game, craft fair. Who knows."

"Perfect," I said. "And I see three RV's to boot. God is on our side."

I turned into an empty parking spot, pulled a Philips screwdriver from the kit. I switched my Iowa plates for a set from Colorado, and climbed back in the driver's seat.

Nadine asked, "What if they notice? If they report the plates they'll know we've been here."

I waved her off. "No one ever looks at their own plates."

Stan shook his head and crossed his arms across his chest.

Two lefts and a right and we were back on the highway. Along the way there were signs directing us to the Sod House Museum, No Man's Land Museum, and half a dozen other tourist traps.

I noticed the roadside billboards had suffered damage and thought a windstorm or small tornado must have swept through the area. On one of the brightly-colored, larger boards a lightning strike or a gust of wind had partially torn the overlying ad in the shape of a thunderbolt. It reminded me of Leah's art. I smiled at first, but the damaged sign struck a hollow feeling inside me that lasted long after passing the sign.

I pulled into a Blue Lion just north of Buffalo, Oklahoma. Stan tended the pump while Nadine and I made a bathroom stop and bought some essentials. Nadine had chips, a magazine, and a diet soda, I had selected a couple cans of an energy drink and a big bag of Corn Nuts. I glanced to see if Stan was done pumping, then looked at the cashier. She had a tattoo of stars on her neck, three studs in her right ear, and a pierced nose. I said, "All this plus pump number three." I noticed Nadine, digging in her purse. I said, "I got it."

"I know." She found what she wanted and in a single move, waved a Blue Lion discount card across the scanner. I grabbed her wrist and jerked it away, but it was too late.

The register pinged. "One dollar three-cents savings," said a robotic, female voice.

"What the fuck are you doing?" I cried.

"Language," monotoned the cashier, a silver Jesus cross dangling between her breasts.

"Ow! Let go!" Nadine pulled away.

I fumed. "What did I say—"

Stan walked in. "What's going on?"

"Nadine scanned her card." I leaned into the counter and said to the girl, "Can you cancel that? What she just did? Can you delete it?"

She flinched. "What? I don't know. Why would I?" Her face reddened. "I can cancel the sale."

"Shit," I said.

"One more of those"—the cashier glowered—"and you'll have to leave."

Stan slid between Nadine, me, and the desk. "Okay. Not the end of the world. Why don't you two go outside. I'll settle up." Staring poison at each other, neither Nadine nor I moved. Stan showed us out.

We walked toward the LeSharo, bickering as we went.

"You two get in the camper," Stan called from the station door. "I gotta make a pit stop. Think you two can cool it for that long?"

Nadine opened the passenger door. "You said credit cards."

I walked around the front of the camper and jumped into the front seat. "Card!" I held out my hand. "Give me the card."

She sat motionless in her seat, looking forward. I made a grab for her purse. She yanked it away, spilling the contents on the floor. "Oh, great. Nice work, ya jerk."

"Give me the card."

She was deliberate, painfully slow in picking up the make-up, pens, and half a dozen other pieces, each of which had to be carefully examined before she replaced it in her purse. She'd kept the blue card for last.

Stan opened the service door and got in. "Oh, good. No felonies in the last five minutes."

I had her card in hand, bending it back and forth. "All cards matter. They can track us. *Whenever you scan, kneel to the man.*" I threw the two halves on the floor.

"Drive the camper, Max," Stan said. "Before the cashier calls the cops." He sat down. "You two complain like a couple of crows."

Over the next ten minutes the tension turned into an Oklahoma twister without the radar changes. Stan rubbed his chest and sighed deeply. I looked in the rearview mirror. His breathing looked off and his color too. A small, dark bottle came out of his pocket and from it, a small, white pill. He slipped it under his tongue, put the bottle away, and leaned back.

"Stan, are you all right?" I asked.

"Will be in a minute." And he was right. Ten minutes later his breathing had steadied, but he still looked washed out. A while after that, he sat up, peered forward from the back seat, and pointed. "Look at that. A whole store sells nothing but beef jerky. We gotta stop."

I said, "There's a ton of salt in that shit."

"Oh, to hell with that. I never seen a place special like that. One time ain't gonna kill me."

"All right—"

"If he's stopping," added Nadine, "then I want a Dairy Queen."

I didn't want to do anything for Nadine, not after the stunt she pulled with the discount card. The entire trip was at risk now because she had to save twenty-five cents on a bag of chips. "Where the hell are we going to find that in the middle of No Man's Land?"

"Right there." She leaned back. The sign was visible through her window, about a quarter mile away.

"Perfect," Stan said.

Defeated, I turned the steering wheel.

We got back on 64 westbound. Stan worked on his second piece of Southwest Beef Jerky. I one-handed a medium vanilla cone dipped in chocolate. Nadine spooned an Oreo Blizzard so fast she gave herself a Queen-freeze headache. I asked Nadine where else she had used the Blue Lion discount card.

"When we stopped for gas, yesterday," she said.

"St. Joseph." I sighed and looked at my outside mirrors. "Keep an eye out for cops."

Nadine clicked out of her seatbelt. "Look for yourself. Stan and I are playing cards."

I checked my speed. "Aren't you sick of Rummy by now?"

"Yeah, we are." She walked to the dining area. "That's why we're playing strip poker."

"We are? Hang on," Stan said. "I've got a marked deck in the drawer."

"For chrissakes." I adjusted the rearview mirror. "Stan, no! You'll have a stroke."

"Yeah, but I'll die happy."

Nadine said to me, "You can put the mirror back on the road. We're using the cowboy and cowgirl dolls Stan bought."

"Dolls!" I scoffed. "Are you shittin' me?"

"There's always a catch," grumbled Stan.

The hands went back and forth early, but in time Stan emerged as the better player. "Blouse," he said.

"Stan! You're a perv," Nadine said. "Besides, you don't get to pick."

"Okay, Max is the judge. Who says what to take off?" Stan asked.

"Winner picks. Loser strips."

"Fine." Nadine pouted. "You want to see my breasts." She pulled off her shirt.

Stan's jaw dropped. "Nadine."

"Oh, right. Forgot." She put on the shirt. "Where's the doll?"

The LeSharo rolled sluggishly along the monotonous Oklahoma landscape. The engine felt most comfortable at fifty-two miles per hour. Angular sunlight showed off a layer of dust on the antiquated dashboard that I'd not noticed before. I rubbed my hand across my face and thought, *so this is freedom.* Driving down narrow highways marked by tar lines and alligator cracks, constantly humiliated by mothers and grandpas who passed me because I was a drag-ass. Another "whoop!" from the back: I'd become a caretaker for two people, a burden I'd have never seen coming, not in a million years. *Jonah, my ass,* I thought. *I'm still Ahab. And I'm driving a white whale.*

Later, we got to Boise City, located at the far west end of the panhandle, the last stop before we headed southwest to New Mexico. We were almost out of diesel, so I pulled in at a Truck Stop just inside the city limits. Stan and Nadine walked into the store. I yelled after them, "Grab me a Coke. And no discount cards."

Without turning around, she whipped me the bird, backhanded. "Suck on this instead."

CHAPTER TWENTY-SIX

Nate

Mila and Claire were hungry so we stopped at a burger and custard place down the road. We ordered at the counter, took our number, and slid into a corner booth, the girls on one side of me, Brooke on the other. I caught up on school, boys, sports, and the escapades of Bullet, our family dog. Claire and the dog were inseparable, and we were sure Bullet thought of Claire not as human, but rather a fellow canine. Brooke and I listened as the girls assumed the bulk of the conversation. I gave her hand a squeeze and wondered what it would have been like to have Austin here.

The face of Max Cherhasky flashed in my mind and, not for the first time, I wondered whether my desire to pull him back from the brink was solely for his benefit, or mine. After all, Nadine was the primary focus of my assignment, not Max. And yet I'd been working the case as if they were equally important. In the last three days I'd found myself thinking *Max is not Austin* all too often, or maybe not often enough.

If Rick Atwater knew that I was making a connection between my son and Max, I'd have been immediately relieved of duty, brought back to Milwaukee—a shuffle-and-staple agent for the rest of my career. But there were unmistakable similarities between the two boys. Both were good athletes, Austin more so than Max, although that might have been different had Max not given up basketball when he moved to South Dakota. From what I'd been told, he was musically gifted. No one would've described Austin that way, though he played a decent trombone for the marching band. Most importantly, both grew up lacking a stable father figure. Max, because J.R. had no instincts for fatherhood. Austin was similarly deprived, but for different reasons. I could blame it on the demanding nature of my job, but that would have been a cop out. I missed most of Austin's eighteen years because I was a high-functioning alcoholic. Through the countless bottles of vodka and gin, I was able to meet life's challenges and demands. In all ways except one.

The food was surprisingly good, or maybe it was just the company. It was almost time to go. "Anyone for ice cream?" I asked. Both the girls got the flavor of the day. Brooke and I passed, but I cleaned up whatever the girls couldn't finish.

Back at the airstrip, they dropped me off. I waved as they drove away, my throat thick and raspy. I coughed a bit, loaded my luggage into the plane, and completed an inspection. Refueling was next, then a final check on weather. I pointed the Cessna 172 down the runway and hit the throttle.

Except for a little turbulence about an hour out, the flight was smooth. The sun set and I flew the last half of the trip after dusk. Then my cell rang. I got news that put me into a special kind of darkness.

"Hello, is Nathaniel Bauer available?"

"Speaking. Who is this?"

"Blain Baker." The skin on my neck crawled. Why was he calling? "Captain, Iowa City—"

"Yes, Captain Baker, what can I do for you?"

"I have some bad news," he said. "You left us information on who your marks might be traveling with, one Stanley Dettmann."

"That's correct."

"I'm at Kitty Dettmann's home right now. She's dead. Single shot to the forehead."

I closed my eyes. "The sonofabitch."

"No signs of struggle by the victim but the place has been

ransacked. Seems the perp was looking for information. Left $326 in the kitchen drawer. Then he went upstairs, where your traveler lives. My guess: he's got personal information on Stanley."

"You have the name I gave you a couple days ago? Antoni Kopec?"

"That's who we're looking for, but he's probably long gone. They're putting time of death at two p.m., give or take. No witnesses. Neighbor saw a dark-green sedan with white license plates earlier."

"That's him. That's his car, a Buick, four years old." I paused, swallowed hard. At the time I had talked to her, she had less than two hours to live. "God, this is awful."

"Copy that. I'll call you if I get anything else."

Rosecrans Memorial Airport is not close to St. Joseph proper, so I got a few granola bars from a vending machine and slept in my plane. Thinking about Kitty and how she died kept me up half the night. Luckily, there was no alcohol at the airport, because the image of her with a bullet in her head was enough to drive me to drink. The next morning, the sun in my eyes, I woke up stiff and sore in a dozen-odd places. After two Ibuprofen and a trip to the terminal facilities I felt less-than Monday-morning human, which wasn't good considering it was still the weekend, day five of Max and Nadine's not-so-Excellent Adventure. I was anxious too. The next call from Lance was going to be key. I needed direction for the next flight.

Kopec's whereabouts remained unknown, and that stuck in my throat like a bitter pill. It had now been over eighteen hours since he killed Kitty. What information was he working on? Given the wide-open Internet and the mob's extensive connections, I wouldn't doubt he had access to the same intelligence as me, and almost as fast.

Just before eight a.m. Lance rang. He asked where I was and how I was doing, then gave me the latest on Kitty's murder; scant new information except for bullet ballistics. "Hang on," he said. Someone had handed him a fax. A pause, then: "Boom! Another hit on the Blue Lion. Yesterday afternoon. Buffalo, Oklahoma. Same user, Nadine Farmer."

"Thank you, Nadine…" Then it struck me. Kopec was trashing the house for a reason. "Lance, put a trace on another card. Stanley Dettmann, Iowa City, Iowa." I swore under my breath. "I should have thought of it hours ago. Get back to me ASAP."

I looked for an airstrip in the Oklahoma Panhandle, but found nothing useful. An alternative in northern Texas was close. My gut said their direction was southwest, so Dalhart, Texas, worked best. Accounting for wind speed and direction, I would be able to cover the five hundred forty miles by lunch, which would get me in just ahead of heavy weather coming in from the southwest.

An unexpected thunderstorm delayed my take-off from Rosecrans for forty-five minutes. The backlog of arrivals and departures took another hour before my number was called. A minute later I was airborne. After the storm passed, good weather held. I was halfway to my destination when Lance called again. Stan Dettman had used his credit card to purchase sixty-one dollars' worth of beef jerky in a town at the tip of the Oklahoma Panhandle called Boise City. Lance had also called Iowa City for an update on Kitty. Again, nothing more, but a tag had been placed on Stanley's Winnebago, and the title dropped. The vehicle was now registered in the name of Max Cherhasky.

CHAPTER TWENTY-SEVEN

Max

Driver's fatigue was setting in. With a blazing sun boring in and no tint on the windows, the afternoon drive had been particularly tough. We found a small restaurant and ordered a meal. Stan got salad with a piece of blueberry pie. I had a burger and fries. Nadine a Northwest Wrap. There was little to no conversation. It had been a long day, and after the fight at the service station, we stayed out of each other's way.

The meal was rejuvenating. I decided New Mexico was within our reach before sundown. Stan fell asleep in his second-row seat, snoring softly. Nadine swept her finger across her cell phone, feet on the dash, her wedding ring glinting in the setting sun.

Apropos of nothing, she asked, "What is it with you and your father?" Suddenly, she sat up, feet on the floor. "I mean, it goes back, long before they found your Mom. *And* before I showed up."

Reluctantly, I agreed. She shifted and turned toward me.

"You want to hear why?"

She nodded.

I rubbed the stubble on top of my head. "Really? I don't enjoy reliving nannies when I was five, or going to boarding school for seventh and eighth grade."

"You did?"

She appeared genuinely interested, so I added, "I don't really remember the first two housekeepers, but the third one, her name was Judy Jennings. I loved her. She was there from third to sixth grade. If I ever had anyone close to a mother, it was her. She was kind but kept me on my homework. My best grades ever. Great cook. She liked me too, believe it or not."

"What happened?"

"J.R. fired her."

"Why? Did she want more money?"

"No, nothing so minor as that. She was outspoken, especially about me. She followed his orders to the letter with everything, but he was an absentee father, and she called him on it. I remember those exact words. Wasn't two weeks and she was gone. I pitched a fit. Like I said, I loved her. A few weeks later I was gone to boarding school. I hated it and got kicked out for putting bullheads on top of the urinals in the dormitory bathroom. You know, looking forward, so they'd be watching you while you pee."

"OMG. The whole fish?"

"The whole fish."

"Eeuuww! That's disgusting." She pulled on her hair. "I'm almost afraid to ask. The next one, eighth grade?"

"Different school. Different scam. Do you know what an M-80 is?" I asked.

"A huge firecracker."

"About a quarter stick of dynamite. I flushed a live one down the school toilet. It went off and caused some wet asses in the teachers' bathroom next door. My dad had to pay a fine on that one, or whatever it's called." I straightened my arms on the wheel. "Looking back, he got off easy. Killing Mom and shipping me off. The fucker."

"He is a fucker." She looked forward for a moment, still tugging on her hair. "Well, then it's not all me."

"Where he and I are concerned, it's very little you. Nothing personal. You and me, we're just, I don't know. I hate to say we're alike—"

"Oh, god no. Don't hang that on me," she blurted. "You're a pompous ass."

"Thanks a lot." I smiled a little.

"You're more like your father."

"Hey! That's a cheap shot. Besides, I can't pick my parents.

You married him. You had a choice"

"Shit. Don't I know it."

I went right by a speed trap near Clayton and didn't see it until it would have been too late. My reflexes, concentration, and eyes were gone.

Nadine searched ahead and found Corrizo RV Park for our overnight. We paid, parked, and hooked up. I sat down at the dining table and connected to the free internet, catching up on the news about my father's murder trial. I skimmed through a couple posts. Because it was the weekend, not much had happened. He was still in Rapid City, South Dakota, awaiting his trip back to the state of Wisconsin. The third article was more in-depth, with a tag at the top that stopped me cold. It listed the charges against J.R. Cherhasky, which included hiding a corpse and accessory to murder after the fact. I read further. There was no mention of a murder charge. How could Nadine have gotten things so wrong? The article said there were no witnesses to Madelyn Cherhasky's death. An unnamed person had apparently helped in removing the body from the house and dumping it into Red Wolf Lake. How the victim had died was not known. J.R. knew, I was sure of that. But if he was going to name anyone else as a party to the murder, he'd implicate himself, and the case against him would be much worse.

I had no idea what to make of the charges. It was possible the authorities knew J.R. had done the deed but were withholding information from the public for strategic reasons. What had my father told them? Is that why they were after me? I dropped the phone in my lap and stared out the rear window. J.R. knew about leverage. If he could reduce the charges by naming an accomplice, he'd do it and not lose a wink of sleep.

I searched "Nadine Farmer missing" and got an entire page of hits. The headlines took me by surprise. She was in the forward cabin, looking for a station on the small TV bolted over the windshield. Stan was there too, helping her with the controls. I tapped the most recent story. A television station from Rapid City reported that authorities had noted Nadine missing

Thursday. According to Nathaniel Bauer, FBI agent assigned to the case, her whereabouts remained a mystery. Though foul play was not suspected, there was "concern for her safety and anyone with information…"

The name of the Federal agent rang a bell. I looked through the video and found a shot of him; it confirmed my suspicions. He was the same guy who'd been in our house during a raid on my father's business almost a year ago. I scrolled down to look for any mention of my name. In a few lines at the end, concern was raised regarding Max Cherhasky, also missing. His life was not thought to be in danger, but the timing of his disappearance on the same day was suspicious.

I went to a second listing. The story was a little different, but the details were the same. Nadine was the primary subject of the search, not me. None of the stories mentioned robbery, the four missing watches, or the $10,000 bank withdrawal. I felt deflated, defeated. I was the brains, the leader! Why was Nadine so important? Did her signature on the WPP contract carry more weight than mine? Maybe. I was a minor at the time the WPP went into effect. There was a logical explanation, I was sure, but for all the sand in the high desert I couldn't think of one. And it rather pissed me off.

Stan chuckled. His feet up, he nibbled on jerky and watched *Seinfeld* re-runs.

Rather than say anything about the online post, I took my phone to Nadine and pointed at the screen. She read silently for fifteen seconds, her fingertip scrolling once.

Her eyebrows went up. "See? Told you. If the FBI can't find us, that shooter won't either."

Night came. Stan took his pills, pulled out his hearing aids, and went to sleep. The sleeping arrangements up front were the same, but there was no visit from Nadine. The bad vibes that started when I grabbed her wrist had not gone away, and I wasn't about to offer the olive branch. I slept poorly for a good part of the night. I couldn't get my mind off Nadine, but not for the reason I would have guessed. She wasn't learning the rules.

We were on the run, and she was acting as if it was a road trip to the beach or a Beyoncé concert. I thought I could make her respect the danger. But if bullets ripping tree bark and exploding luggage wasn't enough to turn her head, then nothing would.

And where did the gunman fit in? For all the ambivalent feelings I had about federal law enforcement and "the man" in general, I couldn't see a guy like Agent Bauer involved in a plot to kill us. So, who was the shooter? Who was he after and why? Maybe it was a case of mistaken identity. Nadine sensed she might know the man, yet not know him, and that led in only one direction. I shivered.

I'd expected too much from Nadine, that was my fault. The time to cut my losses was upon me. The FBI was determined to find her. Someone else had tried to kill us. I wasn't going to end up a dolphin in a tuna net.

CHAPTER TWENTY-EIGHT

Max

Finally, by the next morning, I'd settled on a plan. The scheme was no more than a contingency, that's what I told myself, a way to protect my interests should we part ways in the middle of an argument. I split the cash down the middle. Half went in the withdrawal envelope she got from the bank, the other half in the lining of my backpack. If she figured it out, I'd argue I was only taking her advice and dividing the cash.

If I had any second thoughts about the fairness of what I was doing, I had that figured out too. She owed me. Escape was a precious commodity, and I had guided her out of two, no, three traps. First, from the claws of small-town America and a life she'd grown to despise. Moreau's population of over 3,000 people was more the three times that of her home town, Walnut Creek. She was born and raised there, a town in Northern Wisconsin known for lakes and logging. Mom and Dad had six kids, wedged into a five-room home without exterior siding, central heating, or a front porch. When she said she wanted to "go back home," I knew she meant Wisconsin and not the family Colum.

Second, I'd taken her away from a terrible marriage to my father, Jeremiah Roman Cherhasky. Yes, he was in jail, and I'd had nothing to do with that. But even from there he could still intimidate her. She didn't have the personal strength to break free on her own. I couldn't give her a piece of paper that said "Divorce," but at this point it hardly seemed to matter.

Third, the Feds. This dodge wasn't a done deal, but getting

out of the WPP was never going to be a walk in the woods, we both knew that. Without me, Nadine wouldn't have made it past the front porch, much less escaped Moreau. So yeah, I'd given her good value for the money. She ought to be happy to get away with half the loot.

Rather than crawl over Nadine's sleeping area and risk a confrontation, I went out the passenger door. I pulled out my burner cell and dialed a number. It rang twice.

"Hello, this is Leah."

Her voice in my ear had me right back in her studio. A wave of regret surged through me. I could smell her hair mingled with acrylic paint, could almost feel the coarse edge of her painter's pants on my fingertips, the heat of her breath on my neck.

"Hello? Who is this?"

I ended the call. Suddenly off balance, I took a deep breath, then reentered the camper via the galley door. Stan was up, cup of coffee in hand, his bunk already broken down to the dinette set, which was where he sat. He looked a little dragged out.

"I didn't sleep for crap." Stan massaged his chest with an open hand. "Woke up middle of the night. Felt like someone was sitting right here."

"Did you take your pills?"

"In a minute."

Nadine stirred. I jumped into the bathroom ahead of her; brushed, combed and washed; then exited a couple minutes later. Nadine took my place, the two of us passing and not a word was spoken. There was little to find for breakfast. The milk was gone, so I ate my cereal dry. I held the raisin bran box up to Stan and asked, "Join me?"

He shook his head. "Already had some Teriyaki jerk chicken, which is about the only food left in the LeSharo, I might add."

Nadine came out of the bathroom.

I said, "We'll stop for food at lunch."

Nadine rummaged about the galley. "And what am *I* supposed to eat until then?"

"There's an egg in the frig, and a little cheese," Stan said.

"Don't have to worry about my weight when I'm traveling with you guys." She turned on the stove burner. "We should stop in Clayton before we leave."

"Moving out in ten," I said. "We can shop anytime."

She dropped the frying pan on the stove. "We wouldn't be in such a hurry if Leah was here."

Had she heard me on the phone? I had to think back on the call for a moment to remember if I'd mentioned Leah's name. I said, "I want to get some miles behind us before it gets too hot."

Nadine cracked the shell and dropped the egg in the pan. "There's your father again. Gotta make good time."

"Somebody's got to save your ass," I said.

Stan groaned. "Ass, ass, ass."

Nadine said, "Yeah, well who asked you?"

I stood and put my finger in her face. "You did. You —"

"Stop!" Stan held up his hand. "Not another word." He got up and threw his coffee out the door. "Thought I signed on with adults. When they arrive, let me know."

The spatula whacked the pan and Nadine's egg went from over easy to scrambled. I stepped past her and broke down the forward sleep area. She finished her egg, cheese, and water breakfast, and had barely the time to brush her teeth before I disconnected from the water service.

We headed into the desert, going south parallel to the Texas border. The wind came up gradually throughout the morning and rocked and pushed the camper all over the road. Sand blew across the highway. An hour out, Stan said it was time to "tap a kidney." It was many miles to the next town, and even decent-sized hamlets may not have a gas station. The terrain was boring as a Sunday morning, high desert all around with an occasional fence line or pine tree, more commonly low grass and sagebrush. Stan spotted a short strip of boulders and said to pull over.

I steered the Winnebago to a stop. Stan climbed out first and disappeared behind the rocks. I got a glass of water, stood in front of the hood, and scanned the horizon. The clouds were paper-thin and very high overhead, but dark to the west. Sand blew under my sunglasses. I blinked my vision clear and looked for Nadine. It looked like she was still playing Solitaire on her phone in the passenger seat.

"Stan," I called. "You done? Let's go." Earlier, Stan had mentioned something about an enlarged prostate and sitting too much, so I gave him a minute more. I went inside, rinsed my eyes with water, and grabbed a towel.

"Shouldn't he be back by now?" Nadine asked.

I threw the towel on the table. "I'll go get him."

Following Stan's path around the rocks, I found him as still as the stones, a couple feet from the rock face. He didn't turn when I approached. His chest rattled with every breath.

"Stan, you all right?" No answer, not even a twitch. I moved a few steps closer, the rocks on my right were about chest high, tapering away from us down to nothing after ten feet. "What the hell, man, you see a—"

Then it was there. The warning I'd heard only on television or in the movies, was now only feet away: the rattle of a Prairie Viper, coiled in front of Stan, its forked tongue flicking.

CHAPTER TWENTY-NINE

Max

My worst nightmare in the flesh, ready to strike. My stomach seized into my chest. My head slithering through a grey, hazy whirlpool, I stumbled into the boulder to my right, then dropped my head onto the stone until my vision cleared.

"Stay away," whispered Stan. "Don't…"

My voice was but a feeble croak. "Yeah," I backed up. Once away from the snake, I collapsed to my knees. Nadine came running from the camper.

"Max, what the hell. What's the matter?"

I raised my hand to stop her. She was six feet away, but didn't retreat. "What? Is it Stan? Did something happen?" She bolted forward.

I stumbled toward her, grabbed her around the waist, and brought her down. "No, don't. Rattlesnake," I panted. "Two, three feet from Stan. We can't… we can't do anything, or it'll strike."

Nadine sat up, wide-eyed. "A snake? We gotta help him."

"Are you crazy?" I growled. "We're miles from a hospital. One bite from that thing and I'm dead."

"We can't leave him there."

We both stood up.

"What do we have?" Sweat slicked my palm as I worried the stubble on my head. "To sneak up on a snake and knock it away? What? Fast. Think!"

"I don't know," she said.

"I'm not talking to you," I snapped.

There wasn't a stick or a tree or a stone as far as the eye could see; nothing except sand, brush, and boulders. My gaze went to the LeSharo. I ran.

"Where are you going?" Nadine yelled. "Get back here, you coward."

The radio antenna, a long skinny metal tube held down by two rubber stays, followed the line of the windshield next to the passenger-side door. I pried and pulled on the antenna. "Come on, you bastard." With a snap, the bottom half gave way, but it separated from the top leaving a piece that was only eighteen inches long. Something a child might poke at a frog.

Nadine stepped closer. "What the hell?"

I threw the useless metal to the ground. "You're being loads of help." The sun glinted off the golden buckle on the skinny belt around her waist. I said. "A belt." I took off my shirt, handed it to Nadine, and said, "Roll this into a ball, as tight as you can." She looked at the shirt, a blank expression on her face. "Do it," I hissed, then pulled the belt from my jeans; a woven leather type without holes. While she held the rolled shirt, I fashioned a leather loop and wrapped it around the cloth ball. Then tightened the belt and clipped the buckle. It swung like a cowboy's lasso.

I grabbed Nadine's arm and told her the plan. She was to whisper instructions to Stan so he would know when to run. She nodded and went to Stan. I went around the far side of the boulders, eyes down, looking for more snakes. There were no more reptiles, but the area I had to traverse was strewn with rocks and boulders of all kinds and sizes. Walking would be treacherous. One misstep and I'd fall to a venomous end.

On hands and knees, I crawled over the rock bed to where I'd last seen Stan and the snake. I peeked around an edge of granite and saw Stan, his face pale and drawn. Suddenly, the snake was there, looking away from me, but only five feet away. Bile scorched my throat. The snake sounded the alarm. My arms collapsed. Scuttling backward, I wiped sweat off my brow and blinked to clear my vision. It didn't work. The rattle sounded again. It pierced my skull like a shard of glass. I put my hands over my ears. The ambush had turned on its heel; the snake was waiting for me, I knew it. I imagined the viper's fangs, the gaping mouth, coming at my face, the split second before it nailed me right on the chin. I held on to the closest rock and puked.

Wind-blown sand stuck to my face. Stomach empty, I pressed my forehead against the granite and gasped for air. Somehow, the retching settled me down.

The rattle, again.

Back on all fours, the lasso dragging alongside, I looked over the lowest stone and saw Stan, sweating, shoulders slouched and breathing hard. If the snake didn't get him, the heat soon would. Slipping forward, I glanced up; he nodded slightly. I gathered the belt, swung it in an arc over my head, and hit the snake from its flank. The bundled shirt hit its mark. The viper splayed. Stan turned and ran. But I had overplayed the strike. As the belt flew out of my sweaty hand, momentum took me belly-down across the rocks.

I planted my palms, looked up, and froze. With unbelievable quickness, the prairie rattler had recovered. We were eye to eye. The tail rattled. My teeth chattered. The slithering forked tongue, the pulsating nostrils, the cold, flat eyes. I recalled a lesson from somewhere, grade school maybe—don't move. Snakes see motion. Stan had just proven that. *Now,* I wondered, *who would save me?* I couldn't count on Nadine, and Stan was too old and exhausted to be any good. I half expected to hear the camper start up and drive away. My arms ached. The rattler coiled back and—

Crack!

I flinched. The snake went sprawling, then lay motionless in the sand. I flopped onto my side. Stan stood over me, a handgun still aimed at the snake, Nadine right behind.

"A gun! Holy shit," I gasped. "Where did that come from?"

"Had it right along." He lowered the barrel. Clearly, the viper was dead.

I went to my knees, my attention no longer on the snake but on the revolver hanging from Stan's hand. The cylinder with its chambered rounds, the well-oiled barrel put a shiver through me that came from a place deeper than even my fear of snakes. I sat back on my haunches and said, "Thanks." I must have glared at the gun, because Stan said:

"Did I scare you? Sorry if I did, but it had to be done."

"Yeah, I know." I pointed. "Those things always scare me."

He looked at the revolver, bemused. "I know how to handle it. It's always in a lock box. You didn't even know it was there."

I stood up. "But I do now, and I don't know if I can sleep at night knowing that thing is riding along."

"Well, get me to California. Then you'll sleep like a baby and so will I." Sweat dripping from his nose and gasping for air, he said, "Let's go. My chest is tighter than bark on a tree."

Sand swirling all around, Nadine and Stan walked back to the camper. I retrieved the belt and joined them. I started the camper and watched as Stan put the gun back in its box. He slouched into a chair and begged for the air conditioning, which was already on.

"Then turn it up," Stan said. "I can't breathe."

"Did you take your water pill?" she asked. "Or was it all the damn sand, blowing around?"

He nodded, and pointed at the air vent.

Nadine redirected the vents at him. I got back on the road. Stan slipped a pill under his tongue and fell into an uneasy slumber. My history with hand guns went back to a time almost before memory. As with most of the bad things in my life, it had to do with my father. The image of the snake flashing before me was replaced by visions of my childhood home in Walnut Creek, Wisconsin, the green and white Victorian house on Red Wolf Lake. I couldn't go back there, not to that place and time, and a horror I'd buried years ago. Stan couldn't understand where my aversion to handguns came from, and there was no way I could explain it to him. Another thing he didn't know, the first chance I had, the gun was going to disappear.

By mid-morning, we made our first fueling break but there was nowhere to buy groceries. I promised to stop at the first store within eyeshot. Four hours after leaving Clayton we made it to my goal, Highway 60, the road that would take us through the mountains. We stopped in Fort Sumner for lunch. Stan got out to use the bathroom and looked like he had rallied a bit. His skin was dry and his breathing regular. Nadine and I ordered at a take-out joint. They bagged our orders to keep blowing sand out of our food while we walked back to the LeSharo. We offered a bite to Stan, and he took half my burger and some of Nadine's fries.

Still, Stan wasn't himself. "The air isn't right. What's goin' on?"

I grabbed my phone. "We're pretty high up already. Elevation, four thousand feet."

"Jesus," Nadine said. "No wonder, hey Stan?" She got no response, then repeated, "Right, Stan?"

"Yeah, whatever..." he said.

Lunch done, we headed west into more, high desert. Doing sixty-five miles-per-hour thirty miles out of town, I heard a loud *thud*. The camper pulled hard to the right. I came off the gas and tapped the brakes. The entire vehicle shook. The camper was fighting me. We veered headlong for the ditch.

CHAPTER THIRTY

Max

The edge of the asphalt grappled with the tires. One second I was in control, the next the steering wheel wanted to break my wrists. The camper shook and wavered in the crosswind. Nadine thrust her hands onto the dash and screamed, waking Stan. The LeSharo teetered like a slowing top. Finally, I tamed the vehicle and managed an uneasy halt, two wheels on pavement, two off, the camper listing to the right. A pick-up passed us going the other way but didn't stop.

"Blown tire." Stan straightened. "Right rear. Lucky it wasn't front or we'd a been ass over elbows in the ditch. Did you hit something?"

I didn't think so. I looked in the mirror anyway. But in the blowing sand, who could tell?

Nadine undid her seatbelt, rested her forehead on the dash.

Stan's feet had swollen while he slept, so he had trouble getting his shoes on. He wouldn't be any help in a sandstorm. I said, "You come out, take a look, show me where the jack and tire wrench are stowed, then back in here." He didn't argue.

While I got to work on the flat, he snuck around to the back and started on the vinyl cover that protected the spare tire mounted there. Nadine came out with hats and bandanas to ward off sun and sand. She asked after Stan. I pointed around the rear. She found him struggling, sweating and gasping.

"Stan," Nadine exclaimed. "Leave that for Max."

I got up from the flat to see what was going on. He stopped wrestling with the vinyl and leaned a shoulder into the spare, a hand pressed to his chest. "Dammit, dammit… dammit," he gasped and put on the bandana.

"Stan," Nadine asked. "What's the matter?"

"There's… a little… pill bottle… in the frig. Get it."

She looked at me. "There's something wrong. He looks… bad. Like a ghost."

"I told him to take it easy," I said bitterly. I was irate with the tire, the weather, and the rusted tire bolts, which hadn't budged since I started working on them. "Get him inside."

"He wants his pills."

"Then get him his pills and get him in the camper, for chrissakes."

She growled something and stomped away.

Stan came around from the back of the camper, his hand on the side of the vehicle to guide his steps, feet dragging in the gravel. "Got to get…"—a gasp— "out of this."

I dropped the tire wrench and shoved a hand under his arm. "Holy shit, Stan. Let's go. Nadine! The pills."

The galley door slammed. She came back to Stan and put the small, dark bottle in his shaking hands. He removed the cap and tipped it. The tiny pills dribbled off his palm and disappeared into the gravel. "Oh Christ, no. No!"

She took the bottle. It was empty. "Damn. Max, he spilled them."

The wind stung my eyes. I felt danger in the air, the unsteady vibration of fear beneath my feet. "Are you kidding me? Well, find them. He only needs one."

She got down on her hands and knees and dug her fingers into the gravel. "I can't see them."

I put the wrench down and crawled next to her.

The tablets had vanished in the dust. Fingers bleeding, her painted nails chipped, she scraped and clawed at the earth. She spotted one and cried out, then it was gone. She got a tiny pill between her fingertips, then fumbled it away.

"There!" I saw a flash of white. "Where'd it go?" Gone.

She dug again, harder, streaks of red etched in the roadbed. I saw the color too, and thought the blood was my own. I stopped abruptly and inspected my hands, my fingertips. Playing the guitar had given me callouses on the tips of four fingers on my left hand. The skin was unharmed. On the right, my fingers were sore, but not bleeding.

"Are you looking at your fingers?" she asked. "Help me." Then she found one—it stuck to her blood-crusted fingertip, a little, white pill. "Stan, I got one. But it's bloody. I'm sorry." She put it in his palm.

"Good." I found another pill and put it in the bottle. "Now get inside." I crawled back to the flat tire. For the third time, the tire wrench went on a bolt and… nothing. I could knock the horns off a mountain goat before that bolt would crack. I moved on.

Stan faced away from the wind and placed the pill under his tongue. She capped the bottle, took him by the arm, and guided him toward the door. As they went by, I slammed the tire wrench into the ground and looked up.

"Stan, when's the last time you had this wheel off? The bolts are rusted; I can't move the fuckers."

"Can't you see he's sick?" Nadine snapped. "Figure it out yourself."

Nadine and Stan disappeared into the camper. Two of the four nuts finally gave way, but by then one wrist and my back were in pain. I stood and stared at the wheel, then turned away from the wind, trying to think. Sam Robel, a friend from Wisconsin, had used Coke to loosen a rusty trailer hitch. There was half-a-bottle in the cab. I stuck my head in the door to retrieve the cola.

"Stan says his chest hurts," Nadine said.

"Did you give him one of those pills?" She said yes. "Well, give him another one." I slammed the door and went back to the wheel. Careful not to waste the precious liquid, I rubbed the cola into each bolt, then sat back and waited. The Coke dried quickly in the heat, so the bolts got two more soaks, and then the wrench.

I pulled, pushed, stomped on the wrench with my foot and still no go. Another dose of cola, then it was time to go inside for a break. I was stunned by Stan's appearance. He looked as if he was standing in the midday sun—sweating, breathing hard, pale. "Didn't the pills help?"

"Only for a minute or two," she said, as she dabbed his brow with a moist cloth.

"Your heart pills?" I gasped. "Do you have another bottle?"

"Gotta... lay down," he said.

I broke down the dining area, put the cushions into place. "Come on, Stan. Over here."

He looked kindly at Nadine, touched her hand, and tried to straighten in the seat. Even with our assistance, he struggled. We laid him on the bed, but lying flat only made him worse.

"Can't turn on the engine. Not until I know if I can get the tire changed. We might run out of fuel." I pulled out my cell phone.

"No service," Nadine said. "I already tried."

I threw the phone on the counter. "I'll go try the tire again."

She shook her head. "How long do you think?"

"How should I know? It'd be done right now if it was up to me." Stan groaned. We both looked at him. I went out.

The two remaining bolts were dry again. Sweat stained my shirt and dripped off my chin. I moistened the bolts one more time. With a *crack* the bolt broke free. I lost my balance, tumbled forward, and scraped my forehead on the fender. Feeling strangely elated, I got up off the ground. With a final soak, the final bolt gave it up as well. The spare was next. Though not a repeat of the rusted disaster, the bolts had never been removed and were stubborn. I rolled the spare to the work area. Blinking hard against the sand, I changed out the tire and put the flat on the tailgate rack. Not a minute too soon. The winds were rising.

I opened the driver's door, threw the jack and wrench on the floor, and got back on the road. "Jesus, this sand is the worst shit I ever saw." The mask peeled off my face, a brown bandana dangled from my hand. I wondered what the sand might do to the engine. "How are you doing, Stan?"

I barely heard him over the engine and the howling wind. "Awful... bad."

"All right." I turned the fan on full. "Nadine, keep an eye on your cell. As soon as we have service—"

"I know," she said. "Search for a hospital."

Ten miles later the phone lit up. Nadine did her search. "Okay, okay. Santa Rosa, there's a hospital on the south side of town.

When you see Highway 54, take a right. We're about forty miles from the front door."

I glanced at her cell. "What's all over your phone?"

"Blood, Max, it's blood." She showed her open hand, palm up, the fingertips oozing.

"Jesus." My hand scrounged in a storage compartment and found a wet wipe. I tossed it to her. "It'll sting. Check the glove box. Maybe some bandages. Or in the back."

"Nope. I already looked." She tossed the wet wipe on the dash. "And I washed them already."

"Forty miles," I whispered. "Shit." Visibility was terrible. Clots of sand blew across the road like a brown blizzard.

"Stan, Stan, stay awake," Nadine said. There was a soft groan. "Max, you better hurry."

"Are you shittin' me? I can barely see the road."

CHAPTER THIRTY-ONE

Max

The floating compass on the dash rotated to northeast. I tapped it a couple times, thinking it had gotten hung up; but it didn't move. The turn onto Highway 54 had us doubling back into the sandstorm and away from the mountains. "What the hell," I said. "We're going backwards."

Nadine came forward, suddenly confused. "What do you mean?"

"Couldn't you have found a place west of here?" My jaw tightened. "We're losing time three times over."

Stunned, Nadine covered her mouth. "Are you serious right now? I found a hospital, the closest one. Maybe not the best for you, but you're not the one who's sick." She drew closer and lowered her voice. "And if we don't get there soon, it might not matter."

Surprised by this, I turned and looked at Stan. "Holy shit."

All at once, the blowing sand had disappeared. The westerly wind was still gusting, pushing the LeSharo all over the road, but suddenly there were clouds overhead, heavy, dark, and low. A minute later, the camper was assaulted by sheets of rain drops, heavy and huge, that hit so hard I thought they would shatter the windshield. The roof rumbled. The windshield wipers smeared rather than cleared. I had to slow down.

By the time we passed the sign for a hospital ahead, Stan was no longer responding to Nadine's voice. He'd stopped sweating, but his breaths came in erratic short bursts, and his lips were a dusky blue.

The signs for the Emergency Department were bleary in the

rain. I parked close to the ED entrance and blew the horn. A nurse came out of the doors and directed me into one of the ambulance bays. I rolled down the window and yelled, "We have an old guy in the back. He's not breathing right. Needs help right away."

Two ED personnel put an oxygen mask on Stan, then transferred him inside where he was seen immediately by a doctor. An EKG was taken, intravenous fluids started, and blood work ordered. Stan was in no shape to answer questions, so Nadine and I answered for him. Barely responsive at first, Stan rallied for a short time, long enough to hear the report from the doctor, a middle-aged, slender redhead with a full beard. Nadine and I were going to leave the room, but Stan asked us to stay. The doctor said, "We're in a tough spot." He mentioned congestive heart failure and heart attack. Stan's lungs were full of fluid and his kidneys were giving out.

"Okay, Doc," Stan said through the oxygen mask. "Am I gonna make it?"

"You're making it now. Hang tough," the doctor replied.

"Okay." Stan closed his eyes and said, "Guess I was wrong."

Nadine took his hand. "About what?"

"Time. Thought... I had time." He stopped to take some air. "Turns out, the one thing I don't have." He coughed. "And I can't buy more."

She squeezed his hand. "Don't you be talkin' like that."

He squeezed her back, weakly. "Nadine, even through a sandstorm, you look like an angel." He coughed again, wet and deep. "That woman in California gonna be mighty put out if I don't show."

The remains of the sandstorm were etched into the creases of Stan's face. There'd been no time to wash them away, so now they stood out against his bloodless skin like the stripes on a zebra. I said, "Stan, what I said about the tires and... I wasn't mad at you. I shouldn't—"

Stanley's face went slack. His eyes rolled back. The blood pressure numbers on the monitor turned red. The pulse flashed 117, then 145.

"He's going out," the nurse said. "Call a code."

The doctor rushed in and told us to leave.

We left Stan's room, fighting a stream of nurses and technicians going the opposite direction. Someone showed us to the waiting room. On the overhead, the announcement repeated: "Code 4, Emergency Department, Room 2..."

We sat down in the molded plastic chairs. I looked at the clock. We'd been at the hospital half an hour. It was almost suppertime. Ten minutes after Stan closed his eyes, Nadine and I went up to the desk and asked about him. The secretary couldn't give us any information and said that the doctor would come out when he was free. She noticed Nadine's bloody fingers and offered band aids for them.

Nadine reached for the bandages and the woman saw the fingers more closely. "How on Earth did you get so chewed up? They must hurt like hell."

"Digging in the gravel for Stanley's heart pills. He spilled them."

The woman looked up at me and asked, "How 'bout you?"

Embarrassed by the pristine condition of my hands, I put them in my pockets. "I'm fine."

Nadine said thank you and we sat down again.

I felt sick. "He's not going to make it."

"Don't say that." She scowled at me. "How do you know, Dr. Cherhasky?"

"Even if he does, he'll be here for days, weeks." I leaned forward, elbows on knees. "We can't do that."

She looked at the door leading to the Emergency Department. "We have to. We're all he's got."

"What are you talking about? We're not his family. We're not responsible. We gave them Kitty's number. She'll come down."

"With the cats?" She crossed her arms. "So that's it? You're going to walk out of this hospital while they're in there pushing on Stan's chest? La La Land will still be there if we're a few days late."

I cradled my face with my fingertips. "You still don't get it. We're looking for a place to hide, you and me. We can melt into the asphalt in California. Here in New Mexico, once this storm clears, we'll stand out like horns on a hog. The feds are after us.

Someone wants us dead. If we sit still, they'll have our ass. You wanna risk that?" I stood up and pulled the keys out of my pocket. "We can't do anything for Stan. They'll take good care of him. We gotta go."

There was a long silence. "You coming or not?"

Her face flushed a shade of red that would have matched her hair back in Moreau.

CHAPTER THIRTY-TWO

Nate

The Saturday afternoon flight from Missouri ended up giving me a good ass whoopin'. By the time I made Dalhart, Texas, I was battling a nasty crosswind and diminishing visibility due to blowing sand. I'd never run into anything like it and hope never to see it again. The landing was harrowing, my hands white-knuckled on the yoke. As I taxied up to a spot next to the hangar, I had visions of my Cessna doing cartwheels down the tarmac. Two men ran out from the diner, opened the hangar door, and fired up a large ATV. They towed my Cessna inside to join six other planes, safe from the sandstorm. When the door finally closed and the howling wind a little less obtrusive, Roger and Patrick introduced themselves. I thanked them for their help. Patrick grabbed a box off a stack behind a counter and said, "You'll need one of these."

It was an air filter, and he was right. Until that moment, I hadn't thought what a flight spent in swirling, driven sand would do to my engine. I removed the filter on my plane and got the shock of my aviation career—the element looked as caked and calcified as an old barnacle. Another five minutes in the air may have been my last. My stomach went sour. There'd be no more flying until the sandstorm passed.

For a place so isolated, the terminal was a pleasant surprise. I found out it was a frequently used stop-over for pilots flying cross-country. The grill and coffee shop were comfortable; a good thing, as I was not the only stranded pilot. The décor was cowboy spats and lassos hanging on the walls—typical Texas, but unlike a lot of places I'd been in, not too pushy about it. I liked the boot spur handles on the beer mugs, even though mine contained a root beer float. I took a seat, looked briefly at a menu, then out the tall, panoramic dining room windows. I struck up a conversation with two fellow pilots who told me blowing sand and high wind went hand in hand around Northern Texas on a fairly regular basis, especially in spring.

The diner had Wi-Fi so I got on my laptop. Some good news from Lance would have put a better spin on the day, but no dice. After the hit on Stanley's credit card in the Oklahoma Panhandle, the trail had gone cold. So, there I sat, within one – or two-hours' flight of virtually anywhere in Eastern New Mexico, but nowhere to go. I was grounded. The weatherman on the overhead flat screen said the storm would change to thundershowers that would last through the night and well into Sunday. I tried studying aeronautical charts of New Mexico, but without a specific target, it was hard to keep my concentration.

My cell phone rang. It was Brooke checking up on me. I said I was just about to call her, which always came out sounding lame. The girls were at a friend's house and doing well. Their ride back to Appleton had been uneventful until Mila let slip that her sister had a boyfriend.

"When was she going to tell us?" I asked. "Claire's too young. Who is he? When I get home, I'll have—"

"Nate, slow down," Brooke said. "She's fine. The boy, we know him, he's a good kid. We'll talk when you get home."

I paused for a moment, then said, "Boyfriend. She's thirteen. How old is he?"

"He's a grade ahead. Aaron Harrison."

I had a vague recollection of the boy and the name, but that was all. "Okay, you'll keep an eye on her, I know."

"You're such a worry wart."

"And Mila, she's good?"

"She's good. How's the hunt for the wandering witness going?"

I told her I needed a couple of breaks, and if I didn't get them soon, my switching-to-the-plane gambit was going to look like a bad decision. She told me the breaks would come, the weather would clear, and she had confidence in my instincts, which was more than I could say for myself.

Dalhart had a limousine service that transported pilots and passengers stranded at the airport into town then back again when weather permitted. I paid the fee for overnight on the hangar space and caught the Saturday night special, along with four couples, into Dalhart. The town was shut down, much like the effect a blizzard had in Wisconsin. The nine of us checked into the same hotel. I got a bite to eat at the attached restaurant, then went to bed.

Sunday morning. Day six. The wind was relentless. The morning weather report showed a line of thunderstorms covering large portions of New Mexico, Oklahoma, and Texas. I thought of Max, Nadine, and Stan and wondered how they were doing in this mess. Over the last several days, I'd gotten to know my-man Max, and my guess was he'd have pushed on. Picturing the old Winnebago sputtering through the high desert, I remembered the air filter from my plane and shivered. A thirty-year-old camper could easily breakdown in weather like this. If it happened in the middle of nowhere, it would be a catastrophe. Max and Nadine might survive. I wasn't so sure about Stan; his age alone had me worried. And Kopec would love nothing better than a stationary target.

Breakfast was gratis at the hotel. I hadn't done anything to work up an appetite, and when I'm on edge, the last thing I wanted was a heavy meal putting an anchor in my belly. The morning weather report left little room for optimism, but what difference did it make? There was no point in flying without a destination. But it had to be slowing Max and Nadine too; in the end the storm was worse for them than it was for me.

I spent the rest of the morning arranging a taxi ride to a couple of AA meetings, one right after breakfast, the other in the afternoon. Unfortunately, the forecast told me I could schedule both without fear of losing flight time. I worked out in the hotel exercise room twice, showered twice, and I was still stir-crazy. Finally, the weather lost a little of its intensity. I took the shuttle back to the airport and ate supper at the diner. Lance wouldn't be at the office, so I didn't call him. I knew he'd let me know if anything came up.

About an hour later my phone rang. It wasn't Lance; he had a ringtone all his own. The girls and Brooke did too. The name on the phone was still familiar.

"Hello, Blain," I said. "How are things in Iowa City? You pulling an evening shift?"

"Filling in for a friend. Pretty quiet, but then it's Sunday, and my shift just started. And you?"

"Waiting out a thunderstorm, Texas panhandle." I groaned. "Started out as a sandstorm. Christ on crutches, you ever been in one of those?"

"Hell no, and don't ever plan to."

There was a voice in the background. "Captain Baker, call on line two."

"Tell them to hold, will you, Chuck? I'm on the phone." Blain came back. "Sorry. Anyway, the point of my call. I was just talking with the medical examiner for Guadalupe County in New Mexico. Bad news. Stanley Dettmann is dead. Cardiac arrest in the Santa Rosa hospital."

"The former owner of the camper," I said. "The guy traveling with my people."

"One and the same. He was brought to the hospital by two young adults—"

"Max and Nadine."

"Probably. He was in rough shape already when he got there. They hung around long enough to check him in, then they split. Sheriff patrolled the area, but by the time they knew to look, they were gone. They gave Kitty as next of kin, and when they called her number, well…"

"When she didn't answer they called you."

"Right. Thought you'd want to know. I'm sending another

team over to the house for one more look around."

"Thanks, keep me posted."

Though I'd never met Stanley Dettmann, I felt responsible for his death. If the pick-up in Moreau had gone as planned, Max and Nadine would never have gotten to Iowa City, and Stan and Kitty would still be alive. Had the Dettmanns been alone in the world? The background information on both of them was thin; there'd been no mention of children.

This case was getting more unpredictable. I was hundreds of miles away from the subjects of my assignment and grounded by my decisions. Even before the sandstorm, I'd been little more than a formless shadow in Max's rearview and hadn't changed the trajectory in Max and Nadine's lives at all, not since the raid on their house on Red Wolf Lake anyway. The similarities between this case and the Cordell kidnapping were scant indeed; nevertheless, I was hounded by an unshakable sense of deja vu. It was beyond the realm of logic, so naturally that's exactly how I tried to explain it. The Cherhaskys and the Cordells had very little in common. The Cherhaskys were wealthy once, the Cordells still were. Troy was the President and CEO of Cordell Oil and Gas, and had all the trappings that went along with that office. His wife Adriana was lovely, not as young or stunning as Nadine but smart and well spoken. The two had been married for twenty years when I last met with them at their vacation home in Egg Harbor, Wisconsin. Already, their only child, seventeen-year-old Charlotte, had been kidnapped, snatched off the street by her captors as she left an exclusive high school in the Milwaukee area. The ransom wasn't financial, not exactly. The "only thing" that would bring their daughter back was the relocation of a pipeline that had been built across the northern edge of the largest marsh and waterfowl preserve in the state. Cordell had already been successful in fighting off numerous legal challenges to the continued use of the pipeline. Unwilling to accept the dictates of the court, eco-terrorists had kidnapped the girl and pledged to hold her until Troy Cordell publicly agreed to move the pipeline. I looked at this set of circumstances from several different angles.

Outside of the single-child household and the obvious trappings of wealth, I couldn't see a parallel between the cases or the families.

By eight p.m. the skies had cleared, and the winds had calmed enough for me to take off. Santa Rosa had a little-used air strip outside of town, but there were no landing lights. Visibility was excellent. I could fly there in a few hours, but I'd have nowhere to land. I hit the table with the side of my fist and rattled the cup and saucer. The rest of the coffee shop startled.

"Sorry," I said, and held up a hand.

Hopefully, I would need my plane's nine-hundred-mile range in the morning. I went out and filled the tank with fuel and wiped down the dash and upholstery. Most of the interior surfaces had a fine layer of sand that had found its way into the hangar. If I went back to the hotel, I might lose time in the morning. Resigned to another restless night, I climbed into the pilot's seat.

CHAPTER THIRTY-THREE

Max

I turned left out of the hospital lot, heading south out of town. My eyes darting from one mirror to the other, I watched for a nurse, a doctor, or a security guard rushing out of the sliding door, calling us back. What would the hospital do when they discovered we had bolted? They might call the police, but for what? So far as they knew, we were good Samaritans. And without a license number or vehicle identification, there'd be very little to go on. *What about outside security cameras?* I thought. I'd never checked for them. Does every hospital monitor their parking lot? *Of course, they do.* "Damn," I grunted. Nadine started but didn't look at me. Then I thought, *what good are cameras in a thunderstorm?*

"Where are you going?" Nadine asked. "We need food."

"Get the hell out of Dodge. Food can wait."

She tipped her head back and laughed. "You're going to hide this big, old camper out in the middle of a wide-open desert with no other traffic?" She lowered her chin. "Yeah, that'll work. You'd be better off hiding in traffic."

I stared straight ahead and said nothing.

"If one person in that hospital saw us leave," she said, "we're toast. And do you really think it's smart to go back into the middle of nowhere, night coming, no food and two bottles of water?"

I slammed on the brakes and stopped in the middle of the road, a bitter taste in my mouth. "All right, we go back." I turned the camper around and headed back to town. As we passed the hospital, Nadine rubber-necked a long look. I said,

"I never got to tell him I was sorry."

"Who? Stan? About what? Leaving him there?"

"No." I pinched my eyebrows together. "About the wheel. Yelling about the damn bolts. I wouldn't have done it if I'd known."

We passed the County Sheriff Department without incident, found Main Street and a grocery store. Nadine was starving. We passed several restaurants; she made the case for stopping. I pulled into the FireSky Grocery parking instead, pulled a fifty-dollar bill from the envelope, and handed it to her. "Don't be too long. I'll wait." She snatched the money from my hand and slammed the door. Sitting quietly gave me a chance to settle down and process the guilt Nadine had laid on me. The rain lightened. I thought we might even see the sun once more before night came.

Ten minutes later, Nadine exited the store with a shopping cart full of food and a flat of bottled water. I helped her load it into the camper. I sucked down a bottle of water, then took another with me to the driver's seat. We headed toward the highway. When I turned onto Highway 54, I noticed, two blocks behind, a sheriff's cruiser making the same turn. My earlier confidence was rattled.

"Shit. I knew it," I said. "Cop, block or two back, and me with a goddamn gun in the back. I don't have a license for that thing. If he stops us and searches the cabin, I'm screwed."

I scanned ahead and saw a sign for an RV park on the right. I looked to the heavens and whispered, "Thank you." It was near sundown and no one was manning the front office. I backed the camper into the second empty spot. Shutdown was quick. We waited. The cruiser entered and patrolled the park. I motioned Nadine out of the front seat to the back table. I turned on the light over the stove and sat down next to her. The cruiser crawled by but did not stop.

I let out a sigh, propped my elbows on the table, and put my head in hands.

Chewing a piece of gum she'd gotten from the store, Nadine checked the bandages on her fingers. "None of this would be a problem if we'd stayed with Stan."

I didn't look up. "We wait, twenty, thirty minutes. Then I'll take a short walk, look around. If it's clear, we leave."

Nadine opened a magazine and slapped it open on her knee. I checked the Internet for any news about my father's case, but found nothing. When time was up, I grabbed the lock box that contained the gun, left the camper, and found a dumpster. The hard, plastic case made a sickening *thud* when it hit bottom. A quick walk to check for the cop turned up nothing. I climbed back in the LeSharo, started the engine, and drove away. A fine layer of sand had somehow found its way inside the camper and covered everything from carpet to coffee cups. Nothing was clean. I didn't know if I could sleep on dirty sheets. Highway 54 was a secondary road and fit our needs perfectly: light traffic, two-lane highway more often used by locals than tourists. But in the middle of New Mexico's high desert, hotels were as rare as dairy farms, and there was no Internet to do a search.

Nadine moved to the passenger's seat. "There was a place half an hour ago."

"I'm not going backward, not again."

"God forbid." She snapped her gum. "We *should* go backward, all the way to the hospital." Her voice wavered. "What if he made it? He's wondering where we are. Where his 'friends' are."

"He didn't make it." I squirmed in my seat. "You saw him. He was good as gone when we left. Sorry, but it's the truth."

"Thank you again, Dr. Cherhasky. Where'd you get your diploma, Walmart?"

"Up yours." I was distracted and suddenly confronted by a confusing set of road signs. There was still sand on the road, making lane markers difficult to see and the pavement slippery. Impulsively, I took a left.

"Up yours, too," answered Nadine. "Why did I ever leave Moreau with you? I must have been crazy. No. I am crazy." She got up from her seat, went to the back of the camper, and sat down.

Over the next thirty miles, the road varied from solid asphalt to pothole hell. I wondered what could have happened to the highway that would cause this kind of damage? The road got narrower. There were no signs, no houses, no traffic. For the first time, I was lost.

I had to slow down or risk damaging the suspension which, if it was anything like the right rear wheel, was half iron, half rust. Breaking down out here after sundown would be a disaster, and possibly deadly.

An hour later, the camper creeping slowly along, I finally thought to check the compass. I slammed my fist on the dash. Nadine startled out of sleep. "What?"

"East. We're heading east. The last turn was wrong. Damn it." How had I missed the compass reading for so long? The headlights caught a reflection a quarter mile ahead. I stopped the vehicle and checked the signs. "New Mexico 285. No way!" I opened the map. "Oh, screw me to the wall, we've been on a county backroad." Too exhausted to go on, the map collapsed and then so did I—into the second-row seat. A Sunday from hell: a confrontation with a viper. A sandstorm. A flat tire and rusty bolts. A heart attack. *A death, for shit sake.* The day filled with nothing but suck. My head ached. My legs ached. I needed to close my eyes. I wanted a bed. "That's it. I can't do another minute. We're stopping here." I broke down the seats into the forward bed and left Nadine to her own devices.

The next morning, I stepped outside to get some air and noticed for the first time how grimy the LeSharo was. A veil of fine sand streaked by rain made it look like a reptile. If the air filter looked the same, or if any sand had found its way into the engine, well, what was the point of worry? We were hell and gone from a garage. The mechanic I'd hired for the trip was probably dead. And even if I found a shop in the middle of New Mexico, the chances of finding parts for a vintage 1980 LeSharo were less than zero. So, I'd *run with what I got till it don't got no more.*

I stepped inside and rocked Nadine by the hip to wake her. "Daylights burning. Let's go." I told her of my plan to drive to

Roswell, catch the highway there, and go west. "Make up for lost time. Gonna be a better day."

"Can't get no worse," Nadine said. "And helping Stan is not lost time."

Nadine sat in the passenger seat. No coffee, no make-up, and a bad night's sleep did not a happy woman make, and not one I wanted to mess with. The highway was straight and well paved. Still, she fidgeted. "I don't understand you," she said.

"Please, Nadine. It's too early." A poor attempt at staunching the heat coming off of her. And it was there, I could feel it, see it, hear it in her verbal tics, a click of the tongue. And her hair! "Will you stop that." I said. "Tugging on your hair won't make it grow faster."

"Save your breath. I'm not listening." Seconds later—a puff of air from her nose. And through it all, her constantly restless legs. I waited for the next barrage.

A mile later I saw a way out. Roswell was not far. "We need gas," I said, even though the gauge said half. I had to get away from her, even if it was only for a few minutes.

I pulled into a station. Roswell was fully awake, what passed for morning drive time was about at its end. The sky was high, not a single cloud, the day quickly warming. Nadine grabbed her phone, tapped the screen, and put it to her ear. I tended the pump and washed the windows. I asked who she'd been talking to.

"No one." Eyes flushed pink, she put her phone in her purse. "Max, we have to go back to Santa Rosa today... now. If we find out Stan is dead, fine, we move on. It'll take a day, maybe less, but we have to do it."

She was backlit by the morning sun. I squinted. "We've talked about this. Think of the time. Think of the gas. We're already over budget. No. Get over it."

She reached into the front seat, grabbed my backpack, and threw it on the ground. "The money."

"What?"

"My money, from the bank. I want it, all of it."

I blinked. "What for?"

"I'm leaving. I mean, I'm staying… I don't know what I mean. But I'm not going with you."

"Now wait—"

She kicked my backpack. "The money. Now."

I pointed at the ground. "It's in there. The bank envelope." I took a step toward her.

"Stay back!" she cried, loud enough to draw attention from customers at the other pumps.

I put up my hands. "Fine. But you're making a mistake."

"Oh, you know about mistakes? Well, so do I." She found the envelope and shoved it in her backpack. "Not the least of which"—she pointed at me—"was marrying into the Cherhasky clan." She slammed the door. "Goodbye forever." She turned and walked away.

"Nadine, wait." But she didn't. She marched away from the station. Away from me. She did not turn around, she didn't break her gait, she didn't even turn her head.

CHAPTER THIRTY-FOUR

Nate

I was up with the sound of another plane, throttle full, rolling down the runway; I was still stuck in Dalhart. Nothing against Texas, but this was not what I had in mind when I got the Cessna. Thirty-six hours and more of nothing but waiting. It was driving me crazy, if not to drink. It was not that the people of Dalhart were not good hosts, they were. Let's face it, had they not pulled my plane into the hangar the night of my arrival, the sand may have grounded me right into next month. But it was time to get back to my appointed rounds.

There was no wait for take-off. I got off the ground and head-ed west into the blue skies and light winds of New Mexico. The flight to Santa Rosa took just over an hour. The airstrip looked deserted: no other planes, no personnel running the port, only a single building with restrooms and shelter. The windsock was near motionless and the visibility unlimited: ideal conditions. I taxied to the end of the runway; not bothering to arrange for land transportation into town. Max and Nadine were long gone, and it sounded as if they had left unobserved. Interviewing towns-people would be wasted time. I decided to stay where I was and wait for more information to direct my pursuit. It was Monday, so the Milwaukee office would be fully staffed, and Lance nicely rested from the weekend, ready to sift through whatever new intel was out there.

The next several hours went by more slowly than death by quicksand. When I couldn't wait any longer, I phoned Lance, if for no other reason than to talk to someone. He had only one thing to pass along. The Oklahoma State Police reported a stolen license plate on a camper from Colorado visiting the panhandle area. Whoever took the plate made a mistake, they replaced it with one assigned to Stanley Dettman, Iowa City, Iowa.

I shook my head and mumbled Max's name.

"What's that?" asked Lance.

"Nothing, nothing. What plate am I looking for?" Nate gave me the details, promised to call with any updates, and rang off.

Now that J.R. Cherhasky was back in Wisconsin and charges filed, I was hoping he would, for once in his life, do the right thing and plea the charges. If there was no trial, Nadine wouldn't have to testify, and the contract on her life would probably be cancelled. She couldn't be compelled to testify against her husband, of course, but the mob obviously wasn't willing to take that chance. My other thought, the greedy and more delusional of the two, was that a plea was the only way for J.R. to reconnect with his son.

So, there it was. I had lost a son through neglect and self-absorption. The same script was playing out before me, only this time it was J.R. Cherhasky walking down that road. While I didn't expect Max's end to be the same as Austin's, it could turn out just as painful. I'd have given anything to have one more chance with Austin. J. Roman still had a chance with Max, but he'd have to take the plea deal first.

Another hour of waiting. More doubts crept in. Where was Antoni Kopec? How close was he to Max and Nadine? Did they understand the danger? I knew the answer to none of these questions except the last, and it was no. I thought of Leah. She thought Max knew more about his mother's death than he was letting on. And the confidence she had in her synesthesia convinced me she was acting on more than a hunch.

I needed Sam and Nadine to make another mistake. And yet, it couldn't be the kind of error that would get them killed. Some mistakes could cut both ways. Kopec was tracking them along with me. But how would he find out about Stanley's death and Max and Nadine's last known location? The medical examiner had only made a couple of calls. One, to Blain Baker, the other to…

Suddenly, my chest caved. I dialed the number of the Iowa City P.D. and got the watch commander on the phone. "Get a detective over to Kitty Dettmann's house, right now." I told him what to look for. He said he'd call me back pronto when he had the answer. I rang off, swearing at myself. How had I not thought of it before?

I did a visual inspection of the Cessna. It was covered with streaks of sand, but otherwise holding up well. My phone rang. It was the detective sent to Kitty's home.

"Jack Quarles, Iowa City P.D. calling from the Dettmann house. I've got good news and bad news. Which do you want first?"

I dropped my head. "Give me the bad."

"You guessed right," Quarles said. "There's a message machine on Kitty's land line. About a dozen hang-ups, probably telemarketers. We found a bug—"

"Shit."

"I hear ya. Must be foreign. Nothing I've seen before."

"Kopec," I said.

"I'm having my guys disconnect it now. But whoever set it up probably knows what I'm about to tell you."

"Go on."

"Two calls last night from the hospital in Santa Rosa about Stanley Dettmann." I groaned. Quarles went on. "And then this, just this morning, someone named Nadine called from Roswell. Quite emotional. She rambled a bit, but it sounds like she had a fight with someone named Max. She apologized for leaving Stan behind in the hospital, said it was Max's fault. She wanted to go back and check on Stan, but Max wouldn't let her. Apparently, he's hell-bent on California, taking the highway west, she didn't say which one. Then the time ran out and she hung up."

Frantically, I scribbled the essentials of what Quarles said. "Goddamn it," I said under my breath.

"What's that?"

"I said good work, keep me up to date." I hung up and got in the plane. I was still the only one on the strip, so the skies were wide open. The Cessna lifted confidently upward. I turned south.

Roswell was less than an hour away, but that Polish bastard had an entire night's head start and was working with the same information I had. From the beginning, I imagined us traveling on parallel lines: our paths were headed in the same direction, but if I was clever, quicker, smarter I'd get to Max and Nadine before Kopec. Whether I was none of those things, or all three, it didn't matter. The bug in Kitty's phone cleared my head, and what I didn't want to admit before was now obvious—our paths were not parallel, they were merging ever closer. Now, my job was to make the confrontation happen on my terms, not his.

CHAPTER THIRTY-FIVE

Max

I hit the brakes, cursed, then checked all my mirrors. I'd been doing fifty-five miles-per-hour through a thirty-five zone, in a camper with stolen plates. I leaned back into the headrest and tried to relax. Twenty-four hours earlier we'd been a threesome; now I was alone. It wasn't my fault. Who could blame me for the health of a man I'd known less than a week? I got him to a hospital as soon as I could, and in the middle of a sandstorm. Then Nadine walked away and cut my cash position in half. So, yeah, I was a little distracted, but the cops wouldn't care if they pinched me for speeding.

As far as Nadine was concerned, it couldn't have ended any other way. Why had I ever thought otherwise, that was the mystery. Then I looked down at the backpack, remembered the money, and how I'd deceived her. I felt cheap. I needed some music, but the radio was nothing but static, the antenna laying in the sand hundreds of miles away. There was a cassette deck in the dash. But I'd never seen music on tape, much less owned one.

What was wrong with me? The highway was clear, the sky high and blue. I should've felt free now, unfettered, but I didn't. Instead, I noticed everything. The camper creaked and clicked in a hundred places. I worried it was the first sign of the next breakdown. My mind should have been clear, not muddled and directionless. Nadine had been a constant aggravation, but a distraction too. A half hour later, I had a sudden need to talk to Leah for just five minutes. She answered after the third ring. She was at the studio, I could tell by the music playing in the background.

"Hello, this is Leah."

I couldn't speak.

For a moment, there was a silence, then, "Max? Max, is that you?"

I opened my mouth and choked on an utterance.

"Max, come home—"

My eyes burned. I ended the call, wiped my nose on my shirt-sleeve, and drove on.

The wind was nothing like the day before. Still, a wisp of sand streaming across the road reminded me of the bum spare tacked on the back of the LeSharo. I was well into the morning when I saw a sign for Carrizozo. I'd stop there, have the spare changed, and the wheels checked.

Carrizozo was a small town built at a crossroads of two high-ways. On one of the four corners I found Temple Fuel and Tire. Given the lack of cars parked in front and two open bays, I was optimistic about a quick service call. I pulled off the road, parked under a canopy for the shade, and walked in the open front door to a small, unattended retail area. I called "hello" a couple times, but no one replied. I walked into the garage where I found two mechanics working on an exhaust system.

The shorter, heavier, greasier of the two walked from under the car. Wiping grime from his hands as he drew closer, the man looked tired already, and it wasn't yet lunchtime. We grunted our greetings. His dark blue shirt was dirty and fit him poorly, barely covering his melon-shaped belly. He tipped his chin up at me and said, "Yes?"

"Ah, hi, I'm Max Cherhasky." He was still too far away to shake my hand. "That's my camper outside. I need a new spare."

The man glanced out the bay door. "Okay."

I stepped forward. "How long will it take? I'm in a hurry. Going through the mountains."

"Montañas." His eyes were pools of indifference. "Today."

"Oh, great," I said enthusiastically, trying to inject some energy into the conversation, if not the establishment. The other mechanic had stopped working. I looked at my phone for the time. "Before lunch?"

His muddy brown eyes found mine. The name on his shirt said "Red" though I couldn't see why. There was no such color anywhere. "No. Finish this. Then eat. Then siesta. Then do tire."

The town was so small I had seen both city limits with a single glance. There wasn't another service station on the main road. It was Red or nothing. "Okay," I said. "Soon as you can. I'll leave it here in case you can do it sooner."

Red shrugged. I left my cell phone number with the key and requested a call when the work was done. Just down the street from the service station I saw a sign for a small café. There was little traffic and very few parked cars, so the somewhat dated and dinged green sedan sitting near the intersection caught my eye. Stranger still, the driver was in the car, head down, intent on something on his lap. A couple blocks later, when I'd arrived at the café, I took another look. The man was still in the car. Odd, I thought, on a day when the temperature was in the eighties.

The window air conditioner in the café was blowing like a Kansas twister but there was little cool air to show for it. Still, the seating was comfortable and the room airy. I could survive the next couple of hours here. I started off with a coffee, asking for a menu only when the waitress became impatient. Eating a meal wasn't in my plan, but she was hovering, so I ordered the simplest item on the menu. The soup arrived, too hot and rather tasteless. Hunched over the bowl, I added crackers to give the broth a little substance, and started to eat. The lunch hour passed and still no call. It was time to light a fire under Red.

On the walk back, the green sedan was gone. Why it bothered me, I didn't know, but nevertheless I was relieved.

When I arrived back at the service station my worst fears were realized. The bay doors were open, the office empty, the work area deserted. "Siesta time is over," I said to myself. There was no sign of Red and his lacky, so I started the job myself. The spare came off the back of the Winnebago, then I made a racket by dropping the tire iron. I rolled the dead spare into the shop, went back to the camper, and popped the hub caps off; each one clanged on the concrete. There was rust on all the bolts on all the wheels, some worse than others. Finally, Red emerged from a back room, his eyes barely open. He didn't look pleased.

I held up the wrench and smiled. "Thought I'd get a head start. Hope I didn't wake you." I became the most obnoxious helicopter customer possible, hovering over Red and his assistant, whose name I never learned. Quite a few of the bolts needed penetrating oil to crack them loose. All told, it was another hour and a half before I got out of town. As an afterthought, I asked them to check the air filter. It was a disaster, but they didn't have a replacement, so I had them clean the old one. The filter was caked so heavy with sand they had to knock off the first layer before compressed air could break through and finish the job. The element was far from ideal but so much better than what I'd drove in with. I'd dodged another bullet.

Driving west again felt like victory. I was more confident of the vehicle now; the open road was running straight and true—all-clear to the west coast. There was virtually no other traffic. All I'd seen were two trucks going east and a Buick that came from behind and blew past me in a blink. So quick, in fact, I hadn't time to spot him in my rearview mirror. I blamed that on the afternoon sun, which was right in my face and blinding even with sunglasses. The car quickly disappeared ahead of me.

I passed the time humming tunes, putting lyrics together in my head. I thought to record some of the melodies into my cell phone, but then remembered all I had was a burner, and a recording app was not included. An envelope from the glove box became my note pad. As the words came to me, I wrote them down, the shimmering asphalt sliding under the hood as if I were gliding. The words stopped when I became aware of my fingers, holding the pen with ease. Nothing at all like Nadine's bandaged fingertips, blood oozing underneath. Eventually, she'd heal, and she'd be able to say that when Stan needed her most, she did her damnest. I couldn't say the same. A sign marking the White Sands Missile Range, site of the first nuclear explosion, went by on the left. A bit later, a car had pulled off the road. As I approached, I could see a man standing on the far side. He looked fine, but what was he—

The steering wheel wrenched in my hands. Then I heard a *pop!* Or was it the other way around? The LeSharo veered hard over the centerline. I cried, "Damn it, Stan, not again." I dropped the pen and put both hands on the wheel. Then another *pop!* more screeching metal. *Two flats at the same time? Come on!* The camper shimmied, veered hard off the road, and thumped onto its side. Searing facial pain. My shoulder crunched. Then there was nothing.

CHAPTER THIRTY-SIX

Max

The sound of breaking glass startled me. Someone or something was pummeling the windshield from the outside. The windowpane shattered, shards of it on me and the dash. The LeSharo was on its side, engine off, and someone, a balding man kneeling on the ground, was trying to get me out of the cab.

"You okay?" he said.

I lifted my head, then tried to move my arms and hands. The scene wasn't registering. *What is this place?* I thought. *Why can't I move?* I tried to get upright by pulling on the steering wheel. I pushed feebly on the seat.

"Seat belt," said the voice. "Buckle. Push button."

I heard the words but didn't understand. Seat belt. Seat belt. There was a strap of some kind across my chest. Without conscious thought, my thumb fumbled about, pushed down, and released the latch.

A meaty hand with thick fingers reached through a hole in the windshield and yanked the belt off me. He grabbed a mittful of my shirt and, with a tremendous force, extracted me from the camper, my shoulders enlarging the gash in the glass as I passed. My left foot wedged between the seat and steering wheel. With barely a pause, the man took hold of one of my shoulders, twisted my torso, and jerked me out like a weed in a flower bed. I screamed in pain. The man paid me no mind. My shirt in tatters, shoulder aching, I was dragged a short distance and sat on the ground, my back propped against a car door.

Head lolling in the heat, I said, "Thirsty. Water?" I squinted through slits. The stocky frame trudged back to the Winnebago and entered through the windshield like a badger into a burrow. The wind burned my skin. My thirst grew, but I was relieved to have someone there to help. I might have gone hours without seeing another person.

"Where is passenger?" he yelled from inside the LeSharo.

Something broke inside the camper. A glass? A window? I flinched. Then there were more sounds of thrashing, no, trashing the interior. "What the hell," I whispered. The man opened the passenger-side door and climbed out of the cab. This was my Good Samaritan? There'd been no mention of help on the way. I thought of calling 911 myself.

He walked toward me, a feral look in his eye. "Where is she?" The accent was heavy, Eastern European.

I shaded my eyes. "Who?"

He grabbed my left hand. "Don't try screw me, skinny one. The girl, Nadine Cherhasky." He twisted my wrist and cargo-tied it to the door handle. "Now, you no run. Tell me where she is, I let you go. You no tell"—he fixed me with a bitter gaze—"I use police training...I learn good, from the worst." He growled and laughed in the same breath.

Everything about him was round and broad, even his pock-marked face. He didn't appear to have anything I could call a neck, and his eyes were empty and as cold as a polar vortex. This was the guy, this was the man Nadine had recognized. My stomach seized into my throat.

"Last chance. You tell?" I didn't know what he was talking about, and I told him so. He shrugged, pulled a set of keys from his pocket, and walked to the trunk. He must have had some trouble opening it, because he swore in a Russian-sounding language and pounded the lid two or three times.

I reached for my cell phone, and using my right thumb, dialed 911.

An operator answered, "What is your emergency?"

The trunk creaked open. The man scrummed about, looking for something. I hoarse-whispered through a thick throat, "Help me, Highway 3-8-0. I think he's going to kill me." I turned down the volume, silenced the ringer, and tucked the phone upside-down behind my shirt and under the belt.

The man slammed the trunk shut and returned with a hand axe. I slammed my spine against the car. My voice trembled. "An axe?" I tried to smile. "No trees out here."

The corner of the man's eye twitched, a glassy look of antic-ipation in his eyes. "Dat's true, about trees. But useful still." He spun the axe in his hand. "And please, call me Tony." He grabbed me by the shirt and pulled. "Stand."

"You've got it wrong, Tony." A choking fear rose in me. "I'm Max Cherhasky. Nadine Cherhasky, she's not here."

"This I know." He tapped the blunt end of the hatchet against my forehead. "Tony must know where she is. Then you go."

"But I don't know—" With a stunningly quick swing, Tony slapped my face with the back of his hand. I tasted blood.

"Please, no lies. Is very upsetting." Tony paced in front of me, then tapped the fender next to my right hand, pointing out several somewhat parallel hash-marks in the metal. "I not want to add another. Bad for trade-in, you know. He grasped my free hand, separated the small finger from the others, and asked, "You ready to lose finger… for her?"

So much flashed through my mind in the next seconds. I was right-handed, true. But a guitarist could do without a small finger on the right more easily than on the left. *What the hell am I think-ing!* This guy wouldn't stop at one finger, not unless I gave him what he wanted. And what then? He'd probably kill me anyway.

"Where am I going to hide her?" I screamed. "And I didn't kill her and bury her out here in the white sand."

Kopec ran his finger across the blade and shrugged. "I try, be reasonable." In one quick swing, the axe went up, and down.

A flash of pain ricocheted from my hand to my shoulder and back again. I screamed. Writhing back and forth, I tore against the plastic shackle. Neither hand moved. Tony's grip on my right hand was more like a vice than the half-inch cargo tie on my left. I squinted at the bloody fender and saw my severed finger lying inert on the trunk lid. Kopec wedged the hatchet handle across my throat and thrust his knee into my groin. I doubled up and retched. An airplane engine, I thought I heard an airplane. *Responding to my 911*, I thought. But it was so far off, and then the sound passed by and was gone.

"Where?" grunted Kopec. "Or another finger? You choose."

"I... don't... know."

With no sense of bitterness or resignation, Tony said, "Very well." He exposed my ring finger on the bloody fender.

"Please, no!" I pleaded.

He raised the axe.

I slammed my heel into the arch of his foot. Lips stretched across his teeth, his face was a rictus of pain. Hobbling backward, he went to one knee. The hatchet dropped to the ground. He massaged the foot. A minute later, he regained his weapon, then his feet, and limped toward me. The impassive look on his face was gone; he was now a snarling wolf. Without warning, he swung the blunt end of the hatchet into my left kneecap. For the second time in days, my leg felt like exploding. I cried out, the knee far more painful than the severed finger.

"Do again, I kill you." He snatched my right hand. "You raised price. Not just finger." He squeezed my hand like an anaconda. "Now I cut at wrist."

"No!" I gasped, "I'll tell you. She's in Carrizozo." He yanked at my hand again. The pain in my knee so severe I could barely speak. "No. I left her... there. We... fought."

Tony tightened his hold. "Carrizozo. No. I watch. Not see girl." He patted my cheek with the side of the hatchet. "You got guts, I give you that. But no brains, too bad. So, what you do California? Why go there?"

"Music." I looked down. "I sing. Play guitar."

Kopec pushed out his lower lip. "So now you play." He raised the axe over his head. "With one hand."

Chapter Thirty-Seven

Nate

In the pilot's seat, back where I belong. Even if it extended to no more than the modest dimensions of the cockpit, I was in control; and there was no better way to make up for lost time and lost ground than by flying.

My heading would take me just west of Roswell. All along, Max had shown a decided preference for minor, remote highways. It had served him well in the more populated states, but now, in wide-open New Mexico, he had driven himself into a corner. In spite of the manic events of the last twenty-four hours, I believed his near-psychotic desire to get to Los Angeles hadn't changed. If so, the only sensible option was state highway 380. I'd checked ahead for airstrips from Carrizozo to the Arizona state line, which was as far as I thought he could drive during daylight. In Socorro, he'd have to pick up Highway 60 again; given his vehicle and lack of experience in that part of the country, it was the only logical choice.

Flight time to Highway 380 was an hour. Max would be driving through Lincoln County first, then west of Carrizozo he'd enter the county of Socorro. I called the Sheriff's Department from each, starting with Lincoln, and asked to speak with the dispatcher. The request was clearly a curveball because the officer who took the call put me on hold, came back, and put me on hold again two more times. When he came back for a third stab at it, I stopped him.

"Hold on. What's your name, officer?"

"Ted Simmons, Sergeant."

"Great, Sergeant," I said. "Can I give you my contact information for the FBI office in Milwaukee, Wisconsin? It'll make it easier for you to check me out." I gave him Lance's name and a direct line. "I need your help. If the dispatch receives any unusual calls along 380, I'd appreciate an immediate heads-up. I'm tracking Max and Nadine Cherhasky—"

"Hold on." I could tell he was writing. "Go on."

I gave him a description of Max's vehicle, the plate number, and a warning about Antoni Kopec. "Polish National hired by the mob, driving an older, green Buick." I gave him physical descriptions of Max, Nadine, and Kopec, my phone number, and told him to call if I could be of further assistance.

The call to the next county west, Socorro, went more smoothly. They clearly had more experience with law enforcement from outside their jurisdiction. I gave them the same rundown on the case in a quarter of the time, then turned on my police scanner and monitored both counties from eight-hundred feet.

By mid-morning I was approaching my waypoint west of Roswell. There was nothing happening on the ground below, on the radio, or my phone. I turned ninety degrees and followed 380 westbound, dropping to five-hundred feet to get a better look at any vehicles I might spot. I slowed my air speed to one-hundred miles-per-hour and still made Interstate 25 by lunchtime, bypassing Capitan, Carrizozo, and Bingham as I went. Traffic on 380 had been light, pick-ups mostly, a few eighteen wheelers, and even fewer campers, none of which I could mistake for a forty-year-old Winnebago. Somehow, I'd missed him. He could have stopped in one of the towns, but a prolonged layover would have been so unlike him and so unlucky for me. Most likely I'd overrun him, but Max had surprised me before, so I decided to turn north up to Highway 60, in case he'd made better time than I expected. Except for a stunning view of South Baldy Mountain, the trip proved fruitless.

I broke out a couple of energy bars and an apple for a late lunch and doubled back to 380. I had just turned east toward Bingham when the scanner stopped on a 911 call from Socorro County. Details were sketchy, but the source sounded rural, the closest cruiser twenty minutes away. I stayed on the call and dialed Socorro dispatch. The tenor of the room had changed dramatically, I could tell by the background noise. Besides the voice I was talking to, I could hear an operator, speaking urgently but, from what I could tell, getting no response.

A patrolman took my call. "We have an open mic 911. We're playing it back. The guy's name is Matt, or Nat. Last name unintelligible —"

"Max! Max Cherhasky. Where is he?"

"We don't know. He left the phone open so we're trying to nail it down. We can hear muffled voices, yelling. Something's going down, but we don't—hold on…" The patrolman paused. "The call is coming from east county area north of the missile range. The caller dropped a clue, said 'white sand,' which probably means the White Sands Missile Range. That's all we got."

"Get out there. Get out there now or your caller is dead," I said. "Antoni Kopec will be there too, I'm sure of it. Professional assassin. Watch yourself."

"Yeah. We heard."

"Call me back with whatever you get. I'm flying east over 380 from I-25."

I throttled up to maximum. There was a tail wind, so my land speed was well over 160 miles-per-hour. I passed an eastbound semi and a pick-up like they were standing still. I was alone with the desert, the plane, and the highway. The scanner chatter was constant on the 911. The State Troopers were more than ten minutes out, rolling at high speed.

What do you call a nightmare that happens on the brightest of days? I was fully awake and thinking only of Max and Nadine. And still my mind was back in the richly appointed library of Troy Cordell's Door County mansion. The negotiations with the eco-terrorists had reached a critical stage. We had negotiated with the mother-son kidnapping duo for over a week. All I had to do was wrangle a concession from Troy on the placement of the marshland pipeline and we'd have his daughter back safe and sound. Tracking down the terrorists after that would be our concern, not his.

But somehow all the rapport I'd built with the head of Cordell Oil and Gas had vaporized. He refused to agree to any compromise whatsoever. "Negotiation is capitulation," he said over and over. Every argument, every plea for sanity that I threw at him, he deflected with the same reply. He would not soften his position, not even for Charlotte. "It sends the wrong message. I can't do it. What do I do the next time they have me over a barrel? Give them the keys to my company?" My ears burned. "And what message does it send to your daughter?" I asked. "She's going to figure it out someday and ask you why. Lots of luck when that happens, because you're going to need it." Troy paused and turned away. "She'll understand." The discussion was over. Charlotte's fate and mine had been decided.

Seven minutes later, I was over the scene—an upended camper on the south side of the road, another car parked nearby. I swallowed an acidic burp, slowed my plane, and circled south.

There was a large hole in the windshield of the camper. The car's trunk was open, a man with his head buried inside. Sitting on the ground, head down, legs splayed, was a young man with his left hand bound to the back-door handle. Whether this was Max and Kopec, I couldn't be sure. Was it a 911 call in progress? Absolutely. Except Nadine. Where was she? Dead inside the camper, maybe. I'd found online pictures of old Winnebagos, and this one fit the bill.

Then, a scene bloomed in my mind like a patch of thistles, the barbs threatening to stab me with the slightest move. I was back in northern Wisconsin. My partner, Caleb Lambert and I had knocked on doors, talked to farmers at milking time, and canvassed patrons at the local restaurant. Charlotte Cordell was being held in a dilapidated cabin far off the nearest road in the wilds of Marinette County. We called for back-up, and went to the backwoods hideout. Waiting at a safe distance, we never once considered the possibility that the son, Jeremy, might be out hunting. He approached the cabin from our back. Before I saw or heard anything unusual, Jeremy had put the sights of his .22 rifle on Caleb. The surprise was complete, but not beyond managing. Caleb and I were separated by fifteen feet, both of us with our sidearms ready. Caleb ordered him to drop the rifle.

Jeremy's face contracted, his eyes wide and wild. He was in his early twenties, thin, with long, dark hair, but that's not what I was seeing. Jeremy didn't look like Austin, but there was something in this kid's eye, a tilt in his hip that stopped me. I had the kidnapper dead-to-rights, my Glock trained on his chest. He was actively threatening my partner, but I couldn't pull the trigger. I repeated Caleb's order, told Jeremy to drop his weapon. Instead of complying, he called out "Mom!" and fired. Caleb's wrist exploded. The report from the rifle shook me from my trance. I returned fire and knocked down the shooter. Joan Robinson had appeared in a cabin window and saw her son collapse. She opened fire. I knew Charlotte was in the cabin, but I had to provide cover for my partner, who was bleeding profusely from his arm. I fired twice. The first round missed. The second found its mark and dropped her to the floor with a nasty shoulder wound.

I went down range half a mile, banked, and turned into the wind. Highway 380 stretched in front of me straight and flat. Distance would hide me for a while, but the roar of my engine would be a giveaway. I made my approach and turned the key. The prop went still, the engine silent. I focused on relaxing my grip, positioning my feet on the rudder control and brakes. The last time I'd done a deadstick landing, I was still in flight school. That was years ago.

CHAPTER THIRTY-EIGHT

Nate

My wheels touched. Even without the engine I had too much speed. I tapped the brakes. If I drew Kopec's attention away from Max too soon, I'd lose the element of surprise. I coasted as close to the wreckage as I dared. The man with an axe let out a burly cry of pain, and stumbled backwards. The face of Max Cherhasky was easy to spot. Facial hair, his profile wet with sweat, scalp almost as bald as Kopec. I pulled my sidearm, left the cockpit, and ran toward the camper. Max doubled over in pain. One of his legs appeared to be lame or in pain or both. The deadstick landing had done its job. Neither Max nor Kopec was aware of my presence.

Then Kopec had Max stretched somehow, his right hand lying like a leg of lamb on the already-bloodied fender. I propped my shoulder against the back end of the camper. The sun was in my face, the angles all wrong. Max stood between me and Kopec. No chance for a kill-shot, barely an opening to wing him. To change my position, I'd have to run around the back of the camper, wasting seconds, precious seconds. Declaring my presence could create a hostage situation. Kopec had an axe, a gun no doubt, and could use Max as a shield. I was struck with an overwhelming sense of emptiness. I was present, and I was not, a feeling that had haunted me so many times since the death of Austin. Time measured out in long seconds, pouring into a vessel of lost chances that could never be filled.

I blinked hard. My brain begged for a whiskey and water. I needed whiskey, just an ounce, to settle my hand, my mind, my soul. The desert heat played games with my vision. Steam hissed from the LeSharo's radiator, the pungent odor of anti-freeze singed my nose, its bittersweet taste coated my tongue. For lost moments, it was Austin standing next to the car. I wiped the sweat from my face. *Good God, don't do this. Don't leave me out of this fight.... He will not allow it,* I thought. *The Power Greater than I will—*

Kopec growled, then raised the axe over his head.

I blinked again, aimed, and fired.

The 9mm slug chinged off the axe handle and sent it flying. My second shot missed. Kopec howled, dropped his arm, and ducked behind Max. I rushed the Buick. Kopec drew his firearm, then ducked toward the open, passenger-side door.

"Max, down," I yelled. "Down."

I crouched low beside the left rear tire, my Glock poised at my shoulder. "FBI, Kopec. Sheriff on the way. Drop the gun."

The passenger door slammed. The engine started. With Max bound to the right-rear door, Kopec slammed on the accelerator. Sand kicked off the wheel into my face. I rolled, aimed, and put a slug in the driver's door and front tire. The car slowed but didn't stop. Max screamed, tried to hop, then collapsed. Dragging Max, Kopec steered toward the road. I had one shot. The bullet exploded the head rest on the driver's seat, but incredibly, missed the driver. Two more shots through the window stopped him. He lunged through the passenger's door, and scrambled to the front of the car. His arm was extended on the hood; he drew a bead on me. I could see little more than the crown of his head. I rolled, stumbled, and leaped toward the trunk.

Max was in a bad way. I crawled to his side. He could barely move, from blood loss and pain, and who knew what else. I shot the handle off the door. Max yelped, then collapsed onto the sand.

I sent a few rounds in Kopec's direction. Max and I sat in the shadows of the car, which meant Kopec had the sun behind him, a clear advantage. I hovered over Max's near-motionless body. The only thing between us and death was the trashed Buick, my Glock, and the ticking clock. Kopec had to make a move. He would know the Sheriff squads were minutes away, so he couldn't wait us out. In spite of my aviation glasses, the sun was blinding me at all angles.

I heard even less. He had to be in a near panic, but then so was I. Then I saw it—movement in the shadow, or rather the roofline shadow—it was no longer an unbroken, smooth line in the sand.

I crab-crawled toward the still-open passenger door, pointed my Glock at the roof of the sedan, and filled it with holes. The shadow moved no more.

CHAPTER THIRTY-NINE

Max

I opened my eyes to the smell of bleached sheets and maple syrup. A breakfast tray sat on the hospital table next to my bed. A bulky dressing had turned my right hand into a bulbous club that throbbed in time with my pulse. The head of the bed was elevated. My lips were chapped, my tongue like leather. While looking for something to drink, I caught movement in the corner of my eye. A man with a familiar face was in the chair next to me. "I know you. What's your name again?"

"Hi Max. I'm Nate Bauer. We met almost a year ago—"

"Yeah, I know. Saw you in the story about my father. Don't you ever go home?"

"Appleton is a long way from here, even for my Cessna," Nate said. "And I haven't finished my job." The ice water was out of reach. He stood. "Let me get that. How you feeling?"

"Like roadkill, 'cept I'm not dead, I guess." I pushed myself up with my left hand and took a long drink, then slipped my right leg off the bed. A long, stiff brace went from mid-thigh to mid-calf, immobilizing my left knee and weighing me down like an anchor. The Velcro straps were pulled so tight it might as well have been a cast. Word from the orthopedic surgeon had not yet come as to whether I would need surgery on my fractured kneecap. "Job not done? Kopec is dead. What else is there?"

"The biggest part, actually." Nate leaned forward. "You don't look too bad, all things considered. A little pale, but then again you lost some blood. Careful with that left shoulder, by the way.

It dislocated while Kopec was dragging you around. They fixed it in Emergency after they gave you some pain medication. It'll be swollen and sore for a while. Why don't you have breakfast. The nurse said she'd give you a hand." He chuckled at his own joke. "I'll be back in an hour, and we'll talk."

When Nate returned, I was in street clothes, a set of crutches propped on the wall. The surgeon had mostly good news. The kneecap was fractured but not bad enough to require an operation; only the brace for six weeks and close follow-up. I could leave today.

Nate agreed, good news indeed, but then added, "But let's face it, you're showing a lot of wear and tear, and you've been on the road for only a week. God knows what a month might do." He sat down and told me that Stanley was dead; never made it out of the Emergency Room in Santa Rosa. I dropped my head and said I was sorry to hear it, but I'd assumed as much. "What you probably don't know is that Kitty Dettmann was shot a couple days ago. We think Kopec did it. She was probably protecting your whereabouts."

I deflated like an old tire. I looked at the bandage on my hand. *And I was worried about a finger*, I thought. An awful, helpless feeling overwhelmed me; I had to sit down. After a moment of silence, Nate continued with the latest on my father's case and the charges against him: the incarceration in Wisconsin, an eye witness, a public defender.

"Not to interrupt," I said, "but you've obviously mistaken me for someone who gives a damn. Jeremiah Roman Cherhasky can rot in whatever hole they dig for him, and I won't lose a wink of sleep. In fact, if not for my temporarily fucked up circumstances, I'd be there with a shovel, helping them dig." Had J.R. told the prosecutors anything about the day of my mother's death? I wanted to ask Nate about the charges, and if they were able to hang the murder on J.R. or just the disposal of a corpse business. But I had to be careful. If I was too curious, it would sound suspicious.

"I get it." Nate stood, his gestures now more urgent. "I really do. But there is another life on the line and it's my job to make you see the danger…" He paused. "For her."

I sucked on my teeth. "Nadine."

"Nadine. She knows too much about the wrong people. Or the wrong people think she knows too much. And yes, we could put her back in Witness Protection. But you've made your position on that clear. Just between you and me, I don't see her living alone, in a new city, with no friends. She wouldn't make it. And your father's former business associates do not want her to testify at trial."

"That's what Kopec was all about? He was after Nadine?"

"Yes." Nate gazed out the window. "And Kopecs are a dime a dozen."

I frowned. "Then why are you talking to me? You should be looking for Nadine."

"That's what I've been doing for the last week. You just happened to be with her." He turned, scrutinizing me. "You look a little deflated. But if you turn me down and go your own way, or my plan doesn't work, that's exactly what I'll be doing—looking for her."

Then something hit me. "You mean, you're not going to relocate me?"

Nate said there was no interest in shackling me to another relocation effort. I was stunned. Leah had been right all along. I could've kept all ten fingers, Stan would still be alive, and Kitty too. And Leah, she wouldn't have had to see me as a self-absorbed idiot. The feds didn't race across eight states to catch me. It was Nadine they wanted; I was an afterthought.

Bauer went on to say the WPP does not, cannot keep anyone in the program against their wishes. It was America, after all. I shook my head in disgust. Kopec had put the whiff of death in my nostrils, and I couldn't shake the smell. Nadine could end up on a deserted highway with the likes of Kopec at her throat. I didn't want that on my conscience. "You said something about a plan."

The trail on Nadine had gone cold, she was off the grid. As of right now, Nate had no leads. Plucking her out of the middle of the New Mexico desert didn't seem likely, so the only logical approach was to avoid a trial altogether. To do that, J. R. Cherhasky would have to plea to the charges. The prosecutors had gone to him with a "deal" and a guaranteed sentence, but he wasn't playing ball. "Your father, I'm told, is a remarkably stubborn and self-centered man." I guffawed at that. Nate went on. "I still think we have a shot at this, but there are only two people who can talk to J. Roman and get him to change his mind. And one of them is lost somewhere in the high desert."

The realization dawned on me slowly. My shoulders drew back. "Oh no. Fuck no. Anything but that. I said I'd never see that bastard again, and I meant it." And seeing him under these circumstances would put me too close to the day he killed my mother. I didn't know where his head was at, but after a week in lock-up it had to be bad, possibly desperate. Just seeing my face could trigger him into saying something we would both regret. That was a scene I had to avoid. I felt my eyes moisten.

Nate watched me closely. "Max, if you don't talk to J.R., they'll keep coming for her. Now, if I get to her first, she *might* be okay." He eyed my hand, my leg. "I mean, look in the mirror. If not…"

"I just cannot fucking believe it." For the first time since news of my father's arrest, I put my face in my hands and wept. Wept for a person I barely remembered because I was so young when she was cruelly, suddenly torn from my life. Wept because I was trapped by the sonofabitch who had killed her all those years ago. Now he had the drop on me again.

Nate sat down and waited.

"All right. I'll try." I wiped my face with a handful of tissues. "But I got no transportation. The camper is totaled and it wasn't insured."

"No problem. Ever flown in a Cessna?"

———

The novelty of riding shotgun in Nathaniel Bauer's Cessna 172 wore off within an hour. My right hand and left knee throbbed in perfect time with a headache that began right after take-off.

I swallowed a pain pill and tried to put my mind on something positive, but it was no use. Over and over, the terror of being at the mercy of Kopec pushed all other thoughts aside.

The past three days were a blur, and reconstructing them became near impossible when the pain pill kicked in. I realized I didn't know what day it was. Nate told me it was Tuesday. Nadine and I had left Moreau a week ago. I closed my eyes and waited for the pills to catch up to the pain. I slept for long portions of the flight back to Wisconsin. During the first leg of the trip from Socorro to Topeka, Kansas, when Nate caught me awake, he'd quiz me about Nadine and where he might look for her if the meeting with J. Roman went south.

The late-afternoon sun reflected off Nate's wings as we set down to refuel. He taxied up to an area next to the guest hangar and shut down the engine.

I tried to straighten my spine. The sudden movement made me woozy. "Oh shit. I slept too long." I squinted out the windshield. "We're stopping?"

Nate told me yes, and asked how I was holding up.

I tried to move the fingers on my right hand, then my left leg with predictably bad results. Nate said we'd made good progress. "We're over halfway; over eight hundred miles behind us. Only about five hundred left for tomorrow." While I stretched, Nate took care of fueling the plane and filing a flight plan for the morning. A taxi took us to the closest hotel. I asked for a separate room because I thought I might be up and down, and I wanted my pilot to get a good night's sleep. We got a bite to eat and turned in early.

———

The next morning, I thought I'd beaten Nate out of bed. His room was dead quiet when I limped by his door on my way to the lobby for a cup of coffee. I drank half a cup, refilled, and was headed back to my room when Nate came through the front doors.

I paused. "Where the hell were you? Out for a walk?"

"Nothing that healthy," Nate said. "AA meeting. I cannot believe people can smoke and drink Coke at six-thirty in the morning."

"You're in AA?"

"Yeah, saved my life. Ready for some breakfast?"

We skipped the free breakfast at the hotel, and got a real meal at a restaurant across the street. I had slept pretty well and woke up with a decent appetite. Nate looked up from his breakfast burrito skillet. "This is going to be a big day. Have you thought about how you're going to do it? The talk with your father."

Without looking at him, I cut into my ham using just a fork. "Please stop calling him my father. Roman will do."

He poured cream in his coffee. "No problem."

"No." I stabbed the meat and put it in my mouth, then buttered my toast, a tough job done one-handed. Nate didn't ask again, so I said, "I've been ignoring it. Trying something new, no planning this time. I throw them out in the first ten seconds anyway. Damn OCD. Besides, I think better on my feet."

Nate said for more than eighteen years no one had known J. Roman better than me. If anyone was going to make him change his mind, I had the best shot. I knew where his buttons were.

"Born too pretty," I said. Bauer stopped eating for a moment and looked at me quizzically. "That's what Grandma said about him, Roman. She was crazy, too. Died when I was eleven or twelve. Some of the stories she told me were mean and nasty; used to scare the shit out of me."

Nate asked what made the stories so frightening, and why a grandmother would tell such stories in the first place, especially to her grandson?

"Her favorite topic was her son, but she would go hot and cold on him like, I don't know, an old bathroom sink. You know the kind with separate faucets—that was her. One minute he could do no wrong, Albert Einstein and Steve Jobs rolled into one. The next, born too pretty, never had to work for nothing, married a good-for-nothing woman—"

"Wait...what?" Nate asked. "She said that, about your mom?"

"Oh, yeah. She and Mom never got along. I was too young to remember much of it, but both Roman and Grandma used to say so. It must've caused big problems. And remember, it was already a mess after Grandpa screwed Roman on that business deal." I took a bite of the eggs. Nate took a drink of coffee, leaning into the story, waiting for the details. "Way back, Roman, right out of college, he had a little money so he bought three service stations from Grandpa. They were making money; looked like a good deal for both sides, except for one thing. There was a new highway in the works and once it opened, the old highway would be a backroad to nowhere. The stations wouldn't be worth the ground they were built on. Grandpa knew about this new road, Roman didn't. Grandpa got top dollar from his own son for a business that turned out to be the cream of the crap. Of course, the new road went in and the stations went belly-up."

Nate frowned. "You're not kidding."

I shook my head. "All straight-up Cherhasky family history. Roman never forgave Grandpa. He said it wasn't his fault if Roman didn't know about the new highway." I was waving my hand too much; it started aching so I set it on the table. "Then it got worse. Roman picked up the pieces and made some good business moves. That made Grandpa look smalltime."

"By doing what?"

"Making a lot of money, or making more than Grandpa did. That was too much for the old man. Grandma said Roman was better at everything than Grandpa. Made him jealous of his own son."

Nate sat back. "This kind of background is priceless. You have good instincts. Trust them. Remember, he doesn't know you're coming to see him. That's a big advantage." Nate put down his fork and knife. "Even so, you're going to have to be tough and smart, clever, and even cunning." He took a sip of coffee. "But he knows you, too. So it's not going to be easy."

CHAPTER FORTY

Max

By nine a.m. we were in the air, heading northeast to Milwaukee's Timmerman Airport. Wednesday's flight was shorter by far, and I was awake for most of it. We talked about Kopec, how he'd shot out my tires. The description of his brutality was brief. I'd forgotten some of it, and wanted to keep it that way. I must have blanked out after Nate shot the axe out of Kopec's hand. According to the doctor in the Emergency Department, I probably had a concussion. The whole left arm was sore, my wrist especially, but compared to the hand and the knee, it was nothing. Some of Nate's descriptions made me shiver. A deep sense of dread crawled up my throat when I thought of Kopec and what he would've done had Nate been even a couple minutes late.

"You left some very good friends in Moreau," Nate said. "I found that out."

I shrugged my right shoulder. "I had friends in Walnut Creek, too. Sam, Diane. I think you know them." Bauer said he did. I looked away. "The first time is the toughest. Leaving, I mean. But I didn't have anything to say about the first one, did I?"

"No, you didn't." He nodded. "I interviewed a very lovely woman in Moreau. She was mending a broken heart by ripping the soul out of the canvas in her studio." He looked sidelong at me. "I'll never understand how you left her behind."

"Can't even explain it to myself." I shifted in my seat, uncomfortable with the conversation. "Going through AA, that must be tough."

"Why do you say that?"

"J.R. knew this woman," I replied. "You probably know her too. Deborah Manticore, married Willard Manticore."

"Absolutely. Always felt sorry for her, stuck in that family."

I said, "She went through AA three times before it took."

"AA's not tough, alcoholism is. I've seen it rip up more lives, more families than I care to remember."

"Why did you go in Wichita? If I'm being nosy, just say so."

"Not at all. I'm a big supporter of AA, that's why I go, to help those at the meetings, and to remind myself of who I am. I have to keep working at it, just like everybody."

"They have the Twelve Steps, right? What's the toughest one?"

"That's easy. Number eight and nine." He checked the gauges on the dash. "Make a list of persons harmed, then make amends."

I nodded. "Yeah, the list, no problem. But the face to face—don't know if I could do it."

Nate watched me. "Why do you ask?"

"No in-flight entertainment," I said. "Too much time to think."

"And you're thinking maybe you've got some bridges to mend?"

"Yeah, if they haven't been taken out altogether. You know, then what?"

"You're stuck in my plane, so I'm going to give you some advice. Give those people a chance to be bigger than you think they are. It's a compliment, whether they accept it or not." He changed our bearing slightly. The wind shook the plane. "Accept what you can't control, that's another principle."

I looked down, doubtful. "Yeah, maybe."

"Don't wait till it's too late. That was my mistake."

"What do you mean?"

Nate leaned toward me a bit and raised a finger. "Not like your situation at all. My son, Austin, was drinking in high school, and what else—I don't know because I wasn't there. Working too much, drinking when I wasn't working. A high functioning alcoholic, that's what they call me. Well, you know what all that *high functioning* did? It isolated me, so when Austin got into trouble, he saw the old man boozing it up and said, *why not?* Austin died when he was seventeen. He and a couple of his friends were out getting high in a car. Austin was in the backseat, but when a car wraps itself around an oak tree, where you're sitting doesn't matter."

I looked away. "Oh my god. I'm sorry, I shouldn't have asked…"

"Not at all. It's a story I've told many times. If it helps someone else, then it's worth it. I joined AA and quit drinking right after his funeral. Too late for Austin. Hopefully not too late for my two daughters."

"So, what's this high functioning thing about?" I asked. "That means you can drink and no one can tell you're drunk? I knew a girl like that back in Wisconsin."

"No. More like I was drinking and doing my job at the same time. No one knew except Caleb, my partner." His fingernails dug into the yoke, but the plane remained steady.

Curiosity gets the better of me too often; I overstep and regret it afterwards. "Sorry."

He dismissed that with a brief wave. "No problem. It's a good question. Fact is, I thought I was different from all the other millions of addicts out there." He shook his head. "Arrogance, never ends well."

He was telling it straight, I could tell, right down to the last, miserable detail.

"Austin paid the price for my sins. Caleb, too."

"Your partner? What happened to him?"

He unloaded again—everything from the stake-out, which actually happened less than an hour's drive from where I grew up, to Caleb's crippled hand and his forced retirement from the agency. "My job suffered too. They knocked me down a few pegs, took me off field work for almost six months. I didn't complain. Just doing penance, and always will be." By that point, Nate's voice was so small and soft that I had to strain to hear him over the sound of the engine.

"Looks like you're back now," I said. "This thing with Nadine and me."

"Yeah, my first since the kidnapping. Was supposed to be an easy assignment. Turns out, there's nothing easy about it."

223

"I suppose that's on me," I said.

"Yes. You and Nadine and Kopec."

"Sorry."

"You don't owe me anything," he said. "But you owe, son. You owe."

The ride from Timmerman Airport to the jail took thirty minutes. Nate had arranged for a government car to be available on our arrival. He'd been in contact with the Asst. U.S. Attorney assigned to the Cherhasky murder case. Nate briefed me on what might be offered to Roman by way of a deal if he changed his mind and pleaded guilty.

We parked in a spot reserved for federal employees and took the elevator to the fourth floor. There was a man talking on a cell phone as we exited the doors. He was rather diminutive, slight of build in a three-piece suit, with glasses, a jarhead cut, and no facial hair. He ended the call and introduced himself as Roger Wendell from the D.A.'s office.

"Walk with me," Roger said. "I'll take you to the interview room. He doesn't know you're here." He punched a keypad and opened a door. "This way. You must be Max." He held out his hand; Nate shook, then I did too. "Nate has told me about you. Obviously, we have an interest in a plea here." He set his briefcase on a table and opened it. "You don't have to know the specifics, of course, that's our job. But you may want to have an idea of what's on the table." He pulled out a file and closed the briefcase. Nate and I came closer.

"This is the indictment," Roger said, hand on a packet of papers about a dozen pages thick. "The charges have to do with the unlawful disposal of a corpse and hiding a corpse. We think he killed her too, but we can't prove that, so we're seeking the maximum sentence without parole."

"Can you make it stick?" asked Nate.

"Probably, but there are extenuating circumstances. The

murder happened so long ago, some of the evidence has lost its luster. The eyewitness saw the disposal, not the actual shooting."

"So, you know she was shot?" I asked. That hadn't been in any news reports that I'd seen.

"That's right." Roger clasped his hands. "We would agree to parole in fifteen with good behavior. FYI Max, your father—"

"Don't call him that," I said. "I've disowned him."

"Okay. The prisoner will be shackled during the interview. I'll be on the other side of the one-way glass, right here. Do you want Agent Bauer in the room with you?"

I glanced at Roger, then Nate, and finally through the one-way glass at J. Roman, who was already in the interview room. I said, "No. I can handle him."

J. Roman was seated at the table in the chair away from the door. Bauer looked at me before opening the door and asked if I was ready? I nodded. "All right," Nate said. "I'll go in first. You stay back for a second." Bauer entered the room and shut the door. I listened to the conversation via the intercom. "Roman Cherhasky, we meet again. I'm Nathaniel—"

"I know who you are, Bauer." Roman tilted his head back. "Don't tell me you're the reason they dragged me all the way down here. I got nothing to say to the F.B. fucking I."

"Thought you might say that, so I bought someone else. He's got something to say to you. You got one shot at this, so make it count." Nate turned his head. "Okay, come on in."

Roger opened the door. Nate stepped back. I walked in. Roman's eyes widened. "Son, what are you—"

"You can…" My voice cracked. "Call me Max." He was man-acled at the wrists and ankles.

Roman's eyes darted away. "Max, oh. All right."

Nate motioned for me to sit down and said, "You two have some ground to cover. I'm a third wheel." He looked at me. "I'll be right outside the door."

"Can I get a water?" I was talking to Nate, but my eyes were on Roman. I pointed my chin at my father. "You look"—I cleared my throat—"like crap."

Roman's grin was snarky, the one he always used when he thought he had the upper hand. "Look in the mirror. What the hell happened to you? A car crash?"

I felt a blush. "Camper."

Nate set a plastic cup of water on the table and exited the room.

"Oh." He yawned. "You all right?"

"Never better." I sneered. "Hope I'm not boring you."

He shrugged. "Where'd it happen? That why you're here?"

"New Mexico." I took a sip.

"Don't bullshit a bullshitter," Roman huffed.

"So, don't believe me. I don't care." My bandaged hand rested on the table, my left in a fist on my lap.

"New Mexico." Suddenly, I had his attention. "You left Nadine in Moreau for chrissakes? Alone!"

"Of course not. She was with me for a while. I dropped her in Roswell a few days ago."

Roman's jaw went slack. "Jesus H. Christ. Who's watching the house? I've got..." He stopped himself. "Someone could break in."

I laughed derisively. "Oh shit! That's perfect. Not 'where's Nadine? Is she all right?' Not 'Did you break your leg?' Not 'What the hell were you doing in bum fuck, New Mexico?'" I laughed again, then stared at my father, who looked confused. "And the watch collection, the Piagets, the Rolex, et cetera, you were going to mention a second ago, not to worry. I took them. But why should you care? Can't wear them in the slammer."

Roman moved to raise his hands but was stopped by the shackles. "Hey, innocent until proven otherwise. We still live in America. Don't you forget it."

I lowered my brow. "That's how you're going to play it? No apology. No remorse for any of the pain. The lives you've ruined."

"Well, yeah, sure. The mob was a mistake. But you're going to be good. And I will be too. If you're worried about the charges, I've seen the evidence. They got squat."

"What they got or don't got is not the point. The point, dear ol' Dad, is who you killed."

Roman's expression sagged. "Son... I—you know we're being taped."

"Max! My name is Max." Already, I was off course. I was there to get him to plea, not to relive my mother's death.

Roman flinched, then found some iron in his jaw. "How dare you ask me that question? Don't forget who you are. And don't forget—"

"Are you out of your mind?" Panicked, I cut him off. "I've given up on forgetting." I took a breath and lowered my voice to a whisper. "You and I know there was another person in the room that day, someone who can finger you for the murder. And Nadine knows the guy who helped you dump the body. I'll bring her back and she'll testify. Then it's game over."

He stared at me for a long moment. "She won't."

"She will," I countered.

Roman pursed his lips. "You wouldn't."

"I will. You doubt it? Your old friends from Chicago are out there right now trying to kill her because, just like you, they're afraid of her. Imagine that, all you big, strong men, afraid of a little redhead don't weigh more than one-hundred fifteen pounds." I felt a little more confident, so I sat back. "But not a surprise. You've never cared about anyone except yourself."

Roman's face reddened. "Why should I? Me? Care about a woman who has barely looked at me for the past year. And now I find out, she left town the minute I was arrested!" He leaned forward. "Is she going to file for divorce?"

I licked my teeth. "Don't know. It's never come up."

"So, it's implied, that's what you're saying." Roman yanked on his handcuffs. "I knew it before you even walked in here. Probably got a lawyer writing up the papers right now. If you think I'm going to bat for an ex-wife who won't give me the time of day, you might as well go back to strumming that guitar, because just like before, no one's listening."

Roman looked at my hand. "I'll bet they did that." I said yes, a hit man nearly killed me. Roman said, "Yeah, well, imagine if I go to prison; it'll be hell on earth. I'd be toes-up before the laundry got done. Ever think of that?"

"For about two seconds. Then I remembered Mom."

Roman's face flushed. "You better watch it, boy. If my memory suddenly clears, you could be in some hot water."

If I reconciled with this jerk, my self-respect would be gone. In a way, that thought made the rest of the interview easier. "You're all bark and no bite. Go ahead, shoot yourself in the foot. Add murder to the charges." He blinked. After all this time, I wasn't about to give anything away.

The air in the room was stifling. Roman clenched his hands. "Why are you really here? Not like you, is it, to take Nadine's side. Chalk and cheese, that's you two. And let's face it, you never invest a nickel's worth of time unless there's a pay-off at the end."

"You taught me well." Roman's eyes were flat, like I was looking at a reptile. How had I not seen it before? Had he changed that much after less than two weeks of incarceration, or was it me? I saw the legacy of my grandfather in the deep lines on Roman's face. I said, "But here's the difference. When I walk out the door, I'm not looking back. Not making the same mistakes you did. You remember Sam Robel? He told me not to become another J. Roman. I almost did. Now I'm settling debts."

"Well, well, well." Roman smirked. "Just as I suspected. I have to look out for number one. No one else is, was, or will. So, cut to the chase. What's in it for me?"

"You've avoided a murder rap. They offered you a plea deal on a reduced charge. Take it. Nadine won't have to testify, the mob will cancel the contract on her, and they won't mess with you in prison. You get the satisfaction of knowing you saved her life. Think of it as payback for the life you took twelve years ago. You might even get some self-respect."

"And what about you?" he asked.

I knew what that meant; it was a threat.

I paused for a sip of water. I needed an answer that would stifle any idea that J.R. had about having the upper hand and, at the same time, not raise any suspicions from Nate or the D.A. "As long as you're behind bars, I'll be fine."

An acidic frustration burned in Roman's eyes. "And how much self-respect do you think I'll have once they get ahold of me in the big house? They're offering twenty years," said Roman. "Jesus Christ, I'll be an old man."

"Fifteen with good behavior. And 'will be old.' That's a laugh. That ship has sailed, man. But better old than dead."

Roman's face worked like dough on a baker's board. I thought he would cry. I didn't want to be there to see it, because I didn't want to feel sorry for him.

"If Nadine dies, the blood of two women will be on your hands," I said. "Can you live with that?" My fingernail scratched at the table. "Here's your chance at redemption, the only one you're going to get. Don't be a fool." I burped something sickish. "For once in your life, prove your mother wrong."

The veins in Roman's neck bulged. I'd hit the mark. I leaned forward and pressed my advantage. "Why did you do it?"

Roman turned his eyes away and shook his head. "I didn't." His voice was weak, wheezy. "I didn't."

My neck and face were on fire. I waved at the window, pushed my chair away, and got up.

The shackles tensed at his wrists. "Sit your ass down. We're not done here."

"You were done a long time ago. Take the plea deal before it's too late." I sneered, "Have a crappy life." Then I limped out the door.

Chapter Forty-One

Max

The flights back to Roswell, New Mexico, took two days, the same as before; but they seemed easier, so I thought I must be healing. Talking to my father hadn't produced the desired result—he would not take the deal. But that wasn't why I decided to join Nate on the search for Nadine. The fight we had in Roswell, the way we parted ways, was bothering me more since the interview with J.R. His callous disregard for everyone except himself was a brutal reminder about where I came from, and how easy it would be for me to go back to that ugly place. Nate's description of the menace still hunting her down rang true. And the money, her money, that I carried in my backpack weighed me down more and more every day. I had to give it back.

Nate decided to start at her last known location and pick up the scent from there. I couldn't get out of Milwaukee soon enough, and only a veto from Nate prevented us leaving immediately following the end of the interview. The day had been a long one, and Nate would not extend it by flying again. We stayed the night in Milwaukee and left Timmerman Field early the next day.

It was a cloudy day; not ideal flying weather but it wouldn't slow us down. After we settled in, Nate asked me about only one part of the interview. "What did Roman mean when he said you might get in hot water? What was that about?"

My toes curled. "I don't know. Maybe he thinks he can hang me for breaking and entering. From the night we raided the Manticore boathouse last year."

"Old news. We knew about that last summer."

"Yeah. I think the bars are messing him up." But I knew that wasn't it. Roman wasn't talking about last year. He was going back a lot further than that.

We arrived in Roswell on Saturday morning, rented a car, and proceeded to canvass the local hotels. Our picture of Nadine was dated, she was still a long-haired redhead, but it didn't seem to matter, all those interviewed were sure they'd not seen her. We moved on to restaurants, asking if she'd been either a customer or looking for a job. She didn't have a lot of money, and the last job she held before we left Moreau, one of the few jobs to match her skillset, was waitress. I tried to go on as many stops as I could, but the knee immobilizer and my bandaged hand was slowing us down, so sometimes I stayed in the car. There wasn't time to cover all of Roswell Saturday, so we got a hotel room and stayed the night.

Sunday morning, I purchased a cane. Even though I had to use it in the wrong hand, it was easier than using crutches. We covered the rest of Roswell in short order. It appeared Nadine had wasted no time getting out of town.

"What's your gut telling you?" Nate asked. He and I were sitting in the car, parked in the shade of a tree, air conditioner on. "You know her best. Is she hitchhiking home? Heading west?"

"My gut don't know jack." I gazed down one of the dusty streets. "This is not a big city. Someone should have seen her. And once you see her, you remember her." Nate raised his eyebrows, agreeing. "Was there a second hit man on our trail?" I rubbed my forehead. "Is that possible? Jesus Christ. And if this Kopec bastard snuck up on me..."

"Max, slow down a sec—"

"No really, I know her. She doesn't pay attention to... anything." A chill brewed in my chest. "Or hitching, she'd take the first ride, and god knows what kind of dirt bag might have—"

"Max, stop. This isn't helping. Take a breath. Stay focused. There's no reason to suspect another hit man. Not yet."

I exhaled. "It's only been what, four or five days? Go west. Go home. She's got just enough crazy to do either." I tapped my fingertips on the dashboard. "California, though, that was my dream, not hers. She never had an idea to go there until she heard me talking. From Roswell, I'm not sure she would know how to get there. Going home, sure, but which one? Moreau? Walnut Creek? I think she has enough sense to stay away from Wisconsin, but then again, when you put her feet to the fire…" I shrugged. "Based on what she was saying right before we split, I think her first move would be Santa Rosa."

"Why there, if Stanley's dead?"

"She didn't know that when we split. Neither did I until you told me." I bit on a fingernail. "I knew, but I didn't. And Nadine didn't want to believe it."

"All right. You have an appointment with your surgeon in Socorro tomorrow." Nate pulled away. "We'll fly there today. See the doc tomorrow morning, then fly to Santa Rosa right after."

The surgeon wouldn't budge on the knee immobilizer—I was married to it for another month. But he was okay with the cane, and the bulky wrap on my hand was replaced by a much smaller, easier to manage version.

Crosswinds made the flight into the unmanned airstrip at Santa Rosa a rough one. Then we had to wait for a taxi for a lift to the only car rental place in town. We started our rounds at the hospital where we got our first positive identification. The receptionist at the front desk recognized Nadine even before I mentioned her new haircut and color.

"Oh, it's got nothing to do with the hair." The woman looked in her early forties, dark skinned, and attractive. "It's those eyes. Can't hide those now, can you? Unless you're wearing sunglasses, and she wasn't."

Nate asked for more details: what was she was wearing? How long did she stay? Did she mention where she was going? The woman remembered nothing of importance except she asked about the cafés in town.

I said, "Our next stop."

Then he smiled at the woman. "Which are your favorites?" She mentioned three restaurants, which Nate wrote down.

While Nate drove, I did an internet search and looked at the menus. Two of them served ethnic food, one Tex-Mex, the other Chinese. The third had an American menu, "classic greasy spoon," I said. "She doesn't know an enchilada from egg drop soup. My guess, if she's going to work any of these joints, it'll be Harry's Café because she'll understand the menu. Take a left at the next light. Halfway down the block."

The first thing I noticed about Harry's Café was the veil of rust weeping down from an air conditioner propped in a high window on the side wall. The name of the restaurant was in bold blue letters, a foot high at waist level and punctuated by the rust. There were parking spots in front of the Harry's sign, all unoccupied. The building was long and narrow; the front had room for two double-hung windows flanking a single-pane front entrance. Nate helped me with the door.

A single table was occupied by an older couple and two men were sitting at the counter. Nate and I took two of the six empty stools. The waiter was tall and gangly and had his grey-streaked hair pulled into the shortest ponytail I'd ever seen. He wore an egg-and-coffee-stained apron as if he were a cook, but didn't appear to be working the grill. Nate asked him if the owner was available.

He wiped down the counter. "Depends who's asking."

Nate reached into his pocket and showed his credentials. "We're looking for someone. Wondering if she might have stopped here." He gave Coffee and Eggs (he never introduced himself and had no name tag) a quick look at Nadine's picture. His nose twitched. "I'll go get him."

Harry didn't need his hands to open the double-swing kitchen doors; his belly did it for him. His name was embroidered on his t-shirt and his apron too, the latter had a bacon-and-pancakes graphic he probably got online. He had a three-day growth on his face, a white towel tossed over his right shoulder, and a waddling gait. He took a look at us, squinted with one eye, and said,

"Who's the Fed?"

I shot my thumb at Nate. "That would be him."

"Okay, maybe we can clear this up so I can get back to work. I got a lunch rush to contend with."

I looked over my shoulder at the mostly empty tables and smirked.

"Absolutely." Nate grinned. "We're looking for this woman." He showed Harry the picture. "It's important we find her. We know she's been in Santa Rosa."

"This is a pretty out-of-the-way place." Harry dabbed a bit of sweat with a corner of the towel. "Pretty woman like this comes here, it's usually because she wants to be left alone."

"Maybe so," Nate said, "but she may not be aware of the situation. There are some very nasty people looking for her, people with lots of money who will pay to have her killed."

From halfway down the counter, Coffee and Eggs interjected, "I knew it. I told you, Boss."

"Shut up, Donald. Go out back and unload the frozen food like I told you."

I said, "We don't think she knows she's being hunted."

Harry's eyes widened, then he bowed his head. "Killed! I knew it was too good to last. Just hired her two days ago and already she's my best waitress."

Coffee and Eggs snorted as he walked by.

Harry gazed from under a unibrow. "They won't find her. Here? In this little, back-water town?"

"They found me on 380, north of White Sands." I held up my right hand. "This hand would be completely gone, and I'd be dead if it wasn't for Agent Bauer."

The corner of Harry's mouth hooked down. He shifted his girth and looked at the clock over the cash register. "Her shift starts in fifteen minutes. Want to look at a menu?"

"Why not," I said. Coffee and Eggs reappeared; we gave him our orders. Meat loaf dinner for Nate and fried chicken for me.

"Do you think she'll try to run when she sees us?" Nate asked.

I thought for a moment. "No. This town isn't going to wear well. Won't take long, she'll want a way out." I took another look around the café. "I wonder where she's living."

"Not with ol' Coffee and Eggs over there," Nate said. "I'll bet the farm on that."

I laughed.

Halfway through our meals, Nadine walked in a back door. We heard Harry's voice tell her about "visitors up front." She came through the doors, shoulders slouched, without a trace of surprise on her face. Ignoring me, she cast her gaze on Nate and said, "What took you so long?"

"Hello, Nadine," Nate said. "Good to see you again. Been worried."

Her hair was washed, still brunette, with a barrette holding it off one ear. There were no wait-staff uniforms at Harry's, Coffee and Eggs had made that clear. Nadine wore jeans, a blouse, and tennis shoes. "Yeah, well, I can take care of myself." She glanced at me. "Guess I have to." Then she saw my hand, the cane, and the straightened left leg. "What happened to you?"

"Remember the guy that shot at us in La Crosse?" Of course, she did. "He shot the camper out from under me in the middle of the desert. When he didn't find you in the Winnebago, he went nuclear."

She wiggled her fingers. "He did that?"

"I wouldn't tell him where you were."

She looked at my leg, extended sideways. "Is it broken?"

I shrugged. "Just the kneecap. Another month, good as new."

"He's lucky to be alive. We'll tell you all about it." Nate wiped his mouth, called for the check, but she made no move to come along. "Nadine, we have to go." He told her about the mob, the contract, and Kopec's failed attempts. "There'll be more like him, and they're coming. Maybe not right now, but tomorrow..."

CHAPTER FORTY-TWO

Max

The flightpath north-by-northeast from Santa Rosa into Colorado started out smooth and clear. The sight of high cirrus clouds sweeping in from the northwest an hour into the flight was a good sign. But soon after, we outran the good weather. The wind picked up and visibility dropped. After three hours of flying we approached Limon, Colorado, a town Nate knew from a previous visit. Flight conditions had deteriorated by then, so he put the Cessna down at the local airport. There was a decent hotel nearby, and a good AA chapter he could attend that evening. The director of the Chapter was a personal friend who met our plane at the airport and drove us to the hotel. He then whisked Nate away and left Nadine and me alone.

I was still living out of my backpack; I assumed as much for Nadine. We had passed a laundry on the first floor. I put all my clothes (save the stuff I was wearing) into dark or light bags, threw them over my shoulder, and went next door to Nadine's room.

I knocked and called her name. She snapped, "What do you want?"

"Ah, listen, I'm going to do some clothes… in the laundry. Wonder if you, I mean I could do some, if you have anything. You know, since I'm—"

"Just a minute," she said through the door. The chain dropped. Her arm appeared through a crack in the door, a bulging laundry bag in hand. "You know about whites and colors?"

She closed the door before I could answer. The mini-laundromat was down the hall. Neither one of us carried a lot of clothing, so I was able to combine our wash into two loads. I went back to a reading room where they had a "Leave-one, Take-one library," and found an old paperback to read.

The spin cycle finished; I transferred the clothes to a dryer. After that, I folded each piece best I could. On the flight up from Santa Rosa, Nadine had sat in the shotgun seat next to Nate. I was in the back. Nate and Nadine had an on-again, off-again conversation, but she hadn't shared a word with me. The exchange at the door made it clear she was still angry, and yet there I stood, folding her clothes, putting her bras and panties together in a neat pile. Taken together, I had no idea where our relationship was at.

I went back to the room and threw my clothes on the bed, then knocked on her door and said, "Laundry service."

She opened the door. The empty laundry bag sagged over my forearms. On top, I had carefully stacked her clean laundry, which I extended toward her like some kind of peace offering to a princess. Nadine nodded in a prim, neutral way. "Thank you." She took her clothes and was about to close the door.

"Uh, are you eating alone? I asked. "I mean, Nate said he wouldn't be back until later. They have a restaurant here."

She held the clothes close to her chest. "I don't think so."

"Oh." I looked down, crestfallen. "Okay, then." I limped away.

"Max, wait. Let me put these down." She stepped away, then came back. "You pay."

"Yeah, sure."

Even though the High Plains Café looked rather busy, we were seated immediately, albeit at the worst table in the place. I tried to make light of it by saying, "Table without a view."

"Good times," was her reply, obviously tinged with sarcasm.

The waiter bought the menus and took drink orders. I remarked on the limited selections. She shrugged. "I like that."

I asked why.

"The places that keep it simple do it best. The longer the menu, the crappier the food. Where would you rather buy your guitar, Walmart or a guitar store?"

"Good point."

The waiter returned and took the orders, then the menus, and left.

I had a lot to say to her, but I couldn't look her in the eye, so I rearranged my silverware. "I know what you must think of me, and I don't blame you. But I'm glad we found you, and… I'm glad you're okay."

She took a drink of her wine. "Max, it's never going to be the same—"

I held up my good hand. "I know. I know. Let me finish. Please, or I'll screw it up."

She put down her glass.

My throat tightened. "You were right about Stan. We should have stayed there until we knew… what was going to happen." I pulled my bandaged hand off the table and put it on my lap. "Did you hear about Kitty?"

"Hear what about Kitty? No!" Her eyes flared. "Tell me. Is she all right? What happened?"

The candle's flickering flame suddenly dimmed. There was no good way to break this kind of news, no words to soften an assassination. "She was shot, last week, by Kopec. The guy that was after us." I held up my bandaged hand. "The guy who did this. They figure Kitty wouldn't give him the information he wanted, so—"

"He shot her. Oh my god. That sonofabitch." She looked away. "She was already dead when Stan went in the hospital? He was more alone than I thought."

"Yeah. Then, in Roswell, I don't know what I was thinking. I left you…" I reached into my back pocket, removed an envelope, and put it on the table. "I know this doesn't make it right, but I'm sorry."

"What's this?"

"The money. I took it from your backpack." I stared at the envelope, still not wanting to meet her eyes. "It's all there, as close as I could count."

She took the envelope. "What? You stole from me? When?"

"Before you walked away. I don't remember. Buffalo maybe."

She opened the flap, took a glance inside, and said, "It's not that easy, Max." She grabbed the bundle of bills and threw them at me; the money splayed to the floor.

A passing waiter stopped in mid-stride and asked, "Is there a problem?"

"No. No problem," Nadine said in a matter-of-fact voice.

"What are you doing?" I leaned over my knee immobilizer and tried to collect the cash.

She crossed her arms. "Are you serious right now? You're asking *me* that question?"

With my one good hand, I struggled. "A little help here?"

"Sure." Nadine moved her water glass to the other side of the table, to give me room to stack the money. "There you go. You missed some twenties." She pointed. "Over here."

They lay right next to her chair. I got up, put the money back together, and sat again. "Jesus, you could have said 'no thanks, asshole' and sent the same message."

"I don't think so. The punishment should fit the crime." She raised her glass of wine. "Cheers."

"I'm trying to apologize."

"Well, I'm not having it." She took a second drink. "More wine."

The food arrived and, except for the mandatory banter, we ate mostly in silence. While we were waiting for the bill, I said, "There's one more thing, I was in Milwaukee last week. I tried to talk to Roman about taking a plea deal, so there wouldn't be a trial. It's the only way the mob will call off the dogs."

Finally looking at me, she put down her fork and knife. "Did it work? I haven't heard anything about a plea."

"No. I pulled out every line I know. Even brought up *his* mother." I threw my napkin on the table. "Let's face it, everything I've done the last three months has been a waste, and for the last three weeks—roadkill on the interstate. Not even the vultures look at me."

She pointed at the bandage. "You can still play guitar. And it's not like you'll never walk again, so quit whining." She spoke in a tone that used to make me angry, but she was entitled.

I looked down. "I wasn't talking about that." I'd hoped she'd understand about my hand and knee and how they were the price for not giving her location away. "Roman thinks you're going to divorce him. He's already pissed about it."

"Maybe I will."

I leaned toward her. "You have to talk to him. Tell him a lie. Tell him anything as long as he gets off this divorce thing. Give him a little hope and he might cop a plea." I repositioned my aching leg. "Once he signs off on a deal and they lock him up, you can do whatever you want."

She tidied the stack of cash and put it in the envelope. "Sounds pretty messed up to me. And frankly, as of a week ago, I've stopped listening to you. So, don't waste your breath."

The four-hundred-mile flight to Moreau on Tuesday was a long one. We had to fly around bad weather in northern Colorado and fight head winds after that. Nate reminded Nadine she couldn't stay in town for long; her life was still worth a lot of money to "your husband's former associates." There was no mob interest in me, so I could do as I pleased. Still, Nate wondered what my plans were. It was noisy inside the Cessna, so all three of us wore headsets. I said my California plan was postponed. A lot depended on Leah and how she reacted when I got back to Moreau. Come fall, a local college, maybe.

Nadine had been silent for a while, strangely so. I leaned forward and saw her eyes were moist, almost tearing.

"Nadine, what's wrong?" I asked.

She rubbed her eyes. "What's wrong! Are you serious?" She turned and looked at me. "You're free and clear, well whoop-dee fucking doo. The FBI just told me I have to go off and live in some god-forsaken place under a new name. No husband, no family, not even you for shit's sake. And you're asking me 'what's wrong?'"

Nate pursed his lips.

I swallowed hard, tempted to repeat last night's conversation about divorce and J. Roman, but not daring.

"I want to go back to Wisconsin." She looked at Nate. "I don't care what you say, or Max, or anyone else. I have friends there. They'll watch out for me." She cried silently on and off for the rest of the flight.

An hour later we touched down. Very little had been said after Nadine's pronouncement. A government car had been left for Nate's use at the Moreau airport. After lunch, we drove to our residence and went inside. The heat was off, so it was chilly. Nate did a search of the house and neighborhood and saw nothing suspicious. He warned both of us to be careful. Then he called the police department and asked them to keep an eye on the address. Nate took me to a pawnshop where I sold the three remaining watches, the proceeds of which I used to purchase a used Jeep Wrangler. Nate had work to do and an AA meeting, so we parted ways for the rest of the day. My final destination was an art studio behind the Thrift Store, but I had another stop ahead of that.

I slipped out of the Wrangler in front of Trevor's house. There was movement in the front window, someone in the living room. I limped up the gravel driveway, onto the concrete stoop, and knocked on the door. Mrs. Manning's face widened in recognition. "Oh my god, Max Farmer. It's you!" Her eyes reddened. My "disguise" hadn't fooled her. "We heard the worst. What happened to your hair?" The she looked down at my hand and the leg and gasped.

"I'm still supposed to be using a cane." I tapped on the knee immobilizer. "It's a long story. By the way, it's Max Cherhasky now."

"Cherhasky? For god's sake, you changed your name? What on earth for?" She invited me in and moved aside, to give me room to pass. She crossed her arms, as if getting ready for a cross-examination. But the look on her face, surprise, joy, concern, all in one, was so disarming, I had to laugh. I stepped inside, begged off an explanation about my name until later, and asked about Trevor.

"You just missed him," Mrs. Manning said. "He just drove to the Thrift Store." She leaned closer. "Don't say I said so, but I think he likes being around Leah more than working there."

"Who wouldn't?" I replied. My stomach turned into softened Jell-O at the sound of her name.

She tapped me on the shoulder. "You... of all people." Again, she asked what had happened to me. I promised I'd give her the full story another time, then backed out as gracefully as I could.

After a drive of five minutes, I hobbled in the open garage door of the Receiving Department and saw Trevor sorting kitchen utensils. "Trevor, you handsome bastard." I opened my arms. "Where you been?"

Trevor looked up and squinted at my back-lit silhouette. "Max, is that you?"

I skipped forward and hugged him. "Of course, it's me, you big oaf. How you been?"

"You're in one piece, I guess." He leaned back. "Why are you limping? And the hand? You get runover or something? I heard you were dead."

"That's a pretty close guess. I'll tell you about it." I sat heavily on an old sofa. "First you. How was graduation?"

For the next half-hour, Trevor did his sorting thing, first with silverware, then sports equipment, while he and I talked ourselves up to the present day. I found out I'd graduated in absentia. Trevor had my diploma at home. The story about Nadine and me and our brush with death at the hands of Antoni Kopec took longer than the actual event. Trevor wanted details and stopped me with questions frequently. "You're lucky to be here."

"You got that right." I leaned in. "I got a lot wrong before I left. You know better than anyone. Leah, too." I paused a moment, grabbed a few baseballs, and tossed them into bins. A couple of salespeople walked by. I said, "Did she ask about me?"

"Who?" Trevor asked.

"Leah, after I left, did she"—I shrugged—"I don't know, mention my name?"

"No... but I'm sure she missed you," he added quickly. "What you doing? Making the rounds?"

I shook my head. "Making amends, if it's not too late. You're my first stop. I'm sorry, man. It won't happen again."

Trevor smiled from his perch on the chair. "Not to worry. Christ, you've saved my ass so many times. Remember Tugger? Now there is someone who's been asking for you, and not in a good way. He's the one that said you were dead. And he was smiling when he said it."

"Tugger Jonsson—what a blockhead." We hugged again and made plans to meet later. I took a deep breath and headed for the back hallway. "I got another stop."

CHAPTER FORTY-THREE

Max

The passage from the Thrift Store to Leah's Studio was only fifteen feet long, but it felt like a mountain trail at 15,000 feet. I couldn't get my air, and the closer I got to her door, the heavier my chest. I stopped for a moment and wondered if I was cut out for this making amends thing. My effort with Nadine had been terrible. I'd done better with Trevor, but only because he would always let me off the hook.

Click. Click. Click. The sound came from a plastic wall clock. The time was wrong, the second hand stuck at the nine because of a dying battery. I stepped away, worried the timepiece was a symbol of what my life had become. My steps grew shorter as I approached the door. The sign said, "It's Open, Come In." Was I too late? Had she buried me in a deep layer of her canvas and cut the thread? If time had stopped in the hallway, perhaps not. A small bell hanging on the handle announced my arrival.

The studio was quiet. No music playing—that meant Leah was not creating at the moment. I called her name and heard the sound of a pen hitting a desktop. But it wasn't just any pen drop. This tap was peculiar, purposeful, the kind heard when the hand holding the pen was suddenly in the moment.

The faint odor of the acrylic paint was doing nothing for my head. A wall divided the makeshift foyer from her work area. I waited. Her hand, the painted nails, were the first to appear, grasping the molding at the end of the partition. Then, her hair and a single eye, crystal blue.

Her brow went up. Slowly, she came fully before me, a hand to her mouth as if seeing a ghost. Seconds later her arms were around my neck. "For chrissakes, where have you been?"

"Well, I…"

She put my face in her hands for a moment, then hugged my neck again and tipped her forehead into my chest. "What happened? Why didn't you call?"

"I did, but…" I tried to swallow. "I couldn't say anything."

She looked up at me. "So, it *was* you."

Embarrassed, I nodded. "There's so much, I don't know where to begin." I grasped her arms and stepped back. "You haven't changed, thank god." As always, there was paint everywhere. I dabbed a finger in a spot of green on her shirt. "It's always like you've walked through a rainbow."

She smiled shyly, then ran a few fingernails across the stubble on my head. "You've changed quite a bit." She glanced sideways and held my hand. "What about this bandage?"

We found chairs to sit, mine high enough to accommodate my knee immobilizer. I promised to tell her the whole story down to every sordid detail, but not today. I told her a twenty-minute version instead. "In short, a cross-country cluster-fuck in the worst sense of the word." I paused. "I had the feeling you recognized my voice when I came in."

"Of course."

"Then why the hesitation coming around the wall like you did?"

"Because the word around town is that both of you are dead. Some hit man had it in for you and that's why you bolted." She pushed a curl off her face. "Then Trevor told me maybe it was true, about the mob."

"Who was spreading the shooter story?"

"Everybody knows. I've heard it from three people already. One of them was Tugger. He wanted to be sure I heard it from him. Thought I'd be impressed if he could throw some shade on my ex, especially the heavy stuff. Definitely enjoying himself." She rolled her eyes. "That creep has been trying to date me for years."

"He has it in for me." I told her about the keys-in-the-gas tank affair. "I can take care of him. Just give me the word."

"Oh, sure you can. With a bum hand and a leg that don't work. Stay away from him. He's got the worst halo I've ever seen."

"Halo? Like on an angel?"

"Sort of, but he's no angel."

"Listen, Leah, there's something else, and it's important."

She turned toward me, her clear eyes the opposite to my muddy thoughts. Her mouth was fixed not in a smile, but in a way that said 'take your best shot.'

"I'm serious," I said. "I'm not always, but this time I am."

"I know."

I moved my left leg even though it wasn't bothering me. I should have gone with my first impression. This making amends thing was not my jam. The restaurant scene with Nadine was evidence enough. Now, I faced the most important person in my life, and I didn't even know how to start.

"I want you to know…" I rocked a bit. "What I mean is." I stood and rubbed my forehead. "Gawd, I'm terrible at this."

"At what? A minute ago, you were talking a mile a minute, but that was about the trip, facts, details. This must be about something else."

I shook my head and smiled, but inside I was a wreck. She was reading me right down to the laces on my shoes. "You're something, really. These pictures." I threw my chin at the gallery. "It's like you break a vein open and whatever is going on inside, you bleed it out on the canvas." She laughed a little. I asked, "What's funny?"

She stood and pointed. "The one on the floor next to you. There's blood on that one. I cut myself pulling a couple of the strands. Maybe that's what I'll call it, *Acrylic in Blood.*" She looked down at her hands. "Couple of the more recent ones I got carried away." She had bandages on her right hand too. There were probably other wounds; not visible but just as real. She picked at the tape on her finger.

She was the adult in the room. While I struggled to begin a sentence, she had told me everything about the last three weeks of her life with a single painting. "You were right; I should never have left. I was so messed up."

She sat and rested her hands on her lap. "You were in shock. You found out that the camper story about your mother's death was a lie. Your father had been deceiving you for all those years. I'd want to get away from him too." She looked toward a picture on the wall. "The first time I saw him I knew he was trouble, nothing but heartache and pain for everyone around him."

"Yeah, I was running away." She handed me a tissue to dry my face. "The first time you came to our house, I thought Roman was on his good behavior. We were only together for a minute or two. Did he say something nasty?"

She took a tissue of her own and twisted it in her hands. "It wasn't anything he said or did, not exactly. And I'd seen him before."

"You never told me that."

She looked directly at me. "Months before you introduced us, I saw him shopping with Nadine at the hardware store."

"Did you talk to him?" I asked.

"No. They were in the same aisle as me for a minute. Then I saw him in line at the check-out, that's it."

"I still don't get it. Did you hear something? Was he talking trash to Nadine?"

"If we're doing confessions, then I have one too." She unwrapped the tissue and flattened it on her knee. "I'm a synesthete, Max. I see auras around people, a sort of colored mist. I've learned to read them, what they're saying about the person, their emotions and attitudes mostly."

"Before you even talk to them?"

"Yes."

I didn't know what she was talking about. What next? Reading palms and Tarot Cards? I stood. "Come on, Leah. Don't mess with me. Not now."

"I'm not," she said. "Everyone has an aura; most people can't see them, but I can. And they change. Yours is greenish-blue most of the time. It goes up and down from day to day; we all do. But when you talk about you mother's death it shrinks... a lot." She paused. "I should have told you a long time ago but... I was afraid you'd think I'm a freak." She folded the tissue. "Because of that, I don't tell anyone about it, or almost no one."

That was it. That's how she could read me, read a room, it finally made sense. "It's called syna-what?"

"Synesthesia." She said it's more common than most people knew, and varies. Some synesthetes see numbers as colors. Others associate words with smells. She looked down. "If you don't want to see me anymore, I'll understand."

Truth demands truth, and hers was calling on something deep inside of me. I squeezed the hand she offered me, elated that she hadn't closed the door on our relationship, and dreading what it demanded of me. "I have something too." I let go her hand, turned, and took a step away. "Same deal. If you want to call it off, I'll understand."

"What is it?"

I turned toward her and saw both worry and compassion on her face. "I've never told this to anyone. One other person knows, you'll be the third." I rubbed the side of my face. "Leah, I knew all along." I could see she wasn't following. "The bullshit about the camping, the bear, I knew it was a cover story years ago. I've never told anyone."

"How did you find out? J. Roman didn't tell you."

"He didn't have to. I was in the room when she died."

"Oh my god." She stood and embraced me for a long time.

I could have ended the confession right there, and she would have assumed I was an eye witness, a child traumatized by seeing his mother murdered. But there was more. I put my hands on her hips and gently put space between us. "I haven't finished. Sit down"

We sat again. Our thighs weren't touching, but she was close enough to give me the courage to continue. I wondered if our auras were mingling. What happened when two people became emotionally entangled? Did colors mix? Did yellow and blue become green?

I began, "First of all, I wasn't four when it happened, I was six. I always lied about it because I remember the day so well, and I figured if I made myself younger, my memory would fade somehow. That worked for shit. And, this is even dumber, I thought people would be less likely to suspect a four-year-old kid than one who's six."

Her eyes narrowed. "Suspect them of what?"

"Getting to that. Anyway, J. Roman used to beat my mother, not frequently but when he did, it was awful. Finally, it got so bad, Mom went out and bought a handgun for protection. She hid it in a drawer in the bedroom."

She leaned closer. "Oh, no. How did you know? Did you find it?"

"No," I said. "I didn't know until the day it happened. I don't know what set him off, but J. Roman was in a rage. The argument started in the kitchen. I was in the living room, so they moved to the bedroom, you know, so I wouldn't have to watch. You know what? That was worse. Hearing the threats, the anger, and then lamps crashing against the wall. It scared the shit out of me. I thought he was going to really hurt her. I don't know if I thought he'd kill her. That isn't a thing you think about when you're six. But bruises and pain and crying, I knew about that. I couldn't take it anymore. I opened the door, walked into the room, and—dead quiet. My mother was in a shamble. I can still see her lips quivering, arms shaking; she had the gun in both hands, aimed at J. Roman.

"She begged me to leave, but I couldn't move. I'd never seen a handgun before. Her eyes were on me. Roman lunged for the gun, wrestled it free, and turned it on Mom. I ran forward and swung my fist. The gun went off. Mom collapsed, I suppose. All I remember for sure is the smell of the gun and the sound of her falling behind the bed. I never saw her again." I dropped my head. "After that, my brain was in a fog. Somehow, I ended up at Grandma's house."

Tears streaming down her cheeks, she stroked the side of my face. "You've been carrying that since you were six." Her voice was a whisper. "That's the real reason, isn't it? That's what you've been running from."

"I'm sorry, Leah." I slid closer and took her injured hand in my good one. "For the hand, for the blood on the canvas, the blood on the floor." My eyes burned. I blinked. "For being a coward. For leaving. For everything —"

She put a fingertip to my lips, and said, "Forgiven."

I let out the rest of my breath and cried. Wept in her arms until the pain and emptiness and loss had spun their worst. Then I collapsed in her embrace.

250

CHAPTER FORTY-FOUR

Max

The next day, Leah came by for a visit. I watched from my bedroom window as she approached. The lawn was an embarrassment: tall grass in some areas, nothing but dandelions and weeds in others. There were flyers and letters spilling out of the mailbox, so she stopped and collected them.

I had invited her over, but the plan for the day revolved around Nadine, not me. Leah knocked on the door; Nadine answered and offered to call me. Leah said not to bother. She was there for some girl talk, and I was not invited. She'd start out by asking about the ten-day escape across the country, how it must have been an awful experience. She hoped Nadine would want to vent, but that wasn't what she said at the door. Like she'd been trained at the Actor's Studio, Leah played the conflicted one, as if she were the one who needed advice.

Nadine took the mail from Leah, invited her into the living room, and offered her something to drink. She asked for "diet whatever." I listened from my bedroom, waiting for my cue. Nadine was surprised and confused by Leah's appearance at the house because she asked, "Sure you don't want me to call Max?"

Leah's voice, "Oh, definitely." The plan, in fact, called for me to make a brief appearance at some point and take my dismissal like a man. Leah and Nadine settled in. I limped down the hall, then acted surprised. "Oh, Leah. Hi. Why are you here?"

"Talking to Nadine about disgusting habits in the American male," Leah said.

"I will definitely pass on that one." I headed for the door, then stopped. "Speaking in general, not specifics, right?"

Leah raised her eyebrows. "No particulars. Peg-leg men, last names starting in C, that's it."

The girls laughed. I left the house.

I had a new smart phone in my back pocket. The burner cell was in the trash. I climbed into the Wrangler and headed for my meeting with Nate Bauer. He would want to know about my discussion with Nadine and whether she would talk to J. Roman. The rendezvous was at Riverside Park, five minutes away. There was plenty of parking. A couple of older fellows were fishing down at the water's edge. A small group of Canadian geese roamed about, song birds flittered in the trees. The breeze was a little cool if you were in the shade. Nate was sitting at a picnic table. I took a spot next to him and said there was little to report.

Nate was no fountain of information, either. There was nothing new on another hit man out of Chicago, or whether there'd been a change in the contract on Nadine's life. J. Roman was as silent as a northern lake in October, and the District Attorney refused to change the plea deal. Nate was flying back to Wisconsin early tomorrow. He asked, "Do you think Nadine will come with me?"

I looked across the river and said that Nadine hadn't listened to me at all. "She's still pissed at me, and I can't blame her." I wasn't even sure she would cooperate with the WPP. "What happens then?"

Nate shrugged and said they would try to convince her otherwise. If not, she'd be on her own, and "up to her ass in alligators."

"That's on me. She never would have left if not for me." I stretched some tension out of my neck. "It still might work. I have Leah working on her right now."

"Smart move. I hope she works fast. I have to leave tomorrow come hell or high water."

There was shopping to do and errands to run. By the time I

finished it was after lunch. I walked through the kitchen and down the hall before spotting Nadine in her bedroom, a suitcase open on the bed in front of her. I stopped at her door. "Going somewhere?"

"Yes. Milwaukee, with Nate. So are you. Get packing."

"Well, all right." I turned, pumped a fist, and headed back out the front door.

"Where are you going?" Nadine called.

"Buy some munchies. Nate's in-flight food service sucks."

I parked on the side of the convenience store and walked in. All the gas pumps were occupied, a camper pulling a boat on one side, a couple bikers and a car on the other, so I thought to gas up after shopping. Filling a blue handbasket with bagged salty stuff and bottle drinks didn't take long. I charged the sale and went out the door. The car and camper were gone. The bikes remained. I took a closer look, and recognized one. I turned the corner of the building. Tugger Jonsson was next to my Wrangler chewing tobacco, a foot on the front bumper, his yellow teeth dingy even on a sunny day.

"Hey, Tugger, seems like just yesterday," I said. "But that can't be. I've been gone for two weeks."

"We all thought you was dead," Tugger said, leaning into his knee.

"What's the old saying? Rumors of my death have been greatly exaggerated."

Tugger's friend, a fox-faced, skin-flinty, dark-haired guy, picked at a sore on his arm and chuckled.

"Shut up, Billy," Tugger said. "It'll only make for more of his bullshit."

I put the food in the front seat and pointed at Jonsson's shirt. "Could it be *two* weeks? Because, that stain on your shirt, I think it's the same one."

"Which reminds me. You owe me forty-five dollars."

"For what?"

Tugger poked his chest with his thumb. "I had to buy a special tool to get the keys out of my gas tank."

"Sorry." I opened my palms. "Flat broke. Besides, you were

harassing my friend. You got off cheap."

"Cheap!" Tugger cried.

"And another thing. If I hear about you bothering Leah again, I'm going to put more than keys in your tank."

Billy stopped picking and looked up, eyes wide. "Easy, Tug. Easy."

"No one talks trash to me." He brought his foot off the bumper. "No one." He spit tobacco juice on my windshield.

I held my ground next to the driver's door. "Tug, don't be an ass."

Jonsson moved his bulk with surprising agility, came close to me, and slammed both palms into my chest. I toppled to the ground. Had I had the use of both legs and both hands, I wouldn't have fallen. But...

Tugger grabbed my shirt, stood me up, and slammed me twice against the Jeep.

"What was that about Leah?" he snarled.

"Stay away from her."

He slammed me twice again. "Say what?"

"Stay"—I grunted—"away."

Jonsson spat on the rearview mirror and put me into a choke hold. His grip was frightening. The world started to fade. I wind-milled my right arm over the top of Tugger's forearms, broke the grip, then brought my elbow back to his jaw. Tugger staggered, but only for a second. Before I could escape, his huge right arm had me in a headlock. A series of left hooks pummeled my face and head.

I reached up from behind with my left hand, hooked a finger in each of Tugger's nostrils, and pulled as hard as I could. Tugger fell backward over my bad leg, thumping his shoulder and head into the asphalt.

———————

Early Thursday morning, we were back in the Cessna. I settled in to my backseat cocoon and gazed out at the southern horizon. Almost directly below us, the Badlands slipped past. I hadn't planned on ever going back to Wisconsin. And seeing Leah had sprung something loose at my core, a coiled, overwound piece of mainspring. When it broke free, I was nearly shattered. But through some kind of white magic, Leah had controlled the blow. Now, I wanted to find out if I could see my way with her.

Ironically, it was Leah who put us back on the plane to Milwaukee. She had done her job well, had convinced Nadine to go to her husband and tell him whatever it took to gain her freedom. Nate and I filled her in on the details of the plea deal, so by the time we arrived at the federal Courthouse in Milwaukee there was little more to be said by the D.A. With the attorney, Nate, and me observing from behind the one-way glass, Nadine took a seat opposite J. R. Cherhasky. Since his talk with me, he had somehow cleaned up, straightened up, and brightened up. Nadine had followed Leah's suggestion to dress with class but also in a way to remind J. Roman of the striking woman he was married to.

Nadine had done well. A walnut-brown summer blouse fit her form, the color to show off her eyes, two buttons undone to reveal her tan but not much more. White slacks and strapped, low heels. J. Roman noticed more than just the clothes. He commented on her short, dark hair right away.

She touched her hair, then her throat. "I know. I don't like it either. I can go back to my real color. And it'll grow out in no time." She combed her hair with her fingers. "Not my idea anyway." He didn't reply, except with his eyes, which were hard and cold. She shifted in the rigid seat. Her voice was warm. "How are you, Roman? I've been thinking about you every day."

The interview room was the same as before. A single desk, two chairs, and an overhead light. One of the walls had the one-way glass and the access door. A penitentiary guard stood next to Roman.

"I'll bet you've been thinking," he growled. "Where's your lawyer?"

"What? Why would I need a *lawyer*?"

Roman dropped his chin. "Okay. Play it your way. No, I don't like it, not at all."

"Don't like what?" she asked.

"Your hair. That color, for chrissakes. And who told you to cut it? One of your new *boy*friends?"

"Boyfriend! No, I don't have a boyfriend. I'm married to you."

"Whose idea was it, then? The hair."

"Well, but… it doesn't matter, it'll be long and red in no time, the way you like it." She touched her throat again. "I wore your favorite blouse. You remember. The buttons?" She bit her lower lip. "I asked about one of those visits they have for married people. What's it called? A…"

Roman lowered his brow, thought a moment. "A conjugal visit?"

Behind the glass, I asked, "Did she? I didn't hear it."

Nate shook his head.

"Yes, that's it," Nadine said. "I couldn't remember the name." She tilted her head down and looked up at Roman. "But they said they don't have that here. No room, whatever that means. After all," she purred. "We never needed very much… room, I mean."

Nate scratched his ear. "Where is she going with this?"

"It's been such a long time," she said. "I don't think you realize how lonely I've been for you."

"Now there's some bullshit." I crossed my arms. "But I don't think he's picked up the scent."

"And I've been so worried about you, stuck in this prison. It must be awful." She bit on the tip of a finger. "They told me about the deal, Roman. Why don't you take it? The names I gave them a year ago, at the interview in Green Bay, they're going to use them you know, whether I testify or not." She stopped and studied his face. "I know you haven't forgotten about that."

Nate tapped me on the arm and said, "I'm not sure Nadine can see it, but Roman *has* forgotten about that, about the interviews from a year ago."

The federal lawyer agreed. "Our investigation is informed and guided by her testimony prior to the WPP placement, and it's made the case against him much stronger. If she adds new testimony to that, he'll be facing more time. Roman is looking into one massive blackhole."

I was struck by her sophistication. "She's playing him like a fiddle."

Roman repositioned his shackled wrists. "Is that why you came here? To remind me of old history? Because if that's it, our little talk is over."

"No. No!" She extended a hand, as if to touch his. "I'm sorry. It's just. Well, you might as well know. Max told me you want a divorce, and it broke me up. I couldn't sleep. I —"

"He told you what?"

Nadine took a tissue out of her pocket. "I knew I would need this." She dabbed under both eyes.

"Nadine, look at me. What did Max say?"

In the view room, Nate said, "That guy is cold. But Nadine is Oscar material."

I nodded. "She reversed the divorce thing and put it on him."

"Who came up with that?" asked Nate, pointing at me.

I shook my head. "My guess, the brain behind this act is torturing canvas back in South Dakota."

"Torture." Nate moved closer to the window. "Kinda like what we're watching right here."

Nadine blew her nose. "He said you sounded like you were fed up with everyone, including me, and that you were going to divorce me. And I thought, of course because of what I said to the lawyers last year. You're upset. If I could just explain. But then I thought the only way I can change your mind is if I see you. So, I flew here…and…" She covered her mouth, red lipstick smearing the tissue. "Oh, Roman you can't divorce me. Please, not now, not ever." Then the tears came. J. Roman studied his wife's expression for a long time trying, it seemed, to find the crease in her face that would reveal the flaw in her story. I watched for it too. It never showed. Her mascara ran. The guard in the room offered her his handkerchief, which she accepted.

"Visits are allowed in the penitentiary," she choked between sobs. "I could come. Have your lawyer put you in a place in Wisconsin, so it's not too far." She sat straight and took a cleansing breath. "Say something, please. Or I'll die, I really will, Roman."

Finally, he pried his lips apart. "You came here because you thought *I* was going to divorce *you*?"

She nodded vigorously, then paused. "Well, yes, of course," she said, as if there were no other possible explanation.

J. Roman paused again for what seemed like forever. Then he turned his head toward the guard. "Get my lawyer." He squared his shoulders. "I'll take the deal."

Nate let out a huge breath.

I bowed my head and grabbed the back of a chair. "Yes. Yes. Yes."

"Oh, Roman!" Nadine stood and moved to give him a hug, then stopped short. Looking at the guard, she asked, "May I?"

"A quick one."

She put her hands on his face and kissed his lips.

"Where are you going now?" Roman asked.

"Back to Moreau to get my things. I'm coming home."

Chapter Forty-Five

Max

The next morning, fully rested from a good night's sleep in a downtown hotel, Nadine and I stood near the front door of a restaurant, waiting for Nate Bauer to arrive. The streets were wet from an early-morning rain, the air fresh off Lake Michigan, and the clouds clearing. The plans for the day had been hammered out the night before. Nate was flying home to Appleton. Nadine and I had tickets on a commercial flight to Rapid City, South Dakota, with a stopover in Minneapolis.

Breakfast was going to be a goodbye meal for us and Nate. I paced nervously. Though I wouldn't admit it, I wasn't looking forward to parting ways with Nate. The encounter with Kopec had shook me from my moorings and set me adrift. But the time I'd spent with Nate put me on a course I could recognize as my own, not some trumped-up vision of retribution and independence. The California Plan, I now realized, was about getting away from my father and his misplaced arrogance, not a vehicle taking me toward anything I really wanted.

I'd misjudged Nate at the start. Even after he'd saved my life, I had my doubts. It was only after the flights home—the conversations about AA, Austin, and my own emotional minefield—that my opinion changed. I wasn't sure what our relationship had become, I only knew when I talked to Nate I felt better and wiser, a sense I'd never had with my biological father.

Nate arrived five minutes late, shook hands with me and hugged Nadine. We went inside, sat down at a crescent-shaped table, Nadine in the middle, and ordered coffee. Nadine was the first to express regret at our parting, which I quickly echoed. Looking at the menu, Nate told us not to worry, we might not be rid of him yet. He complimented Nadine, for the third time, on how she "handled the interview, whether you were telling the truth or not." He put up a hand. "That's not a question. I don't want to know."

"He's right," I said. "You were awesome."

Nadine shrugged one shoulder and took a sip of coffee.

Nate said even though J. Roman had signed the plea agreement, sentencing could take months. Should Nadine have a change of heart about a divorce, she shouldn't show her hand until her husband was incarcerated in his new, permanent home.

I asked, "Can they put him in a place where the mob can't get to him? Some kind of protective custody?"

Nadine side-eyed me. Nate dropped his menu on the table. "Good question. Surprising though, coming from you. You don't care anymore, remember?"

I slapped a sugar packet on the edge of the table, then ripped it open over my coffee. "He's not 100% rotten. He signed off, didn't he?"

"Yes," Nate said. "Yes, he did."

"So, can you?" Nadine asked. "Put him in a place like that?"

"I'll ask Roger Wendell to talk to the board that assigns prisoners," Nate said.

Nate insisted on paying for the meal, for which Nadine and I were quietly grateful, short of cash as we were. We walked out and said good-bye at the taxi stand. Nate had a car to drive to Timmerman Field. Nadine and I were going to catch a taxi to Milwaukee Mitchell Field.

"Thanks, Nate," I said. "For everything."

"Keep in touch." He patted me on the back. "Both of you. I'll text you my number."

With a handshake and a hug, we parted ways.

The flight home went without a hitch. I made several conciliatory remarks in-flight and during the layover, but there was no sign of capitulation from Nadine, not an inkling that at some point I'd be back in her good graces. Then, somewhere over the middle of Minnesota:

"No one's looking over my shoulder," Nadine said, apropos of nothing.

I looked up from my book. "What?"

"That's the best thing, I think. I'm going to have my own money, my own car, my own place. Do you know I've never lived by myself, like in an apartment or anything, ever? I've always had a bunch of brothers and sisters. Then roommates, cuz none of us could afford to live alone. It was J.R. after that. I never had my own life, that's what I'm saying. Now I will."

I closed the book. "Living alone ain't all that great from what I've heard. And remember, the money from Cherhasky Capital is gone."

"I'll get a job, it'll be enough. The WPP will help me move back. I already asked." She took a drink of water. "Free to do as I please. When I woke up this morning I realized, once J.R. signed, it was like *I* was released from prison. What's that called, reverse psychology?"

"No, it's more like irony. Reverse psychology is a little like what you did in the interview. Put the divorce idea on him. That was brilliant. Someday he'll be sitting there, all alone in his prison cell, bored out of his skull and all of a sudden, it'll hit him like a migraine from hell. He'll be so fuckin' mad he won't know whether to shit or go blind."

She laughed. "Oh my god, where did you ever hear that saying?"

"Sam's old man, Jim. He's got a million of 'em." I noticed the bandages on her fingertips were gone, the scabs healed on all but one of the fingers.

She settled back into her seat. "We're flying in the wrong direction, but I know Wisconsin isn't far off."

"Walnut Creek?"

"I don't think so. Crivitz maybe. Get a job, maybe even buy one of those little condos on the flowage. That would be a dream."

We managed the airport in Rapid City without delay. Fifteen minutes after disembarkation we found Trevor, who'd come down from Moreau to drive us home. He was full of questions about the interview, and when Nadine responded with a verve and lilt in her voice that I hadn't heard all day, I was ready to strangle both of them. I settled for watching the greening fields instead. We were almost back to Moreau, a forty-five-minute drive, before Trevor had a question for me.

"Why was Tugger Jonsson asking about you last night?"

I raised my good hand. "I don't know. Last I saw him we were talking about Leah. He did bring up the incident with the keys. Expected me to pay up."

"Maybe you should," Trevor said dramatically.

"Hell no. He started it." I waved him off. "You just have to keep your eye on him, then he's harmless."

"I tried to pay for you, but he wouldn't take it." Trevor shook his head. "He's twice your size, man. You could hit him with a fence post and he wouldn't blink. You better be careful."

Trevor dropped us off. Nadine and I took some time to settle in and finish a light meal in front of the TV. Then we sat down at the small dinner table and decided what to do with the house. We were faced with two absolute but contradictory facts: First of all, Nadine was not staying in Moreau. Her plans were set; in her mind she was already packed.

For my part, I wasn't going anywhere. The surprised expression on Nadine's face was no surprise at all. I thought about how things had turned on a dime; me, most of all. But there it was, and here I would stay. For now, Leah was my who, what, and where. Simple as that.

Another truth: I could not buy out Nadine's part of the house. Even if I assumed, under the most generous interpretation, that I held a half interest, there was no way I could come up with the cash. And Nadine's name appeared on the deed, mine did not. Legally, I might not be entitled to *any* equity at all. Selling the house wouldn't be the end of the world. I'd get a job, find a cheap rental, and go to community college in the fall.

Nadine was pragmatic if nothing else, and in this case, more generous than she had to be. Maybe it was her way of acknowledging my role in getting her together with Leah (yes, Nadine had figured it out). She said we should avoid the lawyers and agree to split the proceeds of the sale down the middle. Her only stipulation was I pay all the fees, taxes, and charges associated with the transaction.

We shook hands.

———————————

Later that evening, after I watched the Twins beat the Red Sox, I gave in to an urge for a pizza take-out, which I ordered from a restaurant on the Town Square. I called down the hall to tell Nadine I'd be right back. "Do you need anything?" I asked. She stuck her head out of the bedroom door and asked where I was going, and could I drop her off at the Walmart? She was desperate for razors, shampoo, and hair conditioner.

I stopped the Wrangler near the front door of the store. She went inside alone. In less than ten minutes she was out front, flagging me down. I picked her up, a plastic bag in one hand, a paperback in the other. She shut the door and buckled up. I glanced at her as I drove away.

"This is a first. You have a book." I bent forward to see the title. "*The Poisonwood Bible.* I'm impressed."

"It was on the discount rack. Two bucks." She looked directly at me. "I used to read all the time, before I met your father."

"Nadine. The deal, remember?" I took a breath. "It's like if I call you Mrs. Cherhasky right now. Which I wouldn't do."

She looked out the side window. "Oh, hell no."

I had to drive three sides of the one-way streets around the downtown square before I got to the pizzeria. Lining the outer circumference and illuminating the sidewalk were streetlamps, spaced every thirty feet. Every other light had a bench; those without a bench had a tub as big as a Jacuzzi, full of flowers. The inner square had the ubiquitous bandstand, rarely used except on Saturdays for the farmers' market, protected by old trees and new paint. I stopped directly in front of the restaurant, but Nadine asked me to back up a spot. She wanted to start reading her book and needed light from the streetlamp.

I did as she asked, then got out of the Jeep. The bandage on my hand was now a gauze sponge and two pieces of tape. The immobilizer was still on, but I had to admit, I wasn't strapping it on properly, and I put weight on the leg without a second thought. I left the cane behind.

The rumble and smell of a rusted and abused pickup with a hole in the exhaust came counterclockwise around the square. The driver gunned the throttle down the short straights and didn't bother with the STOP signs. The windows were down. I could hear two men, laughing over the muffler's roar.

I shut the door on the Jeep. The pickup pulled alongside. Tugger was driving. He tried to lean forward, but he was wedged against the steering wheel by his beer belly.

"Hey, Max, out on a date with your new girrrl—friennnd? What a perv, dating your own moth—er."

The guy riding along cackled, "That makes him a real-life motherfucker."

Tugger punched the steering wheel and guffawed. After a closer look I recognized his friend. It was Ronny Morgan, a guy who'd dropped out of school and, over the last year, had worked in half-a-dozen minimum wage jobs around Moreau. He'd finally broken out of that circuit and landed a decent-paying job at the ski factory in town.

"Past your bedtime, isn't it, Tugger?" I replied.

Ronny grinned and got an elbow in the shoulder for his trouble.

"Max, let's go," said Nadine. I took it to mean get the food and let's get out of here. The tone in her voice suggested something else, something urgent, but I missed it.

"It's been real." I limped toward the front door.

"Max!" said Nadine, with an edge in her voice. I kept going. I wasn't going to let Tugger deny me a pizza.

The exhaust belched and the pickup inched along with me. Tugger yelled, "Hey you, don't walk away from me, you moth-er-fuckin' runt. I'm talkin' ta you."

"My pizza's getting cold," I stopped and turned. "Besides, come on, Tugger. You've gone down twice. Haven't you had enough?" I stepped up to the restaurant door. The engine roared. Tires squealing, Tugger pulled away. He took a left, then another left around the square. A seed of anxiety bloomed in my belly as I went inside. Maybe if I got out of sight, Tugger would get bored and leave. I went to the cashier, picked up, and paid for the pizza.

As I came out the door, my eyes searched, ears listened for the truck, but the square was peaceful. I loosened my grip on the pizza box and took two steps toward the Jeep. A growl erupted from halfway down the block. The rust bucket backed out from between two other trucks and turned on its lights. Tugger revved the engine and trained the high-beams on my Wrangler. As quickly as I could, I moved toward the driver's door. Nadine called my name and then, "It's Tugger. Look out!" His tires squealed.

"I know!" I grabbed the door latch with my bandaged hand and pulled. My fingers slipped.

The engine's roar gelled in my ears. The high-beams blinded me. White flashed in my head. Tugger howled. Accelerating, the thirsty engine, the gaping grill, were feet away. There was no time.

"Get out," I yelled. "Nadine, get—." She screamed.

The pizza dropped. I dove to the ground. Iron shrieked. Glass shattered. The engine stopped.

Tugger had T-boned the Wrangler against the light standard.

I peeled myself off the street. "Nadine!"

CHAPTER FORTY-SIX

Max

My ears were ringing, my knee throbbing from the fall.

Tugger had missed me, but destroyed two vehicles. Stunned by the violence of the collision, I stood too quickly. I put a hand on the crumpled fender of the Jeep and shook my head. The Wrangler had been demolished, the driver's side mangled and flattened. I could barely see where the truck began and the Jeep ended. The radiator steamed and hissed. Some kind of dark liquid streamed from under the engine. There was no movement anywhere. Tugger was draped over the steering wheel, his mouth and nose dripping blood. Ronny Morgan had disappeared.

"Nadine!" I cried. I couldn't see her through the windshield. Her seat had been ripped from the floor, shoved sideways and forward both. The airbags had gone off and covered the deranged interior like a deflated parachute. But, where was she? I stumbled around the wreckage to the sidewalk. Her door was half-open and crunched against the light pole. I called her name again, rushed around the door, and found her motionless form splayed across the concrete like every police-chalk drawing I'd ever seen.

I tried to go to her side but the knee immobilizer stopped me. I tore off the Velcro straps and threw the brace aside. Finally, I thought to call 911. By the time I had the operator, there were people streaming out of buildings all around the square. I knelt beside her. A pool of blood mushroomed on the sidewalk from a laceration on her forehead. Her legs were in an unusual position, and I wondered about broken bones. I didn't move her except to gently shake her shoulder. I said her name and told her to wake up, but got no response. I sat back. An oily wetness tumbled in my stomach.

Another body lay motionless under the rear bumper of the Wrangler. Ronny had a head wound that didn't look fixable in this world, and maybe not in the next. He'd not been wearing a seatbelt. After flying through the windshield, he must have gone head-first into the Jeep, then rolled onto the pavement. I crawled next to him. He wasn't breathing.

Sirens blared in the distance.

———————————

Thirty minutes later, I was sitting in the Emergency Department of Moreau Memorial Hospital, giving my statement to the cop who'd driven me there. They'd quickly CAT scanned Nadine's head, chest, neck and abdomen. She'd sustained what the doctor called "multiple trauma," and there were no surgeons in Moreau trained to handle her injuries. A transfer to Rapid City by helicopter for emergency surgery was arranged.

I had no more than finished telling Trevor about the accident, and he was at the Moreau hospital in the family Subaru. I climbed in for the ride to Rapid City. I told and retold the story, trying to fill the hole in my chest. It didn't work.

The Intensive Care Unit at Rapid City Community Hospital was at the far end of the longest hallway on the third floor. We were directed to the waiting area. Some kind of secretary told us we'd be notified when Nadine was out of the recovery room and if we'd be allowed to see her. Then a nurse came out and gave us an update. Nadine required abdominal surgery, that's all she could say. The surgeon would be out to talk to us soon.

"Stomach surgery," Trevor said. "You didn't say anything about that. What could they be fixing in there?"

I stared at the wall opposite my chair. There was an old, black and white movie playing soundlessly on a TV hanging in the corner, a coffee stand right below it. "No idea. I'm just glad they're not operating on her head. She had a gash, bleeding like stink. I thought her brains were leaking out."

"Oh, man." Trevor cringed. "Don't even say it."

"Thought all kinds a bad shit. Broken neck. Broken back. Jesus, Trev, what did I do?"

Trevor put up his hand. "Stop it, man. Tugger did it. This ain't on you."

It was well after midnight, when a woman with dark hair and eyes, dressed in surgical scrubs, and about the same size as Nadine walked through the door. We stood up. I looked at the ID hanging from her pocket and realized this was the surgeon. Her hair was pulled back into a tight knot and she wore not a speck of make-up. "You're Nadine's family?"

"I am," I said. "This is Trevor."

"Any other family coming?"

"There's no one else in South Dakota. Her husband is in…" I almost said jail. "Wisconsin. She's lost touch with her family."

"All right. My name is Carol Intapp. We finished surgery about an hour ago. She sustained a lacerated spleen in the accident. It bled quite a bit. I removed the spleen and the bleeding has stopped. She also has a bruised kidney, but we didn't need to operate there."

"Bleeding?" I asked. "I didn't see any blood, except from the cut on her head."

"You wouldn't have," she said. "It was internal." She explained where the spleen was located, what it does, and why she couldn't just "sew" it up. "She can live without her spleen. She'll have to take a few precautions. Our biggest worry right now is her low blood pressure. We had to give her blood and a lot of fluids."

"Is she going to be all right?" I asked.

She untied the surgical mask from around her neck. "She's young and strong, except for a few broken ribs—three of them on the left side, right where her spleen used to be—and a pretty good concussion. One of the ribs punctured her left lung. There was blood in the chest. I put a tube in the chest to drain the blood and re-expand the lung. I don't see any other medical issues. We'll know a lot more tomorrow. Healing is going to take a long time."

I asked when I could see her. Nadine wouldn't be awake for some time, but the doctor said I could visit now.

After the surgeon left, Trevor did too. He had to be home so his mother could use the car for work. He got on the elevator. I went in to see Nadine, who they'd put right next to the nurse's station. That worried me. A friend once told me the closer they put you to the nurses, the worse your condition.

I stood at her bedside, an antiseptic smell hung in the air. She had an IV stuck in each arm. A breathing tube in her mouth was attached to a respirator that clicked along with her breathing. They'd covered her in two blankets, leaving only her shoulders, arms and head visible. I gave her hand a little squeeze and called her name. Her eye lashes flittered. For a few precious seconds I saw eyes, but I don't think they saw me. Her pupils moved from side to side, not focused on anything. A nurse walked in dressed in a smock and scrubs, her hair back too, but not as severely as the doctor's. I thought she must be in her forties. "Did she respond to your voice?" she asked.

"Opened her eyes a little," I said. I looked at the sutures in the laceration on her scalp. "Does she have any brain damage?"

The nurse checked an IV bag. "We won't know until she wakes up. The CAT scan in Moreau was normal, so that's a good thing."

I sat down to get out of her way. She checked a plastic bag hanging below the bed. It was empty. "Is that good or bad?" I asked.

She shook her head. "This is for collecting urine. So far, she isn't making any. When this bag starts to fill, I'll feel a lot better."

Right next to the urine bag was a plastic tube that looked like an oversized rain gauge. It was connected to a tube as well, and the dark fluid it was measuring looked like old blood. The nurse said that was connected to the chest tube, and the less drainage in that one, the better.

So now, Nadine's kidneys had shut down, and she was bleeding from her lung. The nurse left. I looked at the monitor over her bed. If the red and yellow numbers meant anything, her pulse was too high and the blood pressure, too low. I pried my eyes away from the hypnotic blip of the heart tracing and wondered if she had enough to get through the night. Whatever the answer, I would be in the room to hear it. I'd left one hospital bedside too soon. That wasn't going to happen again.

CHAPTER FORTY-SEVEN

Max

The clicking, sighing ventilator was like a sleeping potion. I fell asleep in the chair for a couple hours, my head lolling back and forth. I woke up with a stiff neck. My gaze went to the urine bag. It was still empty. For the first time since the accident I choked up. Nadine had survived the trials of life on the road, of a confrontation with her sleazy husband, only to end up on a breathing machine. Whatever aura I had was being snuffed by guilt. I was glad Leah wasn't with me to see it.

Why had it always been a struggle between Nadine and me? Would her answer to that question be the same as mine? The differences we had, the almost daily arguments were trivial when stacked against kidney failure and a smashed spleen. She hadn't played politics or poisoned the relationship between J. Roman and me. We'd managed that all by ourselves. Roman clearly loved her more than me, and I had blamed her for it. I went to the waiting room to make a call.

Remorse was stacking inside me like dirty dishes in a kitchen sink. I needed to call Nate. He said I could do it anytime, but to call at four in the morning? He didn't have my new number so his caller ID wouldn't know me. He may not answer, or his phone could be off. The waiting room was empty, the TV off. I punched the number and counted the rings. A surge of embarrassment came over me. I went to end the call when I heard his voice.

"Nathaniel Bauer." His voice was sleepy but not thick, as if he was used to answering the phone at all hours.

My voice caught for a second.

"Hello?" he said.

"Ahem. Nate, it's Max. I'm sorry to call so early, or late, or whatever it is."

"Max, yeah. What's going on?"

"I'm sorry, but, but…Nadine's been hurt real bad. She's in the hospital. I didn't know who to call."

I could sense he was moving. "Hang on," he said. "I'm going to the living room so I can talk." I paced the room until his voice was back. "All right. Where are you, Max? Are you okay?"

I told him what had happened, the accident, Nadine's helicopter ride, and the surgery. Everything, right down to the failing kidneys. He asked a question or two. I ended with a deep sigh. "Nate, I'm scared."

I heard a water tap running. "You're alone. Your stepmom is fighting for her life. Who wouldn't be scared?"

"I'm afraid she's going to die. Her breathing, her blood pressure, it all looks bad." I paused. "It's all my fault. I couldn't leave Tugger alone. I kept poking him. And now Ronny's dead, and two people are in the hospital."

"Tugger?"

"Yeah, I think he's four rooms down. I don't know what's going on with him. Last I saw, he was unconscious in the pick-up."

"So, here's the thing." His voice was the same as always, sympathetic but matter-of-fact. "You didn't drive the pickup, Tugger did. We'll talk on him later. Second, you're there with her. That's all that counts."

"We were finally becoming like, almost friends. We could actually talk, even after what I did in Roswell."

"I thought you two had talked that out."

"Well, I did most of the talking. Tried to make amends, step nine, like you said. But she never bought it." A janitor went by polishing the floor. I lowered my voice. "And I don't think I'm going to get the chance to ask her again."

"I think you will. It's the only bet you should be looking at." I heard his chair move. "Bet on her. Bet on yourself. She's shown her toughness."

That stunned me, but it shouldn't have. I'd been discounting her for years. It was a habit worth breaking. "Okay. I'll give it a shot." I stood again. "Go back to bed. Sorry I messed up your night." He said he was glad I called and asked for an update when I knew more.

I went back to Nadine's room. The nurse came in a couple of times to check urine output; each time punching "none" in her computer. I must have nodded off for a few hours because the next thing I remember was the sound of Dr. Intapp getting a report from the nurse. I shook the sleep from my head, stood up, and returned the doctor's "Good morning." I listened closely to the conversation but couldn't make heads or tails of the medical stuff. Dr. Intapp motioned me into the hallway where she grabbed her cup of coffee, held it up, and said, "Need one?"

She poured me a cup from the pot in the break room. "Well, Max, she made it through the night. The first is always the toughest."

"When do you think she'll wake up?"

"Today, I hope. She was a little restless last night, so she might be coming out of the coma."

"Coma? I didn't know…"

She took a sip of coffee. "She's very sick. There was a lot of blood in her belly. That's probably why her kidneys are struggling. But she's starting to make urine; that's really good. We get a few more signs like that, and we'll all feel better." I asked about the breathing tube and the one in the draining blood in the lung. "Breathing tube out today." She pointed at the ceiling. "I hope. Chest tube will be a couple more days, then we'll see."

I didn't know if I could eat, but I went to the cafeteria anyway and got something wrapped in plastic and a piece of fruit from a vending machine. I sat down, called Trevor, and told him I'd be staying another night. By the time I got back to the ICU, there was a swirl of activity in Nadine's room. The nurse sent me away because they were in the middle of something. "But it's good," she said. "She's off the vent."

Later that morning, she woke up. I squeezed her hand. She opened her eyes and said my name. I smiled. My vision blurred.

CHAPTER FORTY-EIGHT

Max

A couple hours later, Leah arrived. I'd given her a call right after the doctor left. In her hand was my duffle bag with a change of clothes, toothbrush, that sort of thing. As soon as I saw her, my sense of remorse and loneliness started to fade. She listened, much as Nate had, as I unloaded the details, the smoldering panic and dread of the last day or so. Nadine seemed to have no memory of the accident. It was too early to tell if she was completely "there" or not, not to mention the long-term side effects of her other injuries.

We went in to see Nadine, but she was sleeping, so we walked the long hall for a while. I was still obsessing about step nine and Nadine's stubborn streak, when Leah told me something that stopped me where I was standing:

"She's already forgiven you."

"What? How do you know?"

She tugged on my elbow to keep walking. "She told me the other day, when I came to your house. But I knew even before that. Her aura is a muted yellow, but when your name came up, I saw a tinge of blue. If she was still mad at you, that wouldn't have happened."

I looked down and shook my head. "You don't even know what that means."

She looked at me with a mischievous grin. "I do. There's something else."

I stopped walking again, with a 'now what' look on my face.

"Two things actually. First the good stuff. She's gonna make it, at least I think so." She got me walking, again. "Her aura is strong. If it was fading or wavering, that'd worry me. But it's not."

"That's fabulous!" I paused. "What's the not-so-good?"

"You're not done with step nine." She must have seen my confusion, because she added, "Tugger."

There was no way I could act surprised by this. I'd been watching his room from the corner of my eye all day; I even thought of visiting. But apologizing seemed like a step too far. It wasn't me behind the wheel of the truck. I tried to protest, but Leah stopped me with a tilt of her chin and a raised eyebrow. "You have to talk to him. And you have to do it alone."

———————

I pushed aside the sliding door, and walked into the dimly lit room, curtains drawn, television off, the same hiss and click of the ventilator. I approached the bed and touched Tugger's puffy left hand, splinted and taped, an IV running. There was no response, not even a flick of the finger. I looked at the nurse, who adjusted the pillow under his head. "Can I talk to him?"

"Sure. Whether he will hear you or not?" She shrugged. "He hasn't responded to anything we've done for him. You're his first visitor. Are you family?" I told her no. She left a couple minutes later.

"Tugger, Tugger, how ya doin'?" *How stupid*, I thought. *The dumbest question ever asked of a guy in a coma.* "It's Max. I've come to see you. Yeah, I know." I tried to say it in my lightest voice, the one reserved for picnics and holidays. "Hard to believe, right?"

His face was swollen to twice its normal size, eyes shut, the nose packed with gauze sponges turned black with old blood. His lips were bloated and purple, the breathing tube taped and anchored to his face. Nothing like the guy I saw at the service station. A gown covered Tugger's torso, a blanket warmed his legs. His formidable mass filled the bed. I couldn't see his aura, but I didn't need Leah's sixth sense to know: he was doing worse, much worse than Nadine.

Perched on the wall, a monitor silently traced his life, or what remained of it, a point of light walking left to right, writing the story of his heart until it had nothing left to say. Two poles, three bags of fluid. I wondered at the complexity of it all, and then thought it was nothing compared to a single brainwave. Tugger still had them. A stream of wires stuck to his scalp led to a bedside oscilloscope, which pulsated in a jagged line. Is that what they were waiting for? A flat line on his brain, the single indicator to make everything else in the room meaningless? Maybe he was a potential organ donor. The extraordinary efforts on his behalf actually being done to save someone else's life.

I grabbed hold of the bedrail with both hands, straightened my arms, and dropped my head between them. "Tugger, for god's sake, why? You dumb, vindictive sonofabitch." And though I spoke in barely a whisper, the words reverberated in my head like the accusation they were. The answer was in the question. Tugger had responded to my taunts in the only way he knew. And I'd known it all along. I liked poking the beast.

That thought made me think of Nate. "He figured it out, Tugger," I said. "Nate, I mean. Great wife, two daughters, one prettier than the next, a career. That's where I want to be in twenty-five years." I tapped my fingers on the bedrail. "But for all of that, I could tell a piece was missing." Tugger's face was passive. "Oh, I know what you're thinking." I waved a finger at him. "I only noticed because I know the story—Austin, the drugs, the joyride ended by an oak tree."

A nurse came in, checked Tugger's IVs, and repositioned both of his arms. I was glad for the interruption, the presence of another person in the room to take the pressure off. She asked if I needed anything? I said no.

After she left, I walked to the side of the bed next to the window and peeked out the shades. I told him what Nate had said about AA and the twelve steps.

"You see what I'm talking about, right Tugger?" I asked. "Nadine forgave me, you know." My head turned toward the head of the bed. "No, really!" I paused. "Fine. Go ahead. Laugh..." I walked to the foot of the bed, and threw an accusing finger at Tugger. "Listen, you bastard. You almost killed her." The words soured in my ears. The condescension in my voice amplified by his silence. I put up my hand. "Sorry. Sorry. My bad. Old habits, you know." I grabbed the edge of the bed and said, "Damn it, Tugger, why are you making this so hard?

"Look, all I'm saying, all I'm trying to say is I'm sorry. I know it's probably...it is... too late for you. As you can see, I'm an amateur." I raked my fingers through my hair, now almost long enough to grab. "I'm sorry, man."

The drape pulled aside. I expected to see the nurse again, but felt a hand on my waist.

"Nurse said you might need a little help."

I turned. "Leah." I managed a small, brief smile.

"How is he?" she asked.

"Bad. Nurse said even if he makes it, he'll never be the same."

"That goes for both of you, I'd say."

"Yeah," I said. "Guess it does."

She nodded and took my hand. "Time to go home."

CHAPTER FORTY-NINE

Max

Nadine was eating Chinese take-out, two cartons at a time. No time for a plate, barely the patience for a fork. The way her appetite was running, I wondered out loud if she was pregnant. She gave me a look that shut me up. In the hospital and for a week after, she'd had no interest in food. She was down ten pounds at one point, way too much for someone her size. If she had a taste for something, I ordered it. A rotation of restaurant take-out—pizza, Mexican, burgers, Chinese—was right up her alley. The urge to cook, never a strong part of her personality, had yet to reappear, and she made no secret what she thought of my kitchen skills.

The one-month follow-up appointment with Dr. Intapp had gone very well. She complimented Nadine for her quick recovery, gave her a pneumonia vaccine, and asked her to return in six weeks for a final wound check. Nadine agreed, but I noticed a gleam in her eye that said she had no intention of being anywhere near Rapid City. "Take it easy for the next few weeks. Come back any time you need."

Nadine spritzed soy sauce into a container and talked about getting a divorce lawyer. I said, "Better to get one in the state where you're going to file."

"You mean I have to do it in Wisconsin just because Roman's there?"

"Well, yes, there's that." I mixed my chow mein with the rice. "But you're going to be there too."

Her fork stopped. Her hair was shoulder-length now and she'd dyed it back to her original auburn. She was back, and going back home, and so I told her. The doctor's optimism was the final piece. She jumped out of her chair, walked behind me, and hugged my shoulders. The only question now was where, exactly, was home. Walnut Creek?

She sat again. "No. When I say home, at no time did I mean that shack by Left Foot Lake. I have a friend from high school. She lives in Crivitz. I know her husband too. He did business with Roman for a while, until he found out how crooked he was."

I told her to give this couple a call to see what kind of reception she'd get. She was confident they'd be happy to have her, but not so sure about my new vehicle, a used Bronco, which already had over 120,000 miles on it. "And there's no way all my stuff would fit," she said.

She was right. We'd rent a van and get cardboard boxes through Trevor from the Thrift Store. She was on a lifting limit of ten pounds, so he and I did all the heavy work. Nadine filled the boxes and taped them tight, but when the end of the job was in sight, she got too anxious and went off the chain. "Nadine!" I snapped. "Pick up one more chair, and I'm going to tie you to it."

Seriously, I thought we were doing this too soon after her surgery. But after she got the open-arms response from her Crivitz friends, Perry and Gail Gutierrez, she was determined to head east. I'd never known her when she had nothing. I'd always assumed she could only exist in an all-inclusive world of Gucci, champagne glasses, and party dresses. I was wrong. The prospect of starting over didn't bother her at all.

The ride across South Dakota, through a corner of Minnesota, and into Wisconsin was the quickest two days we'd ever spent together. The anticipation in Nadine's voice grew as we got closer to her new home. Her room in the Gutierrez house was good until she found a job and a place of her own. She seemed to be undaunted by the profound changes coming her way. The Nadine of six weeks ago would've been intimidated by the very idea, much less the act. The transformation made me sad in a way. At the start of our road trip, I resented her dependence on me, thought of her as ice on my wings. But within a week, we were in Roswell, and she was leaving me with nothing but the shoes on her feet and the clothes in her backpack. Her bravery and loyalty to Stan were amazing. My stubborn admiration for her was born right there. It was her best hour. And my worst. After that, we were on equal footing. But for all the changes I'd seen in her, I wasn't sure if she knew what was going on with me. Perhaps that was a part of her I couldn't have.

Perry and Gail were waiting for us with all the enthusiasm and wonder you might expect. One of their best friends had dropped off the Earth and had now returned. We unloaded the van and had dinner. They invited me to stay overnight. I slept well enough, but woke the next morning feeling shallow, low, and anxious. I didn't know if I'd ever see Nadine again, and I didn't want to wallow in any long farewells. After breakfast, within the confines of the front door, we said goodbye.

"Be careful driving," she said. "And say hello to Sam."

I nodded, my toe scuffing at something, or nothing, on the concrete of the front porch. "You have my new number."

"You've asked me a dozen times." A small smile. "Yes, Max, I have it."

"And you'll send me your new address," I said. Cliché's were all I could come up with, to cover a finality I was trying to ignore. For her part, her eyes were still clear, her complexion as pure as porcelain.

"Of course. The minute I move in," she said.

I blinked and sniffled. "Have a good life, Nadine. You deserve it." I didn't want to make a mess of it, so I turned to leave. Suddenly, there were urgent footsteps behind me, a hand on my arm that spun me around.

Her eyes flared. "What's that supposed to mean?" I'd heard that edge in her voice a thousand times, and yet it caught me off guard. I'd never been more sincere. Why was she upset?

"I just want you to be happy," I said.

"No. It's more than that." A huff of exasperation. "'Have a good life.' Don't say that. You're acting like… That's what people say when they're going to Australia, or Mars, or wherever. We're going to see each other again."

Now she had me upset, but I tried not to show it. Old habits… "Sure. Okay, you're right." I paused. "Be good. Be safe. We'll talk."

"Okay," she said sharply. Then, "Okay," again with more affection. "Thank you, Max, for getting me out. For bringing me here." She gave me a peck on the cheek. But it's the hug I'll remember—solid, strong, and freely given.

———————————

Later that day, I arrived at Noquebay Resort. There was none of the Crivitz fanfare because I hadn't called ahead. I wanted to surprise Sam and his family. Just like old times, without a knock, I walked through the back door of the lodge and into the kitchen just as the Robels were sitting down to lunch. I might have said I was greeted with stunned silence, but the sound of silverware clanging onto plates and falling to the floor filled the room. Maybe they thought I was some kind of zombie, returning from the dead. Then there were cries of disbelief, hugs, and the clearing of a spot—my old place—at the table. The meal was a long one, full of questions; only half of which I answered.

After lunch, Sam and I walked the resort. I asked about Diane.

"That's right," Sam said. "You don't know. We found her sister, Jean. She was down in Memphis, living in a trailer park."

"Memphis?"

"I know, right? Turning tricks and strung out on drugs. But we got her out," He said in a monotone. "She's still married to Junior Manticore. He's taken over the Manticore empire, or what's left of it." As if delivering a sermon, he told the story of the old man, Mitchell, and especially Steve, who'd been cooking meth on public lands, with pride and not a little nostalgia. The story was killer, great stuff, but there was little excitement in his voice. And he hadn't answered my question.

"And Diane?" I repeated.

"Well." He stopped walking and looked away. "Well, I don't know. We were together for the whole Memphis thing, and senior year. She's living in Green Bay now, with Fanny and Wes. Working for them too." His shoulders slumped. "Max, I think I lost her."

I'd never seen Sam this way. There was one other girl he'd met last summer. She'd been staying in one of the cabins. They had a summer thing that ended when she had to go home four days later. He was bummed then, but this was beyond that. This was hurt, regret, and worst of all, resignation. I was sympathetic, of course, but I didn't push him for details. Those could come another time.

A bald eagle swept before us and thrust its talons into the surface of the lake. Clutching a small fish, the bird flew right over us, then skimmed the treetops behind the resort and vanished.

"Oh, hey, that reminds me," Sam said. "There's something else. I got it stashed in the attic."

"In the lodge?" I asked. "Next to the bat shit?"

"No. No. The garage. A year ago, you and I were putting down plywood for an attic floor. Remember? We put that little shelf in the rafters. It's there."

I said, "Lets' go."

I followed him up the farmer's ladder—a series of two-by-fours tacked across a couple of exposed studs on the back wall that led to the loft. The attic was open over half the garage; the other half was storage. In the last year it hadn't seen much use. A few stacks of exterior siding took up less than half the space. A couple of wooden boxes full of old crap and found items from the lodge basement were pushed against the far end. Tucked in a corner, we'd fashioned a rafter ledge open toward the peak. Sam slipped his hand into the blind opening and extracted a cloth bag with a drawstring.

"What the hell is that?" I asked.

The knot in the leather string gave him some trouble. "After you left, Diane and I went over to your place, looking for you. But…" He finally had the better of the leather and opened the pouch.

I could see there was something inside. "Yeah, but, but…"

"The place was deserted of course, but someone forgot to lock the side door on the garage. We went in, looking for a clue, a note, anything. On the way out, I saw this."

In his hand was a picture frame. I recognized it immediately. My knees went weak.

Sam said, "I remembered it from your bedroom. The glass is cracked. Someone must have dropped it. That's you and your mom, right? Madelyn." He handed it to me.

Hands trembling, I looked at the faded colors of the picture. "How old were you?"

"Three or four." I sniffled "A few years later, she was gone." I slouched into the center post of a rafter. "This was the only thing I had left of her. I thought it was lost when we moved." Her summer dress went to her ankles. My arm clutched one of her thighs. "See how she tussled my hair? She always did that so I'd smile for the camera." I wasn't sure if I could speak, so I said nothing at all.

Sam said, "Which reminds me. What's with your hair? You never had short hair. I almost didn't recognize you."

"There's a story behind that too." I looked at him. "Tell you later."

Sam had his eyes on something behind me. I hadn't noticed the basketball in the box. He picked it up and showed it to me, my name in magic marker right across the middle. "Found this too, sitting under the porch," he said. "Just needs a little air. How about a game?"

I put the picture back in the pouch and said, "Aren't you sick of losing all the time?"

He turned toward the ladder, ball under his arm. "This time, I'm going to beat your ass."

Acknowledgments

Thanks again to my writers group, Author's Echo for their ongoing support and input. My gratitude to Kelly Huddleston and David Ross and everyone at Open Books for their efforts on my behalf. Special thanks to Mary Anne Hoff. Without her editorial input, this would not be the novel you see here. She put the polish on this piece, but whatever errors remain, they are strictly my own. And, as always, the daily encouragement from my wife, family, and friends is the best reward of all.